Mind Games

Nancy M. Griffis

Quest Books

Nederland, Texas

ISBN 978-1-932300-53-6

First Printing 2006

9 8 7 6 5 4 3 2 1

Cover design by Valerie Hayken

Published by:

Regal Crest Enterprises, LLC
4700 Hwy 365, Suite A, PMB 210
Port Arthur, Texas 7764

Find us on the World Wide Web at
http://www.regalcrest.biz

Printed in the United States of America

Acknowledgements

A heartfelt thanks to Jen and Fat for demanding more chapters when I thought it was all crap. You guys rock! Weezy? You pick the best nits and have endless patience! Love ya!

Love to my Mom and big, squishy hugs to all my friends who put up with my insanity. Y'all know who you are!

Thanks to Sylverre for her editing patience and good humor, and of course, a big thanks to Regal Crest for publishing me.

Prologue
Introductions

IT WAS THE night that broke the camel's back. I remember that it seemed especially dark as I moved toward the flickering blue lights leading the way to the murder. My partner, and I use the term loosely, met me halfway to the scene. I saw the usual cool and unfriendly look on his face and groaned, knowing that it was going to be one of those nights.

"It's about time you got here."

I shot him a dark look.

Jeremy ignored it and continued with a mocking grin, "What, a little deadness gonna stand in your way?"

Though tempted to roll my eyes and sigh, instead I pointed out, "I'm a telepath, not a necromancer."

Shrugging, Jeremy turned into the alley and I followed him to the actual scene.

Forensics had still been doing their thing, but that didn't bother me. I did my job and they did theirs, and we didn't usually intersect. Of course, their evidence was always admissible in court unless someone messed up, while mine... Being one of the strongest telepaths on the planet didn't mean that I was infallible, not by any stretch of the imagination. I was right a lot more than I was wrong, but that didn't mean it never happened. Hence the forensic confirmation necessary for any evidence that I uncovered through the use of my abilities.

Jeremy looked down at the body and started to work his own kind of magic, recreating in his sharp mind exactly what had gone down. I had worked with him long enough to wonder if maybe he was some kind of residual empath, but hadn't gotten up the nerve to actually ask. We'd had a crappy working relationship. Why mess it up with an attempt at friendship that would be rejected?

Again.

Sighing for real at that point, I spent several minutes concentrating on finding anything that would lead us to the killer. I closed my eyes and wished that there was someone to whom I could ground myself. That there was someone to hold onto, mentally and physically, so that I didn't get lost in the tide of psychic debris littering the emotional landscapes that were crime scenes. Or just life in general.

Since there wasn't, I did the best I could. I opened my mind to the area to get a sense of the person who had committed the murder. My gifts center around touch, like an empath's, but there is generally so much emotion fueling a murder that all I have to do is walk around to get a visual of the suspect. I remember there was definitely rage there, lots of it, and it flashed through to me, sharp and undefined. Everything was unfocused, nothing to help identify the perp.

I turned away and headed towards the cordoned off end of the alley, still musing about my non-relationship with my partner. It was understandable for a Psi/cop partnership to be strained at first— Jeremy wasn't the first one who hadn't taken to me right off—but it was different this time. There was something about me that really rubbed him the wrong way and we'd been partners for almost seven months. I'd proven myself over and over, both as a damn good cop and a Psi Agent. I was beyond tired of him not trusting me.

Ducking under the yellow tape, I went to talk with Amy to see what she'd gotten for witness statements, if anything, given the neighborhood. Amy was one of the few non-telepaths who actually trusted us; or at least trusted me. Tugging briefly at her coat, I smiled when she turned around. "Hey, Ames, what's up?"

"Becky!" she returned, green eyes sparking with mischief. "How's Metal Head?"

Snorting at her personal nickname for Jeremy, though I hadn't any idea of where it came from, I answered, "About the same as usual."

"Damn. Sorry, hon," she said sympathetically.

I shrugged. "Nothing to be done. I think, once we close this case, I'll ask for a transfer."

"That bad, huh?"

Nodding, I was about to say something when an overwhelming flash of rage drove me to the ground. I gasped in pain, knees hitting the pavement hard. I barely locked my elbows in time to keep upright, my mind filled with the killer's actions...

He turned back towards the body to gloat, to review his prowess. His image reflected in the puddle, a twisted sight that shimmered with every spate of breeze over it. I languished in the darkness of the vision, struggling to get free, which was nearly impossible on my own, but I slammed my hand onto the rough pavement a few times, the pain breaking me free.

Gritting my teeth, I ground out, "He's still here. Tall, big, red hair, blue eyes, has a faint limp. Still has the knife on him. Going south from here. God! Amy, make sure, not alone! Don't, don't go alone! Very strong."

Amy ran off while I tried to get myself under control, grateful that no one tried to help by touching me physically.

This was the other main reason that my partnership wasn't working. Jeremy had no use for telepaths because he thought of us as freaks of nature. A not-uncommon belief, but damned hard for me to deal with on a daily basis. I needed someone whose touch would ground me, someone whose voice would focus my talents, not someone who wanted nothing to do with me. It was unusual that I hadn't found a partner as yet, most of us bonding and marrying long before our thirties. It was a simple matter of survival, especially to those of us out and about in the world, in dangerous occupations where "normal" humans didn't shield their thoughts and emotions.

Until I found such a partner, I would continue to muddle through the pain and negative emotions channeled from the psychos I hunted. Getting myself together, I staggered to my feet and leaned against the nearest wall, shoving the mental connection to the back of my mind to be severed properly when there was time. There was never enough time in the moment to do everything I needed to do; this would have to wait, as it always did. Struggling with the rage and psychosis, I forced myself in the direction the killer had taken, going after Amy and the other cops as fast as I could. Contact with the suspect was cut off so completely, so unexpectedly that spiked agony claimed me.

I collapsed as it swallowed me in an instant.

WHEN I WOKE, it was in the quiet, serene room reserved at the Precinct for just such occasions. A migraine hovered, waiting to explode if I so much as twitched the wrong muscle. Thankfully, the lights were dim and the only sound in the room a white noise generator.

There was a gentle, soothing touch to my mind and I immediately relaxed, breathing deeply at the mental contact. Sharon was somewhere close; she would take care of me. Sure enough, the door opened only a moment later and quiet footsteps crossed the room, stopping beside the bed. Looking at the soft, round woman who had taught me about my gifts and had a large part in raising me, I smiled wanly. "Hey."

"Hey, yourself," she greeted with a light touch of fingers across my forehead. "About time you rejoined the world, little one."

Frowning, I asked, "How long was I out?"

"Almost ten hours."

"Ten hours?" I was stupefied. I had never had a backlash knock me out for more than a couple of hours, tops.

"Yes. And I've filed a complaint about Detective Morris' behavior," she said, lips tight in disapproval.

"What did Jeremy do?" I asked, dreading the answer.

"He knocked out the killer while you were still in contact. Officer Sanderson saw the whole thing. She said it was deliberate."

Deliberate. Closing my eyes against the latest pain, an emotional one that would take a while to heal, I whispered, "Why didn't he just ask for me to be transferred if he hated working with me so much?"

Sharon's sigh whispered against my hair. "That's not it."

Not it? What else... "Oh, no."

She nodded sadly, her dark hair fell forward. "During the scan, it came out that he was bought off by UnderTEM."

UnderTEM. The organization dedicated to getting rid of telepaths any way they could. Almost a genteel version of the KKK and far more acceptable, given how unilaterally telepaths were distrusted.

For God's sake! My own damn partner, and I'd no clue. How could he have been allied with them, without my knowing it?

The worst part about UnderTEM was the sneaky way they went about things. Not through genocide, oh no, nothing so blatantly evil. Through the discovery and elimination of whatever gene was responsible for the myriad forms of telepathy. They wanted to prevent any future telepaths from being born. They wanted the existing telepaths registered and labeled, herded into centers "for their own protection."

Right. Like the world's never heard that before.

And he was one of them. I tried not to groan. "So what now?"

"Now you have a couple of days off while an investigation into Officer Sanderson's claims begins," Sharon soothed, running her fingers through my short hair.

"No."

"Why not?"

"Because I'm not going to let that...jerk...drive me out of here," I answered firmly. I wanted to use another word to describe my ex-partner, but restrained myself. "I fought to become a cop, and an agent, and I'll be damned if some prejudiced jerk is going to make me leave!"

Sharon smiled. "How did I know that you were going to say something like that?"

Unable to keep the wry chuckle from escaping, I replied, "Oh I don't know. Maybe because your favorite term of endearment for me happens to be 'stubborn mule'? Just a thought."

Dark eyes sparkled at me with humor. "Maybe. And I won't say that I didn't anticipate this, because I did. Therefore, I have a new partner for you. And this time you will tell me right away if it's not working out."

I didn't miss the steel behind the quiet words, nor the mental reinforcement. "All right, all right, I give."

Beaming once more, Sharon said, "Good. I wanted to ask for Officer Sanderson, but she hasn't yet passed her Detective's exam. I did, however, ask her if there was anyone available suited to being partnered with you."

Curious, I questioned, "Who'd she recommend?"

"A Detective Marshall?"

Groaning, I shook my head. "Oh no, no way!"

A slender eyebrow rose. "What's the matter?"

Detective Genie Marshall. Arrogant. Intimidating. Full of anger and a wall on her emotions stronger than some of the telepaths I knew. "There is no way that that woman would agree to be my partner."

Obviously amused, Sharon said, "She already has."

I honestly couldn't think of a thing to say. When I finally reconnected my tongue to my brain, I gasped, "Why?"

"Why don't you ask her? She's outside waiting for you to wake up," Sharon informed me.

"Sharon!" My frantic squeak got another lift of the eyebrow. I couldn't decide which was more annoying: my squeak, or her eyebrows.

"Yes?"

Nearly desperate, I exclaimed, "She can't. Really. I mean, have you met her? Do you think she's honestly capable of being partnered with anyone, let alone a telepath? There is a reason—many, in fact— as to why she hasn't had any partners for the last three years."

Sharon grinned outright as she walked to the door. "I think the two of you would be a perfect match."

Before I could say anything else, she left.

Detective Marshall entered the room a few moments later. The woman I had avoided since first being introduced to her almost a year ago. The woman was feared pretty much by everyone, except the Captain and a couple of veteran cops, and even they gave her a wide berth. I had really only known her through reputation, but that had been enough to help me keep my distance.

Outwardly she was beautiful with long, burnished auburn hair and slanted almond eyes. I have no idea what her heritage was to come up with that combination. She was tall, too, annoyingly tall in that supermodel kind of way. Fortunately, she had some meat on her bones, so I wouldn't develop a complete inferiority complex.

I hoped.

Swinging my legs over the side of the bed somewhat gingerly, I eyed her cautiously as she approached. She stopped a few feet away. The golden brown eyes revealed nothing of what she thought or felt and, of course, there was no way I would scan her. Awkwardly, I said, "Hey. So, um, I hear we're partners now. That's gotta suck. I mean, for you, of course."

A faint smile of amusement surfaced as she echoed, "Of course."

God. Give me something to work with! I thought, almost frantic.

As if sensing my thought, or at least the emotions behind it, she said, "So, is it Becky, or Rebecca?"

"Um, Becky is fine. Hardly anyone calls me Rebecca."

"Okay. You up for getting back to work right away, or do you need the day off?"

I pushed myself off the bed a little too quickly and stumbled. She caught me and I flinched, waiting for the pain. When none came, I stared up at her in amazement. "It doesn't hurt to touch you."

Eyebrows raising curiously, she offered with half a grin, "Usually not, no."

She didn't understand what touch meant to a telepath. A single touch from the wrong person could send a jolt of agony through me, through any telepath. I gripped the strong biceps holding me up and grinned widely as I straightened. Though I could tell she had no idea why I was grinning like a loon, an echoing smile crossed her face.

Maybe she wasn't so bad after all? Maybe that intimidation thing was just a cover for a really nice person underneath. Holding out my hand, I said, "Rebecca Curtains. Pleased to meet you."

Her smile widened a bit as she gripped my hand. "Genie Marshall, and the pleasure's all mine."

We walked out into the bullpen where I was immediately assaulted by the thoughts and emotions of my fellow officers. The steadying touch of her hand to the small of my back brought my barriers rapidly into place. I nodded to her and the hand was removed. Following her towards her desk, I looked around for where I would be sitting.

Before we got there, however, one of the other detectives walked by, sneering at me.

In a split second, Genie's hand snapped out and she shoved him against the nearest wall. "You got a problem with my new partner?"

As he stammered out an apology, I swallowed nervously and thought, So, okay. Maybe the intimidation thing isn't a cover. Well. This is certainly going to be interesting.

—Excerpted from the biography of Detective Rebecca Curtains

Chapter
One

GENIE WAS, WITHOUT a doubt, the most frustrating and aggravating partner that Becky had ever had. Seething, the petite woman strode to the Jeep and kept her mouth firmly shut, unsure of what might fly out if it opened. *Of all the insulting, condescending, outrageous...!*

Becky couldn't even finish the thought, she was so upset.

The object of her ire walked blithely beside her, as though nothing was wrong. Maybe, in that hard head of her partner's, nothing was. As soon as she could think straight, when she could speak to Genie without screeching in fury, Becky planned to let the other woman know, in no uncertain terms, exactly what she thought about the behavior of a few minutes ago. They arrived at the car and Becky automatically went to the passenger's side and waited.

"It's unlocked."

The mild tone only pissed Becky off further, emphasizing the fact that Genie was clueless about what was going on with her own partner.

"Are you getting in?"

Becky's eyes flashed to the taller woman's face and some of what she felt must have shown, because the other woman stiffened. Satisfied that Genie finally knew that something was wrong, Becky answered, "I haven't decided yet."

Crossing her arms over her chest, Genie demanded, "What did I do this time?"

Furious, Becky stalked around the car and jabbed two fingers hard into Genie's breastbone, snarling, "Don't you *dare* take that tone with me! I have never in my life been so insulted! What the *hell* were you thinking of, to tear me down like that? To anyone, never mind other cops! My job is difficult enough without my own friggin' *partner* giving me shit. If we're going to work together, and that's a big damn IF right now, you make damn sure that we're working together. Because I've had enough of backstabbing partners to last a lifetime. Do I make myself clear?"

Jaw clenched, Genie nodded. "Crystal."

"Good. I'm taking a cab home."

Without waiting for a response, Becky spun on her heel and strode down the sidewalk. She needed to cool off before she blew up at some poor cabbie for no reason.

"Becca, wait!"

Ignoring the call, Becky continued to walk quickly away. It wasn't long before her partner caught up, Genie's long legs making easy work of the distance. Resentful that the other woman couldn't take a hint, she maintained her silence.

"Becca, stop and hear me out, okay?"

The sincerity in Genie's voice gave Becky a brief hesitation, but it didn't slow her footsteps. "Talk."

"You know I haven't had a partner in a long time."

"And that gives you the right to—"

Genie grabbed her arm and stopped her forcibly, turning Becky so that they faced each other. Even angry, Becky couldn't help but respond to the other woman's beauty, it was so damn distracting. Shoving the attraction down and thoroughly planning to strangle it dead later, Becky yanked her arm free. "Mauling me isn't going to get you back into my good graces."

Sighing explosively, Genie released her and replied, "I know. I'm sorry. I just wanted to get your attention."

"Well, you've got it. Full and undivided. So talk."

"I shouldn't have talked about you like that. I'm sorry. I just, I didn't know what to say to them," Genie explained slowly. "It's been a long time since I've interacted with anyone other than Captain Carlson on any kind of a regular basis. I think I was just getting too comfortable with you."

Becky's mouth dropped. "That is the lamest excuse I've ever heard in my life! What, you like me, so you jerk me around and insult me?"

Groaning, Genie said, "I'm not explaining this right."

"So do better," Becky ordered, unforgiving. If they were going to have a working partnership, let alone a friendship, this was something that needed to be nipped in the bud. There was no way that she would wonder about someone else selling her out because she was a telepath.

As though reading her thoughts, Genie denied, "Being a telepath has nothing to do with this. Look, haven't you ever just screwed up, accidentally-on-purpose? Like it was too much of a good thing?"

Reluctantly, Becky had to nod. There probably wasn't a soul alive who hadn't sabotaged themselves at one time or another. "Go on."

"I don't have any friends. Most people don't like me, like it's some kind of instinct. I tend to, ah, rub people the wrong way. I don't do it on purpose, but I know what I want, what I can do, and what I expect from others. I don't make any bones about it, and the people who piss me off need to steer clear of me."

"This isn't a revelation."

"I know, I know. I'm not even sure that I have an explanation you'll accept. I certainly have no excuse. But I am sorry. Truly. And not because you're the only person who's made an effort to get to know me in a couple of years, but because you didn't deserve any of what just happened."

The simple statement got to Becky as nothing else would have. Protestations of innocence, or excuses, would have soured her on the other woman, probably for good. But the way Genie took responsibility and apologized reached through and diffused some of Becky's anger. She sighed deeply. "You do know how much it hurt, right? Especially after what I went through with Jeremy? Implying that I'm only a good cop because of being a telepath..."

Wincing, Genie nodded. "I wish I could promise that I won't tick you off again, but I can't. I have a bad habit of speaking bluntly."

Holding up her hand, Becky countered, "I have no problem with plain speaking, Genie, just maliciousness. I won't go through that again. Jeremy was supposed to be my partner. Instead, he sold me out to UnderTEM and tried to kill me because I'm a telepath."

"I swear to you that you being a telepath doesn't bother me in the slightest. You can scan me if you want."

The earnest promise vanquished the rest of her anger. Eyeing Genie warily, Becky warned, "Last chance, Marshall. You screw up like that again, and I walk. No discussion."

Nodding, Genie held out her hand and vowed, "That will never happen again."

After a brief hesitation, Becky accepted the hand.

GENIE WALKED STIFFLY through the busy hall, doing her best to ignore the short woman beside her. Not an easy task, given how persistent she could be, without even saying a word. She might be tempted to think Becca had tossed some kind of mind-control her way, but knew better. In the short span that they'd been partners, Genie's instinctive trust had grown into a certainty.

They arrived quickly at their desks, as anyone who looked at them moved quickly out of the way. Genie sat and forcefully yanked a drawer open, almost pulling it all the way free in her agitation.

"Trying to break the place down?"

Ignoring the snide remark, Genie gritted her teeth and snapped, "What is your deal?"

"*My* deal? Oh, that's rich!" Becca practically snarled back.

Before Genie could respond, the Captain's shouted loud enough to be heard through his closed door. "Marshall! Curtains! Get in here, now!"

Both women stopped glaring long enough to head for the Captain's office. Once inside, Genie leaned against the wall, while Becca sat in the chair in front of his desk.

He stared at them for a long moment, leaning back in his chair. "Is there a problem here, ladies?"

Finally looking up from the floor, Becca answered stiffly, "I'd like to request a transfer, Sir."

Genie barely aborted her instinctive twitch at the announcement, controlling herself only through long practice at not revealing how she felt to anyone.

Lips pursed thoughtfully, Lewis answered, "Request denied."

"Sir, it's within my rights as a PA to request a transfer if my partnership isn't working."

"Sure it is. And it's within my rights to refuse if it adversely affects this department, which it would," Lewis countered, just as firmly. "Look. You two got problems, you solve them on your own time. While you're here, I expect you to work together and solve crimes. That's what you get paid to do, remember? Now get out of here and get me results before we find another dead tourist. You don't even want to know what my ass looks like after the Commissioner got through with it this morning."

Radiating tension, Becca nodded and left the office.

Genie trailed behind trying not to feel like a contrite but confused puppy. She sat back down at her desk and hissed, "A transfer?" Don't you think—"

Becca glared at her as she sat and interrupted, "Let's just get working on this, okay?"

Mouth puckering up as though tasting something unpleasant, Genie nodded abruptly. "Fine."

"Did you get the forensics report?" Becca asked, pointedly keeping her eyes on the small notebook computer she had set on her desk.

After a muffled curse, Genie said, "It's not here. I'll be right back, and we *will* talk about this, Rebecca."

Not waiting for an answer, she stalked off towards the morgue to get the right reports from Jim.

BECKY WATCHED GENIE leave through lowered lashes, making sure that the detective really was gone before slowly releasing her tension. Her roiling stomach felt like one false move would be enough to send it spewing in the wrong direction.

What a week.

Working with Genie was so different than working with any of her previous partners, especially Jeremy. It was like night and day. Morris had despised her because of her mental abilities, not caring what kind of cop she was. Genie didn't care about anything except the fact that being a telepath brought another set of skills to solving their cases.

'Seemed to' being the operative phrase. She should have known better than to trust so quickly, so eagerly. Becky still wasn't sure why they were having such trouble. They'd made a good start, then a few course corrections, and things had been okay. But this last week, things had just started falling apart. She wanted to like Genie, did like her, in fact. She could see that there was a lot more to the woman than most people assumed, but the detective was making it damned hard to get closer.

Pinching the bridge of her nose in a vain attempt to stop the migraine forming, Becky sighed deeply. Her body was in turmoil because her mind and emotions were in turmoil. Forget turmoil. She'd passed turmoil three days ago and was heading straight for murderous.

"Hey. You all right?"

Looking up at Amy's concerned question, Becky forced a smile. "Fine, thanks. How's patrol these days?"

"Same as usual," Amy answered, green eyes still worried. "I thought things were working out between you two. What happened?"

What happened? Becky looked away, towards the hall that Genie had disappeared down. Realizing that Amy was waiting for an answer, she looked back at the patrol officer. "It's a really long story. Let's just say we've got different viewpoints about a lot of important things."

"That happens, Becky. You're still getting to know each other. Cut her some slack, okay? She isn't used to working with others."

Frowning, Becky said, "I've cut her so much slack that it's a wonder I haven't hung myself with it yet! Tell me what's going on, Ames, please?"

Amy hesitated before answering, "It's not really my place to say, but let's get together for drinks tonight. I'll tell you what I can, all right?"

Becky nodded in relief. "Thanks, I really appreciate this."

Smiling crookedly, Amy observed, "Maybe, maybe not. Six o'clock? Benitos?"

"I've got those reports," Genie interrupted harshly.

Becky jumped a little at Genie's voice. Surprised that she hadn't heard or sensed the other woman's approach, Becky kept her gaze on Amy and said, "I'll see you tonight, Ames."

Amy smiled and nodded, then briefly touched Genie's arm in passing.

Genie watched her go, then shook her head as if to clear it of an unpleasant thought before sitting down and opening the manila folder in her hands.

Becky waited. When Genie at last looked up, Becky leaned back in her chair, staring at her without expression.

Seemingly unnerved by Becky's unusual behavior, Genie's fingers tapped nervously on the desk as she reported, "According to Jim, it's the same person. They're using an aluminum blade, which again left traces on the body. Not to mention the obvious factors, of course, of the victim being a tourist and being left in the same position as the previous two."

"And not a whisper of him for me to find. There should have been some trace that I could use," Becky murmured.

"Hey, don't beat yourself up about it," Genie said awkwardly. "It's not like you have to be on the nose every time. No one's keeping score."

Leaning on her desk, Becky countered sharply, "Yes, they are! Don't think that I don't know exactly what people think of me around here. I'm not a real cop. I wouldn't know a clue if it bit me on the ass. I'd never catch a single perp if I weren't a freak. I know what people think and it isn't due to any telepathic powers. They don't care if I overhear, Genie. No, they *want* me to overhear.

"What I can't figure out here is you. After three years of no partners, suddenly you not only agree to getting one, but you agree to *me*. Why?"

Genie stared back at her, stone-faced.

Becky waited, but the other woman held her silence. Mouth twisting in disgust, she stood. "I'm leaving. We aren't going to get anything else done tonight."

"Becca, wait!"

Becky paused from gathering her coat and snapped, "What?"

Uncertain, Genie asked, "See you in the morning?"

Reading something pleading in her partner's eyes, sensing that Genie maybe *couldn't* reach out, Becky visibly softened and replied, "I'll be back in the morning. Let's get an early start, okay?"

"Sounds good," Genie agreed, patently relieved.

IT SEEMED LIKE Becky was always running late. She glanced at her watch, hating that the Center was on California time. It was such a pain to always be calculating what time people would be where. Of course, that was the same problem in dealing with the European and Asian Centers, too. Officially, she only coordinated between the "organizations" that gave refuge to telepaths worldwide, but really, Becky was very in-touch with the Center located in Southern California. It was where she'd grown up, for the most part, and the place she called home.

She had planned to just run home and call Michelle to get

updates from the North American Center, located in southern California. Something that shouldn't have taken more than a half-hour, tops, but then Michelle had brought up some personality conflicts that needed dealing with. That, in turn, had spiraled into a detailed discussion on training placements, for which Becky could ill-afford the time and yet to which she couldn't say no.

It would be so much easier if Becky could just call from her cell phone or the office, but the line at home was dedicated and secure right to the Center. It was just as well that she had no social life. There really was no time for one, no matter how much Sharon complained about the lack of grandchildren in her future. Her eyes caught sight of a news bulletin and despite her lateness, Becky stopped to watch the closed-caption on the viewscreen in the store window, mouth open with child-like pleasure.

"According to the latest report from the World Wide Space Association, the colonists landed successfully on Mars at the recently finished New Geneva settlement site. There were no casualties or injuries on the trip. The children are even expected to start school on schedule, in three days," the newscaster reported, a broad smile on her face. "We'll have interviews with the Captain and her crew, with standard time delays, later this evening."

Becky shook her head in wonder at the news and hurried on to her meeting at Benitos. It had taken forever, but the first joint venture at WWSA had finally paid off. Briefly wishing that she'd been among the colonists, envying their adventure, Becky returned her attention to the less-than-daring evening of conversation with a friend.

Benitos was an old-fashioned, tavern-style restaurant and bar. It was about two blocks from the 31st Precinct, but more of a family place than a cop hangout. She had to head back towards work from home, which was a pain in the ass. When Becky walked in about twenty minutes late, the dinner crowd was firmly under way.

Looking around, she spotted Amy sitting at a table already and moved towards her, smiling at the hostess as she went. Sitting across from the other woman, the customary evasion came easily. "Sorry about that, I lost track of time."

Grinning, Amy said, "Hey, at least you're honest about it."

Becky didn't even think about her need to be secretive about her life. It was simply too ingrained to even feel guilty about. "I try."

The waitress came over to take their orders and, when she was gone, Becky leaned on the table and ordered simply, "Tell me."

Nodding unhappily, Amy said, "It was when she was partnered with Brian Marks, about five years ago. It wasn't a match made in heaven, but they had a good arrest rate. I wasn't here at the time, in the academy actually, but there's still stories about their, ah, discussions. Discussions that you could hear from the next zip code, apparently."

Becky hated the wall that kept her out of the information loop. If she'd been a "normal" cop, she'd have already heard all this. People would've been tripping over themselves to tell her about her new partner.

"Anyhow, despite the arguments, they did pretty good," Amy continued. "They worked together for a couple of years. Then he was killed in a sting operation they didn't even know about. The Feds had set up some big gun-running deal and Genie and Brian were there on an independent tip. Rumor has it that the Feds knew who they were, but let them go in anyhow. Brian went down under 'friendly fire.'

"Genie went nuts. I mean *completely* nuts. As in, they gave her an extended, six-month psyche-leave. Rumor has it that they were involved at the time of Marks' death, but no one's ever been stupid enough to ask. After Genie got back, she refused to work with anyone. I think Captain Carlson let her do it at first just so she'd have something to hang on to, you know? So she wouldn't do anything stupid. By the time I got on the force, she'd been working alone for a couple of years. That was just a few months shy of when you got here."

Well, no wonder, Becky thought wearily. Taking into account that Genie's partner had been killed, of course she wouldn't want to get close or trust Becky right away. Subconsciously, Genie didn't want to open herself up to that kind of potential pain again. Add to that Becky's background as a federal agent and there was no mystery as to why they were having problems.

Sighing, Becky stayed silent as the waitress put their plates down and asked if they needed anything else. They ate quietly, but it was a friendly quiet, enjoying the food and the company. Eventually, conversation started again, and this time it was about casual topics and the woeful lack of a love life for them both.

Towards the end of the meal, Becky's eyes traveled over the room, just taking in the sights and sounds of the bustling atmosphere. How many of these people would give her that "'freak"' look if they knew exactly what she could do?

Probably most of them, she thought unhappily. The days of burning witches at the stake might be over, but there was no getting around the stigma of being a telepath, despite the lack of mayhem on the telepath's end.

"Hey. I thought we were having a good time here," Amy said suddenly.

"Sorry," Becky apologized. "I guess you can take the poet out of the morbid, but not the morbid out of the poet."

Surprised, Amy asked, "You write poetry?"

Shrugging, Becky replied wryly, "For therapy, mostly. Sharon said I should work on getting it published, but it's really just for me."

Just for me. All mine. Soon, soon, soon.

Shuddering at the foreign, vile thought running through her like sewer waste, Becky looked around the room again. Someone nearby was seriously over the edge. Vaguely, she heard Amy call her name, but was too focused on the thought-path to pay attention. Closing her eyes, Becky breathed deeply and cast her mind adrift.

At first it was like being buffeted by the waves in a lake. The mental breeze caught her up amongst all the general, day-to-day living thoughts of the people surrounding her. Then a cold wind swirled around her, forcefully bringing her around and around like a mini-tornado as she was unexpectedly bathed in a truly sick mind. Horror and darkness, lit by a vast intellect, surrounded her until there was nothing to anchor herself to.

Chapter
Two

WHEN GENIE GOT to the restaurant, she had to wade through a crowd just to get to her partner. She saw Amy doing her best to keep them back, but the uniformed officers just stood to the side, watching with identical smirks. Furious, Genie snapped out, "Menson! Branders! Get rid of these people or you'll be doing beat for the next decade!"

At her order, they jumped into action and began pushing the crowd back. That gave Genie the space to reach her partner; she stopped short at the sight. Becca lay on the booth bench, eyes wide open and staring as she lay in the grip of some mental connection. She shook enough of the shock off to whisper, "Oh my God."

Amy joined her and said, "You have to bring her out of it! She won't respond to me at all. I tried when she first went under."

Alarmed, Genie exclaimed, "What do I do?"

Amy eyed her askance. "She's your partner. You should know."

Ignoring the snippy tone, Genie moved hesitantly towards Becca's motionless form. Right. She could do this. She'd had the same mandatory seminar as everyone else when the PAs, all five of the poor slobs, had first joined the Police Department's provisional Psi-Agent division. As long as they had established a rapport, her touch should bring Becca back.

Shit! What's considered a rapport? Does fighting like cats and dogs count?

Somehow, she didn't think so.

Sighing, Genie knelt on the booth bench, leaning over Becca. Supporting her weight with one hand, the other settled on Becca's shoulder, squeezing and rubbing the locked muscles gently. "All right, Rebecca, I know this isn't how I want to be spending my night, so I can only guess that you feel the same way. Wherever you've gone, you need to come on back. It's not safe for you to stay out so long. Even a greenhorn like me knows that."

For a few minutes she spoke in a low, even tone, saying whatever came to mind. Her hand continued squeezing Becca's shoulder once she remembered that constant sensory input helped interrupt a negative mental connection. She bent closer, until her mouth was almost touching the other woman's ear, hoping that maybe the smell of her perfume would help cut through the backlash.

Finally, the wide, staring eyes blinked a few times and Becca groaned, a shudder running through her.

Genie pulled back and questioned softly, "You all right?"

"I think I'm going to puke."

"Did you hit your head? How's your vision? No, wait, maybe you shouldn't move until we get you checked out."

A faint smile crossed Becca's face as she pushed herself up. "I'm fine, Mom. Just woozy from being under too long. And the puking urge is coming from being in contact with that... that...from being in contact."

"What happened?" Genie asked, standing and giving Becca the room to right herself completely. Even knowing that she was hovering, Genie couldn't help but stand as close to her partner as possible. This was the first time that she'd actually seen a backlash and she was more than a little spooked.

Becca shuddered, then explained, "I was having dinner with Ames and caught the most foul echo."

"Echo of what?"

Both women turned towards the new voice. Genie was startled by Sharon's appearance, but Becca didn't seem all that surprised. She watched as Becca wrapped her arms around the other woman in a quick hug and then sat back on the booth bench. Ruthlessly, she squashed the irrational tension when Sharon kept her hand on Becca's shoulder.

"It was a man. He was completely insane, but smart—so smart it was scary." Becca recounted.

Genie rubbed her eyes and muttered, "Beautiful."

"Hey, not my fault. I was just here for dinner and conversation," Becca snapped.

Irritated, Genie demanded, "Did I say that it was your fault?"

Sharon squeezed Becca's shoulder and looked pointedly at Genie. "That's enough, girls. We don't want a scene in public, now, do we? Well, not another one, anyhow."

Gritting her teeth, Genie settled back. "So what did you see?"

"Nothing specific," Becca replied unhappily. "Just, it was so evil."

"It?" Sharon repeated quietly.

Becca shuddered, arms wrapping around her midriff. "I know it was a man, but there was nothing human in that mind."

"All right, then. Becca, come with me. We should regress you to see what details we can find out. Genie, why don't you head home, dear?"

Not surprisingly, the solicitous, somewhat condescending tone pushed Genie's temper over the edge. "I don't think so! She's my partner and I'm sure as hell not going to let you put her through the wringer alone."

Sharon arched a thoughtful eyebrow, but nodded agreement.

The crowd finally dispersed and Amy walked outside with them.

Becca briefly touched her arm and assured her, "You did exactly the right thing, Ames, thanks."

Amy was obviously relieved as she said, "I was worried."

"Well, I'm fine now. See you tomorrow?"

Hesitant, Amy asked, "Is it okay if I tag along?"

After looking to Sharon, who nodded, Becca smiled a little at the younger woman and answered, "Sure."

It was agreed that Becca would ride with Genie in case there was another backlash. Amy had walked, so she would ride with Sharon and they would meet up at the precinct.

Traffic had thinned out, so Genie had no trouble navigating the busy city streets. She glanced over at her partner to find Becca's arm thrown over her eyes. "You all right? For real?"

Becca's arm came down and she smiled wanly. "As all right as I can be, after touching that filth. I'm telling you, Genie, I've been in contact with some pretty sick characters before, but this guy... I mean, the worst was that serial killer in Virginia, did you hear about him?"

Genie nodded. She'd gone over all of Becca's old cases, both to familiarize herself with her new partner's style, and to see just how much of the action the other woman would want to get into. The serial killer Becca was speaking of now, Emile Brown, had killed twelve men and women in horrifying ways before the PA had been able to locate him. That had been Becca's last case with the Feds.

"This thing, this man, he's like a hundred times worse than Brown. It's hard to describe, but I felt like I was drowning in evil," Becca continued, shivering violently.

Genie reached across the space and gently squeezed the back of Becca's neck. "You don't have to do this tonight. Maybe you should take the night and recover from the backlash first."

Shaking her head firmly, Becca said, "I wouldn't be able to sleep anyhow. It's better to get this out of my system."

By then, they'd reached the precinct and Genie parked in her usual spot. It was almost fitting that rain started falling when she stopped the engine. *What a crappy night.* Looking over at Becca, who didn't have a coat, Genie said, "I've got an extra windbreaker in the back, hang on."

Becca nodded and Genie turned in her seat, bending over to grab the extra jacket. Sitting back down, she handed it to Becca. A spate of humor, and a grin, surfaced unexpectedly when the smaller woman zipped it up.

"What?" Becca asked, half-smiling just from looking at her.

"You look like a little kid," Genie observed, her grin getting bigger.

Grinning back, Becca raised her hands and waved them around, causing the extra material to flop around comically. "I am *not* short. *You* are an Amazon."

Genie snorted, reaching across the space and ruffling the other woman's short hair, then froze when Becca stared at her in surprise. Flushing, she said hastily, "Ah, sorry. Just trying to lighten the mood a little."

Becca smiled tentatively, as if relieved that whatever their problems had been, things might actually be getting a little better. "No, that's okay. I was just surprised."

They stared at each other for another minute or so, then Becca sighed. "We should probably get inside."

Genie nodded in agreement, but neither moved to leave. A couple of silent minutes passed as Genie's eyes flickered around the nearly empty garage. "You know...I, ah, I don't mean to be so rough on you. And I'm trying to be better about it. I know not everyone is as thick-skinned as I am, I just forget sometimes."

The roundabout apology brought a smile to, Becca's face. "Apology accepted."

Genie looked sharply at her partner and opened her mouth to deny it, then mentally rolled her eyes at herself. "Thank you."

That seemed to be the signal both had tacitly been waiting for. They left the Jeep and headed into the precinct. Genie was happy to note that Becca stood a little more at ease, after their conversation. She wondered suddenly when the last time her partner had really had something to laugh about had been. If she dealt with crap like tonight all the time, it was no wonder that the other woman was so quiet. It seemed that Becca always had a smile for everyone but herself, and Genie silently vowed to change that.

After signing in and going through security, the two women went straight to the room reserved for Becca. Sharon and Amy were already there, waiting for them.

"Sorry. Got a bit distracted," Genie apologized insincerely.

Becca snorted softly and proceeded further into the room, stopping at the bed. Genie followed her partner and touched Becca's back with what she hoped was encouragement. Becca shot her a grateful look before getting onto the bed and lying back. Turning towards Sharon, Genie asked, "Now what?"

The older woman had turned on the white noise generator and pulled a chair close to the bed. Amy was leaning on the door, as though guarding it from interruption.

"Now you take Becca's hand so that she can remain grounded in this plane, while I take her into the next," Sharon told her smoothly.

There was something about the older woman that bothered Genie, though she'd never been able to figure out what. Something about the way she never seemed to get ruffled, no matter what the circumstances. It always made Genie want to do something drastic. Never more so than now, however. The tentative camaraderie that she and Becca had gained was something she wanted more than anything else in a long time. Somehow, Sharon seemed like a threat to that burgeoning friendship.

Then there was the fact that what they were about to do was something Genie couldn't protect her partner from: the other, unseen realm where no one had any business being. The realm of which, apparently, Sharon was a master. Genie wanted to stop this before Becca was damaged any further. One look to Becca's determined and faintly pleading eyes, however, stopped the protest cold. Sighing, Genie took Becca's hand and waited.

Sharon started speaking, her voice low and soothing. "Close your eyes and slowly start counting backwards from ten."

Genie watched closely as her partner counted backwards: eyes closed, voice soft, relaxed expression. She wondered if this was something that PA's trained for, to be able to get into a hypnotic state just from the right atmosphere and verbal triggers. Filing it under the long list of questions to ask her partner, Genie leaned against the bed, watching.

"You're at the restaurant with Amy. You've just had dinner and are talking with her. What are you talking about?" Sharon prompted.

"Poetry. I write poetry," Becca answered quietly. "You told me I should get it published, but I know it's just for me. That's what I tell her."

"When did you catch the first echo?"

"Just for me. All mine. Soon, soon, soon."

Genie shivered in visceral dread at the sudden transformation of Becca's voice. It wasn't her partner speaking someone else spoke through her.

In a determined voice, Sharon questioned, "What's all for you?"

"Never tell. Gonna rule them all. Every last soul. Need them. Soon. Soon. Soon."

"What do you need them for?"

"*Power. It will all be mine. They will all be mine.*"

Becca's hand tightened around Genie's with such strength that pain exploded in her fingers and hand. The smaller woman's eyes flew open and stared at Genie with a disturbing light that echoed the hottest, bluest part of a flame. Panicking, Genie shouted, "Get her back! Do it now, Sharon!"

Even as Genie struggled not to let go of Becca's hand, the hand that no longer gripped, but squirmed to be free, she heard Sharon talking in that same, soothing tone, trying to bring Becca back from wherever she'd gone. Instinctively, Genie knew that if she let go of Becca, they'd never get her back. She also knew that Sharon's attempts to break through weren't working, because that madness was still all-too-present in the usually gentle blue eyes.

Genie grabbed Becca's shoulder with her free hand and leaned forward, staring into her partner's eyes as she shouted, "Rebecca Marie Curtains! You get your *ass* back here before I kick it! Do you hear me? You fight this bastard and get back here *now!*"

Becca's entire body seized up, and for a moment, it looked to Genie as though she had stopped breathing altogether. Her hand felt like it was on fire, but she ruthlessly ignored it until Becca's eyes opened again and showed nothing but pained confusion. It was finally Becca, and not some monster, staring back at her. That was when Genie howled in pain and yanked her hand free, dancing across the room as though she could outdistance the shooting pain in every bone from her wrist down.

"Genie? Genie, are you all right?" Becca demanded, grabbing her partner by the shoulder.

Genie glared at her and exclaimed, "No! I'm not all right! You were possessed by some demon, and I think you broke my friggin' hand!"

For whatever reason, that set Becca off into a gale of laughter. After a shocked second of staring at her partner like she really had gone mad, Genie smiled. The laughter was clean and free, something that she might never have heard again.

Finally, Becca got control of herself, wiping at her eyes, and gently took Genie's hand, carefully turning it this way and that. Wincing guiltily, she said, "We need to get you to the emergency room. I think you might really have some broken bones."

Sighing, Genie said, "Figures."

Pausing, Becca looked at Sharon, but didn't say anything to the still, pale woman frozen in shock. Genie didn't hear anything, but knew they were having some kind of silent conversation. She had known, of course, that agreeing to this partnership would cause her to deal with some weird shit, but this was so far beyond what she'd imagined that it didn't even seem like the same planet.

GENIE HATED HOSPITALS. Maybe it was a prerequisite to being a cop, because she didn't know a single one who went voluntarily to the doctor. But the ice pack on her hand wasn't helping all that much any more and she was actively looking forward to drugs.

"Hey. You doing okay?"

Opening her eyes to look over at her partner's tense face, Genie nodded. "Yeah, sure. Doing great."

"I meant, how's the pain? We'll be in the ER in no time."

"Pain? What pain?"

Becca glanced at her briefly, then snorted. "Yeah, right."

They arrived at the hospital within a few minutes and Genie waited for Becca to open the door since she couldn't seem to summon the energy to do more than cope with the shooting pain in her hand. "I'm turning into such a wuss."

Putting her shoulder under Genie's arm, Becca countered, "You are not. Now shut up and let's get inside."

Unfortunately, being Friday night, the ER was booked with far more life-threatening injuries than a broken hand. A nurse was kind enough to give them a coolant pack, but it was almost two hours later that someone actually called Genie's name. Becca walked with her to the exam room where they waited another twenty minutes before the doctor showed up.

Taking her hand carefully, he looked at it and whistled. "You did a good job here. What happened?"

"It was an accident," Genie gritted out. "Could you just fix it?"

"Uh huh. That's what I'm here for. I'll be right back." He talked to someone outside the room then returned, saying, "You've got a few broken bones there, so the nurse is going to bring in a scanner and we'll see which bones need to be fused. Once that's taken care of, we'll put a cast on it to keep it steady for a couple of weeks, give you some pain meds, and send you home."

Genie opened her mouth to make a sarcastic remark, something about asking if he'd really gone to med school for that diagnosis, but the nurse arrived with the scanner. It took only a few minutes to determine that three bones needed to be fused. The others would be fine as long as they were given time to heal and kept immobile. Genie nearly passed out from the pain when they spread her hand flat for the fuser. She swore loudly and vocally about what she was going to do to the doctor's anatomy when the blackness faded.

Seemingly impressed with the vocabulary despite herself, Becca couldn't hide her grin as she scolded, "Genie! He's just trying to help!"

"Don't you look at me like that! This is all your fault, remember?" Genie snapped.

"Doesn't handle pain very well, does she?" the doctor observed.

Snarling at the doctor, Genie was about to use her good hand to punch his face in, when the fuser began to work, distracting her. The rays passed through her skin harmlessly, almost pleasantly. Though she'd grown up with the technology, Genie had no real idea of why or how it didn't burn away the flesh when it fused the broken bones together. Of course, as long as it did work, she didn't really care. As the bones had been pulled into the proper placement while she'd been nearly out of it, and the breaks were clean, the fusing only took about ten minutes.

The longest part of the whole process was putting the cast on. It was, apparently, a lot easier to work with than its predecessor of the previous century, but the plexiglass derivative still took time to set. It was almost twenty minutes later when they finished. Most of that time, the doctor wasn't even present. He came back with a small bag just as the nurse finished up. "Take one of these when you wake up, it'll take care of any residual discomfort."

Becca took the bag from him and said, "Thank you for your help, doctor."

"What help? The nurse did all the work," Genie pointed out caustically as she lifted the strange weight on her hand. It wasn't heavy, just awkward and uncomfortable. The pain had already faded enough for her to think clearly again. She was certainly clear enough to notice his scowl at her words, and the nurse's quickly hidden grin.

"And on that note, we'll be leaving," Becca said firmly, taking Genie's arm and pulling her towards the exit. "You're just a libel suit waiting to happen, aren't you?"

Snickering, Genie replied, "But you can't say I don't have a quick wit."

Becca shook her head and snorted. "No, I definitely can't say that."

The drive to Genie's apartment was silent. It wasn't until they were out of the car that either spoke, and then it was at the same time.

"Genie, I..."

"Did you..."

Running her hand through her hair self-consciously, Becca said, "I'm sorry about your hand."

"It wasn't really your fault."

"Nice of you to say."

"You going to be okay getting home?"

Becca nodded. "Yeah. I'm just going to catch a cab. I'll see you Monday?"

Genie nodded as well. "Yeah. I'll see you then."

"Good. Well. Good night, then."

"Night."

Genie watched her walk out the garage exit and sighed, pulling out her keys. As evenings went, this had been on the adventurous side, even for her.

GENIE PARKED HALF a block from Becca's apartment and considered herself lucky to get that close. It was late at night, after all, and everyone was home. Living in a family-oriented neighborhood pretty much guaranteed that. Most of the dwellings in this area were townhouses and garden-style condos. It was quiet as she walked towards the building, with only the occasional traffic noise reaching her ears. Strangely quiet, considering she was in the city.

She hadn't seen Becca since Friday night, hadn't even called the other woman, because Genie wasn't sure what to say. She was a little unsure what had brought her all the way over tonight. Driving with one hand was a serious pain in the ass, and they'd see each other in the morning at work anyhow, but she just had this niggling feeling in the back of her head that she should check on Becca. Since her instincts had rarely led her in the wrong direction, Genie had looked up her partner's address, put on her coat, and headed for the car.

Reaching the front door, Genie pressed the buzzer for apartment 401, Becca's number.

A few seconds later, Becca's startled voice asked, "Who is it?"

"It's me, Genie."

The door unlocked immediately and Genie grabbed the handle, pulling it open awkwardly with the wrong hand and going inside toward the elevators. It was only a few minutes later that she stepped onto the fourth floor. Glancing around, she established which way the numbers went and headed right. The door opened before she had a chance to knock. Grinning at Becca's pleased expression, Genie greeted, "Surprise!"

Holding the door open, Becca motioned for Genie to come in. "What're you doing here?"

"What, not happy to see me?" Genie teased, arching an eyebrow.

"Of course I am. Have a seat."

The small apartment was as far from claustrophobic as it could get, given its limitations; not quite a loft, but near enough to make no big difference. The living room was open and separated on the right from the kitchen only by an island. There was a free-standing wall at the other side of the kitchen that divided it from what was plainly the bedroom, while another stand-alone wall loosely boxed in the sleeping area. Opposite the front door was the bathroom, the only fully enclosed room in the place.

Looking at Becca as she sat on the couch, Genie commented, "This is really nice."

And it was, too. Candles were lit, the flames dancing beneath soft lamplight, bestowing both light and fragrance. The entertainment center was far enough back from the couch so as not to loom, and two large bookshelves lined the wall between the front door and the bathroom.

"Thanks. So ah, what brings you here?" Becca asked, sitting on a beanbag beside the couch.

And there it was; the reason she had come here. Unfortunately, Genie still wasn't sure of the answer.

Into the silence, Becca offered, "You want something to drink?"

Grateful, Genie nodded. "Whatever you've got."

Walking the short distance to the fridge, Becca pulled out a bottle of soda and poured two glasses, returning to the living room and handing one to Genie. She sat on the couch beside the taller woman and asked, "Was that the first time you'd dealt with something like that?"

Lips twisting into a vague semblance of a smile, Genie shook her head. "With evil? No, unfortunately not. With possession? Yeah. And I've gotta tell you, it has seriously creeped me out. I think part of the reason I'm here is to make sure that you're still you. You know?"

Grinning, Becca nodded and sipped her drink. "I know. Truth to tell, I keep doing things to make sure I'm still me, too."

There was an awkward silence as they each thought of what to say next.

Finally, Becca said, "I know we've been having some problems, but I'm real glad you stopped by."

Smiling more naturally now, Genie agreed, "Me, too. And, uh, I know that those problems are my fault, but—"

"No, Genie."

"Becca, let me finish, okay?"

Becca nodded and pulled her legs up to sit cross-legged, leaning forward to give Genie her full attention.

Taking a deep breath, Genie thought for a moment longer before speaking. "I think that we work really well together, complement each other, you know? You smoothe the feathers that I ruffle and all that. And I like you, you're a good person. I just, I have some problems and it really has nothing to do with you, okay? I'm gonna try and... No. I'm *going* to do better by you. I know I've said that before, and I meant it before, too, but this time it's going to stick. And if I start acting like a bitch again, you've got my permission to kick my ass."

Becca chuckled. "I'll remember that."

Dryly, Genie observed, "I'm sure you will."

"So. Now that that's out of the way, how about we go over my ideas about the case?"

"Sounds like a plan to me."

Excerpt from Rebecca Curtains' Journal—Year One

Being immersed in that evil was like bathing in scum, only not as pleasant. I don't know who this madman is, but it's going to take all our combined wits to find and capture him. Unfortunately, I think it's going to be a long, hard road to getting this bastard.

On a more pleasant note, it looks like Sharon really likes Genie. Not that she'd ever let on, well, to Genie anyhow. I have to laugh because I think for the first time, Sharon's met her match when it comes to being over-protective of me. I don't know where Genie gets this streak because we're hardly bosom buddies, at least not yet.

Another thing to add to the Strange list. One of many.

Still, I think this could be good for both of us, Genie and me. I'm going to try and bring her out of her shell some more, maybe get her to interact with the other detectives, though that'll take a while. I'm so glad she came over tonight. I'm still very much in a "wait and see" mode, but maybe, maybe something in my life will go right?

I can only hope.

Chapter
Three

"WHAT THE HELL happened to you?"

Genie looked up at her Captain's voice and grimaced. Her fingers tried to wriggle within the cast, but it was hopeless; they weren't going anywhere. "Wrestled with the devil."

One dark eyebrow rose as the older man commented, "Hope the other guy looks worse."

Snorting, Genie shrugged. She didn't know how he looked, and that bothered her. There was someone out there stalking her city and that just didn't sit right. As Carlson started walking away, she stood and followed him to his office. "Hey, Captain?"

"Yeah?"

"Something came up on Friday. We kinda have a new case," Genie said slowly, shutting the door behind her.

"Kind of?" he repeated.

"Yeah. Thing is, it's something Becca saw, but wasn't able to get enough of a hold on to get details about."

"And you want to check it out."

Frowning, Genie said, "Well, there's nothing we can do to check it out, not yet anyhow. But when it happens, it's going to be big."

"Wonderful. Big and bad, right?"

"Right."

Sighing, Carlson nodded and said, "All right. When you two get definite proof of what's going down, you can push your cases onto Mathisen and Yu."

Smiling in relief, Genie said, "Thanks, Captain."

"What about the tourist case? How's that going?"

Rolling her eyes, Genie replied, "It isn't. We're meeting with one of my CI's this morning, but I don't know if it'll pan out or not."

"Well? Don't stand around here, get on it," Carlson ordered.

Grinning briefly, Genie mock-saluted and snapped out, "Sir, yes, sir!"

His grumbled "Smartass," followed her out of the office.

When Genie reached her desk, she found Becca had arrived and was currently slumped over her desk. Lips pursed in amusement, Genie sat and asked, "Rough night?"

Groaning, Becca didn't even raise her head as she replied, "Couldn't sleep. I was wide awake until it was actually time to come in."

"Naturally."

"Coffee?"

Chuckling at the plaintive request, Genie stood and said, "Why don't you let me get it?"

The lifting of a middle finger was her answer, which sent Genie into louder laughter as she headed towards the break room. The one positive thing to come out of the insanity was breaking through the walls that had come up between them. And while Genie would have preferred it not to have come at the expense of mobility, she was glad that it had come, because it had started looking like it wasn't going to. Which, naturally, would have been her own damned fault because they'd started on the way to friendship so easily. But then Genie's long-standing pattern of not trusting anyone, or letting anyone get close, had kicked in.

Shaking her head at her own stupidity, Genie walked to the coffeepot. Once poured, Genie scooped up some sugar packets and cream, dumped them all in, and headed back to their desks. Placing the mug beside her still semi-comatose partner, she was about to say something, but stopped with a grin. Becca's hand reached out for the coffee, sliding across the desk to grip the hot ceramic. There was another groan as the dark head lifted just enough to start drinking from the mug. Snickering quietly, Genie moved to sit at her own desk.

After a minute or so of breathing in the coffee's aroma and sipping the dark liquid, bleary blue eyes focused and Becca accused, "You're a morning person, aren't you?"

Assuming an innocent expression, Genie said, "You probably would be too if you were running on more than fumes."

Becca grunted, but actually opened the file that she'd just had her head on before returning to her coffee. Frowning, she asked, "Hey. Just had a thought."

"Uh-oh."

"Funny." Becca made a face. "We know the victims are all here for that damned convention, right?"

"Yeah."

"But they're not in the same hotel."

"Right."

"And so far the only common denominators whatsoever is that they're all single."

"Right again."

"What about travel arrangements?"

"Travel arrangements?"

"Yeah. Like, who's the travel agent? Or did they even have a travel agent?"

"Huh. Good question. Want me to look into it while your brain's still trying to connect?" Genie teased.

Apparently satisfied that she'd come up with a new angle, and that she might be able to remain unthinking a while longer, Becca sighed, "Yes, please."

Smirking, Genie rifled through the victim files looking for any information on who had booked the trips for the victims. Sally Mendes, age forty-seven, single, no family, from Chicago: booked her ticket and hotel online. Jack Lall, age thirty-six, single, elderly mother, from Baton Rouge: booked both ticket and hotel through a travel agency in his hometown. Shrugging to herself, Genie pulled out the last file for the hell of it. Cassie Kendall, age twenty-five, single, parents still living, but no siblings, from Miami: also booked through an agency, but not the same one, or even affiliated with the same one that she could tell.

Genie looked up and set the file aside. "Two through an agency, different agencies, and the other online."

Rubbing her eyes, Becca sighed. "Damn. Well, it was worth a shot. Hey. Read the stats out loud to me? In order?"

Shrugging, Genie nodded. First came Lall, then Kendall then Mendes. She watched as Becca's face took on an intent expression and prompted, "What is it?"

Eyes snapping open, Becca leaned forward and demanded, "That's not the right order! Didn't Jim say, hang on..."

Genie waited impatiently as Becca searched through the mess of paper on her desk, pulling one out with a cry of triumph. Genie saw it was a Medical Examiner's report and recognized Jim Randall's handwriting.

"Right! According to Jim, Kendall was actually killed first, even though we found Lall first. So the real order would be Kendall, Lall, and then Mendes."

"So?"

"Well, it's not much of a pattern, but: K, L, M. Order of the alphabet."

Eyebrows rising, Genie demanded, "The perp's going by alphabet?"

Becca shook her head and amended, "Not just alphabet. Age, too. Going up a decade and year each time: twenty-five, thirty-six, forty-seven."

"So our next victim will be fifty-eight, single, and have the last name starting with N," Genie mused.

"And be in town for that convention," Becca agreed. "Male or female, do you think?"

"Start with a man, end with a man?"

"Possibly. I'll call the convention administrators and see if they have an age/alpha listing of their members," Becca said.

"Good. I think I'm going to—" Genie's phone rang before she could finish her sentence. Thankfully, it was a regular, old-fashioned phone since the State was too cheap to pay for Visi-phones. This way, she didn't have to worry about the caller seeing her grimace or if she made silent fun of whoever was on the other side. Picking up the receiver, she answered, "Detective Marshall."

"Hey. It's me."

"What's up?" Genie questioned, glancing at her watch with a frown. "I thought we were meeting at eleven."

"We were. I think you're gonna want to get down to 458 Colsten Avenue first, though."

"Shit."

"Yep. Give me a call later."

Genie hung up the phone, grabbing her coat from the back of her chair as she said, "Come on. There's been another murder."

Startled, Becca nonetheless stood, picking up her own jacket and following her to the Captain's office. Genie ducked in and said, "There's been another murder. Colsten Ave. Just got the call."

"Shit," Carlson groaned.

"That's what I said."

"I'll get the ball rolling."

"Thanks, Captain."

"So who called?" Becca asked as they headed towards the parking lot.

Genie shrugged. "My informant."

"And they know about the murder because...?"

"Because they're a damned good informant," Genie snapped.

Becca refrained from responding angrily; Genie felt the silence like an accusation. She kept her mouth shut and didn't say anything when they ended up at Genie's Jeep. Something was obviously bothering the other woman, aside from the newest tragedy. After unlocking the doors, they both got into the vehicle.

Genie pulled into traffic, trying to figure out how to break the wall. She sighed and said, "I'm sorry. I shouldn't have gone off like that. I'm a little protective about this particular CI."

Becca shrugged. "All right."

"I mean it. I'm sorry."

Looking closely at her, Becca relented. "It's all right. Did you get any details?"

"Just the address," Genie reported, relieved.

THE REST OF the ride to the crime scene was quiet, each woman lost in her own thoughts. On arrival, Becky saw a couple of squad cars in front of the building with their lights set to intermittent. One of the uniforms kept curious onlookers back while the other stood at the door to the five-story apartment unit. Becky frowned and said, "This is the first time he's used a residential location."

"Maybe it's not our guy," Genie answered hopefully.

Shrugging, Becky got out of the car and waved to Jim as she saw him get out of his car.

Tall and fairly well built, Jim had gray eyes and sported long black hair that was always braided. The man crossed the distance to them quickly and greeted, "Hey."

With a smile, Becky replied, "Hey, yourself, handsome. Keeping out of trouble?"

He winked at her and said, "It's been positively dead around the office."

Genie groaned. They just had to have a coroner with a bad sense of humor.

All three went inside to the victim's apartment. Neighbors peered out of their doorways, most still dressed in robes, but no one tried to ask what was going on. Becky sighed. "How much you want to bet no one heard or saw anything?"

Genie snorted. "I'm not taking that bet."

Jim grinned and added, "Depends. What'll you give for odds?"

Shaking her head in amusement, Becky walked through the open door of apartment thirteen and was immediately hit with a blast of emotions. Staggering back, she would have fallen if Jim hadn't caught her. But then she was hit with his surprise and concern and jerked out of his grip. Before she could stumble again, Genie pulled Becky firmly into her arms and murmured soothing words. After a few moments in the settling embrace, Becky took a long, deep breath and pulled away.

"You okay?" Genie asked with worry.

"Fine, just caught off-guard," Becky assured her. Although that in itself was disturbing because she'd had all her shields firmly in place. Shaking her head, Becky continued, "Why don't you take a look around? I'm going to see what I can get, now that I'm prepared."

Genie nodded and motioned for Jim to follow.

Becky drifted through the apartment, looking at the homemade decorations on the walls and the little touches that made the small living room seem comfortable. The comfort was all surface, though, because Becky felt a sense of dislocation from just about everywhere; dislocation and sadness permeated the entire apartment. Her eyes caught sight of the photos lined up on the coffee table and she squatted down to take a closer look. Family photos mostly, with one constant: a man who was in all of them, at varying ages.

Well. At least she knew who the victim was.

Sighing, she stood and headed towards the kitchen where she

could hear Genie and Jim talking quietly as they examined the scene and the body. One thing she'd never gotten used to was seeing death in all its horror. Even as a girl, she'd hated funerals. Of course, the fact that her first two had been her parents,' and then her sister's, hadn't helped matters.

Walking into the room, Becky forced down an automatic shudder and looked at the body on the floor. It was the man from the photos, no doubt about that. His face was a caricature of happiness. Becky knew without even touching him that the killer had twisted that expression onto the man's face. "The killer did that. There might be fingerprints on the man's face."

Jim looked up at her with a nod, making a note.

Genie stood and practically growled her frustration. "What the hell? This man isn't even a tourist, but it's obviously our guy!"

Becky continued to look around the kitchen. Flashes of this man moving unhappily around the room hit her, filling her with depression. "He is."

Impatient, Genie demanded, "Who is what?"

"He is a tourist. This isn't his real home. He spends very little time here, despite the pictures and nick-knacks," Becky said slowly. "I'm betting he's connected with the convention, but in a more detailed way, maybe as part of the actual administration or a committee detail?"

"Getting anything from the killer?"

Closing her eyes, Becky sent her thoughts adrift but, as before, found nothing. "Not a damned thing."

A comforting hand rested on Becky's shoulder. "We'll nail him. Relax."

Rolling her shoulders a little, she smiled gratefully at the taller woman before shifting away. The photographers had arrived and Jim was working his part of the scene. "See anything unusual?"

"Only the location," Genie answered.

"Maybe."

"Maybe?" When Becky didn't answer her, Genie shrugged and returned to her conversation with Jim.

Becky continued her sweep of the apartment, trying to figure out what was bothering her. There was nothing out of place. The apartment was actually very neat and well cared for, if a bit forlorn in her personal opinion. She knew this wasn't the victim's real home; that wasn't the issue. It was the complete lack of psychic residue from the killer, again, that bugged her. Anyone driven to kill left at least a trace of the emotions behind because they were, nine times out of ten, all strong emotions: hate, love, betrayal, pain. The only exception was a hired killer who considered what he or she did to be part of the job. Which left a whole different set of disturbing emotions to sort through.

Shaking her head again, Becky stopped at the door, catching the faintest of echoes: satisfaction in a job well done. Freezing in place, she let her mind drift again, mentally scenting the trail in the hall, following it slowly, fingers trailing the dusty wall to keep her on track. People moved out of her way, fear and mistrust sweeping out towards her, but she ignored it all to concentrate on the tenuous mental thread.

The back stairs saw an increase in the thread, and when she stepped outside, satisfaction gave way to righteousness and a stronger impression of the killer. *Or, not the killer? No, he has to be. It's hard to tell. Young, early twenties, a cool dedication to his work and no remorse for the killings. Beautiful. Only, the killings aren't the real work for him. He's focused on —*

Something slammed between her shoulder blades, sending her crashing to the ground with an astonishing amount of force and agony. Before she could figure out what had happened, someone kicked her. Pain radiated through her stomach. Gagging as she tried to breathe, Becky was kicked in the ribs, where something cracked and then again, in the stomach. Vomiting wasn't high on her list of things to do when unable breathe, but things were most definitely heading that way.

"Hey! Get the hell away from her, you little bastard!"

Genie! Oh thank God! Becky thought in desperate relief.

"Friggin' mind slut. We'll get your kind. We'll erase you, and don't forget it, bitch!" Another blow, to her back this time, and then her attacker was gone, running down the alley.

"Oh, Becca, can you hear me? Are you all right? I need some help out here!" Genie shouted.

Finally drawing in an almost complete breath, Becky opened her eyes and croaked, "Good timing."

Relief etched Genie's features as she hesitantly touched Becky's face. "Damn. He got you good, partner. What happened?"

Keeping her breathing shallow due to the pain, Becky gasped weakly, "I was working. Someone had a problem with it. Gotta admit, could've come up with a better insult."

"What did he call you?"

"The usual: 'mind-slut' and 'your kind,' " Becky sighed, relaxing into the temple massage Genie was giving her. It was a minor relief, but at this point, she'd take what she could get. The sharp, radiating pain in her side and back were difficult to ignore, but she forced her mind away from it by asking, "There was something... How'd, how'd you know?"

Face etched with worry at the abrupt change in Becky's tone of voice, Genie answered, "I was talking to Jim, then looked around for you and you were gone. This isn't the best part of town for anyone, never mind a telepath, so I wanted to make sure you were okay."

A couple of officers had arrived shortly after Genie, and Becky heard them calling for an ambulance over their radios. Strangely, she didn't feel any hostility or irritation from them about her presence, a boon since it was one more thing she would have had to deal with. Closing her eyes to fight a particularly bad wave of pain in her midsection, Becky breathed quickly and shallowly, tears escaping.

"When I get my hands on that little bastard, I'm going to..."

"Arrest him for a hate crime," Becky said firmly, having ridden out the pain. The last thing she needed was her partner going vigilante.

Thinly, Genie replied, "That wasn't what I had in mind."

The EMTs arrived just then and started checking her over. One of them reported, "Four broken ribs, probably a bruised kidney. We should get her to the hospital and make sure there's no internal damage."

Genie nodded. "I'll ride with you."

"No, Genie, work the scene. I want to catch this asshole," Becky ordered, gritting her teeth against the renewed pain as she was loaded onto a stretcher.

"But..."

"Please?"

Genie sighed, then lightly touched Becky's hand. "All right. I'll check in with you at the hospital when I'm done here. Do you want me to call Sharon?"

"She's in California," Becky said, shaking her head. "I'll catch you later."

"Sure. Be careful with her," Genie ordered sharply.

The EMTs nodded easily, obviously familiar with cop attitudes about their partners. Becky's last sight of Genie was the woman standing in the alley, watching her as the ambulance doors closed.

"IS SHE OKAY?"

Genie shrugged. "Some cracked ribs for sure. They're taking her in to check for internal injuries."

Jim's voice was carefully neutral as he asked, "And you're here?"

"Only because she ordered me to be. She wants to catch this guy."

"Well, there's not much you can do. Mick and Shen have bagged up everything that looks suspicious to bring back for analysis, and let me tell you, it wasn't much," Jim commented wryly. "I think this guy was a relative of Mr. Clean or something."

Some of her bad humor dissipated under Jim's steady words. He always managed to calm even the most hotheaded of tempers. Genie had never seen him in a situation that he couldn't talk himself out of.

"Yeah, well, hopefully there's something we can use."

"I'll let you know. Hey, give Becca my best, all right?"

"I will," Genie promised. "See you later."

On her way out, she passed the men bringing in the body bag and grimaced. There would be even more pressure to catch this guy because now, it was really hitting home. This victim might not be a full-time resident, but he *was* a resident. As she climbed inside the truck, she thought about the words that Becca hadn't said. There had been something her partner had wanted to relay to her, but hadn't felt it secure enough to do so.

Taking a quick detour to her apartment on the way to the hospital, Genie picked up an audio jammer and tucked it into her coat pocket. As sound jammers went, it was fairly small, but would work against all but the most sophisticated of equipment. Whatever Becca had to say might or might not revolve around the case, but regardless, she wanted the other woman to feel as though she could say anything.

It took longer to find a parking spot at the hospital than it did to actually get there. Shaking her head at the sad thought that hospitals were always that busy, Genie belatedly pulled out her phone and called the precinct.

"Carlson."

"Hey, Captain. I'm at the hospital."

"What happened?"

"It's Becca. She was bashed at the scene," Genie reported grimly.

"Excuse me?"

"I was inside with Jim. She moved on without me and that's where they got her. I saw the little prick who did it though. Once I'm done at the hospital, I'll work up a composite."

"Good. What did the EMTs say?"

"Some cracked ribs for sure. They brought her in to check for internal injuries," Genie explained.

"Christ."

"Yeah. He worked her over pretty good before I got there," Genie said, unable to help the anger coloring her tone: anger both at herself for not being there, and the perp who had attacked her partner.

"You listen to me, Marshall. You can't be around her twenty-four-seven, this is not your fault," Carlson snapped.

"I know."

"Uh huh. All right. Call me when you know her condition."

"Will do, boss." Genie tucked the phone back into her pocket and headed for the administrative desk. The woman behind the desk smiled at her approach. "I'm here to check on Detective Curtains' condition. She was brought in about a half hour ago."

Frowning, the woman shook her head. "Doesn't sound familiar, but they might not have updated the system yet. Let me call down to emergency."

"Thanks."

Genie looked around the reception area while the woman made a few calls. After almost ten minutes, growing impatient, she walked back over and asked, "What's taking so long?"

"I'm sorry, miss, but we don't have any record of Detective Curtains being brought in," the woman reported.

Pulling out her badge, Genie thrust it in the woman's face as she pushed aside the cold panic within. "I'm a detective at the 31st precinct, and Detective Curtains is my partner. I personally saw her put in an ambulance belonging to this hospital. She's here. If you don't find her in five minutes, I will be contacting the Administrator."

The woman swallowed nervously and said, "I've checked with everyone I can think of, Detective, honest. If she's here, they don't have her listed by name."

Furious, and a little frightened, Genie ordered, "Get me the Administrator *now*."

The woman picked up the phone again and Genie stepped away, forcing herself to calm down. It wouldn't do anyone any good for her to stomp all over the entire hospital administration, much as she wanted to. Taking several deep breaths, Genie had just calmed herself down when her name was called from behind. Turning, she found herself face to face with someone she hadn't expected to see ever again. Shocked, she stammered, "Steven?"

Just as shocked, the blond man nodded dumbly. "Genie? What's going on?"

Bringing herself back under control, Genie said, "My partner was assaulted and brought here less than an hour ago, but seems to be lost somewhere in this facility."

Shocked now for a different reason, embarrassment flushed through the man's handsome features and he apologized, "I'm sorry, Genie. Why don't you come with me? We'll head down to emergency together and ask the doctors down there."

Nodding, she fell into step with him as they walked towards the elevator. The silence between them was awkward. Unable to help it, she turned to her ex-lover and demanded, "You said you were staying in New York."

Flushing again, Steven said, "I did. But then this position came up and it was a better opportunity."

"How long have you been here?"

"About four months," Steven admitted.

Four months? Genie barely restrained herself from cursing, aware of their public location as they stepped off the elevator. She was angrier that he'd lied about staying in New York than about his not contacting her when he came back. Maybe. Shaking her head free from the confusion, she kept in mind that he was helping to find Becca and that was all that mattered.

They talked to four ER docs before finding one who remembered Becca being brought in. Or at least one that would admit to remembering her. It was a young doctor, Carla Jenkens, a resident, who had information for them.

"I told them she needed to get looked at right away, but the other doctors wouldn't listen to me," Jenkens reported, lips tight with aggravation. "I was told to mind my own business and let the more experienced doctors handle things. Handle things. Right. That poor woman was lying on the gurney for at least twenty minutes before I could pester Dr. Romans into looking at her for real."

Genie wanted to find the doctors who had ignored her partner and beat them into the pavement, but first, she needed to find Becca and make sure she was all right. Keeping a firm grip on her temper, Genie asked the young woman, "Do you know where she is now?"

Jenkens nodded. "By the time Dr. Romans got to her, complications had developed and they brought her to surgery. Far as I know, she's still there."

"Surgery!"

"Genie, calm down, we'll get to the bottom of this, figure out what happened," Steven said.

"Oh, I already know what happened here, Steven. What happened was they figured that because Becca was a telepath, she could wait. What's the difference if another mind-slut gets ignored, right? Well, let me tell you something, and this goes for everyone," Genie said, her voice echoing strongly throughout the ER. "If anything happens to my partner because of your neglect, I will personally charge those responsible with Negligent Homicide under the Hate Crimes act. And I'm sure the Police Union would love to get in on the action."

Genie rounded on Steven, golden eyes flashing. "And as for you. Find her *now*. I want to know her condition and which doctor is working on her, and I want to know within the next ten minutes."

Though pale, Steven nodded and immediately headed out of the ER. Genie turned to the young resident and was surprised by the satisfied expression on the other woman's face. "What?"

"Just glad someone finally got to these old boys," Jenkens smirked. Her dark eyes saddened as she touched Genie's shoulder. "Sorry it was your woman who got caught in the cross-fire, though."

Sighing, Genie rubbed her temple. "Thanks. Look, this is my card. Would you mind coming down to the station and giving a statement as to what you saw happen here?"

"Be delighted. Hey, I've got to get. Keep the faith."

It was as Genie watched the young black woman leave that she realized one of the reasons the resident was helping. Chuckling that someone thought she and Becca were a romantic couple, Genie found the nearest chair and sank into it. It was going to be a long, long afternoon.

Audio Excerpt from Rebecca Curtains' Journal—Year One

Ow.

I cannot say that enough. Ow, infinity plus one. Even with the painkillers, I'm in pain. They can't give me too much, or my barriers go down and that would noooot be a good thing. Gonna have to find someone to figure out why shields aren't an autonomic function. Maybe ask Sharon if any of the kids are scientifically inclined and looking for a project. Make it extra credit or something.

I know I was fuzzy on the way to the hospital, and even more when we got here, but I think it took a lot longer for someone to see me than normal. I'm a little out of focus right now without Genie around, but still, I seem to remember a lot of time going by. I'll have to check on that.

If I remember. Of course, that's why I snagged a recorder from a nurse the second I could think at least a little clearly. I know she thought I was nuts, but I had to get down my impressions, even as vague as they are.

First: this guy's on a holy crusade. Lucky us.

Second: he's not really after these people, just scapegoats, a convenient target.

Third: my head really, really hurts, so I think I'm just gonna go back to sleep now.

Well, as soon as the room stops spinning enough for me to feel like I'm not going to vomit.

Again.

Chapter
Four

IT WAS WARM and fuzzy and so comfortable that Becky didn't want to move. Conversely, she also felt restrained and pinned down in a way she couldn't immediately identify. At least she was focused, which meant... "Genie?"

The looked-for response came almost right away. "Right here, Becca."

"Can't see you."

A low chuckle echoed warmly through the room. "Try opening your eyes."

Oh yeah. Probably a good idea. Now if only she could remember how. After several attempts, the right synapses fired and her eyes blinked open. Genie's familiar face hovered directly beside her bed, her hospital bed? "Hospital?"

"Yeah. You were beaten a little worse than the EMTs thought. They had to do surgery to stop internal bleeding," Genie reported, lightly brushing her fingers across Becky's forehead. "How're you feeling?"

Frowning, Becky took inventory and grimaced. Her midsection was wrapped up like an ancient Egyptian mummy, and there were all-over aches throbbing unpleasantly in time to her pulse. "Like I was beaten with a two by four."

Snorting, Genie told her, "Close. It was a tire iron and a metal-tipped boot. Found the tire-iron in the next alley over. The little pissant who did this is in custody. We got him good, partner."

Somewhat relieved, Becky nodded and yawned. "What time is it?"

Glancing at her watch, Genie answered, "Ten forty-ish."

"In the morning? What the hell day is it?"

"It's Thursday."

"Shit. I lost a whole day?"

Genie nodded, leaning against the bed. "That you did. But don't worry, I've been busy enough for the both of us."

"I'm sure. Did you remember to eat?"

Grinning, Genie nodded and answered, "More or less."

"Good, because you don't eat enough," Becky fussed. She grinned when Genie's eyes rolled and continued, "Don't deny my limited pleasure in fussing over you."

"Heaven forbid. Hey, everyone told me to give you their best," Genie said, pulling something out of her pocket and laying it on the serving tray/table.

Becky frowned at it for all of five seconds before figuring out what it was. "Oh yeah? Everyone?"

"Well, everyone who's not an asshole."

Giving them a cover for the coming silence the jammer would bring, Becky asked, "Hey, you mind if I head back to la-la land? I'm feeling kind of wiped here."

"Sure. I'm going to stick around for a while, just make sure you're doing okay. That was a little too close for comfort for me," Genie said honestly.

Surprised, but pleased, Becky smiled. "Thanks."

"No prob." And with that, Genie turned on the jammer.

"Everyone who's not an asshole? Real smooth, Marshall," Becky said with a laugh. She gasped in pain and groaned. "Okay. Now we know. Do *not* make me laugh."

Chuckling, Genie pointed out, "Hey, the truth hurts. So. What did you want to tell me?"

"I got a sense of our killer," Becky reported, yawning again. "He's in his early twenties and thinks he's on some kind of religious mission; he feels righteous. And the victims, they aren't the real targets."

"Not the real targets? They look pretty damn dead to me!"

"I know, I know, but they're more like pieces he's using to fulfill another plan," Becky said. "It's a gambit."

Sighing, Genie rubbed her eyes, muttering, "Christ. So what, or who rather, is the real target?"

Becky shrugged slightly, wincing as even that faint motion set off a throb of heat. "I don't know. It can't have anything to actually do with the convention, they're just salespeople."

"True. If they were lawyers, then I could see the religious mission," Genie joked.

"What did I just say about making me laugh?" Becky demanded, holding her side as she tried not to do just that.

"Sorry. Did you get a physical description?"

"No. I was just about to when I was attacked," Becky replied.

"Hm."

"Hm, what?"

"Nothing."

"C'mon, Genie, I know that 'Hm' and it always means something," Becky prodded.

"Well. What if your attacker was in on it? He sees you getting close to the killer's trail and decides to disrupt things," Genie suggested.

Thinking back to the attack, Becky shivered. She'd come across hatred before, but this had been much more than a generalized hatred for telepaths; it had been personal, no matter what insults the perp had used. It gave her a very creepy feeling.

"What is it?"

"Just thinking about the attack," Becky answered. She saw the guilt flit across Genie's face, almost too fast to notice. "Genie, you can't possibly blame yourself for this!"

Shrugging, Genie said, "If I'd been with you like I was supposed to, it wouldn't have happened. Not only that, you would've gotten a fix on the perp for real. Yeah, I do blame myself."

"Well don't," Becky said firmly. She reached out and snagged Genie's hand in her own. "I'm a big girl and normally, I can take care of myself pretty damn well. I just wasn't paying attention like I should've been."

Genie pulled her hand free to pace around the small room. "You shouldn't have to! I mean, it's not like you're some raving deviant who's going to pry into everyone's mind! I've never met a telepath like that in my life. You all have a more honorable code of ethics than anyone I've ever known! It sucks that you can't even work without someone at your side to make sure you don't get beaten into a friggin' pulp!"

Sighing, Becky closed her eyes for a moment. When she opened them, Genie was back at her side, looking down at her anxiously. Becky managed a smile, hoping to reassure her partner with it, and said, "It's the way of things, Genie. It takes a long time for things to change, you know that. Someone always has to be the scapegoat. It's like that all throughout history."

"It still sucks," Genie muttered mutinously.

Smiling gently, Becky re-captured her friend's hand and said, "Thanks."

Deliberately shaking off her mood, Genie continued, "Anyhow. I talked to Jim and he said that they didn't find any fingerprints on the corpse, not that we really expected any since our guy's been so careful up until now. Vic's name was Donald Natale, fifty-eight-year-old widower with two surviving, grown children. And you were right. He keeps that apartment here for business, but doesn't generally stick around for long. His hometown is New Boston."

"I know everyone in the admin staff at the convention checked out, but do me a favor and look at them again? Maybe run down family histories? God, that's really going to suck with me being in here. Hey, how long am I here for, anyhow?"

"At least three days," Genie informed her. "Your busted ribs were fused, but there was some internal damage that the surgeons had to use Liqui on."

Becky's groan at the news had nothing to do with pain. Now

she'd be out of commission, probably for too long to be effective with
the rest of this case. On top of that, if she'd been so badly hurt that
the surgeons had to use the Liqui, she'd have to re-qualify before
being allowed back onto the streets! While very effective and safe,
the liquid compound that attached to internal organs to speed
recovery wasn't as good as being allowed to heal naturally; it was the
same with bones being fused. Both technologies were generally
reserved for emergency workers like cops, doctors, or fire personnel
who had to be back on the job as quickly as possible.

Shifting uncomfortably, extremely conscious of her wrapped
midriff, Becky complained, "I can't be in here that long! There's too
much to do!"

"You're only job right now is to get well," Genie ordered sternly.
"And if you have any trouble, you call for Dr. Jenkens, all right?"

"Yes, Mom," Becky grumbled.

Genie grinned. "It won't be that bad. I'll keep in contact with
you and Amy said she'd stop by whenever she got the chance. Oh,
and I did call Sharon when things took a turn for the worse, so she'll
be back in town tonight. You should expect her to blow in around
ten. I already cleared it with the staff."

"Great. I'm sure they loved that," Becky sighed.

"Oh yeah. Hey, um, just so you know, there are some staff here
who aren't thrilled with you being who you are. That's why I gave
you Dr. Jenkens' name. She's cool. Although at the moment, she's
under the impression that you're my partner, not just my coworker."

Becky frowned for a minute, not getting the distinction. Then she
gasped a laugh, clutching her side. "She thinks we're lovers? And
just how did that happen?"

Squirming a little uncomfortably, Genie answered, "I kinda got a
little upset when I couldn't find you."

"Oh? Do tell," Becky teased.

Obviously relieved by Becky's easy response, Genie winked and
explained, "When I got here, they played musical patients on me and
you weren't listed. I called down the Administrator in order to track
you down. And oh, God. You'll never guess who the new hospital
Administrator is."

"Who?"

Genie groaned. "An ex-lover of mine."

"Oh, really!" Becky commented, eyebrows wriggling.

"Well, at least it helped in tracking you down. Though I can't
vouch for my people skills once I found out where you were," Genie
said with a wry grin.

"What people skills?"

"Brat."

Becky smirked and repeated her earlier words of, "Hey. The
truth hurts."

"Yeah, yeah. Look, it's time for you to get back to sleep for real. You've got some serious healing to do."

Becky mock-saluted and snuggled back down into the covers. "You be careful out there."

"I will. And I'll be back tomorrow morning, first thing," Genie promised.

"Good," Becky murmured, closing her eyes. She drifted into sleep feeling Genie's thumb brush across her hand.

THE NEXT TIME Becky woke up, things weren't nearly as comfortable. She was achy and confused and irritable. Opening her eyes took less time though, so she supposed there was some improvement. When she did finally open her eyes, Becky saw Amy sitting in a chair beside the bed doing some kind of paperwork. "Hey."

Amy looked up with a smile. "Hey yourself. How're you feeling?"

"Sore," Becky answered honestly.

"I could get a nurse for you," the other woman offered.

"No, that's okay, I'm good for now."

"Well, if you're sure?"

"Absolutely," Becky confirmed. "What are you doing here? Have you been here long?"

"I am actually working right now," Amy said.

"Working?"

"Yeah. Watching you," Amy explained. "Captain Carlson didn't like the way you were treated, so he's making sure there's someone around to be sure you get the right attention."

"How was I treated?" Becky asked, confused.

"Genie didn't tell you?"

"Tell me what?"

Rolling her eyes, Amy ground out, "I'm going to kill her."

"What happened?"

"Some of the doctors dragged their heels in treating you and because of it, things got pretty hairy there for a while," Amy informed her grimly. "I heard that Genie ripped most of the ER staff new ones about the whole thing."

"Wonderful," Becky muttered. *Got a little upset, huh, partner?*

"Yeah, well, Captain Carlson just wanted to make sure that you were properly looked after," Amy continued. "Which is why you need to really tell me how you feel."

"I'm fine," Becky insisted. "Sore and achy, but there's not much to do about that, right?"

Amy stared at her for a long moment as though trying to determine her truthfulness, then shrugged. "If you say so."

"I do." There was an awkward silence, then Becky sighed. "I'm sorry. It's just that in all the years I was a PA for the Feds, I was injured exactly once. Then I come here and it's like, 'Beat on Becky' time, you know? My first partner sets me up and gives me an almost fatal backlash. Then I get sucked into that thing from hell last week, with another backlash no less. And yesterday, or, no, day before, I was just bashed altogether and wound up in surgery. I still shouldn't take it out on you, because God knows I just don't have enough friends that I can stand to lose one from being pissy."

"Hey, I understand. If I'd had a month like that, I'd want to vent a little, too," Amy assured her.

Becky smiled ruefully. "Thanks."

"No problem. So. Did you and Genie go over the case when she was here earlier?"

"Not really," Becky answered. She didn't know where the paranoia was coming from, but she'd always listened to her instincts and they were telling her to keep her mouth shut without that jammer around. Changing the subject, she asked, "How's the studying for the detectives' exam going? Did you want to get together sometime to go over things?"

"That would be great!"

"Consider it done. Well, once I'm out of here that is."

THE CONFUSION WAS gone the next time she woke, but the comforting sense of stability wasn't coming from Genie. Becky wasn't surprised to find Sharon in the chair that Amy had vacated. Smiling, she greeted, "Hi."

Sharon didn't smile as she stood and crossed to the bed. "How are you?"

"Fine. Which you know, because you've been monitoring me."

There was a reluctant twitch of Sharon's lips. "Guilty. But that's just your body. How are *you*?"

Becky shrugged. "Pissed that I wasn't paying enough attention to see the punk who did this coming. Worried that Genie's going to keep feeling guilty for not being there to stop it. Aggravated that I have to be here another couple of days so I can't really work on catching a killer. Otherwise, I'm fine. You?"

"I'd be better if you weren't here," Sharon admitted.

Becky suddenly remembered where Sharon had been dragged away from and demanded, "Did you get to meet with him? Before you turned around to come right back here?"

This time Sharon did smile. "I did. And he's wonderful. His parents are completely accepting and actually very proud that he's a telepath. They've agreed to bring him to the Center for daily training, although that means they have to move. Of course, it helps that we're paying their moving expenses."

"Of course. How strong?"

"Well, he's only ten, so we won't know for sure until after puberty, but I think he'll be around your level."

Impressed, Becky winked and said, "Really. Not many of us around."

"Impudent."

Grinning cheekily, Becky replied, "And your point would be?"

Reaching out, Sharon's fingers ghosted over Becky's head without actually touching. "It would hurt us more than your lost abilities to lose you, Becky. For any reason. You keep us honest, little one."

Surprised by her foster-mother's suddenly serious mood, Becky reached out with her mind and asked, *What's wrong, Mother?*

Eyes still sad, Sharon answered silently, *Nothing really. Joseph has been making noises again.*

Rolling her eyes, Becky said, *Joseph is always making noises. He's a pompous asshole.*

Snorting with sudden laughter, Sharon agreed, *True. The problem is that some are starting to listen to him. And now, with this attack on you, he might actually gain some support.*

Becky frowned. *That can't be right. His ideas are ludicrous, bordering on fascist. Surely the others wouldn't even think about supporting him?*

The others are getting frightened, little one. The violence isn't going away and UnderTEM is getting stronger. You've always been our guiding voice and you've been gone for a long time.

Sighing, Becky looked away before admitting, *Maybe I have been gone too long, but the work I do here is important. You know that. We have to be on the front lines where people can know us, see that we aren't monsters for being what we are.*

I do know that. But maybe the others would be better served with a reminder from you, personally.

Becky nodded. *All right. Once this case is wrapped up, I'll come home for a visit.*

Relieved, Sharon said aloud, "Good. I am going to head back to your apartment. There is a guard outside the room and he'll be there all night from what I understand. Oh, and give Genie a call, dear. She called while you were sleeping."

"And you didn't wake me?" Becky demanded.

Sharon shrugged placidly. "You needed to rest."

Grumbling, Becky muttered, "Busybody mothers."

Smiling, Sharon kissed her cheek and said, "Sleep well, little one."

"Night, Sharon. I'll see you later." Shaking her head in amusement, Becky picked up the phone on the nearby table and dialed Genie's cell phone.

"Marshall."

"Hey, it's me."

Genie's voice warmed immediately as she exclaimed, "Becca! Hey, how are you?"

Grinning, Becky answered, "Fine. Much better, matter of fact. I'm going to see what I can do about getting out of here tomorrow."

"Don't rush it," Genie ordered.

"I won't," Becky lied blithely. "Sharon said you called?"

"Oh, yeah. I drafted a couple of assistants to check on that lead from earlier. Nothing."

Groaning, Becky repeated, "Nothing? Are you sure?"

"Positive. There were some misdemeanors and lots of unpaid parking tickets, but nothing major," Genie reported.

"Great. Now what? We're back to square one."

"Well, yeah. But I did look for our next victim and found five possibles," Genie said. "The Captain has already assigned them all protection."

"There are five sixty-eight-year-old salespeople at the convention? Don't they know they're supposed to retire by that age?" Becky observed with a grin.

"Apparently not," Genie answered dryly. "Oh, and there aren't any seventy-nine-year-olds, so if we don't catch him this time, I have the very bad feeling that he's just going to disappear."

"The pattern'll be completed," Becky agreed with a sigh. Though she knew that something more was going on, she didn't know what. Not to mention that their killer could choose a completely different pattern to accomplish said unknown goals and they'd be none the wiser that it was the same perp. "Wonderful."

"Hey, at least we've got this one more shot."

"I still don't like it."

Changing the subject, Genie asked, "Hey, have you seen the news at all?"

"No. Why?"

"There was a very unpleasant interview with Doyle tonight."

Harry Doyle. The President of UnderTEM. Becky could guess about the content of the interview, but asked anyhow. "Unpleasant how?"

"Well, he wasn't spouting just his usual crap."

"What was he saying?"

"He mentioned as how they've not only narrowed down the telepathic gene, but also ascertained that telepaths are now scientifically proven to be unstable."

Outraged, Becky exclaimed, "He what?"

Genie snorted. "I know. I almost kicked in my TV when I heard the smug bastard. I don't know, Becca. It seems like things are getting worse instead of better. This is bound to create a fear backlash. Why don't your people ever do any counter-interviews? I mean, the only publicity around telepaths is completely negative."

Sighing, Becky answered, "Because we're divided on the whole issue. Some are afraid to reveal ourselves in such a public venue because it would make us visible targets. Some think it would only make things worse, like we're caving to the media pressure. Then there's the whole camp who want nothing to do with society period."

"A separatist movement? You're kidding," Genie said, surprised.

"I wish. Sharon and I were just talking about it when she was here. I'm heading home when we're done with this assignment so I can see for myself what's going on," Becky replied.

"Wow. Um, well, I guess I can see where you'd want to do that?"

Becky could hear the uncertainty in her friend's voice and smiled. "I'm coming back, Genie. I was just going to take a week off. There're things going on that I need to take care of."

There was a brief pause, then, "That *you* need to take care of?"

While Becky trusted Genie, probably more than she should given their shaky relationship, she wasn't about to discuss private matters over an unsecured phone line. "Yeah. We can talk about it later."

Accepting the statement, Genie said, "You should probably get some sleep."

"Don't you mean more sleep? I can't remember the last time I slept this much!" Becky complained.

"Hey, don't knock it, who knows when you'll get the rest again? Besides which, the more you sleep, the sooner you're out of there, right?"

"I guess. I just feel useless."

"Well, don't. Look, I'll be by in the morning so I can get an official statement from you about the attack. We can talk then," Genie suggested.

"Sounds like a plan," Becky agreed. "Sleep well."

"You too. Bye."

"Bye."

Becky hung up the phone and sighed, wondering if the headache were really physical, or if it had been induced by what she'd learned from Genie and Sharon. Either way, her head was beginning to throb in the all-too-familiar cadences of a migraine. Groaning, she closed her eyes and hoped that sleep wouldn't be too far away.

Audio Excerpt from Rebecca Curtains' Journal—Year One

God, I hate politics. Definitely one of my least favorite things in the world. Bad enough I have to put up with Doyle and his crap from the outside, but within my own people? This bites!

I'm going to be here for a few days more, which really, really sucks. I wish I wasn't feeling quite so paranoid about everything, but, hey, I've got instincts for a reason, right? Interesting thing is that Genie's on the same wavelength. It's so cool when she does that, like she knows what I need before I even ask for it.

Though, I am still drugged up enough to know my instincts might not be completely accurate, they're on the ball enough. And my powers aren't that affected by the medicine.

I know, for instance, that Genie is fine at home. All the way across town. By herself. With a maniac on the loose who seems to be playing mind games with us.

Okay. Calming down now from unnecessary hysteria. Taking nice, deep breaths to push back the panic. I don't know where it came from, but the thought of anything happening to Genie...as much as a pain in my butt as she is, I really do like the big goof.

Chapter
Five

THE HOSPITAL WAS busy, even at the early hour of seven in the morning, and Genie had plenty of company in the elevator heading up to Becca's room. She was the only one who exited on that floor, though, and she spotted the young, uniformed guard outside Becca's room right away.

He looked up at her approach and smiled. "Morning, Detective Marshall."

"Good morning. Mansfield, isn't it?"

"It is. Everything's been quiet since I got on. I looked in on her when I first came on duty."

Genie echoed his smile and said, "Good. And thanks, I appreciate it."

"That's what I'm here for," he said firmly.

Thinking that maybe things weren't so bad off, though Amy and Mansfield were the next generation of cops, Genie entered her partner's room. For some reason, Becca looked even smaller than she usually did, tucked down in the hospital bed. As she reached her partner's side, she was pleased to see a healthy flush had replaced the previous pallor. Becca's usually neat hair was sticking up in short spikes, which made Genie grin. Wishing that she had time to wait until her partner woke naturally, Genie briefly shook the other woman's shoulder.

Blinking awake, Becca stared at her blearily for a few moments before smiling. "Hey."

"Hey yourself. You look better," Genie observed.

Taking a few moments to think about it, Becca replied, "I feel better. Actually, I feel almost normal, just some soreness in my ribs."

"Good. But that doesn't mean you're getting out of here today," Genie warned firmly.

Rolling her eyes, Becca grasped the bed control and raised herself into a slanted position. "The doctor is checking me over this morning to see how I'm doing. I'll call you when she's done and let you know the verdict. And how's your hand doing, anyhow?"

Genie shrugged, lifting the cast with a grin. "I don't notice it until I try to button or zip something. Good thing you didn't have my left hand, or I'd be screwed."

"Did I mention that I'm really sorry about that?" Becca offered with a faint grin.

"Well, as long as it's not a preview of you in PMS-mode, you're forgiven," Genie commented wryly.

Chuckling, Becca said, "Nah. I don't get PMS."

"I'll hold you to that," Genie vowed lightly. She pulled out a tape recorder and set it on the bed tray, flipping it on. "Detective Genie Marshall taking the interview of P.A. Detective Rebecca Curtains. If you could recount the events leading up to your attack, Detective Curtains?"

"I had caught the mental trail of the suspect in an open murder case. I followed it down the back stairs of the apartment building, to the alley outside. My eyes were closed to enhance the mental connection, so I didn't see anyone approach. Something knocked me to the ground. I was kicked twice in the stomach and once in the ribs. I heard you, I heard Detective Marshall shout and then my assailant said, 'Friggin' mind slut. We'll get your kind, we'll erase you and don't forget it, bitch!' Then he punched me in the back and left."

"Did you see your attacker at all?" Genie asked quietly.

"No. My eyes were closed the whole time and my arms were up, protecting my head," Becca answered. "But I'd recognize his voice if I heard it again."

"You're sure?"

"Absolutely. He spoke directly into my ear and I'm good with voices anyhow."

"Do you know what prompted the attack?"

Becca sighed. "Because I'm a telepath. The insults, and the fact that when I'm working, it's really hard to mistake what I am, make that pretty obvious."

"All right. Thank you, Detective Curtains. This tape will be transcribed and returned for your signature. When you're physically able, you'll have to make a voice ID on the assailant," Genie said formally before turning off the recorder.

Sighing deeply, Becca flashed a smile at her and said, "Glad that's over with."

"You all right?" Genie asked with concern. The calm recital of what had happened, had her guts twisted all to hell with the guilt that she hadn't been there, and anger that her partner had gone through something so painful.

"Fine," Becca assured her.

She closed her eyes and lay there quietly, which told Genie that she was probably scanning for eavesdroppers. Pulling the jammer from her pocket, Genie turned it on just as Becca said, "Great minds think alike."

"Or we share the same neuroses," Genie agreed, winking.

Perched on the edge of the bed, she asked, "So why are you really taking time off when all this is over?"

"Sharon said that the man who's leading the separatist movement within the telepaths is getting support that he hadn't before. My attack here has given him an edge that she doesn't like."

"So you're going back to show them that you're all right?" Genie guessed.

"Well, that's one of the reasons," Becca confirmed. "The other is to remind them of the reason that I'm out here in the first place. The reason we're all out here. To show non-telepaths that we're not out to invade everyone's mind."

"Isn't that more Sharon's job than yours?"

Becca shook her head and replied, "Not really. Actually, Sharon's main focus is finding new telepaths and getting them to the Center for training."

"Is that how you two met? Did she find you?"

"No. One of the others found me and brought me to the Center," Becca explained slowly. "My parents and sister died in car crashes when I was young. Sharon kind of took over as my unofficial mom when I got to the Center."

"Jeeze, Becca, I'm sorry."

Becca shrugged. "Old news."

"Doesn't mean it doesn't still hurt," Genie said softly.

Becca nodded acknowledgment and continued, "I grew up at the Center and I'm pretty strong in my gifts. There are a lot of people there who respect what I think. There was a lot of opposition to sending me out here at all, never mind as an Agent. It's dangerous for any of us, but especially for me."

Frowning, Genie asked, "Why especially for you?"

"Think of me as an empathic profiler. I *literally* get inside the minds of the perps we catch. I've come close to stark raving mad more than once, as you have personally witnessed," Becca reminded wryly. "Why do you think I have so much downtime after a bad case?"

"Union rules?" Genie suggested, with the hint of a grin.

Snorting, Becca nodded. "And now you know why. It certainly wasn't to create problems between me and the other detectives."

"But, wait. You still haven't told me why the people at the Center would object to you specifically being a PA."

Becca took a moment to mentally check out the area again and, finding no one listening, she revealed, "I run the Centers."

Jaw dropping, Genie exclaimed, "Excuse me?"

Grinning at her partner's shock, Becca repeated, "I run all the Centers."

"But, wait... How? How could you possibly do that and still be a full-time cop?" Genie demanded.

"Well, I do have assistants." The flippant remark earned her an irritated glare, and she apologized, "Sorry, being serious now. Think of me like a council leader. Each Center is run independently, but we have a conclave every quarter, which I head."

"But you're only twenty-eight. How can you possibly hold that much power?" Genie demanded.

Becca shrugged. "I don't, really. I mediate the conclaves. I make sure that none of the Centers are over-burdened. I keep in contact with each Center Leader to make sure things are going well worldwide. It's like anyone who runs an extra-curricular organization. You just think it's more involved than it really is. Those in charge of the Centers are all capable, good-hearted and, best of all, almost *anally* organized, people."

Genie shook her head, trying to figure out what to make of this latest development.

"Hey, it's all right. Look, I don't mind if you want a new partner after hearing all this. But I have to ask that you keep it confidential. My life out here wouldn't be worth squat if Doyle found out about me," Becca said gently.

Indignant, Genie exclaimed, "Of course I don't want a new partner! Jeeze! I just needed a second to take it all in. Give me a break, all right?"

Properly chastised, Becca smiled in relief. "Good. I'm glad."

"Anyhow. I was thinking about the case last night," Genie said, pointedly leaving on the jammer.

"Oh?"

"Yeah. Mostly about the fact that you couldn't seem to get a handle on the perp, and when you finally did, someone beat it out of you. Literally."

Wondering where this was going, Becca asked, "What about it?"

"Is it possible to take physical steps to make someone psychically invisible?"

Becca thought about it for a few minutes. "I'm not sure. Not directly touching anything in the location is a good start. If you don't touch anything, you can't leave a psychic residue."

"So, what? If you've got like, a tarp or plastic rug on the floor, and don't touch any furniture, then that would do it?" Genie guessed.

"It's a good start, yeah. But you'd also have to have a pretty good grip on your thoughts, too. Which most serial killers don't."

"True," Genie agreed. "But what if it's not your run-of-the-mill serial killer doing this? You said yourself that this person has another goal."

"You mean a hired gun."

"It would make a sick kind of sense."

"Problem being that we don't know what that goal is."

Genie held up a finger. "Yet. And we've only got one more shot to figure it out. Assuming this guy's following his own pattern, the next strike will be tonight."

Grimacing, Becca complained, "I really don't want to be stuck here tonight, Genie. I should be with you catching this bastard! What if these people have already had contact with him, but don't know it? I could scan them and save everyone a lot of time and trouble."

"No, you couldn't. Out of our five possibles, only one of them was even slightly amenable to the idea."

"Even when it could save their lives?"

"Even then."

"Great."

Genie squeezed Becca's shoulder. "We're just going to have to catch him the old-fashioned way. We've got uniforms in place at all of their locations to make sure nothing happens to these people. The Captain and I are going to be at the office all night, as everyone checks in. I will call you first thing in the morning to let you know how it went."

Becca sighed. "I don't suppose I have a choice."

Grinning unrepentantly as she turned off the jammer and put it in her pocket, Genie said, "Nope. Not a one."

"Brat."

"Takes one to know one," Genie teased back comfortably.

Smiling, Becca was about to say something when Dr. Jenkens opened the door. Turning her attention to the newcomer, Becca greeted, "Morning, doc. I thought you were showing up later this morning. You know, around noon?"

Dark eyes twinkling, Jenkens replied, "That's only for real doctors. I'm a peon."

"Ah. That explains a lot," Genie said with a grin. Without thinking, she ran her hand over Becca's cheek and said, "Call me on my cell when you're finished here. I'll probably be busy doing last-minute checks for tonight."

Saluting, Becca agreed, "Will do. Be careful."

Genie grinned and walked towards the door.

As she reached it, Becca called out, "And make sure you eat or I'll hurt you when I get out of here!"

"Yeah, yeah," Genie waved her order aside and left the room.

BECKY SHOOK HER head as Genie left and then complained to Jenkens, "She just doesn't take care of herself. Do you know what her idea of a good meal is? One that takes less than five minutes to make."

Laughing, Jenkens said, "Well, at least she's got you to nag her into eating right."

"When I'm around, yeah," Becky agreed sourly. She straightened and assumed an innocent expression. "So. I can get out of here today, right?"

"Sorry to disappoint, but I tend to doubt it," Jenkens informed her. "I'm going to check your stitches and your ribs and then subject you to some more tests. We'll know when the results come back, but I think one more night here is going to be my minimum requirement. Especially since I tend to doubt that you'll rest much once you escape."

"Who, me?"

"Yeah, you. Now then, open your mouth and say 'ah.' "

IT'S A GOOD thing *I drive an automatic,* Genie thought as she parked at the precinct. *Driving a standard car with this cast would be impossible.*

Despite the internal, environmental improvements to cars over the last half-century or so, the general design hadn't changed a hell of a lot. The engines now ran on safe, efficient hydroelectricity, as did all major electrical appliances and generators, but were still on the ground causing headaches, traffic, and accidents. A successful anti-gravity device had as yet to be invented, and until that happened, things would probably continue along the same way for the next hundred years.

Though, considering the horrifying accidents Genie had witnessed on the ground, perhaps that was a blessing.

Glancing at her watch, Genie was glad that she wouldn't be too late. Carlson was nothing if not a stickler for punctuality. Though he really couldn't hassle her this morning, since she'd been getting Becca's statement. Heading towards her desk, she groaned to herself as a couple of Vice detectives walked towards her. Great. Just what she needed to start the day off right.

"Hey, Marshall."

"Nickerson. Bailey," Genie greeted.

"What happened to your arm?" Nickerson asked. The detective was as tall as she was, but thicker, more muscular, and wore tight jeans and a T-shirt to show off his build.

Bailey chuckled and added, "I heard your partner broke it for you."

Genie glared at the shorter man, taking in his ragged appearance with a disdainful snort. "Like you have enough friends to hear anything outside your rock."

"It proves Doyle's point. You know. About the instability of telepaths. They're a nuisance, and if you didn't have your head shoved up your ass, you'd know it," Bailey snapped.

Growling, Genie was about to do something that she'd probably regret when a restraining hand appeared on her shoulder. Angrily looking over her shoulder, Genie found Thomas Mathisen standing there. Surprised at the other detective's sudden appearance, Genie stayed quiet as he spoke.

"Becca's more stable than your sorry ass, Bailey. Why don't you go crawl back under that rock Marshall was talking about?"

Though grateful for the support, especially when the vice cops left because of it, Genie was wary of it, too. The older man had been one of the more vocal opponents to Becca's admittance into Violent Crimes. Having always been a voice of reason and intellect, he'd wielded a lot of power and almost kept the PA from being hired.

Though she hadn't known Becca at the time, she had known Mathisen, and the depth of the black man's vehemence had surprised her. Still did. Unable to keep the suspicion from her voice, Genie said, "Thanks."

Shrugging, Mathisen replied, "Any time."

"Why?"

Mathisen frowned. "Why, what?"

Frowning as well, Genie said, "You were one of the people dead set against Becca joining this department. Now you're defending her. Why?"

Looking at her thoughtfully, Mathisen said, "I wish that I could say it's because I took the time to get to know Curtains and see my prejudice for what it was, but I'd be lying."

Thoroughly confused now, Genie asked, "Then why?"

Smirking slightly, Mathisen answered, "Because after being your partner for not even a couple of months, she's made you practically human. Anyone who can do that has to be as good as they appear to be, no matter their genetics."

Jaw dropping, unsure whether to be insulted or pleased, Genie settled for a mix of the two and punched the slight man on the shoulder. "Jerk."

Laughing, Mathisen said, "You just proved my point. Before Curtains, you'd have decked me for saying something like that."

Joining in the laughter, somewhat ruefully, Genie fell into step with him as they headed towards their department. Reaching her desk, Genie took only the time needed to pull off her jacket and toss it over her chair before continuing on to Carlson's office. She knocked briefly before stepping inside.

Looking up from his paperwork, Carlson grimaced and complained, "Most people wait until I tell them to come in, Marshall."

Grinning, Genie said, "Ah, but I'm not most people, Sir."

"And don't I know it," he grumbled. "You're late."

"I stopped at the hospital first. Got Becca's statement about the attack. I'm going to drop it off to be transcribed in a minute," Genie reported.

"Good. I already talked to Dispatch and they're going to have the portable set up in the conference room by this afternoon," he informed her. "Make sure you're in there by four this afternoon. If I have to hunt you down, I'm really going to be hunting you down, understood?"

Genie saluted. "Sure thing, Captain. Anything else?"

"Yeah. I don't suppose you've finished up your paperwork for the Burman and Dorell cases yet?"

Thinking about the unfinished files waiting malevolently on her desk, Genie answered weakly, "Not exactly."

"Uh huh. That's what I figured. When you're done with the tape, plant your ass at your desk. I want those files done before we get into the conference room," Carlson ordered.

"Yes, Sir," Genie sighed, standing. Wonderful. A day of paperwork. Her favorite thing in the world.

DURING LUNCH, GENIE sat for a while staring into space, thoughts about the case tumbling constantly through her mind.

What did they know? Young man, in his early twenties. Using this killing spree for another, presumably darker, purpose. Or maybe one with longer-reaching consequences? Unable to get a psychic link on him. Knowledgeable about psychics. Knowledgeable about police procedure?

It was the working towards another goal that was bugging Genie. Knowing that their perp had no qualms about killing to achieve said goal meant that he would do so again and again until they caught him. There was nothing to say that he wouldn't disappear from here and start all over again somewhere else, either.

Groaning, Genie turned her attention back to her desk, which looked like a paper bomb had gone off. Half-heartedly, she turned on her desk radio and started gathering up paper. There was a news report on and a clip of Doyle's interview from the previous night came out of the small radio.

"...which is why I'm saying that there needs to be government involvement in the telepath issue. Donations from concerned, private citizens continue to pour in, and they do help inordinately, but these are people who have lives to lead. The government needs to wake up and see that the telepaths are as bad for it as they are for the rest of us."

The interviewer countered, "According to my sources, the telepaths police themselves more thoroughly than we ever could, Mr. Doyle. And there are plenty of people who think that you're only out to make a name for yourself by preying on the fears of the general population. How do you respond to that allegation?"

"It's nonsense," Doyle dismissed. "The population at large *is* my only concern. It's my intention to show the government what evils these telepaths are up to, and I'm going to start by running for office."

Genie jerked upright in shock at that announcement. It must have happened before she turned on the news the night before.

"...by working within the system. I will work hard to get committees formed and the funding necessary to set up the *proper* means to deal with the telepaths so that everyone can return to the freedom that only peace of mind can bring. Freedom of the mind."

"And there you have it. The bombshell that many political analysts say is setting things on fire here in DC. Harold Doyle, son of Senator James Doyle, is going to run for Senate himself in the coming election. According to..."

Nauseated, Genie shut off the radio, unable to listen to any more.

STARING AT THE ceiling was never fun. Staring at a hospital ceiling was even worse. Bored out of her mind, Becky wished that something would happen to take her mind off her boredom. Amy had left about an hour earlier, and her replacement stayed outside other than to check on her when he first arrived. It was now almost midday and the painkillers had worn off, but it was too early for the next dose to send her into Morpheus' grip.

Her ribs pulsed, full force, despite the fact that they were well on their way to being healed. She almost wished that she'd taken Amy up on her offer to keep the lurid romance novel the other woman had brought, that's how desperately bored she was.

Focusing her breathing into slow, deep breaths, Becky consciously relaxed her body. It had been a long time since she'd done any meditation, since before partnering up with Genie. It had just seemed like she never had the proper time to devote to it since then. Picturing the golden light encircling her body, starting at her toes, Becky brought herself through the relaxation meditation.

It started so slowly that at first, she didn't know what was really happening. The gentle darkness she stared at from behind her eyelids shifted, lightened. Glancing around, Becky noticed that she was in a hallway, an apartment hallway, and carrying a gun. Since she did carry a gun, that didn't surprise her. What did surprise her was that it was in her left hand. That was when she noticed the cast on her right hand.

Bemused, Becky realized that she was either seeing through Genie's eyes or having a premonition. The muted ringing of a cell phone sounded and Genie cursed, stopping to turn it off. Getting a better grip on her gun, Genie continued forward, slowly edging down the hall. All the doors were closed except for one, which was open a crack. It wasn't enough to see much of the apartment within, though.

In a surreal fashion, Becky felt as though she was both watching Genie and seeing through Genie's eyes. One moment she could see her partner inching through the doorway and the next, she saw the couch directly to her right as she crept inside. She saw the plastic covering the entire living room floor and tensed. Unfortunately, it was while she was looking through Genie's eyes that the muffled whump of a silenced gun went off. Pain seared into her gut and then again into her chest.

The fall to the floor seemed to take forever and then someone came into her line of sight. There was a mask, but blue eyes, colder than ice, stared down at her. As her life began to fade away, the man said, "This is what happens when you partner with the devil. The righteous will overcome the evil spawned plans of the telepaths. You are a sacrifice to the greater glory. Be honored that your sins will pass away with your death and you shall ascend to heaven."

A scream ripped from Becky's throat as she jerked out of the trance. Before the echo even started to fade, her guard burst into the room, looking for the problem. Wide-eyed, Becky couldn't even speak, her heart feeling as though it was about to stop. In her mind, she could hear the faltering rhythm of her partner's pulse spiraling towards death.

"Detective! Detective, what's wrong?"

Snapping out of the shock, Becky ignored the young man and reached for the phone, dialing her partner's number. She let it ring for almost half a minute, praying that Genie would pick up. She didn't. After hanging up, she tried Genie's cell phone, but got the same results. Becky re-dialed the precinct and was patched through to Captain Carlson.

"Carlson."

"Captain! You have to stop her. She's going to get herself killed!"

"Curtains? What are you talking about?" Carlson demanded.

"I'm talking about Genie!" she shouted. "I saw it! She's gone after the killer and he's going to shoot her. Wherever she is, you have to get her out of there, now!"

"All right, calm down. I'll find her, Curtains."

"I'm on my way in, call my cell when you track her down!" Becky turned to the officer and ordered, "Get your car and meet me out front!"

He nodded, running out of the room.

Grabbing her clothes, Becky painfully pulled them on, finding out as she did so that her stomach and chest were sore from the psychic connection to Genie where the bullets had impacted. Ignoring everything except the driving need to find and save her partner, Becky yanked on her shoes just as a nurse came in.

Horrified, the nurse exclaimed, "You can't leave! You're not due to be released yet!"

Becky ignored the woman and ran out of the room, clutching her ribs.

Chapter
Six

IT WAS A LAST-MINUTE, coincidental kind of thing. She'd just returned to her desk to search for something chocolate when her phone rang. Picking it up, she answered, "Detective Marshall."

"Hey. It's me."

Straightening in surprise, Genie asked, "What's up?"

"I know where he's gonna be, but you gotta go now if you want to stop him."

"What? Where?"

"One-Eighty Saxon Drive. Number fourteen. He's just getting there now, so you might save her."

Gritting her teeth, Genie knew better than to ask him to stall the killer, or how he got his information. She also knew better than to tell the Captain what was going on because it would waste precious time. She just hung up and ran out of the department. The drive seemed to take forever and when she pulled up in front of the address, she saw that the police assigned to protect this woman were nowhere to be found.

Filing that away for a later ass-chewing, Genie went to the trunk for her vest, only to find that it wasn't there. "Shit!"

Looking up at the apartment building, she briefly debated on whether or not to continue. This was, after all, a lunatic that she was dealing with. The hesitation was only momentary and she quietly shut the trunk and ran to the building. Her cell phone dropped out of her pocket as she reached for the door. Bending down to pick it up, she was surprised to find it off. Shrugging, Genie turned it on and replaced it in her jacket pocket.

The front door, which should have been locked, wasn't, and she slipped inside without any problems. Apartment fourteen was on the third floor and, naturally, the elevator was out. Grimacing, Genie started climbing the stairs, keeping an ear out for anyone else as she went. Halfway up, her phone rang and she pulled it out. "Marshall."

"What the hell do you think you're doing, going out there without backup? I'm going to have you riding a desk from here to eternity, Marshall!"

Oh, crap. "Ah, Captain, it was a last-minute tip."

"Oh, I'm sure it was. Don't you go near that apartment until we get there. Where are you, anyhow?"

"One-Eighty Saxon Drive, number fourteen." she reported. "And it'll take you too long to get here, I have to go in."

"No, you don't. Look, Curtains saw you dying, so you keep your ass out, got it?"

Becca saw her death? A shiver ran through her, but Genie said, "I have to go in, Captain, I'll be careful, I promise."

"God damn it, Marshall! Don't you fu—"

Turning off the cell phone and the ringer, Genie continued up the stairs.

BECKY'S PHONE RANG and she instantly answered it. "Genie?"

"No. Your idiot partner's going in without backup as we speak. 180 Saxon Drive, apartment 14. Meet us there."

Closing her eyes as she hung up, she repeated the address to Mansfield, who turned on the sirens and stepped on the gas. In her mind, all Becky could see was the blood seeping from Genie's body. She could hear the slowing heartbeat and shuddered.

"You all right, Detective?"

Forcing herself to open her eyes, Becky answered grimly, "I will be as soon as I get my hands on my partner. Once I see that she's safe and sound, I'm going to friggin' kill her."

Mansfield swallowed uneasily at her pronouncement and kept his eyes on the road.

THE HALL WAS dark, but not too dark to see. As she moved through it, she saw that all the doors were closed. All but the last, which was open a crack. It wasn't open far enough for her to really see inside, though. Pulling out her gun, she unlatched the safety and held it low, silently putting her cast against the wooden door to open it further.

GENIE SAW THE Captain stop short as she dragged her perp out of the stairwell, shouting the Miranda at him and bleeding from a cut to her forehead. She was woozy, but not enough to stop from shoving him down the last couple of stairs.

Looking bemused, he ordered, "Mathisen, Goldstein, get him away from her before she accidentally kills him, would you? And make sure to re-Miranda his ass so there's no problems down the line."

Genie was somewhat surprised when her two coworkers took the suspect from her, even though she'd heard the order. She promptly leaned against the nearest wall for support while she caught her breath. Closing her eyes, she reported, "Mrs. Jennifer O'Neill is safe and sound, Sir, and upstairs in her apartment. Close thing, though."

Gently, he asked, "You all right, Detective?"

Prying one eye open with an effort, Genie replied, "Only if you protect me from Becca, Sir."

Snorting, he shook his head. "Not a chance. I will, however, get an ambulance to fuse the pieces back together when she's done with you."

Waving a tired hand at him, she said. "Thanks. I think I'm just going to collapse here if you don't mind?"

"Go right ahead," he agreed, pulling out his phone and dialing.

She slowly slid down to the floor, using the wall to maintain balance.

"Genie!?"

The Captain stepped away from Genie as he looked over at the new arrival.

Face white with a combination of pain and fear, Becca stopped abruptly, looking down at her partner. Relief was patently visible for all of five seconds, followed fast by fury. "What the hell did you think you were doing? What? Do you think you're some kind of...of...of superhero? Bulletproof? You're the most aggravating person I've ever met! Sir, I'm reinstating my request for a transfer!"

Blinking in surprise, mostly likely at both the abrupt statement and being addressed by the furious woman, the man prudently withdrew saying, "I'm just going to go and make sure the ambulance gets here. Now. Soon."

Genie sighed and waited for the rest of the lecture, almost hoping that her head would fall off first.

AS MANSFIELD PULLED alongside one of the other cars, Becky was out the door and running across the yard before the car even came to a complete stop. She saw Mathisen and Goldstein dragging someone across the grass towards the cars and almost collapsed in relief. Genie was all right. If she wasn't, the suspect wouldn't be walking. Kim Yu stood at the door and quickly moved aside to let her through.

She didn't remember much of those first few seconds except the sight of Genie's face. Her auburn hair had come out of its customary braid, probably from a struggle, and she was bleeding from the left temple. There was a faint bruise along the left cheek that would darken quickly, but she was alive and pretty much unharmed.

After Captain Carlson made a hasty retreat, Becky forcibly got a grip on her careening emotions. Taking a deep breath, she knelt beside her partner and asked, "Are you all right?"

Hesitant, Genie looked up. "I've got a headache, but that's about it."

"Good. I'm sorry for going off like that, but you scared the shit out of me," Becky said. Sighing, she sat awkwardly beside Genie, favoring her ribs, and continued, "You also pissed me off to no end. What were you thinking? I know the Captain warned you about my premonition, he called me and said that you'd gone ahead anyhow."

"I was thinking that there was someone who might not make it until backup arrived," Genie said quietly. "I also thought that the patrol unit would be here to back me up. They weren't, but I really couldn't afford to wait."

"And your vest?" Becky asked quietly.

"I don't know. It was gone from my trunk," Genie answered. "I was going to wear it, Becca, I swear."

Nodding after a moment, Becky said, "Okay, I believe you. So, tell me what happened?"

"After I hung up with, ah, on the Captain, I continued up the stairs. I got into the hall, which was pretty dark, and found the last one was open a crack. I was about to open it when I realized that he was probably waiting for me. I mean, the whole thing felt like a setup *and* I had your warning. It was just stupid to go in the front. So I slipped around back and climbed up the fire escape. Oh, and wasn't that fun with a cast? It led to the bedroom and I looked in first, found the room was empty, except for Mrs. O'Neill tied up on her bed.

"I showed her my badge and whispered for her to stay quiet. Got through the bedroom and found the asshole kneeling on the floor, gun in hand, just waiting for me to show up. He must've been securing Mrs. O'Neill when I crossed the hall earlier. I put my gun to his head and ordered him to drop the weapon. He did. But when he stood, he lurched against me and we wrestled for control of my gun. He kept saying something about me being a sacrifice, that I was going to be blessed with death. Total psychoid, lemme tell ya."

Genie shuddered, apparently remembering just how close she'd come to losing that fight.

Becky squeezed her thigh, feeling the turmoil and exhaustion in her partner, bringing her back to the present.

Smiling gratefully, Genie continued, "The gun got tossed, and then I got tossed, head first into the door frame. For a few seconds I almost passed out, but life-and-death situations have a way of keeping you conscious."

Becky snorted at the dry tone.

"Anyhow, I jumped on his back and drove him to the ground, clobbered him with my cast, come to think of it. Got him handcuffed and picked up my gun. He was suddenly a lot more cooperative. I kept my gun on him and freed Mrs. O'Neill, told her someone would be up soon. I was so pissed that I think I yelled the entire Miranda at him as I brought him downstairs."

Resting her head against Genie's shoulder, Becky sighed, wincing at the pinch in her side. "I was so scared, Genie. I saw you shot, felt the bullets rip into your stomach and your chest. I think I gave Mansfield a heart attack by screaming."

Chuckling, Genie leaned her cheek against Becky's head. "Probably did. You can really get some volume going, girl."

Becky grinned. "You should talk. Look, I know you're still not used to working with a partner, but that's what we are. You have to think about that before you go tearing off into danger all alone. If you get yourself killed, it's gonna hurt me, okay?"

Staying silent, choked up, Genie nodded.

Becky knew that they felt the same, that they'd definitively crossed the line from just work partners, to friends.

"Good. All right, let's get outside and let everyone know I didn't kill you."

Genie stood, then helped Becky up. They reached the door just as the EMTs did, and she said, "I'm all right. Just a cut and some bruises."

"Why don't we check you over anyhow?" the young man suggested.

Sighing, Genie nodded and followed them towards the ambulance.

Becky turned to Captain Carlson, who'd been waiting just outside, and asked, "What about Mrs. O'Neill?"

Grinning faintly, he replied, "I figured you'd want to yell at her in private, so I sent the others up to her apartment through the back door. Can she still sit down?"

Laughing, then gasping in pain as she clutched her ribs, Becky nodded.

Eyes narrowing, Carlson ordered, "You. Ambulance. Now. It suddenly occurs to me that you're supposed to still be in the hospital."

Becky nodded again and walked stiffly towards her partner. She remembered thinking that life with Genie was going to be interesting when they'd first partnered up and grinned. As self-fulfilling prophecies went, it was pretty damn accurate.

GENIE GROANED WHEN her phone rang. All she wanted to do was get into the tub, soak, and then go to bed. Thinking that it was Becky, she changed course and headed back to the living room, picking up the phone. Unlike the State, Genie had given in and bought a Visi-phone when they became available in retail. Taking the option not to view the other person when she saw it was Sharon on the caller ID, Genie picked up the handset and asked, "What is it, Sharon?"

"What the hell did you do to Becky?"

Wincing at the fury in Sharon's voice, Genie replied hopefully, "Nothing?"

"Don't you give me that, girl! Her emotions reached me all the way on the other side of the country, they were in such turmoil. Well. I called her, but she won't tell me what happened. You are going to."

Angered at the presumption, Genie warned, "Now is not a good time to threaten me, Sharon. I've had a rotten night and your little call isn't improving it any. If Becca doesn't feel like talking to you, I'm sure as hell not going to, because I'm already on her shit list. There's no *way* I'm going to dig myself in deeper, thank you very much."

There was a long pause before Sharon asked, "Will you at least tell me if she's really all right?"

Sighing, Genie replied, "She's fine. Just pulled some stitches loose is all. All you need to know is that I was an idiot, Becca came after me, and we're both fine now. Or I will be, if I can manage to get to my tub and then my bed."

Taking the not-subtle hint, Sharon said, "Fine. I'm sorry that I was concerned about Becky and won't bother you in the future."

"Sharon..."

But the older woman had already hung up so Genie's protest fell on non-existent ears. Groaning again, Genie slammed the phone down and turned towards her bathroom, which was beckoning like Nirvana. She hadn't had a mother in eight years, but it seemed as though when she hooked up with Becca, she'd inherited a new one in the process.

Complete with built-in guilt trips.

Excerpt from Rebecca Curtains' Journal—Year One

If she ever does that again, I'm going to kill her! I swear by all that's Holy, I'll hunt her down and make sure she can't scare me like that again! If I never go through a vision like that again, it will be way the hell too soon! I really thought that I'd lost her there. I really thought that she was going to die in that ambush, especially when the Captain told me that she went ahead anyhow.

Okay, calming down now. Or, trying to anyhow.

I've never had a vision like that before. I was always an observer before this, not a participant. This is completely new to me in so many ways that it's not even funny. And I don't know if it's because a) my powers are changing, b) my link with Genie is a lot deeper than I imagined, or c) I was subconsciously monitoring her because she wasn't with me.

I'd heard of others having similar experiences, but it was only with loved ones: siblings, lovers, and parents. I mean, I know Genie and I have finally gotten to be friends, but is that enough to precipitate this kind of mutation to my powers? I wouldn't have thought so.

I suppose it's all for the best if we got the killer off the streets. Still, I can't help but think that if anything serious had happened to Genie, it wouldn't have been worth it.

Chapter
Seven

THE APARTMENT WAS dark, lit only by candles here and there. Gentle music filled the air, classical guitar that was soothing and uplifting at the same time.

Genie sat on the couch and watched her partner meditate. Becca had tried to rope her into it, but Genie was already far too "'in touch"' with herself to want to get any closer. So she'd settled on the couch with a book, but it was lying untouched in her lap. They'd brought Becca home from the hospital just that morning and had spent the day running errands, getting food and clothing ready for the coming week.

Genie glanced at her watch and saw that nearly an hour had gone by since Becca had even twitched an eyelid. How long was this supposed to go on? As though hearing her worry, Becca shifted slightly on her pillow. Genie smiled and dropped her legs over the side of the sofa, leaning forward so she'd be there when her partner came out of it.

When Becca opened her eyes, however, Genie stiffened at the hard, cold look within. It wasn't anything she'd ever seen on the petite woman, and suddenly, she knew what was going on. Without a second thought, Genie launched herself off the couch and onto her partner, pinning her flat with her heavier body weight.

Becca struggled fiercely and started shouting for her to get off. Genie grabbed the other woman's shoulders and shook her, causing Becca's head to snap back. There was no time to be gentle, because Genie knew that the longer this thing had hold of Becca, the less chance of her coming back. Praying that the same thing would work twice, Genie shouted, "Rebecca Marie Curtains get back here! Fight him for your body, damn it! Fight him!"

There were several long, painful minutes where nothing she did worked and Becca continued to fight her. Added to that was noise coming from the hallway where people were pounding on the door. Genie ignored everything. On a last, desperate hope, she wrapped her arms and legs around Becca and clung to the other woman tightly, whispering desperately, over and over, "Come on back, partner, come on back to me."

It seemed an eternity later that Becca stopped shouting and moving, collapsing beneath Genie and crying limply. Genie rolled to her side, bringing Becca with her and tucking the other carefully against her, murmuring soothing words.

Just then, the door burst open and police entered the room, shouting for her to move away. Genie very slowly released her partner and held her arms out to show she was unarmed. Becca rolled onto her back and didn't say anything for a few seconds. Then she seemed to realize what was going on and struggled to sit up and explain. It took almost ten minutes for everything to get straightened out, but finally, it was.

When everyone was gone and the door locked again, Becca was sitting on the beanbag, wrapped in a blanket. She looked like a fragile doll to Genie as she knelt beside the bag. Looking up at her partner, Genie whispered, "You okay now?"

Becca shook her head wordlessly, visibly spooked by the whole situation.

"You want me to stay over tonight?"

There was a nod this time, still silent.

Genie nodded as well and took Becca's hand in hers, rubbing it softly. "I'll stay, then."

BECKY WOKE UP wrapped in strong arms with a leg thrown over hers. She stiffened fearfully before realizing that it was Genie. The remembered awkwardness of the night before made her smile. They'd both been trying to find comfortable positions without encroaching on each other's personal space. Genie was all arms and legs, making Becky's queen-sized bed seem cramped. At some point during the night, though, they'd apparently decided to ignore the personal boundaries and snuggled together.

Her smile faded as Becky remembered why she was currently using her partner as a living teddy bear. God. What a nightmare. She didn't remember much, just that same feeling of being dipped in evil. It had certainly started out pleasantly enough, meditating as she hadn't in a long time. The next thing she knew, she was suffocating in the evil, and then Genie was whispering for her to come back. When that had happened, Becky had realized that she wasn't in control of herself and struggled to get into her own body.

Then there had been shouting and chaos. It had taken a few minutes to understand that the police thought that it had been Genie hurting her. Once she did, Becky had set them straight about what had happened. At least enough so that they'd gone away.

A yawn from beneath her brought Becky back to the present. Wanting to avoid a potentially embarrassing awakening, not to mention being uncomfortably aware of just how nice it was to be held by Genie, Becky slipped carefully out of her friend's arms. She stopped to get the coffee maker going on her way to the bathroom. When she exited the small room, it was to find Genie sitting up in bed and rubbing her eyes with the palms of her hands. It was so cute that Becky couldn't help but chuckle.

Genie stopped and demanded sleepily, "What?"

"Nothing," Becky replied, still smiling.

Returning to the coffee maker, Becky expertly slipped her mug in place of the pot to catch the dark liquid. Staring intently at the mesmerizing flow, she heard Genie get up and head for the bathroom, thumping heavily across the floor.

A few minutes later, Genie joined her at the counter. "How are you?"

Looking up into concerned amber eyes, Becky shrugged, replying, "Back to normal and all systems go. Thanks for sticking around."

"No problem. I've gotta go, though. So I can shower and change."

"I know. I'll see you at the office."

Nodding, Genie hesitated then said, "You're sure you're okay?"

"I'm fine," Becky insisted with a smile. She gently shoved the taller woman away and continued, "Go on. If you're late, we *both* wind up on traffic duty, remember?"

Genie grinned suddenly and snagged the keys off the coffee table on her way to the door. "You're fine, all right. See you later."

As the door closed behind Genie, Becky sighed. Staring into her mug, she knew that she wouldn't really be fine until the maniac trying to destroy her was caught.

BECKY LOOKED UP and winced sympathetically at Genie as her friend sat down and slumped over her desk. "Still nothing, huh?"

Bleary golden brown eyes raised to look at Becky. Sighing, Genie straightened up and answered, "Not a damned thing. He won't confess, big surprise. Refused to be scanned, another surprise. There's no physical evidence to tie him to the other murders. Bastard didn't have the aluminum knife on him and it wasn't in his creepy little apartment, either. Without the weapon, we've got squat on him except kidnapping, B&E, and assaulting a police officer. Which, with his clean record and high priced lawyer might, *might* get him a couple years and probation."

Standing, Becky said, "All right, Marshall, on your feet."

Frowning, Genie asked, "Why?"

Becky wriggled her eyebrows and ordered, "Just do as you're told. For once."

Flushing at the not-so-veiled reference to her barging off without

backup, Genie stood and picked up her jacket when Becky headed for
the exit. Catching up with the smaller woman, she asked, "Where we
going?"

"We are going somewhere to relax for a couple hours. Then *you*
are going home and to bed," Becky said firmly.

"Oh I am, am I?" Genie countered playfully.

Grinning, Becky elbowed her partner and said, "You am."

The weather outside had finally turned towards spring, the rain
clearing out to leave a soft moistness to the air. Even in the city,
things felt cleaner with the break in the weather pattern. Becky took
a deep breath, relishing the fact that there was only a pinch around
her lungs from her mostly-healed ribs. Genie was due to get her cast
off in a few days and by then, they'd both be back up to par.

Unless one of us gets attacked again between now and then, she
thought wryly.

She'd spent a day on the firing range and another going through
too many damned obstacle courses, but getting re-qualified had been
surprisingly easy. Probably because Captain Carlson had let it be
known that he would personally dismember any instructor who
voted her down. It had been a few days since her psychic-ambush
and they'd been working non-stop on getting the case wrapped up.

As she walked with Genie towards the garage, she said, "I have
the perfect place for us to go."

Genie looked at her, good-humored suspicion plain on her face.

Becky assumed an innocent air and assured the taller woman,
"Trust me."

At that, Genie groaned, but it turned into a stifled chuckle
halfway through.

They'd gotten into the habit of parking next to each other, even if
it meant that they sometimes had to park on the upper level decks.
Becky briefly wished for the days of assigned parking that she'd had
with the Feds. When they reached their cars, Becky said, "454 West
32nd Street. Follow me."

Genie nodded and saluted before getting into her Jeep. Shaking
her head, Becky got into her car and started it up. A nice, quiet night
of good food, music, and conversation was just what they needed to
unwind. She knew that Genie would talk about the case, but that was
fine because the other woman needed some serious decompression.
The drive over was fairly short and, as always, it took longer to find
a parking spot.

Becky waited on the sidewalk for a couple of minutes before
spotting Genie coming toward her. Meeting her halfway, Becky
linked arms with the taller woman and led her towards her favorite
hole-in-the-wall restaurant. Café was actually a better description. It
was small and cozy, with booths and tables, old-time rock-n-roll
playing from a jukebox, and a multitude of dishes to choose from.

"Becky! Hey, hon, haven't see you in forever! Who's this?"

Becky smiled and hugged the hostess, then introduced, "Sasha, this is my partner, Detective Genie Marshall. Genie, this is Sasha."

"Good to meet you," Sasha greeted with a smile. "You're in luck, little one, we're pretty slow tonight."

"That's great, thanks, Sasha!" Becky exclaimed. She'd been hoping for just that. The table she wanted was in the back with a view of the whole place that she knew Genie would appreciate. They followed the woman to the table, then ordered drinks.

"This is a nice place," Genie commented, still looking around.

"Yeah, I found it a couple years back," Becky said, leaning back. She grinned suddenly. "I knew you were going to take the seat that shows all points of entry."

"Attribute it to my paranoid personality."

"You? Paranoid? Nah."

Genie stuck out her tongue, then asked, "What do you recommend?"

"Everything. No, I'm serious. Everything here is great. I generally get the veggie lasagna, though."

Genie frowned, thinking hard for a moment. "You're a vegetarian?"

"Not really. But I don't eat meat a lot, just enough to keep my protein going when I'm not in a tofu mood," Becky answered.

Genie grinned and observed, "Tofu, huh? You'd think that in the thousands of years it's been around, they could make the stuff taste better."

Grinning back at her friend, Becky was about to retort when their waitress arrived with drinks. After some indecision, they both ordered. Looking at Genie closely, Becky saw the lines of strain around the mouth and the circles under the eyes and offered impulsively, "Come with me."

Startled, Genie asked, "Where?"

"To the Center," Becky clarified. "It's so restful and quiet there. You'd have a real chance to unwind and relax."

Uncomfortably, Genie said, "I don't think that's a good idea."

"Why not? You need a break, Genie. When was the last time you had a vacation?"

"Uh..." Genie thought about it, then answered, "Last year some time. I think I took a week off after the Janson case. Actually, the Captain told me not to come back for a week or he'd arrest me."

Becky grinned. "That sounds like him. He cares about you a lot."

"I know. And the yelling really shows it."

Chuckling, Becky asked, "So? Will you?"

Genie stared into her soda for a moment before looking back at Becky. "Let me think about it."

"Sure. I'm not planning to leave until this weekend anyhow. I figure by then we'll either have what we need, or have nothing new, and will need a break from the aggravation anyhow."

Genie's lips twisted as she looked earnestly at her partner. "This really sucks, Becca! We know it's him!"

"Yeah, but we can't prove it." Becky sighed. "What are you going to do if we don't get him for the murders?"

Angrily beating her fingers against the table, Genie asked, "What can I do? Nothing. Not a God damned thing."

"I was thinking about investigating who's paying his bills," Becky admitted quietly.

Genie looked thoughtfully at her partner. "Oh?"

Leaning forward, Becky said, "Think about it. He's a data entry operator. There's no way in hell he can afford Masters and Lyon! Someone is footing the bill, and if we find out who, maybe we can find a tie to the other murders. Somewhere. One thing I learned with the Feds is if you follow the money trail, eventually you'll hit pay dirt. Sometimes literally, depending on whose body's been buried."

"And people call me cynical?"

"Yeah well, what can I say? Lifelong member of Cynics Anonymous."

Lips twisting into a wry grin, Genie asked, "So who do you expect to find?"

"I don't know. I've got a few suspicions, but nothing concrete."

Plainly unconvinced, Genie repeated, "So who do you expect to find?"

Becky made a face at her partner's expectant tone. "Doyle."

Genie instantly looked around the area, suspicion clear in her gaze. "Are you insane? What makes you say that? Did you see something that you're not telling me?"

Shaking her head, Becky answered, "It's not that. It's just a feeling, a hunch, that's all."

"Some hunch," Genie muttered.

The waitress came over with their food just then, forestalling any further comments. Genie picked at her food, her appetite plainly gone. Becky reached across the table and lightly touched Genie's hand to get her attention. Almond eyes looked up at her and Becky promised, "I'm going to be discreet, Genie. You are the only one I've told, and I intend to keep it that way. I know he's powerful, but..."

"But you have to look into it," Genie finished with a sigh.

Nodding in relief, Becky said, "I'm going to be careful, so I don't want you to worry about it, all right?"

Reluctantly, Genie nodded as well, in agreement. "Make sure you are. I'm just starting to get used to you."

Quirking a grin, Becky said, "Good to know."

THINGS HAD BOTH improved and gotten worse by the end of the week.

Genie's cast came off and Becky's ribs stopped hurting. Their casework was caught up. Joshua Belladonna, their perp for the tourist murders, refused to confess, and no new physical evidence was found. The DA decided to go with the charges they had, which did not include the four counts of murder pending.

Also erring on the side of prudence, the ADA decided not to go for Hate Crime assault charges against Henry Aldonis, the young man who'd attacked Becky. He was being charged with assaulting a police officer and attempted murder.

"This sucks."

Genie nodded, happily wiggling her newly freed fingers yet again.

"This really sucks."

Another silent nod as Genie carefully picked up a coffee cup, testing her strength.

"He specifically called me a mind-slut! They can't use that as proof that it's a Hate Crime?"

"Your word against his, since I didn't hear it," Genie repeated patiently, for what was probably the hundredth time.

Glaring at her, Becky repeated, "This sucks!"

"Wanna go get drunk?" Genie suggested helpfully.

Becky snorted, reluctantly letting her anger fade for the moment. "No. Thanks, though. I think I'm going to head home and drown my sorrows in a nice hot tub."

Perking up, Genie exclaimed, "Hey! I can do that now too!"

Arching an eyebrow, Becky said, "I thought I smelled something."

"Very funny."

Becky's grin was more genuine as she stood up to leave. "I thought so."

Chapter
Eight

GENIE LOOKED OVER at the small, explosive sneeze that came from Becca and said automatically, "Bless you."

Becca sniffed and reached around to the back seat for the box of tissues. "Thanks."

"You're not coming down with something, are you?"

There was a surprisingly loud, and long, blowing of the nose before Becca faced forward again. "Nope."

Eyeing the used tissue in Becca's hand, Genie asked, "What are you going to do with that?"

"Marry it," Becca snapped. "What do you think I'm going to do with it? I'm going to toss it."

Genie looking pointedly around the front seat of the Jeep. "Where? I don't have a trash container."

Frowning at the other woman, Becca observed, "You're anal, aren't you?"

"I wouldn't say that," Genie protested.

Becca chuckled. "No, of course you wouldn't. Now don't be alarmed, I'm just setting it on the dash for the rest of the stakeout."

Making a face, Genie returned to looking out the front windshield. Since there was nothing further they could do with the tourist killer, Carlson had assigned them to another case before Becca could actually escape to the west coast. It was a simple homicide case, but that department was booked to overflowing, as were the other VC detectives. The Captain had blatantly played on Becca's good nature to keep her around and Genie had had to go along with her partner.

Genie sighed and glanced around at the students in their own little world of college, completely oblivious to the nasty turn the world could take. Of course, that was as it should be. Leaning her head against the headrest, Genie grumbled, "The second worst thing about police work: stakeouts where nothing happens."

Curious, Becca asked, "What's the first?"

After a pause, they looked at each other and answered, "Paperwork."

Laughing, Genie asked, "So if we actually get a day off this weekend, what're you going to do?"

"Sleep."

"What else?"

"What do you mean, what else? What else is there?"

Seeing that the other woman was serious, Genie snorted. "Oh, I don't know, seeing the outside world for a change? Going to the movies? Picking wildflowers?"

"In DC?"

"I was being poetic."

"Oh, is that what that was?"

"Listen, you..."

"There she is," Becca interrupted.

All business again, Genie's gaze followed Becca's motion and saw their suspect walking down the street toward her off-campus apartment. Elisha Udell was twenty-three, black, pretty, popular, and at the top of her class of almost two thousand students. She was also the main suspect in the murder of her sister, Jenna Udell.

During the witness interview a few days before, Becca had sensed something wrong with the young woman. She'd asked some pointed questions, but gotten only vague answers, when she'd gotten answers at all. Then the parents, who of course hadn't wanted to think their daughter could have anything to do with their other daughter's death, had started yelling at Becca for her "groundless insinuations," and taken their remaining daughter home.

Unfortunately, all they had to go on was Becca's hunch, and Genie's concurring suspicions, which weren't enough to even get a search warrant, let alone an arrest. The Captain had been less than thrilled that the daughter of such prominent citizens was now a suspect, but only told them to keep digging. So they were watching and waiting for the young woman to make a mistake. The last couple of days on stakeout had proven fruitless, unless the discovery of some seriously annoying habits could be considered a positive result.

Which no, it really can't, Genie thought with half a grin, picking at a fingernail. *Although it's nice to know that she has no problems with me snoring. And she's not half-bad at I-Spy.*

"Hello. What have we here?" Becca murmured when a young man approached Elisha.

Genie's eyebrows rose when the student enthusiastically kissed the newcomer. "I thought she was single."

"Officially, she is."

"Think her parents object to her bringing a white guy home for dinner and that's why she said she was unattached?" Genie asked with a grin.

Becca snorted, wagging a finger at her partner. "That's a very archaic attitude, Genie, my girl."

"So's murder."

"Nah. Murder's ever-popular. A classic, even."

Genie arched a curious eyebrow at the other woman before returning her attention to Elisha and the man. He was in his early thirties, had blond hair and a nice physique. They were too far away to note eye color or any distinguishing marks.

"I just find it depressing that Jenna, who had her whole life ahead of her, was killed by one of the people she should have been able to trust," Becca announced suddenly.

Keeping her eyes trained on the couple, Genie replied, "It is depressing. Personally, it pisses me off. So. You want him, or her?"

"Oh, I definitely want her."

The somewhat bloodthirsty tone made Genie shake her head in dark amusement. "You got it, partner. Let's move."

Becca picked up the hand-held comm unit and spoke into it. "Designation VC-10, calling in."

"Go ahead, VC-10," the operator responded.

"We're leaving the vehicle to interview a suspect."

"Is backup required?"

"Negative. Will call for assistance if necessary."

"Understood, VC-10."

"VC-10, out."

"Base, out."

They got out of the Jeep and strode up to Elisha and the stranger, who were heading towards the apartment building. Catching up to the young woman, Becca called, "Ms. Udell, we'd like a few words with you."

Scowling, Elisha demanded, "What do you want? My parents already told you that I was with them at the time of my sister's murder. How much more of an alibi can I get?"

Becca crossed her arms over her chest. "That depends. How much more of one can you come up with?"

"This is harassment, I know it is!" Elisha exclaimed angrily.

"Who're you?" Genie asked the man.

Blue eyes flickered nervously between the two detectives. "Uh, David Sumner."

"And where were you last Monday night, David Sumner?"

"Uh, studying with some friends."

"Aren't you a little old to be a student?" Genie questioned.

"You're never too old, right?" When his attempt at humor fell flat, he shifted uncomfortably and continued, "I started late, all right?"

"What friends were you studying with?"

Sumner glanced slightly towards Elisha, but didn't actually make eye contact before he answered, "Just some friends."

"Names and contact numbers, please," Becca prompted in a steely voice.

"Jackie Smithers, Rosie Nader, and Carl Island. Jackie and Carl live in Beldon House and Rosie lives in Gordon Belle Dorm."

Genie smiled thinly as she wrote the information down. "So, David Sumner, may I ask how you know Ms. Udell here?"

"We're friends," he replied.

Genie shook her head and observed, "That was some kiss for just friends."

Glaring, Elisha demanded, "Is that illegal, Detective?"

Genie shrugged. "Not that I know of. Now murder, that is definitely illegal, last I checked. Becca?"

Becca nodded agreement. "Last I knew, yep."

"So why don't you go out and find my sister's killer instead of giving me attitude?"

"Oh, I think we've got the killer," Becca answered in a soft, menacing tone. She moved closer to Elisha who, though taller than Becca, was plainly spooked by the cop's voice and attitude. "Listen up, little girl, because you've borrowed a world of trouble and my attitude is the least of what's coming. Mr. Sumner, I suggest that you stick around town while we check out your alibi."

He nodded, disconcerted, and Elisha continued to stare daggers at them as Becca and Genie turned and walked away. Once they reached the Jeep, Becca growled in frustration. "I know she was involved, even if she didn't pull the trigger."

"You think Sumner did it?" Genie questioned, leaning against the vehicle. She kept her eyes on the two students, who were making definite tracks for the apartment. Elisha had her cell phone out as she entered the building. Three guesses as to who she was calling and the first two wouldn't count.

Becca sighed and muttered, "Who knows?"

"Great. We've gone from morbid to defeated. Anyone ever tell you you're just a roller-coaster of emotion?"

Glaring at her partner, Becca demanded, "Can I have just a minute to wallow? Jeeze!"

Genie tried not to snicker, but a choked laugh managed to escape. When Becca looked askance at her, she repeated, "Wallow? You know, I think that's the first time I've heard that particular word in the course of an actual conversation."

Hands on hips, Becca held the glare for about a half minute longer before dissolving into laughter herself. "All right, all right! I was having a mood swing."

"I thought you said you don't get PMS."

"Brat."

"This is a news flash, how?"

Chuckling, Becca said, "So why don't you check the alibi and I'll keep an eye on Ms. Udell?"

"Base to VC-10, please come in VC-10."

"Then again, maybe not," Becca muttered, reaching in through the open window. "VC-10 here, go ahead base."

"VC-10, you are advised to cease and desist current stakeout and come back to the precinct. Captain Carlson wants to see you."

Wincing, Becca replied, "Will do. VC-10, out."

"Base, out."

After replacing the handset, Becca turned to Genie and asked, "I don't suppose you've got some kind of protective gear on you?"

With a smirk, Genie shook her head. "I've got my vest. You, my friend, are on your own."

"Gee, thanks, partner."

THE NICEST THING the Captain said to them was, "Take the rest of the day off, and when you get your heads on straight, get your asses back here and work the damned case! If I get another call from those parents, it'll be the last case you work in a very long time. I understand that traffic is very short-staffed these days!"

Only a couple of hours later, Becky and Genie ambled lazily through a mall on the way to the movies. They'd already eaten a pizza, and bought junk food to sneak into the theater, which was currently stuffed in Becky's bag. There was a 2D Action Film Fest going on with classics like, *Matrix, Conan the Barbarian,* and *Le Pact des Loupes.*

"I can't believe you actually enjoy watching these things," Genie complained as they neared the theater.

Having never actually heard Genie whine before, Becky snickered. "What's not to like? There's action, romance, and lots of blood. I'm telling you, one thing 20th Century filmmakers knew how to do was put together *great* action films. I don't think today's films are nearly as good."

"But they're flat!"

Becky rolled her eyes. "Just because you don't think you're actually falling over the cliff, and getting a heart attack in the process I *might* add, doesn't mean that you don't interact with the film."

"Interact?" Genie demanded incredulously. "We sit there like lumps and watch a screen."

Becky heaved a sigh as they waited in line to buy tickets. "Are you going to whine through the whole movie?"

"I haven't decided yet."

"Great."

About a half-hour later, they sat in the old-fashioned bucket seats and the first movie began. Becky settled down with a happy sigh, eyes glued to the "coming attractions" of movies that had been made half a century before.

GENIE HAD MORE fun watching Becca than the movie itself. The way the other woman got so into the story, actually squirming in her seat when the hero or heroine got into trouble, was fascinating to Genie. And more than a little entertaining. It wasn't often that they had time to sit back and relax, what with their workload, and being ordered to play hooky was a hell of a lot of fun.

Grinning as Becca winced at what was happening on the screen, Genie got into a more comfortable position and contemplated the woman who'd become such a good friend. It had been a rocky beginning, no doubt about that. Fortunately for them both, they were on a pretty even keel now. Genie was glad that Becca had stuck through her idiocy, even though she still couldn't believe that she'd done it. It was a miracle Becca hadn't murdered her during that first month together.

Becca turned slightly in her seat and caught Genie's eyes. "What's wrong?"

"Nothing. It's a good movie," Genie whispered back.

Smiling broadly, Becca said, "Told you," and went back to watching Keanu Reeves deal with a strange twist on reality.

Of course, Genie, thought, *he isn't the only one dealing with a strange twist on reality.*

She still wasn't sure how things were going to work out. They'd become solid friends, for which she was grateful. They'd recaptured the easy work relationship that had first sprung up between them, which was also a great thing. The only problem that Genie could foresee was if she went and sabotaged them again. She didn't think that she would, but her subconscious was a murky place that sometimes not even she could see the bottom of.

Turning her eyes to the screen, Genie started paying attention, in case Becca decided to quiz her later. And besides, this break from reality was supposed to be recharging their batteries, getting them fresh perspectives. Rehashing her behavior wasn't going to accomplish anything.

Chapter
Nine

THE NEXT DAY proved to be more productive for their time off. They were both refreshed and had ideas about how to proceed. And if those ideas happened to follow along the lines of Becca's plan from before they were kicked out of the office, well, no one needed to know that but them.

Genie set a cup of coffee on Becca's desk and looked around for her partner. The shorter woman was engaged in an animated conversation with Kim Yu across the office. Genie grinned as she heard, "...special effects were so *cool* for the time, you wouldn't believe it!" She sat at her desk and pulled the autopsy file of Jenna Udell. She perused the report for at least the tenth time, but found nothing new.

The poor girl had been shot in the head, at close range, with an antique pistol. The bullet had gone right through her brain and lodged into the wall. There were no unaccounted-for fingerprints in the apartment where Jenna had lived, just her family and a few friends. There was no sign of a struggle, so Jenna had probably known her killer, but that was only one of the reasons that they had glommed onto the sister almost immediately. Sighing, she closed the file and picked up the phone.

Becca approached just then and sat at her own desk, breathing in her coffee before sipping it with a blissful expression. "Who're you calling?"

Genie didn't have time to answer before the other end was picked up.

"Laroshelle Antiques, how can I help you?" an old woman's voice answered.

"Hi. This is Detective Genie Marshall with the DC Violent Crimes division. I was wondering if anyone has bought any old .38 caliber pistols from your store lately?"

"I don't carry weapons, Detective, most of us don't. Try Scotty Hersh on 58th Street. He deals in all kinds of things."

Genie grinned at the disapproval in the woman's voice. "Thank you, ma'am."

"Any time, Detective."

Hanging up, Genie answered Becca with, "I just thought I'd try and track down the gun while you interviewed Sumner's alibis."

Becca nodded. "Sounds like a good idea. Gonna be hard to do, seeing how old it is."

"Yes and no. We won't be able to track it through normal means, but the antique community is pretty small," Genie pointed out.

Lips pursed thoughtfully, Becca nodded again. "That's true. I didn't think about that. Tell you what, meet you at the café for lunch?"

Genie rubbed her stomach. "Definitely. My treat this time, since you got the movies yesterday."

"I never turn down free food," Becca joked, standing. She picked up her jacket and coffee and continued, "See you later."

Genie picked up the phone as she watched her partner move lithely through the busy office. Shaking her head to get her wandering thoughts back on track, she dialed information.

"I TOLD HIM to stay away from her! I knew she was trouble!"

Somewhat taken aback by the girl's passionately negative assessment of Elisha Udell, even if it did match her own, Becky paused before asking, "How so?"

Her wide, blue eyes went wide, and Rosie Nader tugged fretfully on a lock of long blonde hair. She looked like she was about to have a nervous breakdown, but finally managed to say, "Elisha likes to rule the roost, you know? She's into *everything*. Has to be the center of attention at all times, you know?"

Becky nodded encouragingly.

"Well, after David started hanging around her, he changed. He used to be real sweet and nice, but now he's downright mean sometimes. I think they even do drugs, that new designer one that's purple."

"How do you know that?" Becky questioned.

"There's just this attitude they all get after taking it," Rosie explained. "You'd have to know someone who does it. Not that any of *my* friends do."

Amused, Becky agreed, "Of course not. Go on. You said that he changed?"

"Oh yeah. He was always trying to please her. He would do anything for her."

"Even murder her sister?"

The tears welled up again, but Rosie nodded. "As soon as I heard the news, that was my first thought. That she'd finally gotten him to do it."

Frowning, Becky asked, "What do you mean, 'finally?' "

Uncomfortable now, Rosie said, "Everyone knows Elisha hated her sister, always has. I went to high school with them and Jenna was always more popular than her sister. That's because she was just a really nice person, you know?"

"So Elisha has been planning this for a long time?"

Rosie nodded, tugging on her hair again. "At least, it seemed like it. I never actually heard her say it."

Damn. "All right, Rosie. You've been very helpful. One last thing. Do you know if Elisha had access to a .38 pistol?"

"Oh yeah. Her folks own a collection of antique guns," Rosie said. "I saw it whenever I was over there."

Funny how that had never been mentioned by the parents. Becky sighed to herself and asked, "If I need you to make a formal statement, maybe even testify to any of this in court, would you be willing to do so?"

After a long hesitation, Rosie nodded. "Jenna didn't deserve to die like that, Detective, she didn't deserve to die at all. I'll help any way I can."

"That's great, thanks."

Rosie sighed and nodded again before turning to walk towards her dorm building. They'd met on the quad as it was on the way back from the girl's last class of the day. Becky had already met with the other two students. While they hadn't been able to supply any insight into Elisha's motive, they'd definitely supported Sumner's statement that he'd been with them studying from nine that night until one in the morning. Sumner was actually the group study leader, and they'd met in the library where at least fifteen other students had also been studying.

She grimaced, thinking, *So if the murder takes place at ten thirty Monday night and both the suspects have alibis, who do we look at next?*

Her attention was diverted when she caught sight of a tall woman with long, auburn hair across the square. She tried to make sure that it was her partner, but the woman moved out of sight too quickly. Her build and way of moving was just right for it to be Genie, and it wouldn't be unlikely for the other woman to have come in search of her so she jogged towards the building.

Reaching it in short order, Becky found herself in a crowd of kids talking and shouting and laughing, which made it nearly impossible to avoid being contacted. The raucous emotions of those who brushed against her sent Becky reeling. Her shields were locked tight, which was the only reason she wasn't in a huddle on the ground. It took all her strength to keep them in place, and she couldn't spare the extra energy to ascertain if the other woman really was Genie and, if so, to latch onto her through a mental connection.

Looking desperately around the large, open room with its pool and ping-pong tables, she finally spotted the woman. Relieved, convinced that it was her partner, Becky shouted over the noise, "Genie!"

Instead of turning around, the other woman moved into the next room, auburn braid swaying as she walked in the opposite direction.

Grinding her teeth, Becky picked up the pace again and rushed after her. Catching up just as the other woman reached the elevator, she grabbed Genie's arm and exclaimed, "Didn't you hear me shouting for you?"

Even before the woman turned, Becky knew it wasn't Genie from the annoyed feelings that came through the touch, which slammed into her control, weakening it further. Yanking her hand back, Becky brought her emotions under control as quickly as possible. Similar features and the same hair, but the eyes were blue and the mouth thinner. Startled, positive that it had been Genie, Becky stammered, "I'm sorry, I thought you were someone else."

The younger woman grinned. "Obviously. But it's not a problem. You can shout for me anytime, hon."

The southern accent was also definitely wrong, but the twinkling blue eyes were a nice surprise. It had been a long time since someone had looked at her with that measuring glance. Smiling back was nearly automatic, even as Becky flushed. "So long as it's the correct name, right?"

"Oh, absolutely."

As Becky walked back to her car several minutes later, she was no closer to deciphering the mystery of Elisha's involvement in her sister's death. On the plus side, she did have a phone number and a potential date for Saturday night.

GENIE LOOKED AT her grinning partner in disbelief. "You got what?"

"Hey, I haven't been out on a date in months, so just leave me alone about it!" Becca ordered around a mouth full of French fries.

Becca didn't look the least bit apologetic; Genie shook her head in irritation. Bad enough that the other woman drove her to distraction in her dreams, now she was doing so in the waking world as well. Pointedly, Genie questioned, "And just how old is this piece of jailbait?"

Definitely smug, Becca replied, "Completely legal, I'll have you know."

"Did you check her ID?"

"What crawled up your butt and died? It's just a damned date."

"While you were out resurrecting your love life, I was at work chasing down useless leads on antique weapons. Oh, and the Commish paid a surprise visit, read 'inspection,' to the department."

Becca winced. "Ouch. Sorry, partner."

"Yeah, well, it's probably just as well you weren't there," Genie admitted. She remembered LeBlanc's glare at Becca's empty desk and wondered if her partner had personally pissed the man off, or if it was just case related.

"Why?"

"Because he was out for our blood, or our badges, whichever was easiest on him and most painful for us."

Frowning in earnest now, Becca asked again, "Why?"

Genie thought about how best to answer that, wanting to shield Becca from any additional harassment. The telepath hardly needed her protection, but Genie couldn't help herself. She finally settled on a different truth and related, "Because, apparently, the Udells were fairly hefty contributors to his Honor the Mayor's campaign last time around."

Becca groaned.

Unable to help the snide tone of her voice, Genie asked, "Speaking of new information, did you pull anything off the campus besides a phone number?"

After tossing a napkin at her, Becca replied haughtily, "I did, as a matter of fact. According to Rosie, it's common knowledge that Elisha hated her sister. So common that the first thing young Ms. Nader wondered, upon hearing about Jenna's death, was how Elisha had gotten David to do it."

"Oh, really?"

"Really. Aside from that, I found out that the Udell's own a classic gun collection and David's alibi checks out."

"Well, damn."

Becca nodded agreement.

Thoughtful, Genie commented, "So we have motive and means, but not opportunity."

Pursing her lips, Becca asked wryly, "Am I to assume from this morning's visit from the Commish that we've been ordered to find another line of investigation?"

"You might could say so, yeah."

Becca grinned at Genie's disgusted tone, then took a long drink of her water. She stared into space, fingers tapping on the table as she thought things over.

Genie hesitated, wondering if she should interrupt, then decided against it. Instead, she picked up her burger and pondered the interesting fact that her partner was going out with someone who, apparently, looked a lot like she did.

"What did the Captain say?"

Startled by the question, Genie nearly inhaled her food. When she at last breathed normally again, no thanks to the very unhelpful pounding on her back by a passing waitress, Genie croaked, "About what?"

Becca frowned at her a moment before clarifying, "About what the Commish said."

"He was quite the little diplomat. Might even make Commander one day, in spite of the lot of us."

With a grin, Becca guessed, "Told us to keep at it, but be a tad bit more discreet?"

Finger to her nose, Genie nodded. "Got it in one."

"So okay. How do you want to do this then? Not like we *want* to tick off the Commissioner and the Mayor all in one fell swoop or anything."

Genie just grinned and wolfishly attacked the rest of her burger. Thumbing one's nose at The Establishment built up an appetite.

THE UDELLS WERE extremely unhappy when Genie and Becky showed up on their doorstep the following day with a search warrant and a crew of technicians to do the searching.

"I'll have your jobs for this!" Mr. Udell hissed furiously.

Genie shrugged, unimpressed. "Don't know why you'd want them, really, because the pay sucks."

"And the hours are just awful," Becky agreed.

Mouth tightening in anger, he demanded, "Don't you have any respect? We just lost our daughter!"

Softening almost immediately, Becky replied, "And we are truly sorry for your loss, sir, no matter what you believe of us. But we have a job to do, as unpleasant as the truth can be at times."

"Elisha was with *us* when all this happened. How many times do we have to tell you that?" Mrs. Udell demanded, moving to her husband's side.

"Well, about that. Was Elisha with you every second of the night, or was there a period of time where she went off alone?" Becky questioned gently. "Maybe she went to bed early, or said she had to study?"

Mr. and Mrs. Udell looked at each other, dismay and fear crowding their faces. Shaking her head, Mrs. Udell exclaimed, "I won't believe it! Not my baby girl! She couldn't do anything like this!"

"Detective? We've found two .38's."

Becky looked at the uniformed officer and watched as Genie took the evidence bags, opening first one, then the other. She smelled each in turn and the other woman's grimace told Becky everything she needed to know. The gunpowder used in those old weapons was very distinctive. Not like the weapons of today that were propelled without such explosive means, despite the similarities in design.

Sighing, Becky said, "I'm very sorry, but we need to charge Elisha in the murder of her sister. Would you bring her down here, please?"

But Mrs. Udell began sobbing and it was all her husband could do to hold her up while comforting her. Becky looked at her partner and jerked her head toward the stairs. They left the grieving parents and went to pick up the presumed-innocent suspect. Becky knocked on the bedroom door and called out, "Elisha? It's Detective Curtains. We need you to come out of there."

"Forget it! I'm not coming out."

Oh yeah. The sullen tone was exactly what Becky had expected. Call her crazy for even thinking that there might be a shred of regret for what the girl had done. She again rapped sharply on the door. "Open the door, or we'll open it for you."

The click of the lock echoed through the hall and Becky opened the door. There was only a split second's warning before she found herself on the floor beneath a screeching hellcat trying to beat the crap out of her. Raising her hands to protect her face from the nails that had already drawn blood, Becky fought to get the girl under control.

Genie was in motion the moment Becky went down. She grabbed the young woman under the armpits, hauled her off Becky and flattened her to the rug, putting a knee in the small of Elisha's spine. Pinning the back of the girl's neck with one hand, Genie demanded, "You okay, Becca?"

Becky groaned and cupped the side of her head, reeling from both the attack and the fury behind it. "Stitches, I think, but yeah. I'm fine. Next time, you go in first, okay?"

Chuckling, Genie nodded. Turning serious, she looked down at Elisha and pulled the girl's arms behind her back, cuffing the wrists together. "Elisha Udell, you're being charged in the murder of your sister, Jenna Udell. You have the right to remain silent..."

LONG JOGS WERE good for two things: causing oneself pain, and thinking. As she moved through the early morning foot traffic, Genie had many things on her mind. The most prominent thoughts were about her partner; or, rather, her feelings for her partner. It was almost like being in the other woman's presence drained the constant anger and hostility that Genie felt toward the world at large. Not only that, it was just easy to be with Becca, easy and fun.

It didn't matter how many times she mentally kicked herself. Since that first touch in the gray room after Becca's partner-induced backlash, Genie had been hooked. She'd looked forward to every meeting and every word exchanged with the other woman. Even calling her Becca was Genie's way of distinguishing their relationship from others.

A sharp pain jabbed her shin, but Genie ignored it. *What the hell am I going to do? Is there anything to do? What am I even thinking about?*

I've only known her for a couple of months!

But time had nothing to do with it. They'd been through a lot in their short partnership, more than some cops went through in an entire career. Was it the telepath aspect of things? Was that why she felt so connected to Becca? Or was it the fact that no matter how much shouting and snarling she did, the smaller woman stood toe-to-toe with her? That, despite the irritation and arguments Genie threw at Becca, the detective didn't seem the least bit intimidated?

How long had it been since anyone had done that? Never, she was pretty sure. The relationships she'd had in the past had been completely separate from her work life. Surface relationships where she'd been content to be someone else. Genie knew that it wouldn't be like that with Becca, which scared her. She knew that if they ever moved beyond work partners and good friends, the other woman would demand all of Genie.

And that was why she was having such trouble. Despite Becca's forgiving nature, Genie didn't think her partner would be so accepting of some of the things she'd done in the past. Of a lot of the things she'd done in her past, if she were being completely honest.

Stopping at the edge of the street, Genie drew in a ragged breath and ground her fingers into the pain in her side. No, it was better to just concentrate on the friendship. With the way she'd screwed up in the beginning, Genie was lucky to get that much. She didn't want to push her luck and lose Becca altogether.

BECKY FROWNED WHEN Genie collapsed at her desk. "What happened to you?"

Groaning, Genie answered, "Went for a jog this morning and damn, I am still feeling it!"

Shaking her head at the response, and now knowing why her partner had been stiff all day, Becky returned to straightening out her files. She wasn't one of those people who could leave things a mess when on vacation, even if no one would be going through her things while she was gone.

"Hey, when are you leaving for the Center?"

Startled by the abrupt question, Becky looked over at her partner. Genie was leaning on her elbows, looking at her intently. Frowning slightly, she replied, "In the morning. I'm calling Sharon tonight to make final arrangements."

Somewhat hesitant, Genie asked, "You, ah, you still looking for company?"

Becky was surprised, but very happy at the offer. "Sure! That would be great!"

"Good. Then, um, I'll just pack a bag tonight, I guess. Do I need anything special?"

"Nope. Completely casual," Becky assured her. "I generally wear shorts and a T-shirt."

"Where is it, anyhow?"

"A small town in Southern California that you've never heard of, I'm sure. Good and hot this time of year."

"Sounds like a nice change," Genie commented wistfully.

"It is! Get your gear together, and I'll call you later tonight with details, all right?" Becky exclaimed, closing her drawer and grabbing her jacket.

"Sure thing. Talk to you later."

Becky waved as she headed out, thoughts whirling as she mentally reviewed the preparations that needed to be made for her guest.

GENIE WATCHED HER partner leave, then walked to the Captain's office. She knocked on the door and headed inside without waiting. She grinned at his customary, irritated look, and sat in the chair.

"What do you want, Marshall?"

"Just wanted to let you know I'll be out of town next week," Genie said.

If he was surprised, it didn't show. "Bring me back some sun, would you?"

Genie grinned at the near-surly request and said, "I'll do my best, sir. You have the number?"

"Yeah. And don't worry," he assured her dryly. "I think we can run things without you for a couple of weeks."

Keeping an innocent expression, Genie asked, "You sure?"

"Get out of here before I throw you out," he growled in response.

Winking, Genie stood and left the office.

Chapter
Ten

LAX HADN'T CHANGED in almost seventy years, not since there had been a need to expand to accommodate the new model flyers that could span the globe in a matter of a couple of hours. Becky loved and hated airports for the obvious reasons of coming home, and leaving it.

"I hate time changes," Genie grumbled. "I feel like I'm going to meet myself coming back from somewhere."

Becky looked over with a smirk. "As opposed to meeting yourself going somewhere?"

Genie thought about it for a second, then shook her head as though to clear it. "You're just trying to confuse me."

"Is it working?"

"Often."

Snickering, Becky glanced around the busy airport terminal for Sharon. Their flight had been early, strangely enough, and they'd arrived in LAX almost twenty minutes ahead of schedule. Though she was a fairly active traveler, Becky completely understood what Genie meant about meeting up with oneself. It did feel that way sometimes.

Taking out her claim ticket with one hand, she used the other to drag her partner toward the baggage area. "Let's get our things."

"Yes, master. Whatever you say, master."

This time Becky laughed out loud, very happy at the change in her partner. Even though they were less than a day out of DC, it seemed like Genie had dropped a load off her back. She wondered how often someone had actually tried to get beyond the pissed-off, intimidating exterior. Not that Genie couldn't still intimidate her, because she could, but Becky knew now that nothing would come of it. Well, nothing physical, anyhow.

After collecting their luggage, they returned to the food court area only to find that it was past time to meet Sharon. Looking around the busy area, Becky didn't see any sign of the other woman. Frowning, Becky glanced at her watch and saw that it was now almost fifteen minutes past their meeting time. Sharon was compulsively punctual.

Genie squeezed Becky's shoulder and tried to reassure her. "Hey, relax, she's probably just running late."

Anxious, Becky gave the area a light scan. She didn't latch onto any one person's mind, but rather barely glanced over them in search of her foster-mother. She finally said, "Sharon doesn't run late."

"We could page her. Maybe she got the meeting place mixed up," Genie suggested. "You stay here with the bags, I'll have her paged."

Even though she knew that Sharon wasn't in the building, Becky nodded, knowing it would give her partner something to do. It was impossible to see over the crowd at her height, so she went up on tiptoe every few minutes. Not that it helped, really, it just made her feel as though she was doing more than just standing around.

"Becky!"

Turning in surprise at the person calling her name, Becky found Jarrod striding toward her, the worried expression on his face matched her own. He reached out to her long before arriving at her side and Becky caught the jumbled image of a car crash. It wasn't his forte, however, so she had to ask, "Sharon?"

"She was in a car accident on her way here. She's fine, just bruised and shaken up. The doctors at the hospital wanted to keep her for a few hours for observation, make sure that she doesn't have a concussion," Jarrod reported.

"I knew that something was wrong," Becky fussed.

"It was an accident and she's fine," he repeated firmly. "Michelle is with her now, so I could come and get you and your partner. Where is she, anyhow?"

"She went to page Sharon," Becky answered. Just then the page sounded overhead and she grimaced. "Speaking of which."

Jarrod's mouth quirked briefly in amusement as he reached out and brushed his hand over the back of her wrist. "It's good to see you, Becky. You're looking very well."

Smiling faintly, Becky said, "Thanks. I think I'll look even better after the jet lag's dissipated."

"Well, both of your rooms are made up and Sharon has made it plain to everyone that you are not to be disturbed with anything Center-related until tomorrow at the earliest," Jarrod informed her with a grin.

Chuckling softly, she commented silently, *On penalty of a sore bottom, most likely.*

Something to that effect, he agreed, humor sliding over her in a pleasant manner.

"Becca?"

Becky turned at Genie's hesitant use of her name and smiled, waving her friend forward. "Genie, this is Jarrod. Sharon was in a car accident so he's come to bring us to the Center."

"Is she all right?"

"Fine. She should be home sometime this afternoon or this evening."

"Oh, that's good, then," Genie said, a bit awkward.

"Well, let's get this show on the road," Becky suggested, filling in the silence.

Maybe this wasn't such a good idea, Becky thought, careful to keep her thoughts to herself Jarrod's development was something of a surprise and she didn't know just how much he'd grown.

The tension realigning itself into Genie's shoulders and neck caused her to sigh, but then she shrugged mentally. *We can always stay at a hotel if Genie's too uncomfortable at the Center. Even the most liberal of people would probably have trouble being surrounded by telepaths day in and day out.*

The outside air was hot and dry, exactly as Becky remembered. Genie took in a startled breath and Becky grinned, looking at her friend. "Hotter than you expected?"

"It's only April, for crying out loud," Genie exclaimed as they walked towards a new car parked in the pickup lane. "This isn't natural."

Laughing, Becky countered, "Sure it is."

Genie helped Jarrod put their bags in the trunk, then started to expertly, and quickly, braid her thick hair. When it was done, she pulled out a large wooden pin and put her hair up, off her neck. "That's better. Jeeze, if I lived here, I'd probably get this mane chopped off."

"Oh no! You couldn't!" Becky protested with dismay. She loved playing with Genie's hair.

Arching an eyebrow at her partner, Genie said pointedly, "You can say that because your hair is shorter than my pinky."

"And aren't I glad of that in this kind of weather?"

Genie grabbed her playfully, pulling her into a headlock and giving her a noogie. Becky shrieked and struggled vainly against the stronger woman to get free.

Gasping with her own laughter, Genie demanded, "Say Uncle!"

"Uncle! Uncle! I give!"

Still chuckling, Genie released her friend and glanced over at Jarrod to find him staring at them in horror. Defensive, she demanded, "What?"

His mouth closed with an audible click. "Nothing. I'm sorry, I didn't mean to stare. It's just..."

Becky caught his appalled emotions and reminded Genie, "Remember I told you that touch can be painful for a telepath?"

Genie nodded.

"Well, grabbing someone without permission, especially when they aren't expecting it, is enough to cause some telepaths a backlash. When you nabbed me like that, you probably gave Jarrod the scare of his life," Becky explained. She both smiled at Jarrod and sent him a gentle nudge that she really was fine.

Genie shrugged, squinting at Jarrod as she said, "Oh. Well, sorry, then, Jarrod."

He stared at Genie a moment longer before walking silently to the driver's side.

"Don't worry, he'll get over it," Becky assured her, pulling at the door handle.

GENIE CLIMBED IN the back seat while Becca took the front. She half listened to the conversation in front, but mostly her attention was focused on her surroundings; something she always did in a new location. Definitely paranoid, but she always needed to know the escape routes. She didn't know whether to chalk it up to her military training, personal experience, her PD career, or all of the above.

Roughly an hour on the freeway, and Becca hadn't stopped talking yet. Genie grinned faintly as she watched the excessive hand motions of that showed Becca was relaxed and happy. Becca and Jarrod talked shop the whole time, as far as she could tell, exchanging information on people she'd never heard about, and going over budgets of all things. Not exactly her idea of a good time, but it seemed thrilling enough to Becca.

It wasn't long after that, that they pulled onto what Genie thought was a dirt road, but turned out to be a very long driveway. They pulled up in front of a mansion and Genie's jaw dropped as she took in the ornate exterior. It took a few seconds to get over her surprise and climb out of the car. There weren't many residences that could inspire any kind of reaction, but this one managed it. Turning her attention back to her partner, she followed Becca and Jarrod to the trunk. As they pulled out the bags, several people shouted Becca's name. By the time the luggage was on the ground, Genie found herself pushed to the back of a large welcoming committee.

Irritated, she leaned against the car as her partner was exclaimed and fussed over, with the occasional hug thrown in, by a group that just kept getting bigger. When she caught sight of the happiness on Becca's face, however, she sighed and let the anger drain. This was something that her friend obviously needed, even if it did totally point out her status as outsider. Why the hell had she come? This was like being brought to a family get-together.

After several minutes of being wrapped up in her friends' welcome, Becca met Genie's gaze, giving her a brilliant smile that immediately revived Genie.

Grinning at her entourage, Becca exclaimed, "Enough, already!

How about you let us get inside before we melt from the heat?"

There was laughter at her order and people dispersed. Finally, it was just the three of them again, and Becca rejoined her saying, "That's about half the people living here."

Eyebrows arching in surprise, Genie said, "That makes about what, forty people in residence?"

"Forty-three including the kids, yeah," Becca confirmed, picking up her suitcase. "C'mon, let's get settled."

Genie followed her inside and was somewhat relieved to find it a lot less formal than the exterior. The floors were hardwood, not marble or tile, and the walls painted plaster with cheerful murals interspersed throughout. No chandeliers or high-priced paintings adorned the walls, though there were sculptures and handmade pottery pieces decorating various tables along the way.

Overall, the homey atmosphere began to relax Genie, seeping into her almost right away. They parted from Jarrod at the main staircase where Genie followed Becca up, and then east down another hall. They stopped in front of a door, which Becca pushed open, and they walked into the room. "This is your room, mine is right next door. We've got a connecting bathroom."

Genie was relieved to find the room comfortable, not lavish. The bed was a little more ostentatious than she liked, but, hey, she was on vacation. She warned herself not to get used to it. There was a dresser and bookshelf, but otherwise, the room was pretty .bare. "Nice digs."

Becca grinned. "Thanks. I told Sharon to make sure the room was low-key."

"Well, she definitely managed it," Genie remarked.

"Why don't you take a quick shower to get the dust off and rest for a bit?," Becca suggested. "I'll swing by to get you in about an hour?"

Genie nodded and agreed, "Sounds good. What're you going to be doing?"

Rolling her eyes, Becca answered, "Probably wading my way through the rest of the greetings. I haven't been here in far too long."

Genie touched her friend's shoulder again and cautioned, "Don't overdo it. This is your vacation, too, remember?"

Smiling, Becca reached up to squeeze her partner's hand before picking up her suitcase again and heading towards the door. "See you soon!"

Genie waited until the door closed behind her friend before she sighed, thinking, *Well. This is certainly going to be interesting.*

Excerpt from Rebecca Curtains' Journal—Year One

I can't believe she's actually here! Up until the moment that we got on the plane, I kept expecting her to back out. I hope she really does get in some relaxing, though so far I've seen little enough evidence of it. Of course, coming into the middle of a political battle won't be good for my relaxation, and Genie seems to need me to be relaxed, in order to relax herself. One of those little quirks about her that is both annoying and cute, all at once.

I contacted Sharon to make sure that she really was okay, but only briefly so that I didn't wear her out. Thankfully, she was groggy, but fine. I have to grin, thinking about how Jarrod looked when Genie grabbed me like that. I forget, most times, that Sharon's used to us being all touchy-feely, that most telepaths would be appalled. Well, until they realize how close we are. Strangely close for a partnership containing a non-telepath.

Shit. What am I going to do about Joseph and his idiotic ideas? That's the problem with a telepathic society— you can't repress free speech because people know when you do. Not that I would. Well, maybe in his case...no! Don't start thinking like that. Approach this like you do any other problem: with logic, and honesty.

Though I have to say that Genie's "bash heads together first, sort it out later" approach is sounding really good, right about now.

Chapter
Eleven

JARROD CAME BY to get Genie about an hour later, and the detective was less than pleased by the man's explanation as to Becca's absence.

"I'm sorry, Detective, but Becky is in a meeting and simply can't be disturbed," Jarrod informed her. "She wanted me to give you a tour of the Center while she finished up."

Glaring at the impassive man, Genie demanded, "I thought she wasn't supposed to be working, or, whatever, until tomorrow."

Jarrod shrugged, dark eyes mild. "Things come up."

"Right. Is Sharon back from the hospital yet?"

"Not 'til tomorrow. Turns out that she does have a concussion and they want to keep her overnight," Jarrod answered easily.

Suspicious, Genie nonetheless followed him out of the room. She did need to know her way around, after all. It was just as big on the inside as it looked. The second level held the living quarters and guestrooms. The first floor contained offices, studies, libraries, the kitchen, and a large common room. Outside, Genie found a large swimming pool, a vegetable and herb garden, and well-maintained grounds that seemed to go on forever.

"So how did all of this come about, anyhow? I'm not exactly up on telepath history," Genie questioned, when the tour was finished.

Jarrod stared at her for a moment as though trying to determine her sincerity, which Genie figured he probably was. He wouldn't scan her, even if that were one of his abilities, so suspicion was probably his first reaction. Especially considering the prejudice these people put up with. Knowing all that, she waited patiently, sitting in a chaise by the pool.

"Well, telepaths have always been around, just not in any great number," Jarrod began. When she nodded, he continued in a lecturing tone, "Towards the beginning of the twenty first century, more and more of us began showing up until the AMA founded an entirely separate science in 2048 devoted to studying the phenomenon. In those days, the people in the study were practically a laughing-stock to the rest of their profession, but without their persistence, we wouldn't know half of what we do today.

"When it became evident that telepaths weren't going to go

away, people started getting nervous. As usually happens when something different appears, people feared what they didn't understand, despite the added weight of scientific knowledge. An underground movement started that banded the telepaths together. It was easy enough to know who really was one, after all. That was around 2055 through 2060-ish.

"Through that movement, the Centers were started, more as retreats than anything else. A place where people could go when the 'real world' was too much or too dangerous. The first one was in Canada, quite far north of Montreal. And though that made it difficult for people to get there, it also assured them of privacy. The first real Center was built in 2068 and it was during those first few years there that some doctors were allowed to study us. With their help, we figured out how to categorize and train undeveloped telepaths. More was done in that decade than in all the time previous, despite the AMA's support."

Jarrod sighed, looking over at the pool that was filled with laughing young adults and children, the lifeguard watching over them carefully. A sad smile crossed his handsome face as he said, "It wasn't a bad time for those who were at the Center, but the telepaths out in the world faced witch hunts like you wouldn't believe. The persecution for even being suspected of telepathy was incredibly harsh. That's when being a telepath was added to the Hate Crimes act, in 2072, mostly at the insistence of the medical community, believe it or not. The 'humanitarian' activists, like Amnesty International, wanted nothing to do with us.

"Well, by then a few more Centers had popped up around the world as we organized, which was the only way we were going to survive. Funny thing though, the more *civilized* the country, the harsher the climate for the telepaths.

"Personally speaking, my parents found refuge among some of the First Nation people in Canada before making their way to the Center. One of the Elders saw them being harassed and brought us with him to protect me. I was only a boy, but I remember feeling safe for the first time among them. And it was like that all over the world. Still is. Those who lived their lives closest to the Earth, maintaining their traditions, were the most open to this newest development of the human race."

"I wonder why?" Genie murmured thoughtfully.

Jarrod shrugged. "I don't know, but we're grateful to them. The Native American and First Nation people of North and South America are our greatest supporters. Tribal peoples all over the world, really. In any case, that's how the Centers started, and today they're more than a refuge. We bring young telepaths here to train and protect."

Filing away the details of the lecture to think about later, Genie questioned, "What about their families?"

"If the children are under sixteen, we invite their parents to come as well, offer to pick up the moving tab," Jarrod explained. "If they're sixteen or older, it's more like going away to school with regular breaks and vacations to go home."

"Hey! There you two are!"

Genie looked over at Becca's arrival and smiled. " 'Bout time you got here. You aren't supposed to be working until tomorrow, young lady."

Grimacing, Becca took the chaise on her other side and leaned back with a sigh. "Shit happens."

"Like?" Genie asked.

"There's going to be an impromptu council meeting tomorrow. All the Center leaders will be attending," Becca answered, groaning.

Jarrod bolted to his feet. "There's far too much to get ready before they get here! Michelle making travel arrangements?"

Becca nodded.

"I'm off, then. Nice talking with you, Genie," Jarrod said absently, hurrying away.

Genie grinned as she watched him go. "What is he, the majordomo or something?"

Snorting, Becca answered, "Something like that. Jarrod takes care of the physical arrangements of this Center, while Michelle runs it. He's her assistant."

Eyeing her friend carefully, Genie commented, "You look a little beat. Everything all right?"

"Not really," Becca muttered, dejected.

"What's wrong?"

Becca glanced over at the pool, watching its playful inhabitants for a few minutes before answering, "Why don't we talk about it later?"

Genie continued her observation another moment, then shrugged. "Sure. What's for supper?"

"Whatever we fix," Becca answered as she stood. "C'mon, let's see what's in the kitchen."

Genie accepted the hand up, noticing the odd glances from the few adults around them, and then linked arms with Becca out of a perverse desire to shock the others. She heard Becca's snicker and looked at her friend's highly amused face. Innocently, she asked, "What?"

Grinning, Becca asked, "Could you *be* any more obvious?"

Stifling a grin, Genie replied airily, "I have no idea what you're talking about."

"Yeah, right." Becca dragged Genie towards the house. "So. What do you think about the Center?"

"It's big," Genie answered neutrally.

Becca arched her eyebrows curiously at the response. "That's descriptive. And?"

Shrugging, Genie explained, "I'm still soaking things in. I'll let you know what I think in a couple of days."

"Fair enough."

They reached the large, professional-style kitchen and Genie plopped herself down on one of the stools by a long counter. Grinning impudently, she pointed out, "I'm a guest. You get to cook supper."

Chuckling, Becca headed for the large fridge and looked inside. "Hey, how about a salad and some veggie burgers? Something light."

"Sounds good to me," Genie agreed, leaning on the counter. She watched as her partner pulled out the lettuce, cucumbers, tomatoes, and a couple of red and green peppers. After they were washed, Becca scooped them all together and set them in front of Genie expectantly.

Lifting an eyebrow, Genie prompted, "Yes?"

"Make the salad. That's not cooking."

Rolling her eyes, Genie realized that she'd walked right into it. "So, basically, I get to do all the chopping and peeling while you pop the burgers into the oven?"

Laughing outright, Becca nodded and walked away.

Genie stood and picked up the knife that Becca had left, and started cutting up the vegetables. Becca came back with a large salad bowl and started tearing apart the deep green lettuce. They worked together quietly and easily, as though they'd been doing it for years. They had just finished the salad when the timer rang for the burgers, and Becca went to put them together.

Taking the large bowl to the circular table at one end of the kitchen, Genie called out, "Where're the plates and stuff?"

"Over there."

Genie moved towards the indicated cupboard and pulled out two dinner plates. She looked through a couple of drawers before finding the silverware, then brought everything over to Becca and set them down. Genie watched as her friend put the burgers onto the buns and set them on the plates. "Slaving over a hot stove is such a bitch, isn't it?"

Winking, Becca answered, "Oh yeah. A definite hardship. Let's eat, I'm starving."

Genie picked up a plate and headed back to the table.

"Oh, hey, what do you want to drink?" Becca asked, almost jumping up from her seat.

"Whatever."

"How does a cooler sound?"

"Yummy." Genie watched her partner move gracefully across the kitchen, heading towards a smaller refrigerator. Shaking herself out of the quasi-lecherous contemplation, she turned to dishing out the salad. "Hey. What about dressing?"

Becca stopped short on her way back and rolled her eyes as she detoured back to the main fridge. "Sorry. I forgot about dressing. We got French, Italian, Blue Cheese, um, and something light."

"Italian sounds good," Genie said. "And how about some mustard? C'mon, Curtains, you're big-time slackin' in the hostess duties here."

Becca carefully set down the bottled wine coolers and the dressing, then flipped off her partner.

Genie laughed, but didn't offer to help. She leaned back and watched as Becca filled her arms with the coolers, the dressing, and mustard, ketchup, relish and a jar of pickles.

Putting them all in front of Genie, Becca demanded, "That enough condiments for ya?"

"I'll let you know," Genie teased, reaching for a cooler.

"Smartass."

"What's your point?"

"That *is* my point."

The sound of children suddenly filled the kitchen, but though there was laughter, there wasn't any talking. Genie watched as three of the kids from the pool, still dripping and in swimsuits, opened the freezer door, vying for position to get something, a snack probably. Genie looked over at her partner to see her grinning broadly and nudged the other woman. "What's going on?"

Snorting as she shook her head, Becca called out, "Front and center and *verbal*, if you please."

Instantly, the three kids left the freezer and came to stand near them. Becca smiled and ordered, "Introduce yourselves, please."

The youngest, a tow-headed girl of about five, piped up, "I'm Stephanie."

A girl about eight with dark hair said, "Melissa."

The oldest, a boy around ten said, "Jacky."

"Nice to meet you," Genie greeted with a smile. "I'm Genie."

"You're Becky's police partner," Melissa said, eyes wide.

Genie nodded. "That's right."

The boy frowned and said, "You're not a 'path."

"Nope," Genie agreed easily.

"Isn't that lonely?"

Nonplussed by Melissa's question, Genie hesitated and looked at Becca, who smiled, unhelpful. Gathering her thoughts, Genie answered, "Not so's I've noticed. Isn't it noisy being a telepath?"

Melissa looked thoughtful before saying, "Sometimes. But only when I'm tired and can't keep everyone out."

"You really can't hear anyone?" Jack asked, something like pity in his voice.

Genie stiffened instinctively at his tone, but before she could say anything, Becca spoke, her voice harsh. "Jacob Michael Barrons. What have I warned you about that?"

The boy flinched physically from the rebuke and whispered, "I'm sorry, Genie."

Not sure what had just happened, Genie answered easily, "Apology accepted."

"Detective Marshall might be willing to overlook this, but *I* am not. I'll deal with you tomorrow, Jacob. Be in my office by seven."

"Yes, Becky."

Becca stared at him a moment longer before nodding and shooing the much-subdued children out of the kitchen. Morosely, Becca picked at her salad with a sigh.

Concerned, and somewhat bewildered, Genie demanded, "What just happened?"

Sighing, Becca replied, "We have to reach them while they're still young. We have to make sure they understand that they are no different than non-telepaths. That their gifts are a talent, like being able to play the piano, or being an athlete. If we don't, oh God, Genie, can you imagine what an egocentric telepath would be like? What damage even *one* trained telepath, who doesn't feel or believe in our ethics, could do?"

Genie shivered a little at her partner's bleak tone and reached over to grip her hand comfortingly. "Hey, it's okay. I don't think he even realized what he was doing."

Urgently, Becca replied, "And that's exactly what's wrong. He *has* to be aware of his every action. He *has* to know and realize how non-telepaths are going to view his actions, how they'll view him. It's the other side of the coin. Even if he's completely honest and ethical, if he comes across as superior or, or snobbish, he's going to cause himself, and the rest of us, so many problems."

Genie released Becca's hand and leaned back in her chair, looking critically at her partner with a frown. "Is that why you're always so easygoing? I don't think I've actually seen you get pissed at anyone, well, except me. Not in the whole time you've been working Violent Crimes."

Becca shrugged. "That's part of it, yeah. I can't afford to let my temper go, can't let it, or myself, get out of control."

Genie's frown increased. "Sounds like an awfully rigid way of living."

Snorting quietly, Becca observed dryly, "Hello, pot. I'm kettle."

Chuckling warmly, the tension easing a bit, Genie retorted, "Repression: it's a way of life."

Picking up the now-cooled burger, Becca took a bite before commenting, "Finish your supper. I've got something I want to show you."

Smiling, Genie picked up her burger and started eating.

THE SUN WAS well into its slow, inevitable descent by the time Becca and Genie finished eating and left the mansion. They walked quietly, enjoying the peace that seemed to have fallen over the area. All the children had gone in for the night, and only adults were wandering the grounds in romantic twos and threes. Stars began their nightly duties of illuminating the dark.

Genie took a deep breath of the sweet, fresh air laced with the scent of roses and wondered when she'd last been somewhere so clean. She didn't think ever. "It's beautiful here."

Becca smiled up at her and nodded. "I fell in love with this place almost right away."

"That's right, you grew up here."

"Yep. Boy, was I a handful then," Becca admitted with a chuckle.

Grinning broadly, Genie teased, "Little Becca Curtains a hellion? This, I must hear."

Becca shoved her playfully and said, "I think not. I'll let Sharon fill you in on all the embarrassing details. She does it so much better than I, and enjoys it so much more."

Laughing, Genie asked, "So what did you want to show me?"

"We're getting there, hang on," Becca assured her.

They walked towards the edge of the property and, to Genie's surprise, it ended in a good-sized canyon. She peered over the edge and saw the bottom was at least twenty feet down with jagged rock sides. "Nice."

With a smirk, Becca set down the blanket she'd been carrying and sat, putting her legs over the edge. "What's the matter, Marshall? Chicken?"

"Oh, that's adult," Genie commented. She took another hesitant look over the edge, then carefully sat beside her partner.

"Got you to sit down though, didn't it?"

The sun was pretty much gone by then, the horizon barely showing a lighter purple than the black of night. The heat of the day was still baked into the rock and it seeped into them through the blanket.

"Hey."

Genie looked over at Becca. "What?"

"Lie back."

"Why?"

"Just do it, Marshall."

Reluctantly, Genie lay back. With her feet hanging over the edge, lying on the soft blanket and looking up at the endless night, it felt as though she was floating in forever and she gasped in surprise. It was almost frightening to feel this light and free. "Oh, wow."

"Incredible, isn't it?"

But Genie had to close her eyes against the sensation, fear rising sharply to swamp her. She wanted to move, but her body betrayed her and stayed motionless. It brought her back to the sessions of sensory deprivation she'd suffered through in the military. It was far too overwhelming and she was helpless in the tide.

"Genie? Genie, c'mon, answer me, partner!" Becca ordered, leaning over Genie. When she couldn't answer, Becca grabbed her legs and pulled them up, then rolled them both away from the edge, ending up beneath her partner.

Genie clung to her, holding onto the anchor with all her might, glad for the strong arms that surrounded her waist. Eventually, Becca's soft, reassuring voice penetrated and the fear receded. Almost herself once more, feeling the comfort radiating from the other woman, Genie pushed off her friend to sit on the rough, rocky ground. "Sorry, sorry, didn't mean to lose it like that."

Sitting up, still worried, Becca asked, "Are you all right now?"

Genie nodded and gave her a shaky laugh. "I don't think I'll be doing that again *any* time soon, though. Like, ever."

"God, Genie, I'm sorry," Becca apologized. "I never meant to push you into something that would freak you out! You should've stopped me!"

"Becca, I'm fine. And if I didn't know that it would freak me out, how could you? I've done way more dangerous stuff than lie down somewhere with my legs hanging over an edge. You wanted to share something you thought was beautiful with me and I appreciate that."

Though a frown still creased her forehead, Becca nodded and got to her feet, holding down her hand. Genie took it to stand and walked a short distance away from the edge while her partner gathered up the blanket. As they walked back to the mansion, Genie asked, "Did you used to do that as a kid?"

"Whenever the world overwhelmed me," Becca confirmed quietly. "It reminded me that the universe was so much more than my tiny little life here on this planet. I felt connected, I guess. I knew my part in the plan and while it affected those around me, it didn't much touch the universe in general."

Genie nodded slowly. "I can see where you'd get that. It, ah, it overwhelmed me, actually. I felt, I don't know, like I had no part, I guess. That I was insignificant."

Becca said miserably, "That wasn't my intention, Genie. God, I'm so sorry!"

Linking arms with the smaller woman, Genie said, "It's not your fault. It's my own insecurities talking."

It was pretty obvious that Becca didn't completely believe her, but she didn't press.

"So. You were going to tell me what was wrong," Genie said

hurriedly.

"Oh, there's a more pleasant subject."

Genie smiled faintly and offered, "You don't have to talk about it."

"Nah. I should talk to someone so I don't kill anyone at the meeting tomorrow," Becca said wryly. After a minute or so, she continued, "There's a push to bring all our people into the Centers. To withdraw from society altogether. It's never been a big faction, but all of a sudden, there seems to be a lot more support for it than usual. Of course, we've never really had someone like Doyle to organize support against us, either. I might not be able to stop it, if the vote swings that way."

Stunned, Genie exclaimed, "They can't do that! That's stupid!"

"Can I quote you?"

Serious, Genie nodded. "Absolutely. Matter of fact, why don't you bring me in? Kind of like an impartial witness or something."

Becca seemed surprised by the suggestion. "You'd do that?"

Totally serious, Genie agreed, "Sure! I've got too much to lose if you get yanked back."

Becca shook her head, coming to a stop. "I wouldn't leave."

Now it was Genie's turn to be surprised. She stopped walking as well, looking at her shadowy partner standing before her. Even in the dark, the tension was easy to see. "What do you mean?"

"My work is too important to me, and, not to be too egotistical, it's too important to the world, for me to leave," Becca explained slowly. "If I won't let some punk off the street drive me away, why would I let my own people do it?"

They were silent for a few minutes, then Genie asked slowly, "And what would happen then?"

"Someone else would be elected as Leader."

"No. I mean to your people. The ones not on the council. The ones who feel that *their* work in the outside world is too important to leave, too," Genie clarified.

Pursing her lips, Becca answered, "They'd probably stay where they are. Oh. I see where you're going. That this will divide us. I know. I've known that for a while. It would be the first time in our history that we'd be driven into factions."

"Right. And what happens to those of you outside who don't have the benefit of the Centers' protection?" Genie asked.

"We'd be on our own," Becca whispered. "Vulnerable."

After a short silence, Genie pointed out, "You wouldn't be the only ones. It might just be my paranoia talking, but if most of the telepaths are centrally located, how difficult would it be to wipe you all out? Becca, they're doing Doyle's work for him. One simultaneous strike worldwide and the telepath problem is gone, pretty much for good."

"Oh my God."

Genie nodded, but her thoughts had already turned onto something even more disturbing. What would happen to Becca if someone decided that they didn't like the way she was leading her people? And who was there among the telepaths who wanted to wield the kind of power that Becca took for granted?

Looking at her partner's upset face, so vulnerable in the brightening moonlight, Genie vowed to protect the other woman, even if it was from her own people.

Chapter
Twelve

BECKY WOKE THE following morning with a headache. She groaned and turned over in bed, pulling the pillow over her head and praying it would go away. No such luck. When the throbbing grew unbearable, she stumbled to the bathroom between the bedrooms and searched for a pain reliever. Finding a bottle, she took four tablets and stared blearily at her reflection. Even given the excessively early hour, she looked like crap.

She'd stayed up most of the night obsessing over her discussion with Genie, and it showed in the darkened circles under her eyes. Her hair stuck up straight in spikes without the benefit of hair products and her freckles stood out in sharp relief against too-pale skin.

"Ugh." She stuck her tongue out at herself.

Rubbing her eyes, she went back into the bedroom and looked at the clock. It was just after five in the morning. Wonderful. She'd gotten about two and a half hours of sleep. But if she went back to bed, she probably wouldn't wake up until noon and there was far too much for her to do. Then again, she didn't want to look like a zombie for the rest of the day, either.

Making a decision, she turned back around and entered the bathroom. She peeled off boxers and T-shirt, turning on the shower. Becky was just about to get in when the other door opened and she found herself standing naked in front of her partner. Shaking her head at life's absurdity, she grunted, "Morning," and walked into the shower, pulling the curtain into place.

"What are you doing up at this ungodly hour?"

"Hey. I thought you were a morning person."

Genie yawned loudly. "I am. Which is why *you* should still be in bed."

"Can't sleep."

"Know the feeling."

Leaning against the cool tile, Becky suggested, "Why don't you get back to bed? If I didn't have meetings this morning, that's where I'd be."

"Nah. Besides, I thought I'd sit in on the meetings, if that's okay?"

Becky thought about it for a moment, then shrugged. "Sure. Why not? Nothing top-secret going on. Though I'd rather you not be there for my meeting with Jacob."

"That's okay. I'd rather not be there for that one, either."

"I bet," Becky commented dryly.

Yawning again, Genie said, "I'll leave you to your shower, then grab one myself."

The door closed and Becky relaxed into the hot spray pounding over her body. She was starting to feel a little more awake, but not a hell of a lot. Finally realizing that she wasn't going to get any more alert, Becky turned off the shower and dried off before going back into her room. She went blearily through the motions of getting dressed and ready for the day.

Sitting on her bed, staring into space, Becky didn't move at all when Genie entered the room, fully dressed. She didn't really hear her partner come in, but felt her familiar, comforting presence and so didn't leave the strange mental blur that her mind had latched onto.

There was something wrong in her house and she couldn't identify it. Genie sat beside her, touching the small of her back lightly, grounding her. It wasn't the newcomers who had arrived during the night, they had already filtered into her sub-consciousness. No, it was more a sense of...disharmony...of those who made up her extended family. Shaking off the strangeness, Becky met her partner's concerned gaze with a smile. "I'm fine, thanks. There's just, I don't know, something weird's going on."

"Like?"

"I dunno." Becky shrugged and stood abruptly. "The others should be arriving throughout the day. I'm not sure what time the council meeting's scheduled for yet, but probably late this afternoon. Let's get some breakfast and, more importantly, some coffee. I might start feeling human by then."

Grinning, Genie swatted her gently on the backside and stood. "Lead on."

Becky was disappointed when Jarrod and Michelle joined them at the breakfast table. She'd been hoping to have some time alone with Genie. Forcing a smile, she greeted them pleasantly while they set about making themselves breakfast. Glancing at her partner, Becky stifled a grin to see the other woman just as displeased by their new companions. "Michelle. I don't think you've met my partner, Detective Genie Marshall. Genie, this is Michelle Smith."

They shook hands and Michelle said, "Sorry to make Becky work on your vacation."

Genie shrugged. "Long as she gets *some* rest while we're here, I won't be forced to hurt anyone."

Michelle and Jarrod exchanged uneasy looks. Becky rolled her eyes and informed them, "Ignore her. The coffee hasn't hit her system yet and we were up pretty late last night. Or, well, this morning at any rate."

Genie smiled toothily, but it didn't seem to reassure the others any.

Deliberately ignoring her partner, Becky asked pointedly, "So, Michelle. What's the schedule?"

"Everyone's pretty anxious to get this started, so after Nikola arrives around two, we'll gather in the main study."

Becky nodded, sipping carefully at her hot coffee. "Sounds like a plan."

There was some more talking, but the same feeling that she'd had after waking up distracted Becky, and her headache returned. Finally realizing that they weren't going to get much more out of their leader, Michelle and Jarrod left the breakfast table.

Genie lightly touched Becky's arm and asked, "Headache?"

Closing her eyes, Becky nodded. "Throbbing."

Sympathetically, Genie rubbed the back of her friend's neck and said, "You should've gone back to bed. You won't get another chance."

Groaning, both at the release of tension from Genie's magical fingers, and the knowledge that her partner was right, Becky said, "Too late now."

"Don't worry about it. You'll do fine," Genie said quietly, confidently.

Becky looked over at her friend, fortified by the encouragement. "Thanks."

Sharon chose that moment to walk into the kitchen and both women stood to greet the slightly battered woman.

"Sharon! How are you?" Becky demanded, pulling her mentor into a gentle hug.

"Better, little one, thank you," Sharon answered with a smile. "Genie, it's good to see you."

Genie grinned. "Glad to see you're in one piece."

"Relatively speaking," the other woman joked. Turning somewhat serious, she asked, "I understand there's a Council meeting today?"

Becky nodded. "Right after Nikola gets here."

"Have you seen Joseph yet?" Sharon asked.

"No, and it's just as well."

Genie looked from one woman to the other. "Who's Joseph?"

"He's the one pushing for the isolationist policy," Becky explained.

Genie nodded and asked casually, "Been doing that long?"

Sharon shrugged. "He's always been an alarmist, not to mention an egotistical jerk. It's just as well that he doesn't live outside the Centers, or we'd constantly be cleaning up his messes."

"Genie," Becky warned.

Genie assumed an innocent expression. "What?"

"The interrogation stops now, partner," Becky said firmly.

Grinning faintly, Genie crossed her arms over her chest and leaned against the nearest wall. "I have no idea what you're talking about."

Rolling her eyes, Becky said, "Yeah, right. I have to go meet with Jacob now. Behave yourself and I'll see you in about a half hour?"

Genie nodded, but it didn't reassure Becky all that much. Shaking her head, she left them to whatever trouble they might find.

GENIE LOOKED AT Sharon upon Becca's departure, but the other woman poured herself a cup of coffee without signaling that she was even aware of the scrutiny. She looked tired, long hair limp and eyes grayed with fatigue. Concerned, Genie asked, "So how are you, really?"

"I've had better nights. They were going to keep me another day, but Jarrod told me about the meeting, so I signed out. I met up with Michelle when I got in and she told me you two were in here," Sharon answered wearily.

"What's your honest opinion about what's going to happen?"

Sipping at her coffee, eyes closed, Sharon clearly thought over her response carefully before saying, "That depends on a few things. Right now, the numbers are a little more than half against withdrawing. That could change if Joseph has an eloquent moment or Becca falls down on the job."

Indignant, Genie was about to protest, but Sharon held up a hand to forestall her complaint.

"I'm not saying that to be harsh, Genie. It's just that with Becca being gone for so long, people forget. Out of sight, out of mind, you know?"

Snorting, Genie observed, "I thought you people were never out of mind."

Sharon smiled at the attempt at humor, weak as it was. "Happens to the best of us."

"Tell me more about Joseph," Genie requested, settling back in her chair.

With a shrug, Sharon sipped at her coffee before answering, "He's about my age and has always been paranoid. He's also always had delusions of grandeur and an eye on Becca's seat, and I mean that strictly in the political sense."

"Why? Did he hold it before her?"

"Not at all. Unfortunately, the woman who held it before Becca died of cancer."

"I'm sorry."

"That's all right, dear, it was ten years ago. We ran for a few years with the spot open because no one seemed right for the position. When Becca came back from college, well, she was full of ideas, and passion, and by the time the next full council was assembled, it was a forgone conclusion that she'd hold the position," Sharon explained.

"So where does Joseph come into all of this? Why didn't he make his move when no one was in the spot?"

"It doesn't really work like that."

"So how's it work?"

"Did Becca tell you specifically about her position?"

"Yeah. She moves the council in directions that are best worldwide for telepaths. Oversees things, makes sure that everything runs smoothly," Genie replied.

Sharon nodded. "Right. After Melanie, the previous council leader, we didn't really have a direction, but no one seemed to feel the lack. While things weren't great outside, they weren't bad, either. Melanie had slowly been moving us towards integration with the outside, the main reason young adults are allowed to go to college and get jobs pretty much where they want to."

"Wait, wait, wait! 'Allowed to?' " Genie demanded. "Last I heard, it was a free country, regardless of telepathic ability."

"Would you really want to leave your family if they didn't want you to go?"

Genie stiffened, but didn't respond.

Sharon frowned at the lack of an answer, but left it alone and continued, "How much more difficult would that be if you were connected mind-to-mind? Near impossible. When I said 'allowed,' I meant it in a figurative sense, but unfortunately, Joseph would have that become literal. He would keep us all walled up without the choice of making our way into the world. Aside from those like myself who search out young telepaths, of course."

"Which brings me back to my original question."

"I didn't throw you off at all, did I?"

Genie shrugged modestly. "I do this sort of thing for a living."

Exasperated, eyes rolling slightly, Sharon replied, "Honestly, I don't know. It could go either way."

Pouring herself another cup of coffee, Genie returned to her spot near the older woman. Looking at Sharon closely, she questioned, "Let me ask you this. What would happen if Joseph's changes were accepted and Becca went against the tide? What would happen if she stayed my partner and chucked everything else?"

Sharon's mouth opened, but nothing came out.

Groaning, Genie muttered, "Great. Just great."

GENIE MADE HERSELF as inconspicuous as possible while Becca met with various other people throughout the morning. Most of it was meet and greet stuff, like the department functions Genie avoided at all costs. She made herself comfortable on the leather sofa and opened a book, keeping her ears on tone, more than words. None of the people visiting with Becca seemed in the least bit upset or even irritated. On the whole, they were pleased to see her after a long time apart.

Around one that afternoon, Sharon brought them sandwiches and sodas and then, shortly after, Becca said it was time to get ready for the meeting. On the way back to their rooms, Genie asked plaintively, "We're getting changed? You told me I didn't need to bring anything formal!"

Grinning, Becca answered, "Sorry, partner. And it's not really formal, just not *as* casual as we were yesterday and this morning."

"You're evil."

"Just wear your black pants and that rust shirt, it sets your eyes off nicely and seems pretty comfy."

Eyebrows lifting in surprise, Genie asked, "And just how do you know what I brought for a wardrobe, Detective Curtains?"

Becca smirked. "I'm psychic, remember?"

Laughing, Genie shoved her playfully just as they reached the bedrooms. "You can have the shower first."

"Thanks. I think I need a refresher," Becca said gratefully.

Genie continued on toward her room and met up with a man walking toward her. He was older, in his late fifties most likely, with silver hair, dark eyes and the broad build of a former athlete. She smiled politely and would have brushed past him, but he stopped her. "Detective Marshall, isn't it?"

Maintaining a polite smile, Genie nodded. "And you are?"

"Joseph Senders."

"Nice to meet you," Genie said. He stayed in front of her, blocking the way. Stifling a sigh, she continued, "Is there something I can do for you?"

"I understand that you and Becky are partners."

Genie waited for him to make a point. "That's right."

"And that her previous partner worked for UnderTEM."

"Right again." For some reason, Genie wished that she had her gun, her hand hovering where it should be. "Do you have a point?"

He smiled unpleasantly. "Becky hasn't brought anyone to the Center before. Is there something about your relationship that hasn't been shared with the rest of us?"

Keeping a firm grip on her temper, Genie answered, "Not knowing what information you have, I couldn't really say. And you know, Becca might go for all this communication and sharing shit, but I sure as hell don't. I respect peoples' privacy and expect others to do the same."

"I hope you haven't gotten used to working with Becky, Detective. After all, she won't be your partner for much longer," Joseph said before walking past her.

Genie barely restrained a snarl of anger as she watched him walk down the hall. His words had nothing to do with Becca staying at the Center. She knew that from all her years of military and police training, recognizing danger when it presented itself. All her instincts demanded that she neutralize the threat he represented, then and there.

Gritting her teeth, Genie entered her room, careful to lock the door behind her.

BECKY FROWNED AT Genie, who merely returned her look with a mild one of her own. Something had happened in the brief time they'd taken to get ready for the meeting, but she hadn't a clue as to what. Gone was the easygoing friend along for a ride; in her place was someone who felt a lot like a bodyguard. On the walk to the library, and even now, Genie had stayed on her left flank. It was the stance they took when walking into a dangerous situation and needing to keep their gun-lines clear.

Though her frown increased as she realized that, Becky didn't have any more time to think about it. It was time for the meeting to begin and for her to take her place. When Genie took position behind her, standing guard, Becky snapped quietly, "I don't need a bodyguard!"

Genie looked at her calmly and replied, just as softly, "Yes. You do."

Taken aback, Becky reached out to touch her partner's hip. There, under the black sweater that Genie had donned instead of the light shirt Becky had recommended, was a weapon that Becky hadn't even known her partner had brought. Meeting the cool gaze of a trained professional, Becky couldn't think of a thing to say. What the hell had happened to make her partner think that she needed protection here, of all places?

In a split second, Becky made the decision, once again, to trust her partner's instincts. She turned and faced the assembly, leaving security in Genie's more-than capable hands. "It's good to see you all again, though I'm sorry the circumstances aren't more pleasant."

Genie's presence at her back was comforting, even strengthening. Becky took a breath and continued, "There has been a resolution called for by several members. We're here today to begin discussions about what's come to be known as the Isolationist Move. The floor is open. Who wishes to speak first?"

Joseph stood and said firmly, "I do."

Becky nodded; she'd expected that. "Speak."

THE DISCUSSION STRETCHED through six of the most contentious hours in Center history, from what Becca later told Genie. For the first time, the telepaths were divided among themselves. Each council member was a representative of his or her Center, not there to speak their own personal feelings; still, they were human, and opinions were not always aligned. They were voting for their houses, for their people, for their future. Voices were raised and order called for many times throughout the afternoon.

No decision was reached.

Personally, Genie thought they were being too hard on themselves, pushing to make a decision too quickly. Every so often, a shudder ran through Becky and Genie rested her hand on her partner's shoulder. She was hoping it would help dissipate the negative emotions that she knew had to be attacking her partner's sensitive psyche. She noted both cold and fiercely hot looks whenever she did so, and not just from Joseph Senders. The glaring was not going to dissuade her, though; this was clearly a hostile situation and there was no way she'd let anything move her from her partner's side..

When things seemed to be heating up too much, Genie leaned down and murmured, "Now might be a good time for my debut."

Becky sighed faintly, but nodded and stood, calling out to the two current combatants, "Liza, Seamus, please. You're giving everyone a headache."

Her quietly pained voice instantly cut through the argument and both participants fell silent. Dredging up a smile from somewhere, she said, "I know that many of you are wondering why I brought a non-telepath to this meeting, and that many of you seem uncomfortable with her presence. I brought her so we could all listen to a new perspective. Genie?"

Genie gently squeezed her friend's arm before taking a few steps forward. She gave herself a long moment to look everyone over before speaking, not rushing this for anyone. "My name is Detective Genie Marshall. I work in the Violent Crimes and provisional Psi-Agent Division of the DC police. I was approached by Sharon to work with Detective Curtains, to become her partner a few months back. I'm sure that you'll all find it difficult to believe, but at the time, I didn't have a partner because most people find me a little too abrasive to work with on a regular basis."

There were a few chuckles at her wry comment, but Genie maintained her serious air. "I think my previous partner was a telepath, but I don't know. He was never tested, and he died in the line of duty, so there's no way to ever know for sure. But I'd seen

Detective Curtains' work and read her files, and was extremely impressed with her record. You can all be very proud of her. She's caught some of the vilest criminals it's ever been her misfortune to come across, and saved many lives.

"That being said, she's also a huge pain in the ass to work with. She's emotional, intuitive, and likes to leap without looking. She works god-awful hours and has the self-preservation instincts of a lemming." Genie glanced at Becky with a fond grin. As expected, her partner grimaced, but remained silent. "She's also one of the most dedicated officers that it's been my honor and privilege to work with. Before you make your decision on whether or not to recall your people, there are some points that you should think very carefully about first.

"Without Detective Curtains, there would be fourteen serial killers, three serial rapists, and four garden-variety, but very clever, murderers still free. I don't know what sort of work the rest of you do, but if you bring even half the talent and dedication into the world that Rebecca does, we will lose a lot, too much, if you withdraw from it.

"Things are bad for you right now, I get that. Believe me, I get that. Becca is very important to me and it just about killed me that I couldn't get the bastard who beat her up on charges from the Hate Crimes Act." Genie sighed, then continued, "If you leave, you give in to the hate-mongers. What kind of message are you giving to the men, women, and children out there who don't feel that it's all right to be a telepath? Not to mention that you'd be doing Doyle's work *for* him. He's trying to herd you all into 'shelters' for your own good. I don't know about you, but I wouldn't spit on him if he was dying of thirst in the desert, let alone give him his dearest wish.

"So anyway. I just wanted to say that. And to mention that you will lose some of your own over this. Have you thought about what will happen if you do withdraw and those against it ignore your mandate? It's a free world. For people like Becca, you'd be forcing them to choose between their destiny to serve the greater good, and the family they've found here. Personally, I wouldn't want to risk their decision to leave, because when they do, and they will, you'd have to bar the gate against them coming back. And I don't really think you want to do that."

The room was utterly silent when she finished. Genie backed up, taking her place behind Becky and putting her hand back where it always seemed to belong: on her partner's shoulder. Becky's smaller hand grasped hers tightly for a long moment before coming to a decision.

Standing, Becca announced, "I think that Detective Marshall has brought up a good point. We are divided on something that's vitally important for the first time ever that we know of. Whatever decision we make, we cannot make it in one afternoon. We need to have a number of set discussions, with set times, so that non-council members can attend and voice their opinions individually."

Becky looked around the room, biting her lip as she thought something over. After a moment, she said, "I also want to bring up something that my partner didn't say, probably for fear of it being taken the wrong way, but it has to be said. If we are all in one place, we are that much easier to wipe out. We would be a tempting target for anyone with the right weaponry. There *might* be an outcry once the deed is done, but it wouldn't really matter at that point, would it? We'd still be dead."

The silence took on a darker tone at her words.

"I want five volunteers for a committee to get the discussions under way. You can come to me tomorrow. And no, I won't be on it," Becky said firmly. "This is going to be a time-consuming project. I want people who have the time available to give it their all."

Which seemed to be the signal everyone was waiting for to break up the difficult meeting. Genie stayed where she was, leaning against the wall and watching as Becky made her way through the crowd, talking quietly with various people.

Sharon headed over to her after a while and commented, "You're a lot more eloquent than I expected."

Grinning, Genie replied, "I should be insulted by that."

Sharon chuckled. "Not at all, not at all. Just thinking that it was a very, very good idea to have an outside, fairly objective point of view on the subject. I, ah, I also noticed that you're carrying. Any particular reason?"

Silently, Genie's gaze went to Joseph Senders, who spoke with someone at the far side of the room.

Sharon's gaze followed hers and she asked incredulously, "Do you really think he's *that* sort of problem?"

"I'm not going to leave her alone in a room with him. Ever," Genie informed the other woman flatly. Even now her fingers itched to hold the smooth, reassuring grip of her gun, just with him in the room.

Sharon swallowed uneasily, as it sensing the dark tinge to Genie's thoughts.

Genie wouldn't be surprised if Sharon knew that she'd seen a lot of violence in her life. The older woman wouldn't have scanned her, but the wariness in her eyes showed that Sharon could well believe, and rightly so, that Genie had committed more than enough of her own, personal, brand of mayhem.

Finding her voice, Sharon said, "You'll be happy to know that he's scheduled to leave tomorrow."

Genie looked at her sharply. "Where's he going? I thought he lived here."

"No. He divides his time between the Centers. He's like an accounts overseer and, though he can do most of it from a computer, he does need access to the individual files at the Centers."

Genie didn't relax any at the information. She'd relax when he was gone. Until then, she had the feeling that she'd be sleeping with the connecting doors between her and Becky's bedrooms open. She caught Becky's puzzled look and smiled, mouthing, "Nothing."

Becky grinned and shook her head, returning to her conversation.

Genie went back to her guarding as Sharon rejoined the crowd. Time enough to mingle when she didn't feel like there was a bomb waiting to go off.

THE LAST PART of the evening went a lot better than the first, but Becky still found herself at loose-ends when the Center was long dark and everyone gone to bed. Her feet brought her to all the nooks and crannies in which she'd hidden away as a child before leading her to the kitchen. Someone, probably Michelle, had made sure to stock her favorite kind of ice cream. She moved easily without the light, knowing where each fixture and piece of furniture lay by heart.

Settling at the kitchen table with her half-gallon and a spoon, Becky slowly devoured a good portion while her mind roamed from thought to thought. She couldn't even focus her mind, after the way it had been jangled with so much discord for hours on end.

"I thought I would find you here."

Becky looked up in surprise at her partner's appearance. It was well after midnight and she'd snuck into the kitchen to bury her woes in ice cream. Smiling faintly, she motioned to the empty kitchen chair across from her and pushed the tub of ice cream into the center of the table. "Want some?"

Genie nodded and sat down. After taking a couple of bites from Becky's spoon, she commented, "Rough day."

Becky sighed. "And it's just going to get rougher."

"You kept shivering in there," Genie observed softly.

Sadly, Becky toyed with her spoon and answered, "You couldn't feel the emotions. I thought I was going to backlash a few times, it was so strong. The, the acrimony and anger was nearly overwhelming. These are my people, my family. What do I do?"

Genie responded to the desperation in her voice, reaching across the table to grasp one of Becky's hands in her own. "What every parent does eventually. You let them work it out on their own. You couldn't dictate a decision to them even if you wanted to, which I know you don't. You're only one woman, Becca, no matter how strong and good you are. The weight of this world doesn't rest on you. You can guide them, but you can't tell them what to do."

Flushing at the praise, Becky nodded shyly and said, "Thanks, Genie. For everything. You're my rock."

Genie squeezed her hand in reassurance then released it to take another bite of ice cream.

THE DAY OF their leave-taking was decidedly odd, and somewhat upsetting, for Genie. She'd grown unusually comfortable in the Center, far more so than expected, and truly hated to leave. While Becca had been busy with taking care of business, Genie had taken the time to get to know pretty much everyone on the pseudo-campus. The Center's pulse had fallen in line with her own, or vice verse, in a strangely easy fashion.

To Becca, it seemed to be just another time of saying good-bye to those she loved and cared about. Something Genie knew that the other woman was, well, perhaps not used to, but accepting of. Genie had never really had a caring, extended family to say goodbye to before, despite the fairly good relationship with her parents when they were alive.

So when they were surrounded by at least twenty people at the car in the hot California afternoon, Genie felt as though crying should be at the top of her list of things to do. Warm smiles, caring eyes, and fleeting touches from one and all kept Genie in an unsettled whirl. It was Becca's turn to keep her hand at the small of Genie's back in a comforting, solid manner that spoke of permanence.

Finally, it was time to go and they got into the car, with Jarrod once again their driver. Sharon had left to check out news of a potential telepath in Arizona, and Michelle was too busy with Center business to take them.

As they drove away, Genie caught sight of Joseph standing half in the shadows of the Center. He hadn't, as Sharon had promised, left the day after the meeting. According to Becca, there was no longer any danger of an isolationist policy being voted into effect, and therefore, Senders was no longer a threat. In Genie's mind, however, the man had merely made a strategic retreat when things hadn't gone his way. He would jump in whenever the next opportunity presented itself. For now, though, the danger to Becca was moot, since they were leaving. She doubted the man had the balls to try anything long-distance that could be traced back to him.

"Penny for your thoughts," Becca murmured, resting her head against Genie's shoulder.

Genie shrugged, doing her best not to let her guard down any further than it already was. "Just a little surprised at how hard it is to leave."

Smiling, Becca closed her eyes and curled a little closer. "I knew you'd fall in love with the place."

Genie put her arm around her partner's shoulder. "Who said

anything about that? I'm just going to miss the heat."

Poking Genie gently in the side, Becca shook her head. "You can't fool me, Marshall. You loved every minute there."

"Well, I wouldn't mind going back," Genie admitted grudgingly.

"Mm hmm."

Smiling faintly, Genie met Jarrod's eyes in the rearview mirror. He grinned at her and she couldn't help but grin back. So okay. Going back was definitely on her list of things to do one day. That didn't mean she had to be a pushover about it.

She did have a reputation to maintain, after all.

Chapter
Thirteen

THE HEAT OF the steam room soaked into Becky's body and she sighed deeply in contentment.

"We should do this more often."

Snorting at her partner's words, Becky countered, "Considering that we've barely had time to breathe lately, I doubt that 'more often' is the right phrase."

Grinning in response, Genie said, "Case."

"Huh?"

"Case. You know, as in the old saying, 'a case in point'?"

Dark eyebrows arching, Becky asked, "Has anyone ever told you that you're odd?"

Closing her eyes, Genie airily waved her hand. "Familiar refrain and all that."

Becky stretched out on the slippery tile, resting her head against Genie's thigh. It made a good pillow on the uncomfortable surface. Over three thousand years and someone had as yet to design a comfortable steam room. Wasn't there some kind of material that was soft but would withstand the steam and moisture?

"Not really."

"Excuse me?" Becky asked, startled into opening her eyes. Had she said that aloud?

"I said, 'not really.' You were wondering why these things weren't more comfortable, right?"

"I'm not even going to ask how you knew what I was thinking."

Chuckling, Genie said, "It's easy enough to do since your thoughts are always so close to the surface. And you're way too logical."

Becky frowned. "I think that was an insult."

"More like a left-handed compliment."

"Hey!"

Chuckling again, Genie continued, "As I was saying. The plastic would be just as uncomfortable as tile, more so if you count the sticking factor. Metal is definitely out due to that burning-when-hot thing. Stone's not any more comfortable than tile and definitely does the burn thing, too."

Becky stared up at her partner, who was still grinning. "Put a lot of thought into this, have you?"

With a shrug, Genie replied, "Not really."

They sat in comfortable silence, decompressing from the week of insanity that work had been. Rushing around from crime scene to crime scene, while still trying to chase down that damned psychic stalker, had left them both in serious need of down-time. They'd been spending more and more time together of late, even outside of work. When Becky had suggested coming here, Genie had practically jumped at the offer.

"Excuse me, is there a Detective Curtains here?"

Groaning, Becky whispered, "Think I should answer?"

A long-suffering sigh was her friend's answer.

"I'm back here," Becky called out reluctantly.

A woman dressed in the spa uniform came out of the steam. "There was a phone call for you from a Captain Carlson? He said that you and your partner need to get back to work. There's been a development in one of your cases."

"Thanks."

The woman nodded and retreated.

Scowling, Becky complained, "Don't we even get a full afternoon off?"

Genie ruffled her hair, looking down at her with soft eyes. "I think I'm rested."

A flush that was completely non-steam-related suffused Becky's face and she sat up quickly. Had she somehow let slip her growing interest in Genie without even realizing it? When she caught sight of the mischievous look in her partner's eyes, Becky punched the other woman's shoulder. "You!"

Grinning broadly, Genie hopped to her feet and crowed, "You're so easy, Becca."

"Just don't spread it around," Becky muttered to herself as they left the steam room.

THE COMPLETELY TONELESS shout of, "Curtains! Marshall! My office!" graced the air as soon as they walked into the bullpen.

Becky looked over at her partner. "So much for a case development. What did you do?"

"Me? Why do you automatically assume that it's my fault?" Genie demanded. At Becky's raised brow, she insisted, "I didn't do anything!"

"He only uses that tone when you've done something!"

"Any day now, detectives!"

Both women walked towards the Captain's office. Genie motioned gallantly for Becky to go first and the smaller woman mouthed, "Coward." Genie didn't deny the charge as she took her customary spot by the wall.

To their surprise, an unfamiliar man sat in the extra chair in front of the desk. He was dark-haired, with olive skin and gray eyes, and stood when they entered. Genie met Captain Carlson's eyes curiously, but found nothing there to indicate who the man was.

"Detectives Genie Marshall and Rebecca Curtains, this is Mr. Jonas Lipsham," Carlson introduced.

Genie and Becky exchanged surprised looks, instantly recognizing the name as one of the lead reporters for AllNetNews.com, the leading worldwide online newspaper. They shook hands and Jonas said, "It's good to meet both of you."

"Mr. Lipsham is here to do a story on you two," Carlson said bluntly.

Jaw dropping, Becky exclaimed, "But sir, that's impossible!"

Genie was somewhat less gracious about it. "You have got to be shitting me."

"Marshall," Carlson growled, giving her a quelling glare.

Scowling, Genie subsided.

"Now that the pleasantries are out of the way, I want to assure both of you that this piece isn't going to negatively impact either of you, in any way," Lipsham said earnestly.

Becky tried to stifle a grin and failed. "And just how do you plan to do that?"

Genie and Carlson both heard the "counselor" at the end of her question and grinned at the subtle insult.

Lipsham obviously sensed the silent exchange, but just as obviously didn't pick up on what it was about. Frowning slightly, he answered, "We won't be taking any vids of either of you, and your names will be changed as well. That way you won't be identified from the piece."

"Captain, you can't really be serious about this!" Genie's tone bordered on insubordination.

Carlson wagged a finger at her. "Forget it, Marshall. I've been told that this is for positive PR and you *will* cooperate."

Glowering at the reporter, Genie threatened, "If you get in our way, or our faces, this is over. I don't care what the brass wants."

Lipsham stood and said, still with that earnest air, "I can live with that. You won't even know I'm around."

Genie snorted derisively and stalked out of the office. Becky glared at her partner's retreating back before turning to their new tagalong. Just what they needed. Forcing a smile, Becky said, "You may as well come on."

Following her out of the office, Lipsham said, "I understand that you were attacked about a month ago."

"That's right."

"What happened? Was it a case you were working on?"

Irritated, she replied, "I was bashed."

"Bashed?"

Becky stopped short and asked, "You do know that I'm a Psi-Agent, right?"

He stared at her, then slowly shook his head. "I had suggested doing an in-depth article about the lead detectives in this department. I wasn't aware that you were a PA, no."

"Well, if you'd like to request reassignment to another set of detectives, we'd certainly understand," Becky offered sweetly, again moving towards her desk.

Gray eyes narrowed shrewdly at her before Lipsham shook his head and followed her the rest of the way to the desks. "I think this will make the article even better. Especially since you people are so tight-lipped."

In a dangerous tone, Genie demanded, " 'You people?' "

"Telepaths."

Genie almost stood up at the blunt response. "Look, Lipsham, just because you have permission to hang around with us doesn't mean you can be insulting and..."

"No insult intended," he interrupted hastily. "Look, there are reporters who would kill to be in my position right now. Telepaths are the most media-phobic minority in the world, probably in the history of the world! I'm not going to do anything that would expose you, Detective Curtains, but you have to look at this like it's an opportunity."

Becky looked at him sharply. "Opportunity?"

He nodded, leaning on her desk and insisting, "Yeah! With all the crap that Doyle is spouting these days, this will give you a chance to show the world your stuff."

"I could hardly use you as a mouthpiece even if I wanted to, which I don't."

"And I wouldn't let you. But I can report on you and your actions, both as a cop and a PA, objectively, and get people to see the benefits of having telepaths on their side. C'mon, what do you say?"

Becky met Genie's gaze for a long moment, but found no help there. Looking back at the reporter, Becky saw nothing that would lead her not to believe him. From everything she knew about him, Lipsham was one of the edgiest reporters around, always looking for the hottest story. On the other hand, she'd never heard of him doing anything underhanded, or giving in to sensationalism. For the tiniest moment, Becky thought about scanning him, but dismissed it out of hand. Sighing, she acquiesced, "Fine. But like Genie said. You get in the way, you're gone."

Grinning broadly, he said, "Me? Get in the way? Never happen."

Chapter Fourteen

GENIE AND BECCA hid out in the damp, broken down corridor of an old, underground warehouse outside of DC. It had definitely seen better days, as had the rotting, wooden boxes behind which they were hiding. They'd originally been at the airport to drop the Captain off for an annual conference, nothing that the reporter had needed to be with them for, but he'd insisted on accompanying them with a breezy, "Things just seem to *happen* around you two!"

Which, unfortunately, was all too true.

It was Genie's bad luck that this time, she'd been the one to give in. Shortly after the Captain had gone on his way, Jonas had spotted the mobster, Correlli. Before either of them could stop him, the reporter had raced forward to check things out. The man who had slowly been growing on her, had literally tripped over his own feet and crashed headlong into the criminals. She and Becca had followed the drug runners-*cum*-kidnappers here after Jonas had been taken.

So much for an uneventful day in the Captain's absence.

"I'm going to *kill* him!" Genie repeated as Becca dragged her towards the nearest doorway.

"Get in line," Becca ground out, scrupulously looking around. "I told you we should've ditched him this morning!"

Taking a deep breath, hanging onto her temper by a thread, Genie warned softly, "Do *not* start with me, Rebecca. Can you sense their position or not?"

Closing her eyes, Becca calmed her breathing, clearly reaching out for the frightened reporter with her mind. Genie knew that the telepath would be able to sense Jonas, having been in his company for several days.

"They're behind that door. Jonas is at the back and has a gun on him. Correlli's discussing what they should do with him."

"Think there's a back way in?"

Becca shot her a dark glance. "Do I look like radar equipment to you?"

"Shit! Sonuva... All right, time for a diversion," Genie hissed. Making up in force what she lacked in volume, she continued, "I'm going to get their attention. You stay under cover and hang out here.

And call for backup!"

"And just how do you plan to get their attention without getting killed?" Becca hissed.

"Oh, I have a pretty suicidal idea, all right. But it'll work. I know these assholes too well and Lipsham doesn't have a lot of time!"

"Be careful!"

Genie nodded impatiently, waiting for her partner to get under better cover, further back in the corridor. What to do, what to do? Well, there was always the direct approach. She took a moment to get into the right mind-set. Standing, she hooked her thumbs into her pocket and shouted, "Hey, Correlli! Get your *sorry ass* out here!"

There was a good minute of silence before a startled voice called out, "Cahill?"

"Who else do you think it is? The cops? And thanks for the warm welcome, by the way," Genie called out sarcastically. All she could hope was that none of his current thugs had ever seen her as a cop.

After another second, the door opened and Marco Correlli exited the room surrounded by his men, Jonas at the back. She stepped forward, meeting the short man with a welcoming grin and open arms. "What the hell are you doing in DC? It's a little hot for you around these parts, isn't it?"

The blond man grinned back and hugged her. "You know me. I never could resist the kitchen."

"That's why you keep getting burned, Marco," she chided gently. She looked at Lipsham deliberately and asked, "Who's the rube?"

"Frickin' reporter. Can you believe it? I escape the Feds, the local cops, and some news-jockey catches me," he groused.

Genie snorted. "Losin' your touch, Marco."

"I must be. So what brings you here?"

His tone was casual, but Genie knew the automatic suspicion that lay behind the question. It had sure as hell graced her life often enough. Shrugging, Genie answered, "I was casing the place for a friend when I saw you and your boys come in."

"Last I heard, you were still enforcing for the Amazon," Marco commented, dark eyes looking at her shrewdly.

Genie laughed, a hard sound with nothing of humor in it. "You're a little behind the times then. I go on vacation and come back to find out Erin's been sold down-river. Do you know how hard it is to get another job when your reference is all locked up?"

Marco chuckled. "I hear ya. So, what, you still looking for work after all this time? What've you been up to?"

"Taking it easy, for the most part. Had plenty stashed in the bank to stay on a quasi-permanent vacation, you know? Why? You lookin' to hire?"

He glared at Lipsham. "If my guys can't even keep damned

reporters off my trail, then, yeah, I'm lookin' to hire."

She grinned. "How about I get rid of him for you? If I know you, you're on some kind of schedule, right?"

Surprised, Marco inquired, "You'd do that?'

"Sure," she answered easily.

"And what do you want?" he asked, a half-grin edging out.

"What? You think I'd do this for something in return?" Genie demanded, mock-offended. The grin that surfaced as he continued staring at her was brittle and she conceded, "All right. You got me. I heard Benny's looking for a new East Coaster and my bank account isn't going to last forever. Think you can get me an interview?"

He stared at her for a long moment before the half-grin overtook his whole face. "Yeah. Yeah, I can do that. Thanks, Cahill."

Genie took out her gun and pointed it at Lipsham, ordering, "Over here, pretty boy."

One of the men shoved him when Jonas didn't move fast enough and Genie caught him by the elbow. "So how you want it done? Accidental or what?"

"Doesn't matter to me. Have some fun."

Genie leered at Jonas long enough for the reporter to grow visibly uncomfortable, then she laughed. "Don't sweat it, pretty boy, you're not my type."

Joining in with his own chuckle, Marco agreed, "You've got too much equipment between the legs to interest Cahill here, but that doesn't mean you can't satisfy her other appetites."

Just then the sound of sirens became audible and everyone started swearing. Genie met Marco's eyes and ordered, "Get out of here. I'll ditch pretty boy somewhere the cops won't find him."

He stared at her, suspicion once more in his eyes, but the Mafioso ordered his men to move and followed them out.

As soon as they were all gone, Genie turned to Jonas, eyes hard and angry as she put her gun away. She held up a finger and snapped, "Don't say *one word*. I don't want to hear it. Not even when we get out of here."

Becca chose that moment to rejoin them. "I guess we should just stay here so your cover doesn't get blown. Speaking of which, what is your cover and why haven't I heard of it before now?"

Genie sat on the cleanest piece of floor she could find, her mind running back to that dark time. Drugs, men and women bought and paid for, for any desire she'd had, beating and maiming in the name of duty... How she had managed to avoid killing anyone back then was still a mystery, and a miracle, to her. "I worked undercover for about a year as an enforcer to Erin Malkonen."

Becca whistled in appreciation, recognizing the name of one of the biggest underworld bosses in North America.

Genie scrubbed tired fingers through her hair, thinking about

Erin Malkonen, one of the few women to take on the Mafioso clans and not only hold her own, but cut out a nice little niche for herself. Malkonen had employed mostly women for everything she did; the woman's own, twisted version of feminism, though Genie was sure that the old-time movement would've been horrified to know that.

There'd been no details allowed to get out on how the woman had been brought down. All information had been kept very strictly guarded with closed Grand Jury sessions, no media in the court for the trial, and sealed transcripts to protect more than one undercover operative; Genie included. There had been unwitting duplication by both the Feds and local police, which had only come out after the arrest. Of course, it had made the prosecution ecstatic since that meant they had double the proof; not just on Malkonen, but her elite, too.

Looking at her tight-lipped expression, Becca murmured, "That must've sucked."

Genie snorted at the understatement. "One of the worst years of my life. But we put her away and shut down her business, so it works out, I guess. Though I, I kind of lost myself there for a while. I took a few months off after, both to disappear and get myself back together. I knew after that assignment that I was done with undercover work. I wanted something more straightforward. I just wanted to deal with honest criminals, as strange as that may sound."

Becca sat beside her and squeezed her thigh. "That's understandable. You okay now?"

Genie grimaced and answered, "I will be. Correlli just brought back some unpleasant memories is all."

"Speaking of which," Becca muttered. She looked over at Jonas, who leaned against the opposite wall, watching them warily. "What the *hell* did you think you were doing? You could have gotten all of us killed!"

"I wasn't," Jonas answered heavily, guilt plain on his face. "I'm sorry, but when I caught sight of Correlli, I just...it's instinct. I knew he was here for no good reason and I had to follow him."

"How is it that you're not dead by now, as clumsy as you were?" Genie demanded sourly.

Indignant, Jonas exclaimed, "I'm not clumsy! I just had a bad day."

"Yeah. A bad day that almost got you killed," Genie retorted. "A bad day that nearly sucked me back into a life that almost destroyed me. I don't want to be around you when you have a *really* bad day."

"Look, I'm sorry, all right? It won't happen again."

Becca snapped, "You're damned right it won't, because you won't be around to do it again!"

Shocked, Jonas exclaimed, "You can't do that!"

"Yes, I can. You put my partner at risk with your actions and that is something I won't allow," Becca informed him simply. "You've been with us long enough to have plenty of material to work with."

"I was told that I would have three months to observe you," Jonas stated angrily.

Just as angry, Becca countered, "And you would have, had you done as you were told in the beginning."

Jonas looked for help from Genie, but she only grinned and told him, "Don't look at me. She's the boss."

Pursing his lips, Jonas stared at them thoughtfully, then said, "All right. Look, I won't go to your captain and protest, which would, by the way, get me reassigned to you in no time. But. In exchange for going quietly, I want a real interview with you. As a telepath, not just a cop."

Becca shook her head. "I can't."

"If you want me to go away, you will. Look, it'll be an honest piece, I swear. I'm not going to paint you as anything except what you are."

Becca pinned him with a glare. "Which is?"

"A hardworking woman who probably cares too much about the world she lives in, and is part of the team struggling to keep us all from self-destruction," Jonas answered sincerely.

Becca slowly shook her head. "I can't, Jonas, I'm sorry. We're not allowed to give interviews."

"What do you mean, 'not allowed'?"

"Just what I said. Telepaths aren't allowed to give interviews. Do you really think that there would be such a media-blackout otherwise?"

"But *who* doesn't allow it?" he asked, obviously frustrated. "Why are telepaths surrounded by such a, a mystique? *What* are you hiding?"

Sadly, Becca answered, "Just ourselves, Jonas. Just ourselves."

BECKY YAWNED AS Genie pulled the Jeep in front of the apartment building. Her entire body dragged with exhaustion. Even looking at her partner took more energy than she rightly had; getting up to her apartment was going to suck.

"You're awfully quiet," Genie commented.

They'd had to go back to headquarters after Correlli and his bunch had been rounded up, and spent the last three hours there dealing with paperwork and the Feds. It was almost eleven at night and they were both wiped.

Becky looked at her partner tiredly. "I think things are just getting to me a bit more than usual."

"Want some company?"

"Nah. That's all right. Think Jonas will take no for an answer?" Becky asked, hand on the door.

Snorting, Genie replied, "If you were very, very good in a past life."

Becky grinned reluctantly and moaned, "We're doomed. I'll see you tomorrow. Take care."

Genie nodded and waited until Becky opened the front door, stepped inside, and turned back to wave before driving away.

Sighing, Becky went to the elevator and pushed the button, waiting for it to arrive. She was more tired than the day deserved, really, and wasn't sure where the lethargy was coming from. Yawning, she frowned as she realized that it had been a good amount of time and the elevator still hadn't arrived. Pressing the lit button again gave her a near-electric shock and Becky snatched her hand back, surprised.

That was when she noticed the strange, greenish tint to her surroundings and a shiver ran up and down her spine. Was she really here in her apartment building, was she foreseeing something, or had she caught a backlash somehow? She heard the sound of a rattle down the hall and automatically turned towards it. It wasn't a baby's rattle, it was a snake rattle, something she hadn't heard since her last vision quest.

Following the sound, Becky moved down the hall as the lights dimmed, the green edge growing stronger. The emergency exit door swung open for her and she stepped through. Instead of exiting out the back of her building, though, she stepped into a desert landscape. She knew instantly where she was and a sizzle of energy ran through her, all lethargy vanishing. Striding across the hot sands, Becky headed towards the cave where she'd spent her vision quests.

It seemed to take forever to get there, though of course time had no real meaning in a vision. She at last reached the rock outcropping and began to climb, unsurprised to find herself barefoot and clad only in a thin T-shirt and shorts. Her feet and hands grew bloody in the climb but she doggedly kept going, striving to reach the cavern that awaited her.

After climbing for an eternity, Becky reached the cool ledge leading into the cave. A sweet smoke came from inside and she stood, taking a moment to look out across the desert, reveling in the roiling, blanketing heat that surrounded her. The short trip to the Center hadn't quenched her need to be warm; it had merely banked the fires temporarily.

Once inside, she could see with greater clarity than the dark interior would allow in the real world. There was a tiny fire towards the back and on the far side of it, Becky saw the old man. He'd appeared twice before in her life, both at times of major change; one of good, one of bad. Straightening her shoulders, Becky moved forward and sank down by the fire, cross-legged.

The old man's white hair and pale skin glowed in the firelight, his blind, blue eyes somehow missing nothing as he took in her appearance. "It has been long since you've visited, Strength."

Becky nodded agreement. "It has."

"You started down a difficult path when you were younger, but now you hesitate. Why?"

Staring into the fire for a few minutes, Becky whispered, "I'm scared."

"Of?"

Meeting the pale eyes of her grandfather, ignoring their milky film, Becky answered, "Making the wrong decision. Hurting those I'm supposed to protect. Failing my people."

"All true answers, but not the important one," he chided.

Her eyes lowered, but she knew the answer. So did her grandfather, and he waited patiently for her to verbalize it. Ashamed, she admitted, "I'm scared of being hurt."

"Look at me, Strength."

Reluctantly, she did so, surprised by his gentle smile.

"All people fear being hurt, my granddaughter, there is no shame in it. The shame would only come if you allow that fear to keep you from your destiny."

"What is my destiny?"

The smile grew at her near-desperate question and a familiar mischievous look crossed his face. "What you make of it, of course. But know that you are fortunate."

Exasperation filled her at the customary evasion and she demanded, "Why?"

"You do not travel alone on your path. Too many do not have such a luxury. Nourish and protect the bond that even now nourishes and protects you."

"Grandfather, I don't understand," Becky exclaimed. Her head began to pound in a familiar way and her surroundings trembled as though in a silent earthquake. Even as she reached out for him, he signed a blessing over her and everything faded.

"Becca? C'mon partner, don't do this to me, come on back, Becca, please?"

Frowning as Genie's near-frantic voice penetrated the fuzzy darkness, Becky opened her eyes. Worried amber eyes looked down at her and Becky discovered that she was lying on a cold floor, her head in her partner's lap. "Genie?"

"Oh, thank *God*!" Genie breathed, her fingers brushing aside the dark bangs on Becky's forehead. "You were seriously starting to worry me, Becca!"

Frowning, Becky tried to push herself up, but was overwhelmed with dizziness and had to fall back.

"Hey, take it easy," Genie ordered, relief edged out by concern. "You've been out for almost an hour."

Startled, Becky looked around again and saw Jonas crouched nearby, staring at them with a mixture of concern and fascination. What the hell? "We're still here? In the warehouse?"

Genie nodded. "Mathisen came down and gave the all clear, but you passed out. I almost didn't catch you in time. You've been out ever since. He wanted to get you to a hospital, but I told him it was PA stuff. It was PA stuff, right? I didn't like, almost kill you here by accident, did I?"

Smiling, Becky reaching up to grasp Genie's arm and reassure her. "It was PA stuff."

"What happened?" Jonas asked, moving closer.

Becky stared at him for a long moment before answering, "You still want an interview?"

Stunned, Jonas nodded. "Hell, yeah! Why? What happened?"

Offering up a wry grin, Becky replied, "You could say that I had a sudden meeting with an elder of my tribe who gave the okay. It's probably going to wreak havoc but hell, when has that ever stopped me?"

Genie smiled down at her and answered, "Never, that I've noticed."

"That was supposed to be a rhetorical question, Genie."

Excerpt from Rebecca Curtains' Journal—Year One

The shit is about to hit the fan. My goose is gonna be cooked. Boy, oh boy, am I in trouble.

I gave Jonas the in-depth interview to end all in-depth interviews. He's going to dribble it out into a bunch of different articles and his editor is thrilled to death. Well, of course he would be, since no telepath has ever given an interview since the days of psychic hotlines and sensationalism. Jonas has promised it'll be a tasteful and serious thing and unfortunately, I have to trust him to curb his editor on that.

It was nice of Genie to do it with me, though. Totally surprised me, given that she has the naturally reclusive instincts of a turtle being poked with a stick. It probably helped that our names will be changed. Of course, if someone really wants to find out who we are, it won't be horrendously difficult since we give them a location to work from.

Am I trying to be exposed? Do I subconsciously want the world to know who I am, or just my enemies? Is this the modern-day equivalent of throwing down the gauntlet? Probably. I've never been one to shy away from things and this hide-and-seek method of living pisses me off. Genie said that I don't get angry often enough, but she doesn't understand that I can't control myself very well if I let my emotions get away from me. An uncontrolled telepath is a menace to everyone, how often have I said that? It's something that I firmly believe.

Just, sometimes... I really wish I could lose control. Have someone there to pick up the pieces if I did. Not likely to happen, though, so best not to think about it.

Chapter
Fifteen

AllNetNews.com
May 12, 2107

Telepaths. The word summons many of the darker human emotions: fear, hatred, jealousy, distrust. They are surrounded with mystery and live reclusive lives that rarely intersect with most people not of the same genetic makeup. Consistently, Telepaths have refused to give interviews or any kind of statements to the media, no matter what was going on in the world around them. They have lived lives separate and apart, surrounded by the silence of their own fear.

For the first time, that silence is being broken.

Working among the men and women of Washington, DC's police force, these two women do their jobs with dedication and bravery, the same as their fellow police officers. What is different about them is the telepathic talent of one of the women. This talent has helped to save many lives, but despite that, the detective has been attacked and harassed simply for using her gifts to help others.

Observing these police officers was a chance in a lifetime. By the end of this series, we hope that you come away with a feeling of respect and admiration for their steadfast refusal to buckle under pressure, public or private.

(Interview with Jonas Lipsham. Interviewee*names have been changed to protect those involved)

JL: How long have you lived among telepaths?

*Karen: Most of my life. My family was killed when I was just a child.

JL: Can you tell us what a day in the life of a telepath is like?

Karen: There's not really one set "day in the life." We all live our lives according to our individual talents and jobs.

JL: All right. How about a day in your life? How does being a telepath help or hinder you?

Karen: It helps a lot with being a police officer. I can get a trace of the criminals at the scene, develop a composite, both physical and psychological, of the perpetrator.

JL: That sounds handy. But it's not always a good thing, right?

Karen: That's right. A couple of months ago I was attacked on the job because I was a telepath. I was in the hospital for a few days recovering.

JL: Going from specific to general, why did you agree to this interview and why haven't telepaths in the past given interviews?

Karen: For myself, there are a couple of reasons. I've never really thought the policy of a media-blackout was a very smart thing to do. People need more information, not less, if they're going to be educated about us. As for the past, well, we've been worried about what would happen if our faces were plastered all over the news.

JL: One of the reasons you wouldn't agree to pictures for this interview?

Karen: Not really. I think we should be out there and visible. That's one of the reasons why I'm a detective in the first place. But if I want to be able to work efficiently as a detective, I really can't be a public figure.

JL: Would you tell us about what sort of laws telepaths abide by? Aside from the everyday, governmental ones, that is.

Karen: We do have our own laws, that's true. The strongest one is to never use our powers against anyone. Like mentally scanning someone who hasn't agreed to it. We view that as the worst kind of violation.

JL: What happens to those who break that law?

Karen: There's a meeting among the people where punishment is decided, depending on the severity of the violation.

JL: Worst-case scenario?

Karen: (hesitates) Worst-case scenario is the same as any other psychopath or sociopath. We have our share of bad seeds, same as any other people. In that case, we purposely overload the telepathic centers of the brain so that he or she can't hurt anyone that way again, then hand them over to the courts for judicial punishment.

JL: Sounds harsh.

Karen: We won't allow individuals to use their talents to harm anyone, if it can be at all prevented.

JL: Tell me about some of the good that you've done using your powers. If you don't feel that would be betraying a confidence.

Karen: First of all, don't forget that these are natural abilities, not supernatural powers. That's why we generally call them talents, to avoid such a connotation.

JL: Right, sorry.

*Paula: She's done a lot of good with her abilities. Stopped murderers and serial killers and rapists.

JL: You and Karen haven't been partners for very long. How do you feel about working with a telepath?

Paula: I've never really had a problem with telepaths. The few that I knew growing up were always very careful not to use their psychic abilities in obvious ways, almost like they didn't want to scare us by using them. Actually, I get more pissed off than Karen does when someone insults her.

Karen: (laughs) And she's just normally so cool about everything else, too.

Paula: Hey! I am!

JL: Would say that your partnership is enhanced by Karen being a telepath?

Paula: (shrugs) Dunno. It's just part of who she is and if I'm going to accept her as a partner, I have to accept them as well. Besides, she saved my life by using them, so I can't really complain now, can I?

JL: How did that happen?

Paula: I had gotten a tip on a suspect and was checking it out...

Karen: Without backup!

Paula: Yes. Without backup. Which I will never live down. Anyhow, Karen had a premonition about me dying at the scene and was able to relay it to me in time to stop it from happening.

JL: Can you give us some more instances where being a telepath has turned the tide?

Karen: Unfortunately not without going into detail about our cases, which we don't want to do.

JL: I understand. Tell me, what do you think about Mr. Doyle's allegations regarding telepaths and their agenda?

Paula: He's an idiot and his allegations are libelous in my opinion. If he were raving like this about any other minority, he'd've been slapped with a lawsuit years ago. But because telepaths won't stoop to his level, or even defend themselves, it's allowed to go unchecked.

Karen: I think that Mr. Doyle hasn't had any personal experience with telepaths and is afraid of us. I don't know why that's the case, but I'm sure that if he takes the time to get to know us, he'll find that we don't have any agenda except to live our lives, the same as anyone else.

JL: If you had one thing to impart to the public at large, what would it be?

Karen: That we're just like everyone else and really want to be treated as real people. We're not evil and we don't go around peeking into people's minds just for the hell of it. A lot of us don't even have that talent, as a matter of fact.

JL: But you do, personally speaking.

Karen:(shrugs) Yes, I do. And I only use it on the job or with someone's express permission.

JL: What about you, Paula? What would you say to people about working with a telepath?

Paula: That she's just as human as the rest of us and more so than a lot of people I know. She knows what it's like to be instantly judged for being something she can't help.

JL: Thank you both for your time and I look forward to our next interview.

(Please send all questions regarding this article to JLipsham@allnewsnet.com)

Chapter
Sixteen

THE BULLPEN WAS quiet for a change, most of the other detectives at lunch. Becky glared at her frozen computer, but it remained unmoved no matter how many buttons she stabbed with a pen. Giving up, she tossed aside the pen and complained, "I need a vacation."

Genie didn't look up from the file she was going over. "You just had a vacation."

"That wasn't a real vacation," Becky complained, twisting her neck until it cracked loudly.

Genie looked up with a shudder. "Eew! Do you have to do that?"

Grinning, Becky quipped, "I am my own chiropractor."

Genie snorted. "Just don't break your neck doing it. And why do you need a vacation? Lipsham is gone and we're back to normal. Relatively speaking."

Leaning on her desk, Becky said, "I've been getting phone calls from *lots* of people."

"Ah. The interviews."

"Yeah. The interviews."

Giving her a sympathetic look at the sour confirmation, Genie asked, "What happened?"

"What hasn't? I think I've heard more from the others in the last forty-eight hours than I have in the last four years, recent visit to the Center notwithstanding," Becky answered dryly. "So far, I count the votes at about fifty-fifty."

"As in, half are looking to rip you a new one, and the other half are looking to canonize you," Genie guessed.

"You got it."

"You going to set up another committee?"

Becky crumpled up a piece of paper and threw it unerringly at her forehead in response to the facetious question.

"Hey, Marshall, Curtains. You guys got the MacKenzie case, right?" Detective Mathisen asked, walking up to them.

Becky looked up at the older black man with a smile. "Yep. Lucky us. Why?"

Dark eyes sparkling with amusement, he answered, "Because I

think your favorite person is here to see you."

"Oh crap," Genie muttered, looking over at the entrance to their work area to find Shelby MacKenzie standing there looking around.

"Be nice," Becky warned.

Indignant, Genie exclaimed, "Me? She's the one who starts that shit!"

Becky wagged a warning finger at her partner. Since day one of this case, Genie and Shelby MacKenzie, the niece of the victim, had been like oil and water. Although Becky could understand the irritation—MacKenzie was a first-class snob and rather obnoxious to boot—it didn't excuse her partner's behavior. Becky stood and repeated firmly, "Be nice! Ms. MacKenzie? We're over here."

The young woman heard her and started towards them. Stopping at their desks, she looked briefly at Genie, then dismissed her to smile at Becky. "Detective, it's so good to see you again."

Becky gritted her teeth and wondered how on earth she was going to stop her partner from killing the woman. Forcing a smile and pleasant tone of voice, Becky asked, "How can we help you, Ms. MacKenzie?"

"I have my uncle's address book for you, and thought I would check to see if you'd made any progress while I was dropping it off," the young woman replied with a warm smile.

"Not yet. But, as I said yesterday, as soon as we get a lead, you'll be notified," Becky assured her. She took the small notebook computer. "Are there any passwords that we should know about?"

"Not that I'm aware of."

Becky nodded and set the notebook on her desk, noticing with an inward wince that the young woman hadn't moved. "Was there anything else?"

Shelby hesitated, blushing a little as she asked, "I was wondering if perhaps you were available for dinner Friday night?"

Genie coughed, violently, and reached for the bottled water on her desk. Both Shelby and Becky glared at her and Genie stood, muttering, " 'Scuse me."

I'm going to kill her, Becky thought as she watched her partner escape. Forcing aside the aggravation, she produced a polite smile. "I'm really very flattered, Ms. MacKenzie, but I'm afraid it would be a conflict of interest if I were to accept your dinner invitation."

Disappointed, the other woman managed a smile. "I understand. Perhaps when the case is over, you might give me a call?"

Becky smiled politely and echoed, "Perhaps. You have a good afternoon, all right? And if you think of anything related to the case, don't hesitate to call."

"Of course."

Becky watched the young socialite leave, then sank into her chair with a relieved sigh. She hadn't been sure the woman would take no for an answer. Genie came back and Becky ordered, "Not one word, Marshall, or you're dead meat."

Genie replied in an innocent tone, "Wouldn't think of it. Detective."

"Keep it up, Marshall, you're cruising for it," Becky warned, pinning her partner with a threatening look. She picked up the electronic notebook and turned it on. Flipping through the address program, she went through the various lists and groupings. First the business contacts, then the family, and last the friends.

Like his niece had said the day before, the victim had a lot of friends and business acquaintances, though not much family. All the people they'd talked to since the case had opened three days ago had been forthcoming, none of them with anything to hide. Well, not that she'd been able to tell, and she'd been more than open to feeling any kind of hostility or negative emotion that could be had.

"So what do you think?" Becky asked finally, setting the notebook down.

"She's not your type?"

"Oh, very funny."

Genie straightened a little, grinning unrepentantly. "Sorry. I think that maybe we have what it looks like. A random act of violence with a man in the wrong place at the wrong time. I mean, you didn't sense anything from the people we interviewed, right? And nothing psychic at the..."

Their eyes met as her voice trailed off, suddenly on the same wavelength, and they finished together, "...scene of the crime."

"God *damn* it!" Becky swore, running her hands through her hair furiously. What if she'd been wrong? What if the man they had wanted to lock up for killing the tourists wasn't guilty? It wasn't like he had agreed to a scan for them to be sure. And there hadn't been a lot of physical evidence. Okay, there'd been nothing linking Belladonna to the actual murders.

Leaning forward on her desk, Becky demanded, "Is it possible that we, that *I* was wrong about Belladonna being the killer? I mean, he was in lockup when this went down."

Leaning back in her chair, Genie shook her head. "No chance. Come on, Becca, don't go doubting yourself now!"

Becky sighed, self-doubt flooding through her, despite her partner's assurances. "I don't doubt that he was going to kill you. But did he kill the others? Shit, Genie, what if he's not the guy?"

"He fits your profile," Genie pointed out.

"What little bit of one that I have."

Genie leaned forward, frowning her response to the scathing statement. "Hey. Take it easy."

Tapping the desk with her fingers, Becky shook her head. "I can't. This bothers me. A lot."

"Really? Hadn't noticed."

The comment provoked a short, choked off laugh from Becky. "Some detective."

Genie ignored the teasing and said, "So we've got a robbery that ends up in a strangulation, with no physical evidence except forensics saying that it was gage wire."

"Yeah, but what mugger carries gage wire on them?"

"Okay. So we've got a murderer trying to make it look like a robbery gone bad," Genie said with a shrug. "That's what I was figuring on anyhow."

"Yeah, but why? He's got a good business going, but he's not wealthy. He has no jealous exes that we can find, no current girlfriend or mistress stashed away somewhere. No destitute relatives expecting to inherit if he dies. Matter of fact, he's one of the poorer ones in the family," Becky recounted.

"What about political or religious affiliations?" Genie questioned. "Anything in that thing about those?"

Becky picked up the notebook again and looked through it. "First Presbyterian Church on Swanson is noted, but no political groups."

"Great. So we've got an all-around nice guy who's active in his church and has no enemies," Genie observed, tugging on her braid.

"What do you think he was doing down that part of town, anyhow?" Becky wondered. "It isn't the red zone or anything, but I wouldn't think that someone as affluent as him would be in that area after dark."

Genie rubbed her eyes. "You got me. Want to take another look around? See if we missed anything?"

Shrugging, Becky agreed, "Why not?"

"Detective Marshall?"

Both women looked up at the hesitant greeting to find Jennifer O'Neill nearby. Becky shivered at the coincidence of the older woman showing up just as Becky was re-questioning the whole case. It was almost a sign that something deeper was going on, that fate wanted her to take another look.

Genie stood, smiling. "Mrs. O'Neill! How are you? Come, have a seat."

The older woman smiled in return, accepting the seat beside Genie's desk. "I'm fine, dear, thank you. I was in the neighborhood and thought I would drop in and say hello."

Standing to give them some privacy, Becky said, "I have an errand to run, but it was lovely seeing you again, Mrs. O'Neill."

When she accidentally brushed the older woman's shoulder on her way by, a different shiver ran through her, an echo of psychic power running through the contact. Startled, Becky paused to find that Mrs. O'Neill's hazel eyes had widened in surprise as well.

Nonplussed, Becky hesitated, then continued on her way, feeling the eyes on her back until the stairwell door closed behind her.

It had been latent and faint, but Mrs. O'Neill definitely had telepathic powers. What sort and how strong could only be determined by testing, which she was pretty sure the older woman would not agree to. And since she'd lived her whole life without the talent being a problem, Becky didn't see the need to bring it up.

She did, however, wonder if Mrs. O'Neill had ever mentioned her abilities to anyone. Was this a new facet to the case? Had all the victims been latent telepaths? Was that the real reason they'd been killed? It would make a hell of a lot more sense, given what little she knew about the killer's real motive, or suspected anyhow. But if Mrs. O'Neill hadn't mentioned the telepathy to anyone, since she most likely had never realized it herself, then how had the killer known?

Oh Christ. Was the killer a telepath?

Feeling nauseous as something clicked into place, Becky could suddenly see the killer in her mind's eye. Arrogant, manipulative, certain that he was God's equal because of his powers. Almost certainly a genius, on top of being telepathic, and born to wealth and privilege to finish off the egocentric personality. He would think that his talents gave him the right to decide who lived and died. Probably someone in an official position of life and death decisions, the armed forces, or the medical profession, maybe; something that required precision.

So where did Belladonna and Aldonis come into play? *Disciples, most likely,* she decided. *They're willing to sacrifice themselves for a greater cause. The greater cause of serving the killer directly, touching divinity through contact with him, not killing off telepaths. But then, why only latent telepaths? And why pick these specific victims? Disrupting the tourist trade is a sure way to get noticed.*

He was pitting himself against the police to show his superiority — *No... Oh no.* It wasn't the police he was playing with.

Spinning in place, Becky left the stairwell and hurried back to the bullpen, thankful that Mrs. O'Neill was gone. "C'mon. I'm hungry."

Clearly startled by the abrupt order, Genie followed her out of the precinct to the garage. Becky moved to Genie's Jeep and waited impatiently for the door to be unlocked. Buckling up, Becky waited for Genie to start the engine and turned on the radio loud before hauling her partner close. Murmuring into Genie's ear, she said, "Jammer."

Genie nodded and pulled it out of her coat, flipping it on and turning off the radio. She pulled out of the parking spot and asked, "What's going on?"

"Belladonna's not the real killer."

Genie demanded, "Excuse me?"

"He's a disciple, he thinks that he's working for someone with divine powers," Becky explained. She went into her accidental discovery of Mrs. O'Neill's latency and continued with her theory about the real killer. Taking a shaky breath, Becky finished with, "He's doing this because of *me*, Genie."

Jaw clenching, Genie asked tightly, "Why do you think that?"

"He wants to prove that he's the best. I think he found out my position and has decided for himself that I don't deserve it. He's used to being the best. I'm an affront to him, probably on both a personal and a professional level."

"So what now?"

"I think that I should pay a visit to Belladonna," Becky said after a moment. "I think he's the weak link."

"What? He hasn't said a word without his lawyer present, and even then it's like pulling teeth," Genie reminded. "Aldonis is a lot more excitable."

"Aldonis is a lot more passionate about his cause and a lot more careful about protecting it. Despite being a smartassed punk. Belladonna is over-confident. He keeps his mouth shut because if he opens it, the wrong thing is going to come flying out of it and he knows it."

Genie scowled and said, "If you question him, it'll tip our hand. Any other leads we can follow up first?"

Becky bit her lip and hesitated before saying, "Well, I have been doing that research into who's paying his lawyer's fees."

"And?"

"So far, there have been four different dummy corporations."

"Lovely."

"Yeah. I mean, I'm going to keep digging, but it'll take time and I don't think that we have enough time to spend on it."

"You think the real killer's going to do it again."

"He has to. If he's going to prove himself superior to me, he's got to keep going until I look so grossly incompetent that I lose my job. He'll keep going until I lose everything," Becky finished softly.

"You'll never lose everything."

Becky glanced at her friend and smiled, a warmth rising inside at Genie's statement. Thoughts and possibilities started running through her mind before she could put them down. For a few minutes, the noise around them fell away, just like in a corny, romantic movie, as Becky stared into warm amber eyes. Reaching over, Becky rubbed Genie's shoulder. "Thanks."

Genie returned the smile with a fairly goofy one of her own, but only for a moment. Looking suddenly uncomfortable, she changed the subject. "So. What do you want for lunch? Since we're out and about anyhow."

Chapter
Seventeen

GENIE LEANED BACK against the interrogation room wall, arms crossed over her chest as they waited for Belladonna's appearance. Mr. Harrison, the lawyer, was already present and sitting at the metal table in the center of the room. Becca was also sitting at the table, looking soft and demure with her suit jacket off, her blouse outlining enticing curves.

Genie had understood her partner's unspoken cue to look menacing. She'd put on the black leather jacket she always kept in the Jeep and pulled her hair back severely to help paint the picture. Genie looked forward to the Q & A, curious as to how Becca would handle the interrogation. After a few more minutes, Joshua Belladonna shuffled into the room, handcuffs and chains rattling noisily as the guards half-pulled, half-pushed him forward. He sat beside the lawyer and looked first at Becca, then Genie. Genie stared back without smiling until he looked away, plainly uneasy.

Oh yeah. This is gonna be fun.

"Hi there, Joshua," Becca greeted with a smile. "You remember me, right? Detective Curtains?"

The young man nodded silently.

"Good. There were a few things that I wanted to go over with you, just to clarify your statement," Becca said.

The lawyer nodded. "So long as you don't pull any illegal scans, I think we'll be just fine."

Though no one else would be able to tell, Genie saw the flash of tension in her partner's shoulders.

Becca only smiled in response to the insult. Genie wondered that neither man saw the menace in that smile.

"Of course not." She turned toward the lawyer's client. "How long have you been a member of UnderTEM?"

The question plainly startled both Joshua and his lawyer. The young man frowned then answered, "A couple years."

"So you're not real fond of telepaths, I would assume."

A faint sneer twisted Joshua's lips. "You'd assume correct."

"Why not?"

"'Cause you can't be trusted."

"Then what's to say I'm not reading your mind right now?"

"Nothing, I guess. But you can't use it in court," Joshua said confidently.

Becca smiled. "Who said I wanted to use the information in court?"

Joshua demanded, "What're you talking about?"

Shrugging delicately, Becca answered, "Nothing, really. I'm just curious. Was there a particular event that set off your mistrust of telepaths, or did your parents hold this belief?"

"What's that got to do with anything?"

"Nothing. Like I said, I'm just curious. Do you hold any positions in UnderTEM or are you just a member?"

Harrison demanded, "Detective, what's this got to do with my client's case?"

"Just be patient, Mr. Harrison, I'm getting there," Becca said pleasantly. Turning back to Belladonna, she repeated, "Any official position?"

Frowning, Joshua answered, "No. I just hang out there sometimes. Do some errands if they need help."

"Sounds dull."

Cautious, he agreed, "It can be"

"Ever meet anyone there? Make some friends?"

"A few."

"Like who?"

"None of your damned business!"

Arching an eyebrow, Becca said, "I see."

She opened the file on the table and looked through it for a few moments before asking, "How about a Mr. Aldonis? Do you know him well?"

Staring at her suspiciously, Joshua replied, "Don't know anyone by that name."

"Really? Hm." She flipped through the file for a few minutes as though looking intently for something. "Says here that you two know each other."

Joshua shook his head. "Never heard of him."

"Never spent time together?"

"Nope."

"Didn't ever see him hanging out at the local UnderTEM hall?"

"Nope."

Becca looked up from the file and asked pointedly, "Didn't serve time together at the Mendez Juvenile Facility?"

Joshua hesitated, then said, "Lots of guys spent time there. I sure as hell didn't know them all."

Becca shrugged. "No. No, I'm sure you didn't. But considering that you were both in the same dormitory for about two months, it's pretty likely that you at least know him on sight. Isn't that right, Mr. Belladonna?"

"I told you. I don't know him!" the young man insisted.

"I see." Becca looked back at Genie and asked, "Would you mind getting something for Mr. Belladonna and his attorney to drink? What would you like, gentlemen? Soda? Coffee?"

Warily, Joshua accepted, "Soda's good."

"Mr. Harrison?"

"Coffee is fine."

Genie nodded and directed a smirk at her partner. "Play nice, Detective. I want them both in one piece when I get back."

Becca replied, "Of course, Detective."

Genie closed the door behind her and looked at her watch, thinking, *Ten minutes should about do it.*

THE DOOR CLOSED behind Genie with a loud clang of metal and Becky turned back to her prey, the harsh look on her face eradicating any hint of pleasantness. "Now that the guard dog is gone, why don't we get to business?"

Joshua looked at his lawyer for help, but Harrison was equally as disconcerted by her transformation.

"I want to know why you're lying, Joshua."

"I'm not..."

"I want to know who you and Aldonis work for."

"No one!"

"So you do know Aldonis."

"No! I never said..."

"I know you didn't kill those people on your own, because you're not smart enough. I also know that the hanging around UnderTEM is complete bullshit. You're a groupie. You live to be around telepaths because you want to be one. You think he's going to give you his powers, Joshua? You think that he's going to give some stupid little wannabe groupie a shred of his divinity? Think again."

Adamant, Joshua said, "I don't know what you're talking about."

Standing up abruptly, her chair skittering back a few feet, Becky leaned over him, ignoring the lawyer's loud protest. She spoke hard and quiet as she ripped into the breaking point. "He's laughing at you. He set you up to take the fall. You can't even do *that* right, can you, Joshua? You didn't have the knife on you because you didn't do the murders. He doesn't want you to have any of his glory. He doesn't want to share squat with you. He's going to leave you hanging in the wind and you're going to rot in jail without the tiniest bit of credit."

"He is not!" Joshua shouted furiously, jumping up in his chair despite the chains. "He's going to destroy you, and I'm going to be there when it happens. He promised! You think you're so smart, but you aren't! He's got it all planned out and you're going to wish you were dead by the time the final body count comes in!"

The utter silence in the interrogation room was like a weight. Becky didn't need to do an active scan to know that Joshua realized what he'd done. Not only was it plain from the whiteness on his face and his tight expression, but his emotions screamed at her; guilt warring with pride. Keeping her voice hard, she ground out, "And just how stupid am I, Joshua? How high is the body count so far?"

Obviously deciding to go for broke, Joshua started bragging. "He's up to thirteen now and you didn't even know it. He was too subtle for you. You call yourself a telepath? You are nothing compared to him! He is on God's level and will smite you down like the unbeliever you are. Betraying your own people with those interviews was your biggest mistake, but not your last one. Your last mistake is going to cost you what you hold most dear."

"How? What is he planning?" Becky asked furiously.

An evil smile, made all the more so by youth, crossed Joshua's face. "Wouldn't you like to know?"

Genie appeared right then, just in time to stop Becky from doing something she'd regret. She took one look into her partner's eyes and knew that she was too close to the line. There was a silent warning, a mental push, from Genie, though Becky doubted the other woman knew she'd even done it. Taking a deep breath, Becky pulled back and looked at Harrison. "You can bet we'll be charging your client with a hell of a lot more after this little confession. Let's start with accessory to murder, thirteen counts. Threatening a police officer. Collusion to assault a police officer. And, of course, the other charges already against him will stand."

Resigned, Harrison nodded.

"CHRIST, CURTAINS, REMIND me not to piss you off," Carlson said, stopping the interview video.

Shrugging, a little embarrassed, Becky allowed, "I may have gotten caught up in the moment. A little."

"Uh huh. A little. Still. We can use this to try and badger him into revealing those other murders and the bastard who actually committed them."

Genie shook her head. "He won't give him up."

Becky sighed and agreed, "He's too invested in the success of his master. Right now he's satisfied with getting some of the credit while still keeping the identity secret."

"So what do you want to do now?" Carlson asked.

"Well, there's not much we can do until the next move is made. It's a sick game and he's winning. Actually, he probably counted on Belladonna cracking, because otherwise, I wouldn't have known just how high the score was, how badly we were losing," Becky sighed.

"Great," the Captain muttered. He glanced at his watch. "All right. You two cut out for the day. We aren't going to get anything else done tonight. And do me a favor. Watch your backs."

Chapter
Eighteen

GENIE'S NEIGHBORHOOD WAS always on the go. Getting a parking spot was impossible at the best of times, never mind at night once everyone was home. Biting the bullet, Becky pulled into the garage next to her partner's building. She'd have to pay, but at least she wouldn't have to walk far at the end of the night when she left. Climbing out of the car, Becky headed towards the elevator, her partner's security code repeating in her mind as numbers weren't really her thing.

It only took a few minutes to get up to the ninth floor where she turned right off the elevator. Genie's apartment was three doors down from the elevator and Becky knocked on the door. It took a few moments before a muffled and aggravated, "I'm coming!" sounded, and she grinned.

Finally, the door opened; Becky whistled at the sight of her partner all dressed up. "My goodness! You clean up but good!"

Grimacing, Genie ordered, "Get your butt in here and change!"

"Oh, sure. That's all I'm good for, a family buffer." Becky sighed dramatically.

"You betcha. Now get your cute little butt in here."

Grinning in response, Becky stepped inside and headed for the couch where she could see a garment bag hanging over the edge. She'd been here several times over the last few months and she liked the way Genie had it arranged. The living room had a couch along the right wall, a love seat facing the entertainment center and a chair angled off the love seat. The kitchen was on the left and there was a massive shelving unit against the wall, holding plants of all kinds. Becky had as yet to peek into her partner's bedroom, but she passed it on the way to the bathroom every time.

Picking up the garment bag, she looked at Genie and asked, "You sure this is going to fit?"

"Not only will it fit, you'll look great," Genie assured her. "Go get changed."

Rolling her eyes at the impatient order, Becky headed for the bathroom. She definitely had bathroom-envy. Compared to her hole-in-the-wall stall, Genie's bathroom was positively decadent. The tub was deep and sinful, there was a double sink, and it was very tastefully decorated. Becky had to bite back the question of who'd done the decorating almost every time she was in it. She grinned as the thought surfaced again.

A few minutes later, she called out for help, since the zipper was in the back and she just could *not* get it all the way up, no matter what contortions she tried.

The door opened and Genie poked her head inside. "Yeah?"

"I can't reach the zipper."

Snorting, Genie entered the large bathroom, muttering, "Munchkin-girl."

"I heard that!"

Genie laughed and pulled up the zipper.

Goose bumps erupted over Becky's skin as strong hands ghosted along her bared back, pulling the zipper into place. Becky met Genie's eyes in the mirror but couldn't think of anything to say.

Genie broke the spell by stepping back. "I told you it would fit. Now hurry and do your hair, we're late."

Still disconcerted by her body's strong reaction, Becky replied, "Ah, better late than early to these kinds of affairs."

"Not according to my family."

Becky chuckled and turned her attention to her hair as the other woman left. Fortunately, having short hair meant that all she had to do was run her hands under some water, then rub her fingers through the short strands to reactivate the gel and spike it up, and she was good to go. Joining Genie in the living room, she said, "All set!"

"I hate people with short hair."

Sticking her tongue out at her friend, Becky said, "Hey, it hurts to be beautiful, right?"

"Not in your case."

Pleased by the compliment, Becky smiled brightly. "Thanks!"

Genie smiled back and said, "Any time, partner. Now, can we leave?"

Becky shook her head in exasperation; it was worse than being with a small child sometimes! "Yes, yes, yes, already. We can leave. Jeeze!"

THE BALLROOM WAS elegantly decorated, filled with the soft scent of exotic flowers and light strains of classical music. The people talking or dancing were all exquisitely and expensively dressed, beautiful and confident in their world of wealth and privilege. The political and social elite were all present and accounted for, mingling as they had for hundreds of years.

"I can't believe I let you talk me into this," Becky muttered, shifting uncomfortably in her borrowed dress.

Hiding a grin, Genie ran her fingers over her partner's bare shoulder. "Stop fidgeting, you look incredible."

Exasperated, Becky demanded quietly, "Remind me again why we're here?"

"Because I don't have a choice and you're my best friend and partner who would do anything for me?"

Becky snorted in a distinctly unladylike fashion and complained, "Stop with the puppy-dog eyes already, I'm not going to jump ship."

Genie reached out again, this time to squeeze her partner's shoulder gratefully. "Thank you."

"Genie! Darling! I can't believe you actually made it!"

They turned towards the new voice and Becky pasted on a smile as she observed her partner in an element that she'd certainly never expected to see. Dressed in a sleek black evening gown with her hair falling in a loose cascade over her shoulders, Genie fit right in with all the other socialites. Well, if one overlooked her habit of constantly scanning the room for threats and escape routes. Grinning to herself at the observation, Becky paid attention as her name was given.

"Becca, this is my aunt, Janis Whitehall," Genie introduced. "Aunt Janis, this is my friend, Rebecca Curtains."

The older woman smiled and took her hand in a limp handshake. Becky smiled politely and said, "It's nice to meet you."

Dark eyes looked her over with mild curiosity as the hand was withdrawn. "You as well, my dear. I don't believe that Genie's mentioned you before?"

"Ah, well, we..."

"I only met Becca a few months ago," Genie said, stepping in smoothly.

"I see," Janis said with interest. "And how did you meet?"

Genie successfully diverted her aunt's attention with, "Oh, look, there's Senator Westbrook."

The older woman followed Genie's gaze. "I really must speak to him about his donation to the museum. It was nice meeting you, dear. Will we see you at other family functions?"

Other family functions?

Before Becky could reply, Genie did so for her by saying, "I'm sure you will, Auntie."

When the other woman escaped earshot, Becky looked askance at her partner and demanded, "Other family functions? Genie, just how loaded *is* your family?"

Shrugging uncomfortably, Genie answered, "Pretty loaded. My parents were the black sheep of the family because they made their own way instead of relying on the family name and money. But I spent summers at my aunt's house with my cousins. God, was that a nightmare. They were all spoiled brats, the lot of them."

Smirking, Becky observed, "And you're not?"

"Thanks, partner," Genie muttered dryly.

"You are most welcome. How about something to eat? Or don't we get fed at this gala?" Becky asked. She was curious as to why Genie had been reluctant to introduce her as her work partner, but left the question for later.

Genie put her hand to the small of Becky's back to guide her further into the ballroom. "We can sit pretty much wherever we want. Thank God there's no assigned seating this time, so how about over there?"

Becky caught sight of the corner table and shook her head in amusement. "Again with the back to the wall. One of these days, partner, you're going to tell me where and how you developed this streak of paranoia."

Half-smiling, Genie nodded and pulled out a chair, ignoring the not-so-subtle dig for information. "They usually have little quiche things and fruit and whatnot. I'll get us a couple of plates."

Becky nodded and settled at the small table. She was just as happy to be out of the way, uncomfortable in the rich settings, afraid of making some hideous *faux pas*. Watching Genie as the tall woman made her way across the room was an education. She'd always noticed her partner's grace, they worked out together often enough, but she'd never seen her in quite this fashion before.

Every few steps, it seemed that someone stopped Genie to talk. Becky could tell from the body language that pretty much all of the men wanted more than just conversation and a dance, and the same went for a few of the women. Not that it was surprising, but it brought about an uncomfortable feeling in her stomach. It wasn't any of her business who Genie spent the night with, of course, but Becky didn't think anyone in this crowd was good enough for her partner.

Genie returned in fairly short order with food and they chatted quietly for a while so Becky could eat. It seemed that her partner's appetite didn't survive all the glitz and glitter. Once she was satiated, but not too full, she announced, "I would like to dance."

"Not with me, you don't," Genie replied, grinning.

Becky chuckled. "C'mon, Genie, you brought me here. The least you can do is give me a turn around the dance floor."

Genie heaved a long-suffering sigh and stood, holding out her hand. "Would Madame care to dance?"

Winking, Becky took her hand and replied, "*Mademoiselle* would love to dance."

"Ah, ah, ah! I know for a fact that you're six months older than I am," Genie murmured in her ear, sliding her arm around Becky's waist.

They were almost to the dance floor when two men blocked the way. Becky froze as Genie's hand tightened on her waist, and decided to let her partner take the lead. This was her party, after all.

"Something we can do for you, gentlemen?" Genie asked, a thin smile on her face.

"My employer would like to speak with you, detectives."

Becky recognized a bodyguard when she saw one; an ex-spook, in this case.

Genie apparently did as well, and questioned, "And your employer would be?"

"Mr. Harold Doyle."

Eyebrow arching in surprise, Genie looked at Becky, both of them knowing what this was likely to be about.

After a tense moment, Becky nodded and they followed the two men out of the crowded ballroom and through the foyer to another, smaller room. Genie kept one hand discreetly on her partner's back as they walked. Becky easily sensed her partner's unease about being weaponless and silently echoed it. There was only one occupant in the conservatively decorated room and Becky didn't bother to hide her distaste when Harold Doyle turned to face them.

There was a patently false smile on his face as he greeted them. "Ladies. It's a pleasure to finally meet you."

"Too bad we can't say the same," Genie countered.

"You know, detective, if I'd known you were part of *the* Whitehall family, I wouldn't have missed the last police fund raiser," Doyle said with a sly smile. "Janis and I are really quite close, did you know that?"

"No, but that doesn't surprise me. She's not the brightest bulb in the family plot."

Becky warned quietly, "Genie."

Blue eyes centered on Becky as Doyle said, "And we haven't had the pleasure as yet, Detective Curtains."

Becky smiled brightly and held out her hand in challenge. "It's an honor to meet you, Mr. Doyle."

Doyle looked at her suspiciously and didn't take the delicate hand. After a moment, Becky lowered her hand, losing the smile. "Is there a reason that you wanted to talk with me?"

"I suspect that your interviews are probably causing as much trouble among your community as they are in mine. You need to stop them."

"No."

"No?"

Becky looked him straight in the eye and repeated, "No. We've been silent too long while people like you have filled the world with hatred and fear. I might not be the most popular person in the telepathic world right now, but that doesn't change the fact that I'll do what I think is right for them. Part of that includes showing the general public that we are nothing to fear. If I do nothing except show this to others by example, I'll consider my job well done."

"And just how well can you do your job if your identity is released to that same general public?"

Becky shrugged. "As well as I can. I'm sorry, Mr. Doyle, but threats don't intimidate me. As a matter of fact, they tend to make me work harder."

"You misunderstand me," Doyle said coldly. "I don't threaten."

"I haven't misunderstood anything, but I think you have. I will not back down from this, or anything else that threatens my people. The truth needs to be known, and that's what I'm doing."

Smiling unpleasantly, Doyle said, "The funny thing about the truth is that most people don't really want to hear it."

Becky smiled sadly. "You really believe that, don't you? I feel sorry for you, Mr. Doyle, living with such hatred in your heart. It must be very lonely. Genie? I need some fresh air."

Genie nodded and unobtrusively stayed behind her, blocking Becky from any possible danger that might come from behind. She doubted that Doyle would be stupid enough to try anything in such a public place, but couldn't be sure. Hatred was an irrational emotion and she'd definitely seen just that in his cold, dead eyes.

They passed by the guards, who eyed them warily, and headed outside. Genie gave her valet ticket to the attendant and they waited on the hotel steps in silence. Once inside the truck, Becky collapsed against the seat and closed her eyes, mildly nauseas from the confrontation and Doyle's ill-concealed hatred.

Genie prodded quietly, "Hey. You all right?"

Becky nodded, smiling faintly. "Yeah. Just, next time, let me pick the night out, okay?"

Genie smiled back. "You got it, partner."

Excerpt from Rebecca Curtains' Journal—Year One

Well, tonight was both good and bad in so many ways that it just boggles my mind. Seeing Genie dressed like that did nothing to reinforce my decision to keep my hands off. She was so beautiful, it was incredible. I really wanted to dance with her.

Which leads me to good and bad point number two: Doyle. He's out of the woodwork now, that's for sure, and I have a vocal, powerful enemy.

Yay me.

The good news is that I know it up front. He won't be a hidden enemy, which makes me a little less wary of him. Not much, but a little.

What is it Grandfather calls me? Strength? I can't decide if he's being a real smartass (which does seem to run in the family) or just knows something about me that I don't. Spirits are kind of funny that way. Being unattached to the world at large makes them great observers, but it also gives them a view of things that has nothing to do with our reality.

God. Look at my life. I have a partner who I could easily fall in love with, but can never have. A psycho serial killer who happens to be a rogue telepath trying to ruin my career and probably kill me in the bargain. Enemies at work and at large who would like nothing more than to see me go down in flames and, along with me, every other telepath.

Yay me.

Chapter Nineteen

DARKNESS AND EVIL. Suffocating. A well of black tar, bubbling over and miring her in place. Through the blackness was nothing: no light, no reprieve, no hope.

"Listen to my voice."

A string of lies set within a web of deceit. She tried to scream, tried to move, tried to escape. Futile. Hopeless. Nothing could break the hold; she would remain in hell forever.

"Becca!"

Pain ripped through her at the anguished cry of her name: agonizing, electric pain that slammed into her. Need to scream, need to escape!

"Becca, please, come on back! Oh God, Becca, *please*!"

Heart stopped. Breath stopped. Muscles frozen.

"*Breathe,* God damn it! Don't you *dare* die on me!"

Dragging in a long breath at the harsh command, Becky's eyes snapped open, her gaze fixing automatically on Genie's tear-stained face. Her partner's eyes searched for any sign of self or spirit. After a few more ragged breaths, Becky croaked, "What happened?"

Sagging in relief, Genie loosened her death-grip on Becky's shoulders and answered, "You caught a backlash as bad as I've ever seen, partner. You stopped breathing. I thought... I thought..."

Becky reached up and wiped away the tear-tracks on her partner's face. "I'm all right. Help me up."

"Forget it. You are staying put until the ambulance gets here," Genie ordered, keeping her hand on Becky's shoulder.

"Genie, I'm fine. There's nothing physically wrong with me."

"Then why did you stop breathing?" Genie demanded. "No. You're staying right here if I have to sit on you."

Sighing, recognizing the intensely stubborn tone that she'd become far too well acquainted with over the last several months, Becky subsided with an irritated glare. She could hear the siren of the ambulance outside and knew it wouldn't be long before they got into the apartment. It was a good thing that Genie had been over for supper when the attack had happened, because Becky knew that she wouldn't have made it back without her partner's help. She always responded to Genie's voice, had ever since the beginning of their partnership.

There was a heavy knock at the door. Genie carefully lifted Becky's head from her lap and went to open it. She hovered anxiously as the EMTs examined Becky and reluctantly took their word that her partner checked out fine.

Becky thanked them for coming and promised to get checked out by her doctor the next day. After closing the door, she turned to find Genie seated on the couch, staring at her with an odd expression. "What?"

"I bet if you hadn't mentioned the word 'backlash,' they would've sent you to the hospital to get checked over."

Blinking innocently as she approached the other woman, Becky commented, "I doubt it. There really isn't anything wrong with me."

Obviously worried, Genie observed, "Becca, it's getting worse."

Becky sighed and sat beside her partner. There was no denying it, because Genie was right. The attacks were getting worse, and she had as little clue now as when the first one had happened a few weeks ago. This time, her body's autonomic functions had been stopped, if only for a few seconds. If Genie hadn't been with her, she could have died. Rubbing her eyes tiredly, Becky said, "I know. But I still don't have any idea who's doing it. I can't seem to win against this guy!"

"You could use that guard thing that Sharon suggested."

"No!"

Trying to stay reasonable, Genie pointed out, "She wouldn't have mentioned it if she didn't think it wasn't necessary."

Irritated that her partner wasn't on the same page as her about this, Becky snapped, "I am not going to put anyone else in danger!"

"Fine! So you're just going to let this go on until the bastard finally overcomes you and kills you. Great plan, partner," Genie exclaimed sarcastically.

"This is what I do, Genie, it's who I am. You know that!" Becky countered furiously. "You knew that when we became partners!"

Frustration finally overwhelming her, Genie shouted, "I *do* know that! But you don't have to act like you're the only God-damned one who can fight the evil of the whole God-damned world! Jesus, Becca! When are you going to get it through your thick skull that people care about you? That you aren't in this thing alone? What you said to me about not going anywhere without backup sank into my skull. Why won't you take your own fucking advice?"

They stared at each other for a long time, the tension thick.

Finally Genie said, "When we first became partners, neither of us thought it would last more than a week. Or at least I didn't. But we did it. And it's been the best time in my life, despite all the shit we've gone through. Don't you get it? You're my *best friend*, Becca. I've never had one before, and I don't want to lose you. But you're working my last nerve here by hanging onto this, this pride of yours that *only you* can take care of you. You're human, Becca. When you finally realize that, give me a call."

Becky stared in shocked disbelief as Genie left the apartment, closing the door quietly behind her. Sighing, exhausted from the psychic battle and the subsequent argument with Genie, Becky headed for the bathroom, hoping that a hot shower would relax her enough to let her sleep.

GENIE HADN'T LOST her temper like that with anyone in months, not since hooking up with Becca. She'd certainly never lost it like that *with* Becca. Sighing morosely as she walked towards her truck, Genie wondered if maybe she'd be able to convince Sharon to chime in with a bit more force than she'd been using. Becca had met the older woman's suggestions for a team of psychic bodyguards with open scorn and a flat refusal.

She knew that Becca was being torn in a lot of directions, that there was a lot of pressure for her. Doyle had followed through on his threats to make things difficult. When the interviews continued to air, there had suddenly been people protesting and dogging their every step. The Captain had finally been able to make discrimination and harassment charges stick with the DA. They'd gotten a cease and desist to keep UnderTEM, and any of their members or affiliates, from being anywhere near Becky and Genie, but it had been a battle.

Genie had been trying to make things easier on her partner, but there was just too much at stake for things to keep on the way they were. Their unknown assailant had upped the ante by trying to actually kill Becky in the last two assaults. It had only been blind luck that Genie had been present both times to bring her out of the backlash.

She shuddered, remembering the way Becky's body had arced up in a spine-stiffening arch as the smaller woman's mouth opened in a silent scream. The only thing she had been able to do was hold her partner, make sure that she didn't choke on her own tongue while in the grip of the seizure, and talk to her, try to bring her around. It almost hadn't worked this time. Genie had felt Becky's chest freeze and searched frantically for a pulse, but not found one. And then, suddenly, it had come back and the blue eyes had opened.

Those few seconds of no heartbeat had been some of the scariest in her life.

Shivering again, Genie unlocked her car, got in and started it up. Her watch showed that it was almost midnight, which meant that it was only just about nine in California. Pursing her lips, she gave in to the compulsion to protect her partner, especially from her own stupidity, and pulled out her cell phone.

EVEN THOUGH SHE'D only gotten about three hours of sleep, after a lot of tossing and turning, Genie had awoken at her usual hour of six AM. It wreaked havoc on her sleeping patterns, not to mention her emotional state, when she and Becca fought. It was almost nine and still her eyes felt gritty and hot from the lack of sleep. What little sleep she'd gotten had been so chaotic and awful that she'd woken up more tired than if she'd just stayed up.

Sitting on the couch in her old robe, Genie was trying to read the paper and not having much success. She didn't know whether she should go and apologize to Becca, or wait and try to make her point by not giving in this time. For all the fact that Genie was the blatantly domineering one, all sound and fury, it was Becca who steered them along more often than not.

Genie looked up from the paper, startled when her buzzer rang. Leaving the paper on the kitchen table, she tightened her robe belt and peered out the peephole. Becca stood outside her door and Genie stood there a moment, dumbfounded. She ran a hand through her hair, then opened the door, keeping her face and voice neutral. "Morning, Becca."

Subdued, Becca replied, "Morning. Can I come in?"

Genie stepped back, then closed and locked the door after her partner had entered. She followed the smaller woman into the living room and waited cautiously.

"I can't believe you went behind my back and called Sharon," Becca started.

"Someone had to," Genie replied quietly. "You obviously don't care what happens to you."

Sinking into a chair, Becca leaned back and stared at her thoughtfully. After a few quiet minutes, she observed, "You're a pain in the ass, you know that, Marshall?"

A half-smile crossed Genie's face as she sat on the couch. Things would be okay, now that she'd heard that opening. They were back on good footing if Becca could joke about it. "I have been told that a time or two."

"So. After Sharon finished chewing me out, we hashed out the details of getting some protection for me. I still say it's overreacting, but apparently, I've been outvoted."

Keeping her expression carefully expressionless, Genie asked, "Oh?"

Sourly, Becca retorted, "Yeah. 'Oh.' Once Sharon told the council what's been going on, they unanimously informed me to expect a couple of guardians starting tonight. I hope this makes you happy."

"Ecstatic."

"I bet."

Relieved now that the confrontation was largely over, Genie offered, "You want breakfast?"

"Yeah, sounds good," Becca agreed, following her into the kitchen.

"Eggs? Toast? Orange marmalade?"

"I knew there was a reason I kept you."

The genuine teasing relaxed the last of the tension. Genie pulled out the food and cracked the eggs into a bowl. She could feel Becca's eyes on her as she took out the cheese and started grating it into the bowl.

Slowly, Becca began, "So. About the other stuff that you said last night."

Genie kept her attention on the food, mixing the cheese and eggs together. "What about it?"

"I'm sorry. I didn't stop to think about how all of this has affected you," Becca said simply. "Sharon pointed out to me, rather forcefully, I might add, that I might want to take your side of things into consideration. As well as others."

Genie glanced over at her partner and hid a smile at the sight. Becca sat cross-legged on a kitchen chair and looked about fifteen with her hair sticking up in all directions and no makeup. "It's okay. I was just worried about you."

"I know. And I'm really not used to that," Becca admitted ruefully. She scrubbed her head, forcing her hair into further wildness, and peered up at her partner. "I've never really had anyone look after me before. I mean, Sharon's aiways been there for me, but more like an absentee mom, you know? She was always out and about looking for other children to bring to the Centers. I was encouraged to be independent and it stuck. A little too well, apparently."

Grinning now, Genie echoed, "Apparently."

"Anyhow. I just wanted to let you know that, um, well... you're my best friend too," Becca said, awkward. "I'd probably be going nuts if something like this was happening to you, so I understand a little of where you're coming from."

Genie reached over and squeezed her shoulder. "Good. And I'm sorry I lost my temper like that."

Smiling up at her, Becca accused, "You're a big mushball, you know that? That whole, hard-assed, intimidation thing is one big ruse."

Snickering, Genie poured the eggs into the frying pan and started scrambling them. Ducking the subject of her relative hard-assed-ness, she announced, "I heard from Steven yesterday afternoon."

"Do tell," Becca encouraged with a grin.

"He wants to get together for dinner sometime this week," Genie said, sliding some bread into the toaster.

"Are you going to?" Becca asked curiously.

"I don't know," Genie admitted. She scraped the eggs into plates and put one in front of Becca. "You know where the silverware is."

Becca stood and went to get silverware and napkins, setting them on the table before asking, "Why don't you know?"

"I don't know if I want to see him again just because we have history, or if I really want to see him again," Genie answered with a sigh, pulling the jar of marmalade out of the fridge and setting it on the table. She watched in a somewhat horrified fascination as Becca grabbed the jar, opened it and practically poured most of the concoction onto her toast, sans butter. "I swear. If you could get away with living on orange marmalade sandwiches, you would."

Becca deliberately took a large bite. She grinned as she chewed, apparently aware of the sticky smear on her chin. "What's your point?"

"No point, really. Just. You've never explained this obsession you have with it," Genie answered with a grin, buttering her toast and taking a small bite. "Oh. Drinks. Grapefruit or milk?"

Becca looked at her with an expression that clearly said, "Duh," and Genie shook her head in amusement, getting up again and pulling out the grapefruit juice out of the fridge. She poured glasses for them both and set them on the table. "Well? What's the story?"

Smiling wistfully, Becca explained, "What little I remember of my parents is centered around the breakfast table. I didn't see much of them at night because they were busy working or looking after my little sister. But we always had breakfast together and my mom always gave me marmalade toast. As a side dish, don't worry. I don't think that she believed it to be a valid solo breakfast choice either."

Genie chuckled.

"Anyhow, after they died and I was brought to the Center, they didn't have marmalade and I didn't really know what it was called, so I couldn't ask for it. All I knew was that it was in my Paddington Bear books that my mom used to read to me, but Sharon had never read them and after a while I forgot about it. Then, when I was like, fifteen, I was at some tea shop with friends and it was there and boom, as soon as I tasted it, I remembered." Becca shrugged, a little self-conscious. "I do love the way it tastes, but I think it's more of a comfort thing than anything else."

"I think that's nice," Genie said softly.

Looking surprised, Becca asked, "Yeah?"

Genie nodded. "Yeah."

ACCOMPANYING HER PARTNER to the living area, Becky ran over a few things in her mind while Genie looked around. She watched her partner take in the lit candles and the gentle strains of acoustic guitar, then moved to check the thermostat; it was cool, but

not cold, comfortable for Genie, who was used to the lower
temperatures. And since this was Genie's first time doing something
like this, Becky wanted to make sure her friend was as comfortable as
possible.

"So how does it work again? I mean, they aren't even here, on
this coast," Genie pointed out nervously.

Becky pointed and ordered, "Sit."

Genie did as she was told and sat on the cushions on the floor.
Becky sat beside her and crossed her legs, pivoting to face the other
woman.

"Okay. Sit like this. Good. Now, put your hands on my knees.
Close your eyes," Becky instructed softly, then chided, "Relax.
Nothing is going to happen to you. I just need you to ground me like
you always do."

Smiling reluctantly, Genie opened her eyes and admitted
ruefully, "Doing that always freaks me out a little."

Becky was surprised and frowned at her partner. "How come?"

"Because you're trusting me with, with *you*, you know?" Genie
explained.

Suddenly Becky got it. It had never occurred to Becky that Genie
would find the responsibility frightening. She hadn't seen anything
yet that had truly frightened the other woman. Though it was a fear
that she understood intimately, having grounded others many times
before. Taking her partner's hands, she said, "I do trust you. Have
almost since the moment we met. You'll always bring me back."

Haunted golden eyes stared back at her as Genie whispered, "A
couple of times I almost didn't."

"But you did. We're, we're connected. You ground me better
than anyone ever has, including Sharon. You're the only one who can
reach me when the darkness closes around. You always will."

Genie's eyes widened and though she opened her mouth,
nothing came out at first. Finally, she managed, "Wow. Um. Thanks,
Becca."

Smiling, trying to relieve the odd tension coiling in her stomach,
Becky released the strong hands she'd been gripping and said lightly,
"You're welcome. Now then. It's just about time and I need to get
ready."

Genie nodded and again placed her hands over her partner's
knees, warm and solid, grounding the other woman with her
presence.

Becky breathed deeply, feeling the physical connection to her
partner, and the psychic one as well. It was clear and strong, holding
them together as she'd never been connected to anyone else.

Does Genie have talent? Becky wondered suddenly. Was that why
they'd had such an instant connection? The other woman had never
shown any sign of it; not the slightest residual trace of psychic

energy that indicated telepathic ability. Shaking her head, Becky pushed the thoughts aside to concentrate on what she was supposed to be doing. Breathing slow and deep, she opened her mind to the familiar presences reaching for her from across the distance. Joel and Daniel, empath and projector, respectively.

They were brothers, twins, bonded for life through blood and telepathy. Joel's clean, soothing thoughts surrounded her, like a cool, placid lake. Beneath him was the strength of Daniel, literally the rock upon which Joel's foundation was built. They were two of the strongest talents in the world and various Centers called on the twins to provide psychic protection. Joel connected with the victim and Daniel surrounded both of them, projecting the attacks back from wherever they came. Fortunately, there wasn't a big demand for their talents, even considering the global scale on which they worked.

A sudden, additional connection surprised them all. Becky felt Genie, curious and hesitant, hovering nearby, on the outside looking in, even if the other woman didn't realize that she was doing it. Joel reached out after Becky identified her partner, and carefully brought Genie into their circle. Becky swirled around her friend's essence in happy surprise. Daniel surrounded them all, building the invisible walls that would shield her from future attack.

When everything was done, Becky gently sent Genie back to herself. She gave a lingering hug to Joel and Daniel, then heard Genie's voice calling her back to the physical world. Becky blinked, trying to get used to her body again. Things felt...not wrong, exactly...but different than they should have. Opening her eyes, Becky was shocked to find herself draped over Genie, their bodies molded together instead the way they'd started out.

Looking into amused golden eyes, Becky pushed herself up and frowned. "What happened?"

"I was going to ask you that," Genie responded dryly. "And anytime you want to move your hands, feel free."

Suddenly realizing what she was using as handholds, Becky flushed and rolled off her partner, falling to the floor in embarrassment. Looking up, she grinned at her partner. "Sorry about that."

Genie got up and shrugged. "No problem. It's the most action I've had in months."

Chuckling, Becky took the offered hand and hopped lightly to her feet. She vaguely felt Joel and Daniel in the back of her mind and, if she concentrated, Genie as well. "So. Can you do this with anyone else?"

Genie shrugged again, looking uncomfortable with the new turn of events. "Never have before. Goes a long way towards explaining things, though, doesn't it?"

Becky nodded slowly in agreement. "Like why it doesn't hurt to touch you, for one. And why you've always been so successful at pulling me back. I wonder why me?"

Eyebrow arching, Genie questioned, "Does it matter?"

"No, not really," Becky answered slowly. "Do you want to be tested? See if there's any other abilities that you might have?"

"Not particularly. Hey, I'm starving. Can we eat and talk at the same time?"

Remembering how she'd been constantly hungry after first developing her abilities, Becky grinned and nodded. They walked to the kitchen in companionable silence and Genie rummaged happily through the refrigerator, pulling out fruit and cheese. Becky took out a knife and cutting board, and started dicing things up and placing them in a large bowl. In short order, they had fruit salad and cheese ready and went back into the living room.

Genie sat on the couch, pulling her legs up and holding the bowl in her lap. "So. You want to get me tested."

Becky reached over and pulled out a strawberry. "Only if you want to. I never felt any hint of latency in you before now, so it's likely that this is your only talent."

"Which would be?" Genie asked curiously, munching on some grapes.

"Receiving empath," Becky informed her promptly. "Like Joel, except that you can only link to me."

Frowning, Genie questioned, "What's the point? I mean, from what you and Sharon have said, telepathic powers are the next step in evolution. What's the point in being able to link only to one person?"

"I have no idea. I've never actually heard of this happening before."

Smirking suddenly, Genie said, "So I really am unique."

"I've been saying that for months now."

"Among other things," Genie agreed dryly. "So what now?"

"Can you sense me in your mind? At all?"

Genie frowned, obviously thinking. After a minute or so, she shook her head. "I don't feel the least bit different. The only smartass in my head right now is me."

"Then who knows? Maybe it only happens when we're both open to a meditative state."

After swallowing a chunk of pineapple, Genie commented, "Which I try to stay away from."

Becky grinned suddenly. "Hey. I think we've just proven how open-minded you really are, despite all evidence to the contrary."

"Gee, thanks, partner. So. Since your linking thing is done with, how about we go over the Rochelle case file?"

ONCE SHE ACCEPTED the fact that she was mentally linked to three other people, Genie expected to feel different, but that wasn't the case. The drive home was completely normal and she pulled into her parking spot without any sense of being "watched" or "listened" to. Maybe it was only a temporary thing. Or maybe she just didn't have a strong enough ability to even sense that the link was there.

Entering her apartment a few minutes later, Genie dropped her keys onto the coffee table and her coat over the back of the couch. It was suddenly far too quiet in the apartment and she turned on the television for background noise. Becky usually had music going at her place, but Genie had always been one for silence.

She went to the kitchen and filled the watering can, moving towards the greenery that beckoned. It was her only source of nature in a city devoted to modern urbanism. Though she'd grown up in the suburbs, not the country, she'd always been a nature-freak, as her brother had called her. Her thoughts darkened momentarily at the thought of him, but she determinedly pushed it away.

"Hey, there," she greeted the plants softly.

For the next half-hour, she went over each plant carefully, pulling the dead and dying leaves, and talking as she watered them. When she was finished, Genie headed for the bedroom and stripped immediately upon entering, tossing her shirt in the corner and kicking off her pants. It had been a long day and she was suddenly exhausted, even if strangely restless.

Ignoring the feeling with the ease of long practice, Genie pulled her hair free of its customary braid and ran her fingers through it, grimacing when several long strands came out. Snorting, she shook her head and muttered, "Getting old."

Genie turned off the light and collapsed onto bed, closing her eyes. For the first time in a long time, she wished there was someone in her bed so she didn't have to be alone with her thoughts. Having someone with which to distract herself would have been very welcome. Still, there was always her military training to fall back on; with a few concentrated thoughts, as had been drilled into her brain when she was young, Genie drifted to sleep.

Or at least, she tried. It had always worked before, dropping off at a moment's notice, but not this time. She stared at the ceiling for a good half-hour then gave up. Groaning in frustration, she rolled out of bed and shuffled to the living room. Maybe the TV would bore her enough to make her sleepy.

To her shock, there was a man in her living room, already watching television. He was young and cute, with blue eyes and short brown hair. Furious that someone had gotten into her apartment without her knowing it, Genie demanded, "Who are you?"

He looked over at her with a grin that immediately disarmed her. "I'm Daniel. And now I know where I am. I hadn't seen this particular dreamscape before, so I figured that I was in someone else's. How are you, Genie?"

Dreamscape? I'm sleeping?

"Yep," he answered, his grin getting bigger.

"Stop that!" she ordered crossly. "I don't appreciate you being here in the least, let alone reading my mind."

He shrugged and tossed her the remote. "You must have wanted me here or I wouldn't have been pulled in."

Shaking her head as she sat in the chair by the couch, Genie said, "Becca said that I can only link to her."

"Ah, but in dreams all things are possible. The mind is far more relaxed and open than even in a meditative state."

"So why isn't Joel here?"

He gave her an impudent grin and answered, "No idea. Maybe you didn't like him as much as you did me."

She snorted, her humor finally reviving. "Or maybe he just isn't cute enough."

Daniel laughed out loud at the comment. "Well, we are identical twins, so I can't see that being the reason."

"It's funny. I was just thinking, before I fell asleep, that I didn't want to be alone with my thoughts any more," Genie mused. "But why wouldn't I reach out to Becca? I do know her, after all."

He looked at her shrewdly and observed, "Maybe you know her too well. Something on your mind that you need to talk about, but don't want her to know?"

"What, you're my dream shrink now?"

"I've been called worse," Daniel replied, blue eyes twinkling.

Genie fell silent, unsure what to say next.

"Whatever you want to say."

Rolling her eyes, Genie ordered again, "Stop that."

He smirked but didn't answer.

"I like Becca."

Daniel nodded seriously, understanding the import of the simple statement. "What's the problem?"

"She's my partner."

Pursing his lips, Daniel prompted, "And?"

"And my best friend."

"And?"

"And stop looking at me like I'm an idiot!" Genie snapped.

Not in the least intimidated, Daniel said, "So you like her. That's a good thing, Genie, really. I haven't been outside of this dreamscape, but you seem like a pretty lonely person. And what's not to like about Becky? She's a great woman."

"I know that!" Genie wailed, pulling a cushion over her face. After a moment, she flung it away and continued, "First of all, it's against regulations for partners to be lovers. The moment that happens, they get split up. Only for us, if that happens, Becca's left without someone to ground her, and that's just way too dangerous. Second, what if I make this big declaration and she doesn't feel the same way? Then things get awkward, and even if we move on, there'll be this thought in the back of her mind that I'll always want more. Which, of course, I will. Third, and most importantly, I'm a terrible person and it would be the worst possible thing for Becca to get involved with me romantically."

Daniel opened his mouth to speak but she cut him off. "And before you start quoting self-esteem issues behind that last item, I can assure you that that's not the case. I've done bad things in my past. I've... I've killed people in cold blood just because they got in the way of a mission. I've hurt people to get information out of them. Hell, I hurt people just to get money from them when I was young. And all for nothing. Everything I did, everything I thought I was standing for, was a crock of shit. How can I let Becca get involved with me, when she doesn't really know me?"

To his credit, Daniel didn't give her a pat, easy answer. He got up from the couch and knelt before her, taking her hands in his and turning them to look at the palms. "Do you know what I see when I look at you?"

Genie shook her head wordlessly.

"A wounded soul looking for a way to make things better," Daniel informed her quietly. He met her eyes and continued, "Why did you go into the military, Genie?"

Thinking back to those days, Genie sighed heavily. "Because I was young, and stupid, and naïve. I thought that I'd actually be doing some good in the world. Be All You Can Be, you know?"

"And why'd you become a cop?"

"Because I wanted to take psychos off the street."

"But why a cop? I mean, with your background, you could have gone into the FBI, CIA, NSA, or whatever security agency that you wanted to work for. They all would have been thrilled to have you. I assume that you were in some kind of covert unit, which gave you a pretty high security clearance," he guessed shrewdly. "Why a cop? With all the limitations and aggravations, with all the rules and regulations that have to be followed, so thoroughly, why pick that particular career?"

"You have to ask?" she sneered.

Daniel half-smiled and answered, "I'm not a telepath, Genie. I can sometimes sense your emotions, if they're strong enough and we're connected somehow, but certainly not your thoughts. Tell me why you need the rules."

Trapped by his compassionate gaze, Genie yanked her hands away and spat, "Because someone *would* be looking over my shoulder! Because there was no way that people wouldn't know what

I was doing, okay? So I couldn't beat someone up and not get called on it. Because there are limitations all over the God-damned place. Because I've seen what happens when there's no limit to what you can do in the name of a higher cause!"

Daniel rose onto his knees and brushed aside her tears. "Exactly. Which, in my opinion, makes you a good person, Genie Marshall. So reason number three really is about self-esteem. You could get around reasons number one and two not to go forward with this thing pretty easily. Number three, though, not thinking you're worthy of love... That's a tough one."

Swallowing against the tight, hot sensation in the back of her throat, Genie refused to break down.

"Genie."

Looking into his sweet, open blue eyes, Genie whispered back, "What?"

"You are worthy of love, sweetheart. You deserve it, and... I think you need it more than anyone else I've ever met."

His gentle words broke through her defenses and she started sobbing as she hadn't since her parents' death. Genie didn't resist as he pulled her into his arms and rocked her soothingly, letting her cry out the barely suppressed self-loathing and denial.

When Genie woke for real, it was to a tear-drenched pillow and a headache. Clearing her throat, she turned onto her back and stared up at the sun-brightened ceiling. Her strange dream session with Daniel hadn't really solved anything, but at least she knew the real reason behind her reluctance to approach her partner. The real reasons behind her not wanting to let herself feel more than she already did.

And knowing, as the old saying went, was half the battle.

Chapter
Twenty

PAPERWORK. THERE WAS always a crap-load of paperwork to be done, even in the middle of the worst case. Becky looked curiously across the desk at her partner, wondering at how Genie just plowed right through all of it. Report after report, without a break of any kind. It was like someone flipped a switch on in the other woman and nothing could distract her. Suddenly taking that as a personal challenge, Becky leaned back in her chair and asked, "Hey, Genie?"

Genie didn't even look up. "Yeah?"

"Getting a lot done?"

"Uh-huh."

"Taking care of the Roberts casework?"

"Yep."

"Mathisen just walked by with a naked hooker."

"Uh huh."

"Thought I'd pierce my nipple after work tonight. You want to watch?"

"Yeah."

Becky grinned as she waited for her actual words to penetrate Genie's brain. It took a good thirty seconds before the other woman froze, fingers stopping mid-air above the keyboard. Amber eyes switched from the computer screen to Becky's face, which by then had assumed an innocent expression.

"What did you just say?"

"I said, I thought I would pierce my nipple after work tonight."

Genie stared at her for a moment before shrugging. "That's what I thought you said." She went back to work, the faintest of smirks on her face.

Becky laughed outright and snapped an elastic at her partner.

Genie grinned openly as she looked back at Becky. "What?"

"C'mon, Genie, we've been at this for hours! It's time to go home," Becky cajoled.

Sighing at being so badly put upon, Genie replied dramatically, "I suppose."

Becky shook her head and stood, picking up her jacket. As they walked to the door, Becky nudged Genie with her hip. "I suppose that's something the military beat into you."

"What is?"

"Don't show your face until the paperwork is done."

Genie hip-checked her back and replied, "I could confirm that, but then I'd have to kill you."

Becky rolled her eyes. "You want to go for supper?"

Still snickering, Genie shook her head. "I'd like to, but I have plans."

Eyebrows arching in surprise, Becky questioned, "Oh? Do tell."

"Well, tonight's the date with Steven."

"You dog!"

"Hey! We're just going out for old times' sake."

It was Becky's turn to chuckle. "And just which old times will you be reenacting, I mean, remembering?"

"Oh, please. Get your mind out of the gutter, girl."

"Who, me?"

"Yeah, you. Besides, I know this isn't going to go anywhere, even if we were pretty serious when he left."

Curious, Becky asked, "How serious?"

Genie shrugged. "Obviously not serious enough. He got a job offer in New York that he just couldn't pass up."

Frowning, Becky asked, "He didn't even ask you to go with him?"

"Nope."

"What an asshole! Hey, you want me to give him some nightmares?"

Laughter at her partner's quasi-eager tone pushed aside the remembered hurt more easily than Genie would have expected. "No, but thanks for the offer. It's sweet."

They arrived at their vehicles and Becky said, "Well, have fun. And the nightmare offer stands, okay?"

Genie grinned. "Thanks, partner. I'll see you when I see you."

"Huh?"

"Court tomorrow, remember?"

"Oh, crap! I forgot all about that. And what am I supposed to do while you're out being all officious?"

"Oh, I don't know. Work?"

Becky aimed a swat at her partner's head, which Genie easily avoided. Shaking her head, she watched the other woman get into her Jeep, then waved and got in her car. The truck pulled out as Becky started her engine and she sighed for real this time. Well. Since she had nothing to do for a change, maybe she should call Michelle and get her other work caught up. She snorted, thinking that it would probably shock the other woman into a coma.

TEN MINUTES INTO the date, Genie knew that it was a mistake; not a huge mistake, just a minor error in judgment. By then, of course, it was far too late to get out of it, so she smiled at Steven and didn't say anything when he pulled into the restaurant parking lot. She got out of the car quickly, before he could walk around to open the door for her. She was grateful that at least her subconscious had known this was going to be a mistake and dressed her in slacks and a top instead of something really dressy.

It was a pleasant night and, as always, Steven was good company. He had some new funny stories and interesting tidbits about his new job. The food served at the Italian restaurant was great, and the wine smooth and tasty. It was all very...pleasant. And Genie found herself wishing that she'd gone over to Becky's for dinner and hung out watching television instead.

Towards the end of the night, Steven suddenly asked, "This was a mistake, wasn't it?"

Surprised, Genie automatically shook her head. "Of course not. It's been a wonderful night."

"And you've been bored to tears," Steven commented dryly.

Grinning faintly, Genie said, "I wouldn't say that."

"But close enough for government work, right?"

Smiling fully now, Genie reached across the table and took his hand. "I'm sorry, Steven. I really did want to see if there was anything left between us, but..."

"But there isn't," he finished regretfully. "Not on your side, anyhow. Aw, hell, Gene, I was really hoping we could make another go of this. I should've known better than to leave, especially when you were having such a hard time. I was a coward, afraid of how much you seemed to need me. And now I've gotten the coward's reward, because you definitely don't need me anymore."

Shrugging, embarrassed at the reminder of her pleading with him not to leave, Genie said, "You did what you had to do. I get that."

"One thing, though," he said, covering her hand with his.

"What?"

"I still love you," he replied simply. "All that time I was gone, all I could think about was you. I buried myself in work and didn't come up for air until I came back here. Then I was here and I couldn't seem to make myself contact you. I was afraid that you'd hate me, or that you'd moved on. Guess I was right on the last part."

"But not in the way that you're thinking. It's not that I have someone new in my life, I just...moved on."

Steven's lips twisted. "I'm going to hate myself for saying this but, since I'd like us to be friends at least, you do have someone new in your life. You've been talking about her all night."

Laughing self-consciously, Genie asked, "Becca? Steven, she's my partner. There's nothing romantic going on between us!"

"Right. And that's why you flipped out and threatened me at the hospital that day," Steven reminded, shrewd.

"Yes, it is," Genie said firmly. "Becca's my best friend and, yeah, she's a big part of my changing outlook on life, but that's it."

He plainly disbelieved her, but let it drop. "There's a hospital function in a couple of weeks. Would you save me by being my date?"

Grinning ruefully, Genie said, "I'm going to have more dates with you now than when we were going out, aren't I?"

Steven smiled and answered, "It's a possibility. Will you?"

"Sure. Why not?"

BECKY PUSHED ASIDE the book she'd been reading. If staring at the same page for at least ten minutes counted as reading, which of course it didn't. She walked over to the bookcase and replaced the large hardcover. It was an antique, and she took care of it, but she read them all pretty regularly. Genie had nearly been scandalized at her casual treatment of the books; especially the ones she'd actually written notes in. Grinning at the thought, Becky headed for the kitchen to make a late dinner for which she wasn't really hungry.

Her work call with Michelle had been less than productive. About twenty minutes into the conversation, the other woman had observed wryly, "Do us both a favor and don't call unless you can keep your mind on something besides your partner."

Becky had sputtered, "What are you talking about?"

"Right, boss. Tell it to someone who hasn't known you since you were practically in diapers."

A flush had come over Becky as she'd sighed. "Fine. I'm sorry. I'll give you a call tomorrow, okay?"

Michelle had chuckled and said goodbye.

Pulling out a box of pasta, Becky set about making a small amount for herself, knowing that if she didn't, she'd have no energy the next day. Not that she was looking forward to an anti-stimulating day of no partner, but something else could come up. Just because she and Genie weren't working together didn't mean that she wouldn't be working, after all.

This just totally sucks.

Sighing deeply, Becky poured the pasta into the boiling water and poked at it with her fork. It was times like this that she wanted someone to be with her the most. And that nebulous *someone* had definitely taken shape in her mind. Didn't matter how much she tried to deny it, either, because it just wouldn't go away.

"But it's not going to get any more involved, either," Becky said aloud, just to reinforce the determination. They could be many things to each other, but they couldn't be all things to each other. That had to be unhealthy. Somehow. She was almost positive.

The phone rang and she picked up the receiver. "Hello?"

"Hey, there."

Startled by her partner's warm voice, Becky asked in surprise, "Date over already?"

There was a snort on the other side and Genie answered, "And then some."

Becky couldn't help the pleased feelings that bubbled through her, but kept her voice sympathetic. "Sorry, partner."

"Ah, don't worry about it. Have you eaten?"

The almost accusatory tone sent a flush of guilt through her and she answered defensively, "I'm making supper now!"

"At almost eleven? You're gonna be up all night digesting."

"I thought I was the health-conscious one in this partnership," Becky demanded, stabbing her fork into the pot.

Genie chuckled. "Hey, I can't have you passing out without me around to catch you. And I know you don't eat breakfast. You just consume coffee like it was necessary for life."

Snickering as she turned off the stove, Becky countered, "It *is* necessary for life. Or at least consciousness."

"Well, that's your opinion. Of course it's the opinion of an addict, but—"

"Hey!"

Laughing now, Genie said, "I just wanted to see how you were doing. I'll let you eat now."

"All right. You want to hook up for lunch? I could swing by the courthouse."

"Sure. I'll give you a call if we get an early break. Otherwise I'll see you around twelve, outside."

Becky poured the pasta into the colander and said, "See you then!"

"Bye."

Becky hung up and realized that Genie hadn't given her any actual details about the date. Shrugging, she figured that she'd get them later. She was suddenly hungry enough that the small amount of spaghetti she'd made didn't look like more than a bite, so she went to refill the pot with more water.

Chapter
Twenty-One

BORED, BORED, BORED. Spinning her chair around, Becky knew that she should focus her energy on the files in front of her, but she just couldn't seem to concentrate. It didn't help that Genie was in court this morning, again, being recalled as a witness for a case from well before their partnership. She'd probably be gone most of the day, if not all of it. Just as she'd been gone the whole day before, and the day before that, too. Talking on the phone wasn't nearly as satisfying as face-to-face.

She spun around again, her head hanging back, creating a vague, free-fall feeling.

Captain Carlson barked, "Are we boring you, detective?"

Becky almost fell over, she stopped so fast. Snapping upright and slamming her feet to the ground sent a painful twinge through her spine, but she stifled it and aimed for an innocent expression. "Not at all, Captain. I was, ah, just contemplating one of our cases."

"Uh huh." Carlson eyed her pointedly before continuing, "Since you're in such a *contemplative* mood, how about you go down to Vice and *contemplate* on one of their cases? They've got a new one that could use your dedication."

Flushing guiltily, Becky stood and said, "Sure, I'll um, I'll just go right down there. Now. Right away."

"Take Mathisen with you," Carlson ordered shortly before heading into his office.

Surprised by the command, Becky shrugged and headed over to the other detective's desk, but he wasn't there.

Kim looked up at her approach and grinned, dark eyes smiling a greeting. "Mornin,' Becky."

"Hey, Kim," Becky replied. "Where's your partner?"

"I think he ran out of antacids," Kim answered with a smirk.

"I heard that, Yu," Mathisen growled from behind.

Clearly not intimidated, the vivacious Asian woman beamed up at her partner and said, "You were supposed to."

He turned to Becky with a reserved smile. "What can I do for you, Curtains?"

"Captain wants us to head down and check out a Vice case,"

Becky answered. She was a little surprised when the smile faded, and wondered about it, but continued, "Given Genie's, ah, relationship with the guys in Vice, he's probably just as happy that she's not around to go with me."

That brought out a soft rumble of amusement from Mathisen and he agreed, "Probably. They're all hotheads, especially your partner."

"Want me to come?" Kim offered.

Tossing the candy bar at his partner, he declined. "Enjoy your sugar high. We probably won't be gone long."

Becky fell into step with the tall, slender man as they headed towards the elevator, lengthening her strides automatically, much as she did with Genie. Like she did with most everyone, being well below average height. She had wanted to get to know Thomas Mathisen since they were introduced, but he'd always given off very strong "Don't come near me," vibes. Though at least he was polite about it, which was more than she could say for most.

Since being partnered with Genie, however, she'd thought that he was warming toward her, but he'd never approached her. Still, there were always things to talk about, even in awkward situations. "How are Ginny and Gary doing?"

He looked at her in surprise before answering, "Fine. Ginny just got back from camp last week, and Gary's heading off to college in a couple of weeks."

Smiling, she said, "Rutgers, right? Scholarship?"

Pride showed plainly on his face as they entered the elevators and he hit the sixth floor button. "Full scholarship. All we have to pay for is books and meals."

"That must be a big help."

He nodded. "Definitely. He had a couple of places lined up, but Rutgers was his first choice."

"It's a great school, from what I understand," Becky commented.

The elevator doors opened and he motioned for her to precede him. She could feel him watching her, probably wondering how she'd picked up all the personal information. As they turned the corner into Vice, she said casually, "Your partner likes to brag."

Shaking his head, Mathisen corrected, with fond amusement, "My partner likes to gossip."

Becky chuckled. "That, too."

To her relief, none of the men who routinely gave her a hard time were there as they made arrived at Captain Johansson's office. Waiting for the cue to enter after knocking politely, Becky took a quick look around the busy department. Vice had the smallest percentage of women and minorities of all the departments and she'd often wondered if that was part of the unhealthy attitudes a lot of the detectives in this department maintained.

"Come in!"

Becky stepped inside and nodded to the captain, a bear of a man with a balding pate and pale, watery eyes. His strongest feature was his voice, which was sharp and commanding. "Morning, Captain. You wanted me to take a look at something?"

Johansson looked at her sourly, but nodded. "Have a seat, Curtains, Mathisen. And here, take a look at this. Jurisdiction's a bitch on this case because we've got another county, drugs, child porn, and a couple of murder victims. I wanted to kick it to your department in the first place, but I was outvoted."

Becky sat in front of the desk and opened the file the man placed on the desk. The picture on top instantly soured her stomach and she closed her eyes for a few seconds, trying to get it under control.

"Yeah. That was my first reaction," Johansson said sympathetically. "Want a Tums?"

Becky opened her eyes and shook her head. Taking another look at the picture, she murmured, "No, thanks."

There were two victims in the photo: two women stretched out, making one line with their bodies. Their arms were lashed together at the wrists, held above their heads. They were barely dressed in a strip of leather covering their groins and leather masks over their faces, but that was it. The pools of blood that surrounded them came from the obvious slashes in their abdomens and chests. There was no sign of struggle, which meant they'd been drugged or unconscious at the time of the murders. "I'll need to take a look at the crime scene."

Johansson nodded. "I figured. Take the file with you. Let me know if you find anything."

Standing, Becky nodded, then followed Mathisen out of the office.

He shook his head and muttered, "What a way to start the day."

Becky sighed. "C'mon, let's go pick up Kim and head out."

THE CRIME SCENE turned out to be the basement of a strangely normal, two-level home outside the city. Technically, they didn't have any jurisdiction at all, but the local police captain had felt that expert help had been called for. He had, apparently, been very close to calling in the FBI, but since the DC force dealt with stuff like this all the time, he'd called them instead. It was almost a universal truth that cops would go to any other kind of cop, barring IA of course, before going to a Fed.

Which meant that she'd be keeping quiet about her own Federal background.

The house was in an unremarkable neighborhood, a planned one like all the ones built in the last hundred years or so, with yards and children and two cars in most of the driveways. The sensation of being watched crawled up Becky's spine unpleasantly as she headed from the car to the house. Shaking her head, she hesitated just outside, fortifying her mental shields before walking through the front door. Even though the twins gave her a reassuring "hug," letting her know they were still there and aware of her trepidation, without Genie physically there, things could get dicey if she lost control. The connection they shared had faded since that first day and now Becky could barely feel a tenuous thread to her partner.

Fortunately, there was nothing lying in wait for her when she stepped inside. There was a muted sense of comfort, but nothing else. She met Kim's eyes with a forced smile and continued further into the house.

It was nicely decorated, if not richly so, middle class all the way. She followed Kim and Mathisen toward the basement, walking down the wooden steps with reluctance. Going to a murder scene always sucked, no matter how many years she'd spent visiting them. Thankfully, her physical responses were a lot more controllable than when she'd first started. Also thankfully, the bodies had been removed, though the smell of death lingered.

Glancing around the room, she asked one of the local cops, "Who discovered the bodies?"

"Sister of one of the victims," he answered, shaking his head. "She's upstairs in the kitchen."

"Thanks," Becky murmured, making a mental note to speak with the woman.

Drifting through the basement brought no major sense of anything. There was no violence, no horror or psychosis. Without Genie around, she didn't dare do more than a surface scan of the area, not wanting to lose herself in the jangled emotions coming from the cops around her. The conversation between Mathisen and Kim washed over her as a soothing background noise. Their familiar voices complemented each other as they took turns questioning the local cops about the scene and made their own quiet observations.

Suddenly, there was a charge in the air and Becky stiffened, closing her eyes to get a closer sense of what was going on. Tense, eyes still closed, she demanded of the nearest cop, "Did the bomb squad go over this house?"

A young woman answered, "It wasn't deemed necessary."

Danger. Overwhelming danger swamped her. Becky opened her eyes, shouting, "Everybody get out of the house now!"

"What the hell are you shouting about?" Detective Morel, the officer in charge, demanded as he strode over to her.

She met him halfway. "There's a bomb somewhere in the house and only about a minute before it goes off. Get your people clear now!"

He paled and shouted, "Everybody out!"

Of course, most of them had already heard her and were piling

up the stairs in an organized rush. Those who reached the steps first
called out to the other officers elsewhere in the house. Becky,
Mathisen, and Kim were the last ones out and they barely reached
the end of the driveway before the bomb went off.

Becky stumbled the last few feet and was caught in Mathisen's
strong arms. She yanked herself free from him, the contact spiking
sharply through her, and fell to the ground. Her head connected
painfully with the pavement and she skinned a palm trying to stop
the fall. Becky lay there for a minute, listening to the roar of the fire
and the now-frenzied activity around her. Mathisen and Kim stared
down at her, two sets of dark eyes filled with concern.

Kim knelt beside her, hands hovering but not touching, and
asked, "You okay?"

Grimacing as a few aches made their presence known, Becky
nodded and pushed herself up. "I'll live."

BORED. BORED. BORED. Genie sighed deeply, not bothering to
stifle the sound, and earned herself a glare from the Assistant
District Attorney. The woman wasn't someone she wanted to piss off,
but the boredom as things dragged out was absolutely killing Genie.
She forced a smile and returned her attention to her notebook. So far,
she'd won too many tic-tac-toe games to count. She'd also drawn
cartoon versions of Becca doing simple things, most revolving
around no coffee and lack of sleep.

It is a pretty funny combination, she thought, barely stifling a
chuckle.

Court would probably be out in about three more fun-filled
hours, but she seriously doubted that they would call her to the
stand today, either. The prosecution was finally calling his own
witnesses, but she was at the end of the list due to the "impact" her
testimony would bring.

Her eyes drifted towards the accused and her fists curled. If he
got off, she'd be pissed for weeks to come. He'd killed a young,
married couple in order to rob their place, but had waited to do it
until he'd tortured them for a couple of hours. He glanced at her and
Genie let her fury at what he'd done show in her eyes, promising
mayhem if he didn't go to jail. He blanched and quickly looked away.
When the ADA looked at her curiously, Genie's face was a bland
mask once again and she shrugged, indicating that she had no idea
what was wrong with the defendant.

Picking up her pencil, Genie started tracing out Becca's face in a
serious drawing, the delicate features of her partner coming easily to
her as she carefully drew them. She thought about how the eyes
crinkled up when happy, and the near-perfect pentagon formed by
her mouth and cheeks in the same expression.

"Hey. That's good."

Genie was startled out of her almost hypnotic state at the whispered statement, and she smiled at the ADA, whispering back, "Thanks."

She was about to return to the drawing when a sharp pain in her head struck. The notebook and pencil clattered to the floor as she hunched over, gripping her head.

"Detective! What's wrong?" the other woman hissed anxiously.

Gasping at the throbbing in her head, knowing that Becca was in trouble, Genie replied, "I have to go."

She staggered blindly out of the courtroom, ignoring the looks sent her way, holding one hand to her throbbing head and pulling out her phone with the other. Her fingers automatically dialed Becca's number, but there was no answer. Almost panicked, she dialed the Captain's phone number, and found a convenient wall to lean against while it rang.

"Carlson."

"Where's Becca?"

"What, are you psychic now, too?"

"What happened?"

Carlson sighed into the phone and Genie could easily picture him rubbing his eyes as he answered, "I sent her, Mathisen and Yu to a murder scene outside the city. I just got a call that it exploded."

"Is she...?"

"She's fine. Just bruised and shaken up," Carlson assured her hastily.

Relieved, Genie asked, "What's the address?"

He gave it to her, then questioned, "How did you know something was wrong?"

She could hardly tell him that she and Becca were not only mentally linked together, but linked to two men to protect against psychic attacks. It wasn't really something that would go over well. "A hunch."

"Uh-huh."

A grin surfaced at his blatant disbelief and she promised, "I'll call you later."

"Do so."

With that blessing of sorts, Genie hung up and headed for her Jeep.

"JESUS, BECCA, I can't leave you alone for a friggin' *minute* without you getting into trouble, can I?" Genie demanded, finally reaching her partner's side through the chaos. She found the other woman sitting cross-legged on the hood of one of the emergency cars, a small white butterfly strip along the side of her right temple.

Becca grinned up at the taller woman. "What can I say? There's just not enough excitement in the relationship anymore."

Snorting, Genie brushed her fingers across Becca's shoulder and asked, "Are you all right?"

"Yeah. Luckily, we got everyone out in time," Becca answered. She looked over at the smoldering wreck that used to be a house and continued, "I wish you'd been here, though. I didn't dare go deep without you here to ground me."

"So what did you get?" Genie questioned, leaning against the car.

Shrugging, Becca replied, "Not much. And what I did get probably came from the owner of the house before this whole thing went down."

"Well, that sucks."

"Definitely. How was court?"

Rolling her eyes, Genie said, "Boring, as always. I swear, it almost makes me not want to solve cases. I sit there for hours in order to give twenty minutes of testimony. Which, by the way, I haven't actually done yet. Yeesh!"

Becca grinned. "I totally understand."

"So what do you want to do, now that the crime scene's gone up in flames?" Genie asked.

"I still want to examine it, but the fire fighters say it'll be a while before things are cool enough to enter the remains. I might not be able to get anything from the murder, but I probably can from the bomb. Well, I hope so anyhow," Becca amended.

"How about lunch in the meantime?"

"Sounds great! I think I'm about to pass out from low blood sugar." Becca hopped off the car and followed Genie back to her Jeep. They told Mathisen and Kim where they were going and agreed to bring back food for the other detectives. Genie drove to a nearby sub shop, remaining quiet on the ride there.

Looking at her thoughtfully, Becca asked, "What's wrong?"

"Oh, nothing," Genie answered with a faint smile. "Just pondering the strangeness of life."

"Anything in particular, or the whole ball of wax?" Becca prompted gently.

Shrugging as she pulled into a parking spot, Genie replied, "More like the whole wax museum."

"Ah."

"What 'ah'?" Genie demanded with a grin.

Echoing the grin, Becca asked, "Bad date?"

Genie held the door open and countered, "Did I even mention my date?"

"Didn't have to. Transparent as glass, my friend."

"Uh huh. Su-u-ure."

"Let's eat here," Becca suggested. "We can talk."

"We shouldn't be gone too long."

"Humor me."

Grimacing, Genie nodded and they ordered before moving to a hard, plastic booth in the back with their drinks.

When they were both comfortable, Becca ordered, "Spill."

"Geeze. Pushy much?" Genie muttered. After taking a long sip of her soda, she sighed and said, "When Steven left, I would've done pretty much anything to get him back. Now that he is back, I don't want him. It's like a switch inside me was turned off and now all I can see in him is the potential for a decent friendship. Oh, and he says that he still loves me, by the way."

"Ouch."

Stabbing the ice in her cup with the straw, Genie said, "No kidding. Ever wonder why our feelings change? I mean, I was desperately in love with him and we didn't really have any problems in our relationship. We both worked insane schedules, him at the hospital and me at the precinct, but when we were together, we were really together. Even with all that, though, he didn't ask me to go with him. And now that he's back..."

Becca shrugged. "Everyone grows in different ways over the years. What was enough for you before, obviously isn't enough anymore."

"What do you mean?"

"It sounds like you and Steven had a very limited relationship," Becca observed. "When you were younger, that was probably more than enough, since you weren't ready to settle down."

Eyebrows arching, Genie stated, "I am hardly ready to settle down."

"Maybe."

"Maybe? I think I'd know whether or not I wanted to settle down!"

Holding her hands up in a peace-making gesture, Becca said, "No offense, partner."

Genie looked sharply at the other woman. "And how would you know anyhow? I know you don't peek into the inner sanctum of the mind without permission."

"I don't have to. I just know you."

Grumbling, Genie warned, "Don't even think about coming to me when you need advice on your love life, got it?"

Becca's smile turned wistful as she said, "Not to worry. I wouldn't ask you anyhow."

The waitress arrived just then with their pizza, distracting Genie from the strange comment.

Chapter
Twenty-Two

THE HOUSE STILL smoldered when Becky and Genie got back, but the fire was definitely out. The fire engines were gone, along with most of the police. The personnel remaining included one fire team and the arson investigator, who were still going over the scene, Detective Morel, as officer in charge, and Mathisen and Yu.

The yellow crime scene tape had been expanded to hold the entire yard, and additional plastic blockades had been set up. Becky walked around one, Genie trailing behind, and headed for the investigator talking with Mathisen and Kim. She held out the bag of food they'd brought back for the others.

"Thanks!" Mathisen said gratefully, opening it up right away.

As he and Kim divvied up the food, Becky greeted the investigator. "Detective Becky Curtains. This is my partner, Detective Genie Marshall."

"Good to meet you. John Williamson," he answered, taking her hand and then Genie's.

"Find much yet?" Genie asked.

Shrugging, Williamson answered, "There was just enough explosive used to blow up this house. Whoever did it knew exactly what they were doing. They set it so the blast went toward the backyard, so none of the other houses would get caught. I'd say they wanted to get rid of the evidence and went a little overboard, except that it was too controlled to be a mistake."

Becky drifted away from the conversation as Mathisen and Kim joined in. She headed towards the wreckage of the house, opening herself to the area. Something was bothering her, but she couldn't put her finger on it. There was nothing obvious to blame for the unsettled feeling, just...

"You all right?"

Becky jumped at her partner's voice. "Jesus, Genie! Don't sneak up on me like that!"

Arching an eyebrow, Genie asked, "I'd ask how much coffee you had, but I know it's been at least a few hours since your last cup. What's going on?"

Shifting uncomfortably, Becky glanced at the blackened frame that looked like it was going to fall over. It was nothing specific, but she knew their mysterious psychic attacker was behind this. Just as he'd been behind the two murdered women. "It's him."

"Him, who?" Genie asked with a sigh, though she knew exactly who Becky was talking about.

"The 'him' we're linked against."

"Speaking of which, notice that he hasn't so much as sneezed in your direction since linking up?" Genie commented. "Like all cowards, he can't stand the light of day, preferring sneak attacks that you can't fight against."

Becky ignored the words. "He was here. We should get a copy of the local news tape. See if we can pinpoint him."

"Wait. You mean he was *here*, as in, in the flesh?"

Becky nodded. "Yup."

"I'll get on it," Genie said, moving back toward the other detectives.

Shivering as a cool gust of wind slithered down her spine, Becky crossed her arms in a futile attempt to get warm. Things were escalating. She was positive that it wouldn't be long before the telepath attacked in force. The one thing that she had to be sure of was that Genie was nowhere around when that happened. The other woman had just enough telepathic ability to be dangerous to herself because she would, in all likelihood, try and use that scant talent to protect Becky.

Becky couldn't allow Genie to attempt anything like that, knowing personally just how ruthless their enemy was. She had to keep Genie safe at all costs, especially from the other woman's apparent need to protect Becky, whom she couldn't protect.

This was one battle Becky had to fight alone.

VIDEO WASN'T A medium over which psychic energy ran, unfortunately, so they were reduced to identifying neighbors and onlookers the old-fashioned way. It took hours, but finally they'd identified all but five of the people in the crowd. Of them, two were women who could be crossed off right away, which left only three unknown men to find.

Rubbing tired eyes, Genie grumbled, "I think my eyeballs have gone on strike."

"You're not the only one, partner," Becky sighed. Stretching this way and that until bones cracked, she continued, "At least we've got it narrowed down to three."

Genie leaned back in her chair with a heavy sigh of her own. "Have you even figured out what the hell we're going to charge him with when we catch him? I mean, it's not like we can prove that he's behind everything. And the courts won't accept just your testimony, not without some kind of physical evidence to back it up."

That's the least of my worries, Becky thought. Aloud she said, "I know. All I can think of is finding out who he is first, though. We'll have to worry about the rest later."

"I suppose we could stake him out for a while. Play the waiting game. He'd do something eventually," Genie mused.

"Hey. Got those IDs for you."

Both women looked up at Kim's entrance to the video room. She handed three folders to Becky and asked, "So our killer's one of these three?"

"Hopefully," Becky replied, opening the top file and handing a second to Genie.

"None of them have a record," Kim informed them.

Looking over the file, Becky murmured, "He wouldn't."

"Don't stay too late," Kim admonished before leaving the small room.

Late? Becky wondered, looking at her watch. "No wonder our eyes hurt. It's almost ten. Let's get something to eat while we look this stuff over, okay?"

Genie nodded. "Where do you want to go?"

"We could pick up a pizza and head back to my place?"

"Sounds like a plan to me."

Standing, Becky put her hand out for the file and transferred them to the crook of her arm. "I'll stop for the pizza and meet you there."

"Good idea. I need to rifle through my e-mails anyhow," Genie said, rolling her eyes.

Snickering, Becky had to comment, "If you read them every day, you wouldn't have this problem."

Genie quipped, "If I read them every day, I'd shoot myself."

AS BECCA HEADED downstairs, Genie went back to her desk. This late at night, the office was quiet, with the night shift out and about on their cases. Genie nodded to the people she passed and sank into her chair gratefully. It might not be the most comfortable chair in the world, but it was a damn sight better than those hard plastic jobbies in the viewing room.

Flipping on her screen, Genie opened her e-mail and sighed at the number of messages waiting for her. Delete was her favorite button and almost half of them she could do that to without even opening. The other half turned out to be a mix of requests for information from other departments, court appearance confirmations, and replies to her own requests for information.

"You're here late."

Genie looked up at her captain's voice and shrugged. "Just got done in the viewing room, narrowed it down to three possibles."

"This is for that big case you don't know the specifics for, right?" he asked wryly.

"Yeah. Sorry, Captain," Genie apologized.

"So you still don't know the specifics?"

Feeling somewhat squirmy at his pointed tone of voice—he could always make her feel like a lying little shit—Genie sighed. Technically, they did know what was going on, they just didn't know who was behind it. "Have a seat."

"I don't like the sound of that," he said, echoing her sigh. He grabbed the nearest chair and pulled it closer. "What do you know?"

"Someone's been psychically stalking Becca for a few months now. We know he's behind the tourist murders, and he's also behind the two women and the bomb from today. Now ask me what we can prove."

"Nothing."

"You got it. It's for damned sure that his accomplice, that little punk Belladonna, isn't going to give his holy man up."

"Wonderful," Carlson said, unenthused.

Genie grimaced in agreement. "In any case, once we figure out who he is, all we can do is stake him out and hope we catch him doing something he shouldn't."

"Like we have the manpower for that?"

"Like we have a choice?" she countered. "Look, boss, this guy's on a head-trip. He's out to prove that Becca's a piece of incompetent crap, and is going to do everything in his power to discredit and destroy her. If that takes killing a hundred people, in a hundred different ways, that's exactly what he's going to do."

Scowling, Carlson leaned back in the chair. "It can't come to that, Genie. It *won't* come to that."

"That sounds like a threat."

"Just a statement. The Powers That Be won't stand for it. They'll fire her in a second if they get wind about all of this."

"Well, since we're the only ones who know about it, they aren't going to get wind of it, are they?"

"Genie, I've got to think about public safety here. You said yourself that this guy's going to kill again. If he's that focused on Curtains, then maybe taking her out of play is the best thing all around," he suggested helplessly.

Genie's hands clenched into fists. "You can't do that! You know what she's gone through to get here!"

Holding his hands up in frustration, Carlson demanded, "Give me another option, here, Marshall!"

"Just give us another week, okay? Before you say anything to anybody, one more week. We're close to catching this asshole, so close! I know we can wrap it up in a week," Genie promised.

"With evidence, aside from Curtains' visions."

"With evidence."

He stared at her for a few seconds, then nodded. "All right. You've got *one week*. Then I have to tell the Commissioner what's going on."

"Thanks, Captain. I appreciate the leeway."

"Just catch the bastard, Marshall, and everyone'll be happy," Carlson ordered, standing up.

"Yes, sir."

She watched him go with a faint sigh of relief. At least that was one thing they didn't have to worry about anymore. Deceiving one's captain made for very bad Karma. Of course, now they pretty much had an impossible deadline now, but hey, that was what made life an adventure.

THE NIGHT AIR was cool. Becky shifted the box of pizza and the bag of drinks and snacks as she struggled to open the door with her nose. Finally giving it up for a lost cause, she thumped the door with her head and shoved it open. Just as she set things down on the kitchen counter, the phone rang. Swearing, she lunged to get to the damned machine before voice mail picked up. "Hello?"

"It's me."

Smiling at her foster-mother's voice, Becky turned on the monitor and Sharon's face became visible on the 6" by 6" screen. The older woman was smiling as well, sitting at her desk in her office at the Center. Settling onto the couch, Becky exclaimed, "Hi! How are you?"

"Fine, honey, fine. I was just calling to check in with you, since I hadn't heard from you in a while," Sharon answered.

Rubbing her fingers through her hair, Becky informed her, "Yeah, well, it's been insane here."

"Trouble sleeping?"

Becky nodded. "Yep. But only because there's a psycho trying to break me down mentally and destroy my career. Otherwise, everything's just ducky."

With a wry grin, Sharon commented, "All right. Now tell me what's really wrong."

"What makes you think something's wrong?" Becky asked, keeping her face as neutral as possible, given that she'd never been able to lie successfully to Sharon; not even long-distance.

"Besides the fact that you were at the Center for ten days and avoided being alone with me like I had the plague? Not a damned thing," Sharon replied, amused.

Becky sighed. "Okay. Something's wrong. Well, not really wrong, but more like a problem. Kind of. Maybe. Aside from the psycho and all that, I mean."

Chuckling, Sharon prompted, "So?"

"So I think I have feelings for Genie," Becky blurted out.

That got Sharon's attention. "What kind of feelings?"

"Like, you know, romantic-type feelings."

"When did this happen?"

Groaning, Becky got off the couch and roamed the room before coming back to sit in front of the screen. "I have no idea. And it's not like I'm *in* love with her or anything. It's just, maybe, a little more than friendship, a little more than partners."

"What's wrong with being in love with her? She's a good woman."

"I know that! But she's my partner. And if I want to keep her as such, then I can't ever admit to anything but friendship. You know that little regulation that states partners are not to be romantically or sexually involved with each other? There's a reason for it."

"So you're going to let someone else dictate how you feel."

"I don't know how I feel, all right? All I know is that she gets to me, gets under my skin like no one else every has."

"And the fact that she's drop-dead gorgeous doesn't hurt," Sharon observed with a grin.

Becky rolled her eyes. "You aren't helping, *Mom*."

"I'm sorry, Becky, I'm not poking fun at you. All right, not a lot, anyhow," Sharon amended. "If you have feelings for her, then you should tell her."

"It's not that simple."

"Yes, Becky, it is."

Becky sighed and leaned forward. "She's my partner and best friend. I can't lose that. No matter the reason."

Sharon shook her head as she leaned back in her chair. "It's your life, little one, but I think that you're making a mistake."

Becky snorted. "Wouldn't be the first one, and I'm sure it won't be the last."

A half-smile blossomed on Sharon's face. "Like mother, like daughter, huh?"

"Definitely. And now for something completely different. How're things at the Center since I've loosed the lightning?"

BY THE TIME Genie got to the apartment, Becky had the pizza set out on plates, reheated, and waiting in the living room. She let her partner in and immediately knew that something was wrong from the carefully blank expression. What on earth could've happened in the short time that they'd been apart? And why did it seem like the important things only happened during that time? "What's the matter?"

Pulling off her coat, Genie tossed it towards the coat rack in the corner and made a face when she missed. "Figures."

Eyeing her partner as the taller woman bent down to retrieve the fallen jacket, Becky repeated, "What's the matter?"

"Got anything to drink?"

Becky took in the tired tone and nodded, backing off. Obviously Genie wasn't ready to talk about the problem yet. "What do you want?"

"Rum and coke?"

Becky turned wordlessly towards the kitchen as Genie collapsed on the couch. Genie rarely had hard liquor, even mixed with something else, so this couldn't be good. Pulling out the bottle, she poured a generous amount then cut it with the soda. Shrugging, she poured a drink for herself and brought both glasses back to the living room. She grinned upon finding Genie stretched out on the couch, long legs hanging over the edge.

Putting the drinks on the coffee table beside her friend, Becky sat on the floor and picked up her plate, starting to eat. "I heard from Sharon tonight."

"Yeah?"

"Yep. She said that things have been a little better since the interviews started," Becky reported. "People aren't panicked anymore, since nothing bad's happened in response to them."

"Good, I'm glad," Genie said with a faint smile. "How's Jack doing?"

Becky snorted. "Apparently, cleaning the pool for a month took his ego down a couple of notches."

Grinning outright, Genie said, "Probably a good thing."

"Definitely a good thing. The other kids haven't stopped teasing him about it. His new nickname is 'pool boy.' "

Chuckling, Genie reached over and pulled her plate onto her chest. The silence was comfortable as they ate, music quietly filling in the background. When she was done with the first slice, Genie rolled to her feet and went to the kitchen for another, snagging Becky's plate as well. The return trip was just as quick and she took up her former position. "Have I told you that you have a really comfortable couch?"

"Not that I recall," Becky replied, bemused, watching as Genie got resettled.

"You do."

"Thanks."

Another silence fell, but this one wasn't quite as comfortable as the first. Finally, Genie blurted out, "We've only got a week to catch this guy."

Becky froze in the act of lifting the pizza to her mouth. "Excuse me?"

"I talked to the captain tonight," Genie explained reluctantly.

"He said that he can only give us another week before letting the Commissioner know what's going on. And probably what's going to happen at that point is that you'll be removed from duty."

"Great," Becky sighed. She munched on the pizza as she thought that over, then said, "Well, at least we're further along than we were."

"True enough. Did you look over the files while you were waiting?"

"I did. Didn't get anything from any of them, though," Becky replied. "Not a twitch. And Kim was right; none of them has so much as a parking ticket. They're all in their late forties, white males, successful in their chosen professions. I'd be inclined towards Lt. Colonel Jackson because of the profile."

"Profiles are created for a reason, yes. Gimme the file."

Becky pulled it out and handed it over. "He's in a position of authority, works on promotion committees and such, which fits the killer's need for control and influence. He's from a wealthy, influential family, which also fits."

"So it's a good match. Especially given the question of why a Lt. Colonel would be in that neighborhood in the first place," Genie said. "He certainly doesn't live there."

Becky took a sip of her drink and closed her eyes to savor the burn of the rum. "I agree. But then again, neither do the other two. So why do we have an uptown city psychologist, a Lt. Colonel, and a corporate CEO all hanging around an unremarkable suburban neighborhood all at the same time? That's a little on the strange side, don't you think?"

"We could bring them all in for questioning, see what you get off them," Genie suggested.

"Right. I can see that going over well."

Snorting, Genie agreed, "We're going to have a fight on our hands even if they're all completely innocent of anything just because. They'll be indignant, uncooperative, arrogant. Oh yeah. Tomorrow should be fun."

"Well, if I'm going to get canned, I might as well go out with a bang."

"You are not getting canned! We're going to nail this asshole to the wall in plenty of time."

"No offense, Genie, but I'm not going to hold my breath."

Half turning and leaning on her elbow, Genie promised, "I'm not going to let that happen."

Gently, Becky pointed out, "You might not be able to stop it. Genie, I'm not looking for you to protect me here. We'll do the job the best we can. And you're right, we *are* going to get him. I might just be a little unemployed when we do, so you'd have to make the official arrest."

Scowling, Genie said, "I knew I shouldn't have told you about this."

Becky grinned. "Hindsight, huh?"

"You betcha."

When Genie reached for her glass, Becky exclaimed, "Wait!"

Freezing mid-motion, Genie looked over at her partner and asked cautiously, "What?"

"Oh, nothing. I just thought that if you're like this without alcohol, adding it to the mix might be a bad idea."

Genie threw a pillow at her.

Excerpt from Rebecca Curtains' Journal—Year One

Finally! We have some real suspects, even if there is an impossible time frame to work in. I hate deadlines, have I mentioned that? It's not that I suck under pressure, because I don't. I couldn't be a cop if I did. I just hate having people look over my shoulder all the time. And while the Captain won't do that in an obvious fashion, he's going to have to keep an eye on us now.

Maybe Genie was right. Maybe this guy can't stand the light of day, or close scrutiny. That just doesn't feel like the right answer, though. When push comes to shove and I have to burn him out, I don't know if I'll have the strength to do it. Even if Daniel and Joel can somehow help me, I just don't know.

Okay. I'm getting maudlin now. This is Becky. This is Becky when she's had way the hell too much to drink. Time to get some sleep because five o'clock comes awfully early when you had too much to drink and too much to think about.

Chapter
Twenty-Three

AllNetNews.com
June 18, 2107

Due to the overwhelming response from readers, the sixth article in this series is being postponed so that the questions and comments that AllNetNews has received can be answered. AllNetNews is posting your questions in the exact format as received, unless profanity was used. Only the first part of an address will be shown to protect the privacy of each reader. The volume of responses makes answering every e-mail impossible, but we did our best to choose a wide variety.

(As always, feedback is welcome at JLipshim@allnewsnet.com)

Beta_23: I think it's great that you're finally setting the record straight and all that, but what are you all about? What's the history of the telepaths according to you?

*Karen: Our history is the same as many other minorities. We've faced persecution and prejudice for decades now. When telepaths first came into the public view, the backlash was tremendous. Many of us were subject to beatings and death. Even with the doctors and scientists on our side, stating that it was completely genetic, we had no recourse when someone discriminated against us. Things are better today since we have the law on our side, but as happens in any 'new' situation, there are still those who hate us simply because of who we are.

Nina5890: If I was to meet you on the street, how

do I know you won't read my mind? Don't you ever just get nosy about what everyone's thinking? If someone's thinking bad things about you?

Karen: Personally speaking, I'd rather not know. Generally speaking, the amount of energy used to go into someone's mind is very draining. People think that it's just a brief thought and we're there but it isn't. It takes a lot of concentration and power, some of which manifests physically. I've had devastating migraines, physical exhaustion, even been knocked unconscious for hours at a time. Why would I risk any of that just to know what someone might be thinking about me? The answer is that I wouldn't, and I don't.

Idol_74: this whole love fest makes me sick. you're all a bunch of f##ing mind-sluts and I hope you all burn in hell where you belong.

Karen: Gee, thanks. Have a lovely day.

Camper_Stud: Are you single?

Karen: *grin* Yes I am, but I'm not in the market. Thank you anyhow.

Bikrbabe: This is for your partner. Do you get any cr#p just from being partnered with a telepath?

Paula**: So far, not too much. I think most of the cops here know that she's just doing her job. Not everyone's tolerant, of course, but I've only been hassled a couple of times since we teamed up.

Kittyfan888: What exactly can you do, telepathic-wise?

Karen: My personal gifts have always been linked to thoughts. I create a rapport with others that allows me to know what they think. That can be either through touching something that they've handled, or touching the person directly. I also have some precognitive talents, though those aren't the strongest facets of my telepathy.

Jaxm69: What should someone do if they think they might be a telepath?

Karen: The first thing to do is contact your local Telepathic Resource Center. They can arrange for testing and training and let you know what the next step that you should take is.

Lookout48: How do you live with yourself? You're an aberration to mankind and God.

Karen: Thanks ever so for the helpful comments.

Kelsa_01: Do you think everyone'll eventually be telepathic?

Karen: I'm not a scientist so I really couldn't answer that. I don't know why humans are changing like this but there's probably a reason for it in the grand scheme of things.

JackyStar: What happens if a telepath breaks your rules and does something really hideous with his or her powers?

Karen: A council is brought together to judge the accused. If he/she is guilty, punishment is served according to the severity of the crime and then he/she is handed over to the proper authorities. We do not shelter criminals of any kind, regardless of telepathic ability.

MaiaWorld: How many crooks have you caught with your powers?

Karen: Altogether, on a Federal and local level: Nineteen.

Bond007: Where do you all live? Is there someplace safe for telepaths to go?

Karen: Telepaths pretty much live wherever they want. We have places that some make their permanent home while others just go there as retreats, to get away from the world and recharge their batteries, so to speak.

Havnfun56: The world's changing, but not at a fast enough rate, in my not-so-humble opinion. I just wanted to say that I know a couple of telepaths and you're all the best! I'm proud to call them friend and wish I could meet you in person.

Karen: Thank you so much! I really love to hear things like that!

Lyttle1: Are you the telepaths' leader? If not, how does he/she feel about you doing this whole article thing when no telepaths ever have before?

Karen: Telepaths haven't really spoken out before because, as a whole, we believed it wouldn't make things any better. I don't have the complete support of the telepath community, but so far it's been a more positive reaction than not.

Janeygrrl: What's the ratio of women to men telepaths? Does it seem to happen more in one gender than in another? If so, what powers go with which gender?

Karen: Actually, I never thought to ask that, so I'm not sure. Off the top of my head, though, I'd have to say that it's a pretty even distribution. You'd think that the intuitive powers would reside mostly with women, but that's not true. Some of our strongest empaths are men. On the flip side, some of our strongest teleporters and manifesters are women.

Those are all the questions that we have space for today. At the end of each upcoming article, we'll be including three questions.

EVEN IN THE busy, bustling noise of the bullpen, Becky's irritated voice carried clearly. Becky glared at Genie, knowing the other woman was amused by the whole situation, even if she only heard part of the conversation. Wishing she could wring Jonas' neck through the phone line, she said flatly, "There is no way."

Jonas pleaded, "But, Becky, the response to this has been huge! You can't just drop us like this!"

Rolling her eyes at his overly dramatic tone, Becky reminded, "I didn't even want to agree to as much as I did, remember?"

"But you did! And look at all the good that you've already done just by being straight with people. The number of 'burn in hell' e-mails has dropped thirty percent since we first started this. Your point of view is getting across to the public, they're finally starting to see telepaths as regular people, not devils and demons," he argued persuasively.

Becky wondered briefly if banging her head against her desk would help. "I have too much going on right now as it is. I wouldn't have even taken your call, but you had your editor call my captain. That's a little childish, don't you think, Jonas?"

"I use what works," he dismissed. "I know you're under the gun, but so am I."

"Is anyone going to die if you miss your deadline?"

After a startled silence, he replied, "Ah, no, definitely not. Look, just consider it, okay? I'll give you time to think, but we need to strike while the iron's hot, you know?"

"Well, considering that there's another week before the articles you already have finish their run, you've got time."

"Not as much as you think."

"I'm going now, Jonas. I might call you when I have time enough to do more than just breathe, all right?"

"Sure. Thanks."

Becky hung up without saying goodbye. She didn't even need to look to know there was a grin on her partner's face and warned, "Don't you say a word."

"Who, me?" Genie asked innocently.

She glanced over at the other woman; the suspected grin was definitely in evidence if one knew how to look, which, of course, Becky did. "Yeah, you. He wants me to keep going with the whole telepath article thing, turn it into a weekly Q&A column with the occasional feature article."

"Well, why not?"

Horrified, Becky demanded, "Why not?"

"Sure. You said yourself that there's not enough info out there for us regular folks."

"Like you're a regular folk."

Frowning, Genie replied, "Thanks, I think."

"Curtains! Marshall! My office. Now!"

Becky thumped her head against her desk and moaned, "I can't take this right now, I really can't."

"Cheer up. One way or another, it'll all be over in a week."

"You aren't helping," Becky commented flatly, standing and heading for the Captain's office. She took one look at his face and winced internally. That particular expression never boded well. According to Genie, it had heralded more than one detective's return to beat status.

Genie beat her to the punch with, "Yeah, boss?"

"Mind telling me why you found it necessary to pull duty on these people?" Carlson demanded, waving papers furiously at them.

Genie defended their actions quickly, pointing out, "Look, most firebugs stick around, and these three are the only ones who have no *obvious* reason for being there. They don't live there, and it's not a business or retail district so they couldn't have a business meeting in the area. And Becky sensed the asshole behind this entire situation was there at, or near, the time of the explosion. It's a legitimate call, boss."

"Yeah, well, the only problem is that they've *all* got friends in high places," Carlson snapped.

Sympathetic but firm, Becky said, "We figured, but there's really no help for that."

Leaning back in his chair, the Captain eyed them hard for a few seconds, then nodded. "All right. Go on and interview them, but do me a favor and do it one at a time, all right? Get them done and get them *gone*."

"Got it, Captain," Becky agreed, standing up.

They left the office and returned to their desks. Sitting down, Genie asked, "Who do you want to chat with first?"

Becky looked down at the files on her desk and opened the one on top. The file ID photo revealed a handsome man, if one discounted the stony expression. Tapping the photo, she said, "I like him for it. Let's go visit the Colonel."

THE RIDE TO the Army base took about a half-hour and when they got there, it was another fifteen minutes before they could even get through security to the colonel's office. Once there, they were waylaid by the colonel's secretary and told to wait.

"Look. We need to talk with Lt. Colonel Jackson about a murder investigation," Genie informed the woman.

The young officer didn't look impressed. "He's on an important conference call and can't be disturbed. You can sit or stand, but you're not getting in to see him until he's done."

Scowling, Genie was about to make a rude comment when Becky grabbed her arm and overrode her. "Thank you for your help, Corporal. We'll just have a seat."

After sitting in the hard plastic chairs a few feet away, Genie asked, "What are you doing?"

Becky grinned and leaned close to whisper, "She's about to get a surprise visit. Just wait."

A few seconds later, the door opened and an older man in uniform, with a number of medals on said uniform, entered. The young woman snapped to her feet and saluted. He glanced over at Genie and Becky before looking back at the corporal. "These women are here to interview the Lt. Colonel."

"Yes, Sir, but he's..."

"No buts, Corporal. Interrupt him immediately."

"Yes, Sir!"

Becky stood and walked over to him with a smile, holding out her hand. "General Adley?"

He took it and nodded. "Detective Curtains. It's good to finally meet you. How's young Jack doing?"

Genie's eyebrows rose in surprise.

"Jack's doing great," Becky answered. "This is my partner, Detective Genie Marshall."

They shook hands. "So you're the one he insulted, is that right?"

Genie shrugged. "Didn't feel like much of an insult at the time, but I guess."

"Well, my grandson is a bit precocious, so I'm not really surprised. I kept telling his mother that she spoiled him, but what do I know?" General Adley commented dryly.

The office door opened and Lt. Colonel Jackson came out, accompanied by the corporal. In person, there was a commanding presence that couldn't be denied. His eyes were intense and alive as they looked over the detectives. "Good afternoon, Detectives. How can I help you?"

The moment Becky shook his hand, she jerked back, shot through with power so strong and evil, it made lightning pale by comparison. Joel and Daniel immediately came to her defense, but the assailant was already inside their defenses. She reeled under his assault and couldn't fight back under the vicious strike. Everywhere she looked was darkness and despair. The physical world vanished under his onslaught and she staggered blindly through the world between planes, unable to find her way back.

GENIE REACHED INSTINCTIVELY for Becca even before her partner crumpled towards the floor. She grunted on catching her partner's full weight, carefully lowering Becca to the floor.

"Corporal! Call for a medic!" General Adley exclaimed.

The young woman instantly complied.

Genie looked up, pinning the rather pale Lt. Colonel with a glare. "Put him under arrest!"

"For what? Shaking a woman's hand?" Lt. Colonel Jackson demanded.

Adley gave him a warning look. "Why don't you go back to your office? Obviously, Detective Marshall is distressed by your presence."

The other man's lips tightened unpleasantly, but he obeyed.

Genie waited tensely for the ambulance to arrive, running her fingers soothingly through Becca's hair. Closing her eyes, Genie tried to relax enough to make some kind of contact with Becca but there was absolutely nothing there to grab hold of. She couldn't even feel the twins, though she would have expected them to be out in force during such dire circumstances. When the paramedics arrived, she reluctantly released Becca into their care, not knowing what else to do.

"I'm sure she'll be fine," Adley said. "She's a strong woman, or so everyone keeps telling me. Hadn't met her before today."

Genie nodded absently but kept her eyes on the men working on Becca. Finally concluding there was nothing obviously wrong with the detective, they loaded her onto a stretcher to be brought to the hospital. Genie followed them out of the office and down the hall, keeping pace.

At the building exit, Adley requested, "Let me know how she is."

Waving briefly at him, Genie rushed to her Jeep to get to the hospital. She had just pulled out her cell when it started ringing. "Marshall."

"What is going on? Joel and Daniel just collapsed!" Sharon demanded from the other end.

"Shit!" Genie exclaimed. She'd been hoping that they had some kind of lock on Becca, that they would somehow keep her safe. Genie turned on the engine and then her sirens as she pulled out. "I think that she just met the bastard who's been attacking her. We were about to question him about his latest game when she collapsed. She's on her way to the hospital now."

"I'll be on the next flight."

"Thanks," Genie said, suddenly grateful for the other woman's unswerving devotion to Becca. "What do I do in the meantime?"

"Just stay as close to her as they'll let you. Try to keep physical contact and use that bond of yours to reach her."

"I tried!" Genie exclaimed. She maneuvered around a too-slow car by inches, scaring the other driver, who jerked in the other direction abruptly.

"Just stay calm and be there. She'll always reach out for you, Genie, as long as you're there," Sharon stated firmly.

"All right. As soon as I can, I'll be at her side," Genie replied, taking a deep, calming breath.

There was a short, explosive sigh from the other end just before Sharon told her, "If Joel and Daniel come around, I'll bring them with me."

"Call when you get here."

She put the phone away and concentrated on her driving.

Chapter
Twenty-Four

GENIE STARED THROUGH the small window into Becca's ICU room one last time. The small woman was tubed and IV'd and had EKG wires stuck to her head. She looked like something out of a very bad, very old, horror movie. As Genie turned away and strode down the hall, Sharon rushed to catch up.

The older woman grabbed Genie's arm, forcing her to stop short, and demanded angrily, "Where are you going? Becca needs you *here*. You're her only link to the real world!"

"My being here is useless!" Genie snarled. "I'm going to do something about this, what I should've done when this whole thing started."

Sharon gave her a wary look, as if sensing the darkness that lurked close to the surface. "What are you planning to do?"

Genie tore her arm free. "Beat some answers out of the only person who seems to know what the *fuck* is going on."

Stunned, and looking not a little scared by the violence promised in Genie's voice and eyes, Sharon let her go.

THE SHADOWS KISSED her, welcoming her return as Genie moved silently through them. It was a world she'd given up years ago, and yet now it seemed as though she'd never left. Dressed in black, with her hair wrapped in a concealing, matching skullcap, Genie stalked towards her destination. None of this world's denizens so much as even glanced in her direction. If they did chance to see her, they still wouldn't really see her because this was the red zone. Anything you wanted could happen here if you had either the money to buy it, or the strength to take it. If you had both, you were damned near unstoppable.

Tonight, Genie planned to be unstoppable.

Reaching a dilapidated door guarded by a large bruiser, Genie pulled out a hundred and held it out. He took it and stepped aside. She walked into the underground club, the third one she'd been to that night. She came a little closer to her quarry every time, got a little more information.

The music was retro and raucous, a hard-edged rock-n-roll, almost metal, and it assaulted her ears like a sonic weapon. The bodies were plentiful, and hot, and scantily clad, despite the cool temperature outside. Genie seriously doubted that anyone there felt anything at all, never mind the cold. She smelled the drugs wafting through the air and it teased her senses, calling her to slow down and enjoy them, sample the pleasures of the world she'd denied herself for the last decade.

Ignoring everything except the driving need to save her partner, Genie cut a swath through the writhing throng of dancers. A few neatly placed elbows and several swiftly executed boots to the back of knees cleared her a path, even if it did make it easy to track her progress across the dance floor. She knew that her prey was there and that he was convinced that he had the upper hand. She wondered briefly if he would even bother with bodyguards, but didn't really care.

She would get in to see him and demand that he tell her everything. Genie would put up with this information blackout not a minute longer. She should've taken care of it the second the investigation had turned personal. She should have hunted him down after the first attack against Becca. He'd been teasing her all along with the murder tips, saying, "Look what I can do, and you can't." He'd been determined to keep her in the dark, and deliberately made it as difficult as possible to find him. But now he was off-guard and she fully intended to take advantage of that.

Genie reached the stairs that led to the private rooms above the dance area and pulled off her cap, letting her hair fall free. Unzipping her leather jacket exposed her throat and a small amount of cleavage. She didn't know which room he was in, but it wouldn't be hard to find out. When the door closed behind her, the music lowered to an almost human level and she paused a moment to adjust. Genie looked around to get her bearings and spied two men standing guard outside a door halfway down the hall.

Striding over, she came to a stop before them. "I want to see him. You can let me in, or go to the hospital. Your choice."

The guards looked at her like she was crazy; both were half a head taller and outweighed her by a good fifty pounds. One of them said, "No one sees him without an appointment."

Genie stepped forward and looked up at him coyly. "Oh, come on, you won't let me in to see him?"

He shook his head with a grin. "I just knew that a pretty thing like you..."

That was as far as he got, because her elbow slammed into his windpipe the moment his guard dropped, and he collapsed a split second later. She kicked the other in the crotch and he, too, dropped like a stone. She kicked them both in the head, knocking them out to make sure they didn't come in unexpectedly, or call for help.

Pulling out her gun, Genie stepped silently inside the room and looked around, her gaze not missing a single opulent adornment, or the scent of drugs burned into the air. On a large, satin-clad bed, a woman was in the throes of what Genie hoped was a fake orgasm, because it sounded too painful to be real. Shaking her head in distaste, Genie reached the bed and put her gun to the woman's head, who stopped moving the instant the cold muzzle touched her temple.

Genie met the amused amber eyes of the man on the bed as he ordered the woman, "Get off me and don't bother calling for help, I'll be fine. You might want to get some medical help for Jeff and Nick, though. Right, Genie?"

Nodding, Genie put the gun back in her holster and stepped out of the way as the woman scrambled off the bed and grabbed a robe on her way out of the room.

"So. What brings you to my humble abode?"

"Cut the shit, Bowen, and tell me who he is."

Bowen grinned and rolled lithely off the bed, unconcerned with nudity as he walked to the bar across the room. The dim light in the room played well off his muscled body and caught the highlights of his golden-brown hair. "No small talk? You don't even want to know how I've been since we last saw each other?"

"I know how you've been doing, remember?"

"Oh, that's right. You do like to keep an eye on me, don't you?" he observed archly. "Still, it's been a long time since we've had a face-to-face. I thought you vowed never to come back here. That you were going to, what did you say? Oh yes, you were going to 'get out of this fucking hellhole' and that you'd 'kill yourself before ever stepping foot down here again.' Well. Since you're here, and not a ghost, I can only assume that something drastic has happened and you've come to your little brother for help."

Without a word, Genie crossed the distance between them, pulling out her gun as she walked, and held it underneath his chin. Keeping her eyes on his, Genie said, "I won't ask again, Bowen. You're going to tell me who this man is, and where I can find him."

"You would kill me over this?" he asked curiously.

In answer, she cocked the hammer and pressed the muzzle harder into his Adam's apple.

"Huh. All right, Genie, all right, I'll tell you who it is. But you owe me for this, agreed?"

Genie uncocked the hammer and re-holstered it in one smooth motion. "Agreed."

Bowen returned to fixing his drink as he spoke, seemingly unconcerned with the fact that she could have killed him; or that she might still. "I don't actually know his name, just that he's in the army and really high-ranked. He comes down here to blow off steam. And let me tell you, the girls who go with him don't usually come back. Since they're all crack-whores, though, no one really cares."

Genie took out the picture of Lt. Colonel Jackson. "This him?"

After glancing at the photo for a moment, Bowen shook his head. "Nope."

In a hard voice, Genie demanded, "Are you sure?"

"Yeah, I'm sure, Genie!" he exclaimed, exasperated. "Christ! You come in here, assault my best guards, and best friends I might add, probably into the hospital, pull me out of a very enjoyable interlude at gunpoint, threaten to kill me, and then doubt me? That's not him! He's older than that, for one. Has a bit of a gut and less hair. Looks like a grandfather type, unless you're either between him and something he wants, or happen to be the something he wants. If it's either situation, you're pretty well screwed."

"God damn it!" she shouted, spinning and punching the wall so hard that her fist broke the plaster. If it wasn't Jackson, then they didn't have a clue as to who it could be.

"Genie, Genie! Calm down. You're not going to do anyone any good getting all hyped up like that. You losing control is not a good thing, remember?" Bowen reminded, warily stepping back.

Taking a few deep breaths, Genie brought her rage and frustration under control. Bowen was right. Becca didn't have time for her to have a hissy fit. "How do you know when he's going to kill?"

Bowen shrugged, gulping back the liquor. "He tells me after the fact. Likes to brag. Except for that last time. He was bragging ahead of time for whatever reason, almost like he wanted to advertise."

Snarling silently to herself, Genie ordered, "If he sets one toe in any of your joints, I want to know. If any of your people see him, I want to know. And you're going to put together a composite sketch so I know who he is."

Bowen's laugh was short and hard. "You want to use me as a witness? Now there's a first. Good luck getting the DA to accept my word over that of some general."

Genie gave him a wolfish grin and asked, "Who said anything about going to the DA?"

SITTING AT BECCA'S bedside, Genie rubbed her eyes tiredly. It had been almost fourteen hours since her partner's collapse, and she had nothing. Every minute she sat here, Becca slipped further and further from reality, and without her mind, her body was dying. There was just nothing the doctors could do except treat each system failure as it happened. There was no such thing as a cure in this case, other than Becca coming back.

Genie felt them before the soft tapping at the door and stood, turning to greet Joel and Daniel as they entered the room. They enfolded her in their arms and for a few minutes, Genie felt hope, blanketed not by their strength of body, but by their strength of will. Relieved, she thought, *You're all right. I'm so glad.*

We're fine, Joel answered silently, kissing her cheek warmly.

We thought you'd gone off the deep end, Daniel commented, a hint of scolding in his thoughts.

Ducking her head, Genie admitted, *I did, just a little. But I got some useful information out of it.*

Nothing is more useful than getting her back, Daniel pointed out.

Genie sighed and pulled away. She wondered briefly why she wasn't freaking out by the sudden ability to have an actual, mind-to-mind conversation, then decided that she just didn't have the energy. She could freak out later, when her partner's life wasn't hanging by a thread. Just then, she would use every advantage she could get. "I know. Don't suppose either of you care to explain how I can hear your thoughts, when Becca says I can't do that with anyone but her?"

Both men looked startled, as if the thought hadn't occurred to them.

Daniel replied, "It's a good question, but one that can wait for later."

Genie nodded and they all walked to the bed where Becca was fighting for control of her own mind. Just as they took position around the bed, a nurse came in.

"What's going on here? You can't all be here!" she exclaimed, moving towards the call button.

Genie intercepted her and maneuvered her into a headlock, increasing pressure on the windpipe until the woman dropped unconscious into her arms. With Joel's help, she put the nurse in the bed beside Becca. Looking at the men, Genie said, "We don't have a lot of time before she comes to."

They took up position once more and joined hands.

Just close your eyes and think of Becky, Daniel ordered silently. *Think of your bond, your connection, as though it's a physical cord wrapped around your wrist. Imagine that the other end is tied to Becky and you can use it to find her. Just let go of your physical self and follow where the cord leads. We're here to protect and help, to guide and care for you while you do the same for Becky.*

Joel picked up the narration without missing a beat. *She needs you and is looking for a way back. That tie will bring you right to her, if you let it. The two of you are bound together in ways that most people spend their lives looking for. Soul to soul, mind to mind, you exist for each other, to help one another on the Great Path that we all stumble along.*

Listening to the soothing cadence of their thoughts, Genie felt the heavy rope form around her wrist. The rope was rough and scratchy around her tender skin, formed that way by her thoughts as that had always seemed the strongest kind of rope to her. The kind that was used to keep the old navy ships docked: big, and heavy, and strong enough to keep tons and tons of metal in check.

It was stuck fast to something on the other end and, keeping her eyes closed, Genie tugged on it, following it in the hopes of finding Becca. It was strange, moving through her mind like this, like being in a too-warm pool of water that clung almost uncomfortably to her. She went hand over hand, pulling her way through the darkness to whatever lay on the other side of the rope.

That walk through the dark seemed to take forever and was unlike anything else she'd experienced. It almost felt like she was walking in circles, which was entirely possible given the minefield that was her subconscious. Or was she in Becca's subconscious now? Had she already crossed over, or would she stay in her own mind, useless and unable to reach Becca, let alone bring her partner back?

The futility of what she was doing dragged at her. She was no telepath. Even Becca had said that there was no ability except in conjunction with her. She was inadequate to this particular task because of an accident of birth. She was just a normal human being with no special gifts, nothing to make her unique. Her past of violence was coming back to haunt her now, because she knew that she wasn't good enough to save Becca.

Despair coursed through her as she realized that she, too, was now caught in the snare. She'd succumbed to the darkness and was just as lost as her partner. Joel and Daniel were nowhere to be found, their voices gone. That was when she felt the absence of the rope as well and knew that there was no way back. She was trapped as surely as Becca.

"Becca! Becca, help me!"

GENIE'S FEARFUL SCREAM tore through the darkness and arrowed straight to Becky's heart and soul. Without hesitation, she flew towards it, desperate to reach her partner. Suddenly, she could see everything: all the pitfalls, and all the traps. It was illuminated as clear as day, and Becky could not only see her way back, she saw Genie stumbling around blindly, her eyes closed tightly with her hands stretched out in front.

Reaching her partner, Becky wrapped herself around Genie, feeling her incredible depth of emotion and personality and whispered, "It's all right, Genie, open your eyes."

Hope blossomed onto the other woman's face as she whispered back, "Becca?"

"It's me, partner, now open your eyes. C'mon, it's a simple thing you do every day," Becky urged.

Slowly, Genie's eyes opened.

BECKY COULD NOT get rid of the sensation of the tube in her throat, even though it had been replaced with an oxygen mask. The ice chips Genie had given her helped, but the raw skin hurt every time she swallowed. Her body felt like it had been battered to a pulp, and her breathing was still inconsistent. All this for just seventeen hours of being in la-la land.

"What're you thinking?" Genie asked softly.

Meeting her eyes, Becky answered, "That the body-mind balance is a very fragile one and I hurt like hell."

Smiling faintly, Genie said, "At least you're here to hurt like hell."

"Case," Becky agreed with a grin. She closed her eyes, yawning, and continued, "Glad you found me, partner."

"Hey, you found me, remember?"

Becky reached out with her hand and it was immediately taken by Genie's larger one. "We found each other."

"We certainly did."

Excerpt from Rebecca Curtains' Journal—Year One

Genie thinks I'm nuts for going back to work tomorrow, but we don't have enough time for me to lounge around when really, there isn't anything wrong with me that a new psyche wouldn't fix. Talk about fodder for nightmares for years to come. God. Wandering around in that black nothing is something I never, ever want to go through again!

That scream from Genie scared the hell out of me! Once I found her, I wrapped myself around her and drank her in. And yeah, that was taking liberties, so sue me. All I knew at the time was that I was never more relieved to 'see' someone in my life.

I still haven't figured out exactly what happened. The one thing I do know is that Jackson wasn't the cause of that insanity. Was it just convenient timing or are we being watched? Oh, now there's a pleasant thought! It would make sense, though. This bastard knows that we're on to him, so he wants to cast suspicion onto someone else. After all, you can't be the best without getting away scot-free. I'll have to tell Genie, but she's going to be furious about this little revelation, she's such a private person.

God. Genie...

What am I going to do? Sharon keeps after me to tell her how I feel, but I can't, I can't. I can't risk losing her as a friend and partner for the slim chance that she might feel more for me. If she does, shit...if she does feel more, then she's a damn sight better at hiding it than I am. I mean, I know she cares about me, I'm her best friend. But anything more than that is wishful thinking on my part.

It's a way of thinking that I'm going to get over. This latest rescue she did for me is not going to lead me any deeper than I already am.

Oh, who the hell am I kidding?

Chapter
Twenty-Five

THE NEXT MORNING, Becky went through security as quickly as possible, anxious to get to work. She was still a little sore, her voice a bit rusty, but otherwise, a good night's sleep seemed to have gotten her back on track.

"Hey Curtains, good to see you."

Becky looked up from digging in her bag at the comment from a slightly familiar-looking officer. "Ah, thanks. You too."

A little further down the hall, a homicide detective she barely knew greeted her with, "Glad you're back, Curtains."

Becky smiled vaguely and replied, "Thanks."

By the time she made it to her desk, almost every other person she came across had greeted her with a friendly smile and kind words. Sitting, Becky leaned forward on her desk and asked sotto voce, "Did I win the lottery or something?"

Snorting, Genie met her gaze. "If you did, can I have half?"

"Ah, sure," Becky agreed absently, still looking around.

"Hey, Becky! How're you feeling?" Mathisen asked on his way past their desks.

"Fine. Thanks," Becky answered, though she really felt like she'd stepped into the Twilight Zone. Why was everyone being so nice? Not that people were mean to her or anything, it was just that they weren't ever *this* nice, and certainly not so many of them. Glancing over at her partner, Becky was relieved to see the other woman engrossed in a case file, looking and acting perfectly normal.

Finally pulling her attention from the file, Genie leaned back in her chair with a faint smile. "So, you got some interesting information while you were out."

"Oh?" Becky prompted.

"Oh yeah. I took the liberty of going through your e-mails, knowing how you like to keep up-to-date on them," Genie teased.

Becky grinned and flipped her the bird.

"You got a response from State Records. The owner of Lincoln Towers is another corporation called Gerhardt Nichols, Inc. which is in turn owned by Jasper Co. Ring a bell?"

Frowning, Becky leaned back in her chair and confirmed, "Yeah, but I can't place it."

Genie tossed the file in her hand across the desk to Becky, who picked it up. Opening it, she scanned the page and felt her jaw drop at the information revealed on the page. "You're shitting me!"

Grinning broadly, Genie replied, "I shit you not."

"So, what do you want to do? I know you were a bit, ah, wary about going after Doyle," Becky commented, closing the file.

A feral glint entered the amber eyes looking intently at Becky. "Yeah, well, that was before he signed up with the bastard attacking my partner. Now I'm not saying that we take out a full-page ad that he's a suspect or anything, but we should at least go and pay Mr. Doyle a visit."

"We should probably tell the Captain what's going on," Becky said slowly, glancing at the office across the way.

Pursing her lips, Genie looked towards the closed door as well before standing up. "I dunno. Looks really busy to me. Wouldn't want to interrupt, now, would we?"

Getting her partner's drift, Becky agreed, "No, of course not. He hates to be interrupted."

They actually made it to the department door before Carlson called their names.

Grimacing, Genie muttered, "I swear to God the man's got radar!"

"Almost made it," Becky sighed.

Turning back, they walked to his office, Becky shutting the door behind them. Taking in the Captain's stance, with his arms crossed over his chest, and his closed expression , Becky felt her stomach sink. There was something more going on than their trying to sneak out without letting him know. "What's wrong?"

"I need your gun and badge, Detective," Carlson said gruffly.

"What?" Genie exploded.

"Someone tipped off the Powers That Be about the real focus of our killer. I just got off the phone with the Commissioner," he explained. "They're going to start an investigation into 'irresponsible and reckless endangerment of the public at large.' "

"Son of a bitch!" Genie swore.

Becky only sighed and unclipped her badge from her belt and put it, with her gun, on the Captain's desk. "We knew this would happen, Genie."

Glaring at them both, Genie exclaimed, "But we're so close! Captain, can't you say that you didn't see us before we left? Harry Doyle, by way of several dummy corporations, is the one footing the bill for Belladonna and Aldonis. We were just going over to question him and see what shakes loose."

"Oh yeah. Now there's a plan. I let you go out there and then two seconds after you finish roughing Doyle up, I get another call from the Commish, only this time, it's *my* badge," Carlson predicted sourly. "You know, if I didn't know any better, I'd swear that you were trying to dig me an early grave. Since I do—"

"Captain..."

Carlson's glare was enough to shut Genie up. "As I was saying, since I do know better, I'm going to make like you were late this morning, like you always are whenever I need to talk to you. Both of you."

Startled by the unexpected boon, Becky grabbed her badge and gun from the desk, then Genie's arm, and dragged her partner out of the office with a hasty, "Thanks, Captain!"

"Don't make me regret this!" he shouted after their retreating forms.

They moved quickly and silently through the department to the garage. Becky waited impatiently for Genie to unlock the Jeep doors, almost expecting someone to run after them and stop them. Once inside, Genie started the Jeep and tore out of the parking spot, slowing only around the corners while Becky held onto her seat belt and the dashboard for her life.

Once on the road, Becky demanded, "Are you trying to get us killed?"

"Not yet," Genie answered, eyebrows wriggling comically.

Becky huffed in amusement and told her, "I think you should do the talking when we get there."

"How come?"

"If I do it, he'll be too on edge to let anything slip."

"You want *me* to be subtle?"

Chuckling, Becky commented, "Hey, I've seen you among the rich and somewhat infamous. This is not beyond your acting abilities."

"All right, but don't hold it against me if I wind up decking him."

"If you deck him, the Captain gets in trouble, remember?"

"Damn it. Thanks for the reminder." Genie's phone rang just then and she pulled it out of her pocket. "Hello? Hang on."

Becky looked at her curiously as Genie hooked up the phone to play through the speakers. Once set, she continued, "What do you have?"

"General Randall Helms. He's your guy."

"Thanks, I owe you."

"I'll remember that."

Dry, Genie muttered, "I'm sure you will," before disconnecting and putting the phone away.

Becky pulled out her PDA to run a search for information on the suspect the moment his name was uttered. A few minutes later, an extensive file came up and she frowned. "I have never seen, or heard, of this man before in my life. He's certainly never been at any of the Centers."

With a snort, Genie asked, "So you know every telepath who walks through the door?"

Becky made a face at her partner. "Well, no, of course not. But if he had been to any of the Centers, I would have heard about it."

Curious, Genie asked, "Why?"

"How many two-star generals do *you* know that are telepaths?" Becky pointed out dryly.

"Case."

"Anyhow. It says here that he's been missing for the last week. His assistant reported him missing to the base last Tuesday and there's been a quiet search going on ever since."

"A 'quiet' search? How come?"

"He failed his a psych exam last month, pretty badly, from what this says. Looks like our boy is starting to seriously unravel."

"If we had evidence tying him to the scene, we could snag a warrant on the fly and search his place."

"What about your informant?" Becky asked. "Would he have an idea where Helms would hole up?"

Shaking her head, Genie looked briefly out of the side window before gazing back at the road in front. "Can't use him. First, he's not registered. And the reason he's not registered is because he's nowhere near a credible witness; not with his business practices."

"Yeah, but..."

"We can't use him!"

Startled by the vehemence, Becky leaned back against the door and stared at the other woman. Lips pursed thoughtfully, she accepted, "All right, then. We'll go to Doyle's, like planned, and see what turns up."

Genie sighed. "I'm sorry, Becca, I didn't mean to snap."

"It's okay."

"No, it's not."

Becky half-smiled. "Okay, it's not. But you're forgiven."

THE OFFICE BUILDING that housed UnderTEM's headquarters was a glass and metal monstrosity of thoroughly modern design, which in Genie's opinion, meant no style at all. They showed their badges at the security desk and suffered through the security check. She waited tensely for Becky's revoked status to come up, but fortunately, it didn't. The Captain must have been able to keep it off the city books; for the time being, at least.

They rode up to the top floor in a comfortable silence. Becky stood nearly touching her side, a solid block of warmth that Genie soaked in like a sponge. Her emotions were way too near the surface for comfort. The confrontation with Bowen two days ago had taken a lot out of her, not to mention getting lost in the darkness of her own mind. Between all that *and* the fact that they wanted to take Becky away from her, Genie felt like she was going to explode.

She just hoped that she could hold it together long enough to question Doyle without beating him to a pulp.

AFTER WAITING WHILE the assistant announced their arrival, Genie and Becca walked into Doyle's office.

He stood from behind his desk and smiled, greeting, "Good morning, Detectives. This is certainly a surprise."

"I'm sure it is," Genie replied. "We just had a couple questions for you regarding a current investigation. If you have the time, that is?"

Nodding, Doyle motioned for them to sit on one of the leather sofas and then did the same. "Of course. What can I help you with?"

Genie pulled out a small notebook computer and touched an electronic pen to it. "I was wondering if you know of a corporation by the name of Jasper Co.?"

Though he maintained a smile, it suddenly looked just a bit thinner. "Yes, of course. It's a subsidiary of UnderTEM focused on helping needy families."

"That's a very worthy cause, Mr. Doyle. I didn't realize that UnderTEM was so humanitarian," Becca commented, sounding surprised.

Doyle paused for a moment, then took advantage of the seeming diversion. "Why, yes. There are a number of causes we espouse that I'm sure would meet with your approval."

"Such as?" Her dry tone was unmistakable.

Apparently determined to keep their attention on other things, he launched into a public-service-style bull session talking about everything except Jasper Co., and going into great detail.

About halfway through, Genie noticed Becca's eyes glaze over in a not-so-subtle invitation for more and grinned to herself when Doyle fell for it and poured the PR campaign on even thicker. Every so often he glanced at her, but Genie kept a politely interested expression in place. She used the opportunity to look around the office when his attention was focused on Becca and made mental notes when he mentioned two of the four dummy corporations they were investigating. There were no new names of people, unfortunately, but when Doyle wrapped it up about a half-hour later, Genie knew they had enough verifiable connections to get warrants to search his records.

"And there's so much more that we do, I could go on forever, but I'm sure you have more important things to do," Doyle finished, still smiling.

Genie straightened a bit, wondering if he practiced that smile in a mirror for hours at a time, and said, "Thank you, Mr. Doyle, that was, very informative. We appreciate you taking the time to speak with us."

"Not at all, it's my pleasure," Doyle assured them with what looked to be a genuine smile. He walked them to the door and continued, "If you wish to know anything more, I have some more time to go over..."

Genie interrupted hastily, "I don't think that'll be necessary. But if we do need anything further, we'll call you."

"Of course, of course," he agreed.

Genie didn't miss the flash of alarm over Doyle's face as a man walked towards them, though it was quickly hidden. She was left with the impression of practically nothing at all, while looking at the newcomer, which set off all kinds of mental alarms.

Becca was right behind her as she left. Genie's last glimpse of Doyle before the door closed was the unknown man entering the office through another door. She shared a grin with Becca, but didn't say anything as they headed for the elevators. They'd gotten more than what they'd come for and she hadn't even had to beat it out of him.

Genie was pretty sure she was disappointed about that.

"I KNOW HIM," Becky mused, closing the Jeep door and putting on her seat belt.

"The spook?"

"Noticed him too, did you?"

Genie snorted. "Kinda hard to miss. I haven't seen anyone more uninteresting since, well, for a long time."

Becky looked at her curiously, but didn't question the cut-off statement. She pulled out her cell phone and dialed the number to her old partner's office at the FBI building.

"Special Agent Tyler."

"Hey, Ty, it's Becky."

"Becky! I thought you went and fell off the earth!" Rick Tyler exclaimed from the other end.

"Just about," Becky agreed with a grin. "Hey, you busy?"

"Should've known you'd be calling about work."

"Yeah, well, at least I called, right?"

"Right. What do you need?"

"I just ran into someone and can't remember who he is," Becky explained. "Think you can track down any agents who've dropped off the radar in the last eighteen months?"

"Yeah, sure. Which agency?"

"Any of them."

"When do you need the info?"

"ASAP."

Rick groaned. "That figures. Not like I have any of my own cases to work on."

"Thanks, Rick, I owe you and Mara dinner for this," Becky promised.

She could hear the grin in his voice as he finagled, "And the kids."

"And the kids," Becky agreed before hanging up.

"Rick Tyler, as in your old partner at the Bureau."

Becky looked over at Genie, surprised by the tightness in her partner's voice. "That's right. He can track down information like a bloodhound. I'd do it myself, but we can't exactly go into the office right now. Problem?"

"Nope. Not at all," Genie answered, turning on the car.

Wondering about the odd behavior, Becky let it go and suggested, "I think we should hang out and follow Mr. Ghosty."

"What if he goes nowhere? We don't have a lot of time to waste."

"True, but what other leads do we have?"

With a sigh, Genie conceded, "Case."

IT WAS TWO hours later that Becky's phone rang. "Detective Curtains."

"It's me," Rick greeted.

Straightening, Becky asked, "What've you got?"

"We've got four agents who've vanished in the last eighteen months. The first one is Hank Winders. He's forty-three, dark hair and eyes and an explosives expert. He disappeared about thirteen months ago."

"Next."

"Okay. Number two is Jack Myers, thirty-two, brown hair and eyes. He dropped out of sight nineteen months ago, but I figured it was close enough to your mark to include in the list."

As soon as Rick mentioned the name, Becky flashed onto a memory.

Walking down the hall at the FBI, her arms filled with case files, someone bumped into Becky and sent her papers flying. "Damn it!"

"Hey, sorry about that, let me help you."

Becky smiled politely, looking at the man who'd bumped into her, and refused, "That's okay, I've got it."

But he stooped and helped her pick it up anyhow, handing the last folder over with a flourish and then holding out his hand. "Jack Myers."

Thankful that her arms were full so she wouldn't have to shake, Becky said, "Becky Curtains. Thanks for the help."

"My fault in the first place. I'll see you around," Jack said before *continuing on his way.*

"Becky? Becky are you there?"

Shaking the memory away, Becky replied hastily, "What? Oh yeah, sorry. That's him, thanks, Rick. You pick the place and we'll all go out next week."

"All right. But you better be careful. This guy worked *deep* with the military on drug cartels. He's not only been around the block, he probably paved a few," Rick warned.

"Thanks, Rick. I appreciate the heads up," Becky said, hanging up. Turning to Genie, she said, "Well, imagine that. Mr. Doyle is associating with someone who used to work on military operations eliminating drug cartels."

Genie's fingers tapped restlessly on the steering wheel. "Lovely. Well, at least we've finally got a solid connection to this asshole now. Bowen said that the guy after you is military."

"Who's Bowen?"

"I ah, I didn't tell you about Bowen?"

Looking at her partner pointedly, Becky shook her head. "Not that I recall."

Offering a sickly smile, Genie said, "He's my informant. I went down to the Red Zone to get some information."

"Let me guess. You went alone, without any sort of backup."

"Well, it's not like I don't know my way around," Genie retorted defensively.

"That's not the freakin' point, Genie! Christ! When are you going to get it through your thick skull that you can't do that? That you're going to wind up dead if you keep going cowboy!" Becky exploded. She yanked off her seat belt and got out, stalking away.

Genie jumped out of the Jeep and rushed after her. The busy mid-day pedestrian traffic slowed her down, but after a few minutes, she grabbed Becky's arm and pulled her off to the side. "I'm sorry. I was worried about you and not thinking too clearly."

Glaring, Becky pulled her arm free and exclaimed, "That's not going to help me any when you get your head blown off one day because you conveniently forget to call for backup!"

Quietly, Genie explained, "It was the only thing I could think of to do. Look, you don't know everything about me, Becca. I can handle myself."

Becky tried to keep herself under control. "I know, I know. But that's not going to help any if someone clocks you, or shoots you, from behind."

"I can't get into this right now, not with what we have to do. Not if I want to have any kind of emotional detachment here, all right?" Genie asked plaintively. She reached out and hesitantly cupped

Becky's face in her palm, moving closer. "I just, I don't want to lose you over this, or anything. I won't do anything like that again."

Staring into Genie's golden eyes, Becky felt her resolve begin to crumble in the face of her partner's need. She knew, without using even one iota of her abilities, what Genie wanted. Shaking her head, she denied, "Genie, we can't... We're partners. We can't be anything else."

Genie's hand pulled away as though on fire and she straightened to attention. "Right. Sorry. I, it won't happen again."

Becky silently screamed at herself, wanting to tell the world and its rules to go screw themselves, but nodded raggedly. Aside from the non-fraternization rules, they were in the middle of some serious crap at the moment. There just wasn't time to go into anything right then. As she looked away, she saw Myers coming right at them, though he hadn't yet spotted them. "Oh, shit!"

Before Genie could ask what the problem was, Becky grabbed her shirt, stepped back towards the building behind them, yanking Genie down into a kiss.

For a moment, Genie didn't respond, but then she dove into it with everything she had. Her arms wrapped around Becky's shoulders and she pressed her up against the wall. Becky's hands settled firmly on Genie's hips to keep her in place, mouth opening eagerly for more.

By the time Becky dragged her mouth away, they were both breathing heavily. Genie rested her forehead against Becky's and gasped, "I'm guessing that there's a reason behind you jumping me?"

Bringing her breathing somewhat under control, Becky nodded and pointed at Myer's retreating back. "He was, uh, was walking towards us."

"Ah. Right. Okay. Let's go see what Mr. Ghosty is up to."

Chapter
Twenty-Six

BOTH WOMEN SNAPPED back into cop-mode as they tracked Myers across the next few blocks. Fortunately, the lunch crowd was thick enough that they could merge into the back of a couple of groups when he got suspicious a couple of times and turned around. Myers headed into a low-rent warehouse district where they had to keep more and more space between them in order not to be spotted. That's when they lost him.

"I'm going to track him down," Becky murmured.

Genie nodded tensely, keeping an eye out the way Myers had disappeared.

Closing her eyes, Becky took a deep breath and cast her thoughts out, trying to pick him up. She moved around the empty street, hoping to cross his footpath and get centered on him. For a few long minutes, there was no sign and she finally opened her eyes in irritation. "Nothing."

Genie grinned fiercely and pulled out her weapon. "Then I guess we do this the old-fashioned way."

Becky shook her head in dark amusement, muttering, "You're having *way* too much fun here."

"Who, me?"

"Yeah, you."

Snickering evilly, Genie started walking and Becky fell into step beside her, pulling out her own gun as they moved. Becky looked right and back, as Genie looked left and up. The area they moved through was filled with abandoned, decrepit warehouses. The glass from many broken windows littered the ground, as did useless equipment and trash. Becky was positive that she didn't want to know the source of a nearby, extremely foul, smell.

This was the part about police work that Becky liked the least: being on high alert with every muscle tense and ready. It was the time where she had to prepare herself for the possibility that someone could die in a coming conflict; herself, the suspect, her partner, or all of them. It wasn't anything that she wanted to think about, but it was part of her preparation for what was sure to be a violent confrontation.

In the near-total silence, Becky heard her partner's breathing as well as the connection that flared between them on its own, but absolutely nothing from the man they chased. It was almost as though he'd vanished. Was he meeting with Helms somewhere out of sight, or just eluding them? A sense of being targeted ran through her and Becky tackled her partner, sending them both to the ground as gunshots went off. They reached the dubious cover of a large trash bin, each searching unsuccessfully for Myers' location.

"Shit! Where is he?" Genie demanded, looking everywhere she could from their hiding spot.

Becky listened, but had to shake her head. "Too many echoes. I can't get a lock."

"Me either. What about psychically?"

"I'll give it a shot," Becky said, then grimaced again at the pun.

Genie snorted darkly.

Closing her eyes as Genie's free hand rested solidly between her shoulder blades, Becky took in a deep breath and released it. Searching mentally for any sign of their attacker brought no results. There was another round of gunfire, a few of the bullets coming too close for comfort. Flinching, Becky's eyes opened as she huddled closer to Genie, waiting for the shooting to stop.

"Well, we know he's above us somewhere," Genie said, looking up to try and spy their assailant.

"Yeah, but where?"

"Damned if I know."

"Beautiful," Becky muttered. "So we're pinned down, and even if we call for backup, by the time it gets here, we'll be full of holes."

Cocking her head thoughtfully, Genie answered, "Maybe not."

Becky stared at her partner suspiciously. "What're you thinking?"

"That if we time this right, we could get to that overhang, next to that door," Genie answered, motioning towards the warehouse across the way.

"Genie, he can pick us off when we move."

But Genie already had her cell phone out and was dialing. They both flinched as another set of bullets created even more holes in their inadequate shelter. Covering her open ear, Genie said into the phone, "Yeah! I need some help. I'm at...where are we, Becca?"

After the next round of shots, even closer, Becky answered, "Sylvan and Heights NE are the nearest streets, I think."

"We're pinned by a sniper with a serious arsenal in an alley by Sylvan and Heights NE," Genie reported.

Becky waited, watching her partner for good news.

"Thanks. Uh, hurry."

An eternity of too-many bullets later, there was a major explosion that flattened them to the ground. Debris rained all around and, after a few woozy moments, Genie grabbed Becky and they staggered across the ally to the warehouse door. Leaning against the wall, breathing heavily, Genie gasped, "I do *not* want to know how a gang has access to those kinds of explosives."

Becky nodded emphatic agreement and put her finger in her still-ringing ears, moving it around, trying to alleviate the sudden pressure. It popped unexpectedly and she swore at the pain.

Genie grinned. "Impressive. Now what?"

"Now I'm going to find that sonuvabitch."

Wryly, Genie asked, "Which one?"

Becky grinned, feeling strangely free and unafraid. Whatever was going to happen, was going to happen and she would survive it or not. The only thing she really wanted to make sure of was that Genie got through it intact. "Smartass."

Genie peered out the nearest window and replied absently, "Always. And I don't see or hear him."

Sitting on the cold cement floor, Becky looked up at her partner. "This might take a while."

Hefting her gun, and pulling out her spare for extra measure, Genie moved so that her thigh pressed into Becky's back and assured her, "Take your time."

It was a few minutes before Becky could achieve the calm necessary to cast her thoughts out of her body. She wasn't sure exactly how it differed from what she normally did, since the results were pretty much the same, but it was almost like an aerial view-finder; like she was actually outside her body and seeing everything all at once. And, too, she didn't need to actually connect with whatever she was looking for.

It took far less time to locate her search-object than usual, but sucked out a lot of her strength. There was an unexpected echo of help from... Surprised, Becky found herself buoyed up by Sharon, Daniel, and Joel. She didn't spare any time to question their help, just used it to supplement her own failing strength. It took a few more minutes to locate Myers, who was trying to shake off the effects of the blast, which had happened a lot closer to him, than to them. Several rifles and extra clips of bullets lay around him. Sending a quick flash of gratefulness and love to the others, Becky pulled back into her body.

The sluggishness of her limbs told Becky that she'd been gone longer than she thought, as did the fact that she was lying down instead of sitting. The only comfort came from knowing that Myers was just as badly off, maybe more so. She lay there for several moments longer, regaining her strength, then pushed herself onto her elbows.

Genie instantly knelt down. "What happened? Are you all right?"

Nodding, Becky answered, "He's still on the roof, two

warehouses down. I think he's hurt, might have lost consciousness in the blast."

"Best news I've had all day. We don't have a lot of time before someone official comes to check out the explosion, even in this part of town," Genie pointed out.

Becky nodded again and agreed, "Let's go."

They left the warehouse, Becky in the lead, and moved swiftly towards the building where she'd last seen him. Her body felt bruised and battered, and her energy was practically nil, but Becky knew, somehow, that this was the end game. All the twisted games Helms had put them through, were about to be finished. It gave her the extra boost of adrenaline she needed to keep going.

Halfway there, Becky was overwhelmed by an all-too-familiar mind and fell to her knees. The black vile of Helms' thoughts pushed at her shields, trying to find a way in. Gripping her head in both hands, heedless of the indents her hard, metal gun made indents in her scalp, Becky ground out, "Go away! You can't get in!"

Oh, I think I can.

Shaking her head violently, Becky pictured herself swinging a sledgehammer against the other man's shields, replying, *No, you can't!*

"Becca, Becca, what's going on? We can't stay in the open like this!" Genie exclaimed, casting her gaze constantly about to look for Myers.

"It's Helms," Becky gasped.

It felt like someone had strapped a steel vise around her head, and it squeezed mercilessly tighter. She barely felt Genie's arm go around her waist and couldn't spare any awareness on what happened thereafter.

GENIE HAULED HER partner to her feet, dragging Becca the rest of the way to the warehouse. Once inside, she carefully set the woozy woman down, between the shelter of a rusted piece of machinery and a wall. Brushing her fingers through the dark locks, Genie could see that the telepath was completely out of it, fighting an internal battle. Of course, there was still an external battle that needed to be fought and it looked like it was up to Genie to end it. Grimly checking her rounds, even though she knew they were full, she leaned over and pressed a gentle kiss to her partner's forehead, whispering, "Stay safe."

Then she was up and gone, heading for the decrepit stairs in the corner and hoping that Myers was still aloft, and hurt from the blast. The stairs were shaky and unsafe, big surprise there, but she made it to the top without trouble. Once there, Genie took a good look around and found shelving units blocking her line of sight. Some were partially filled, others were empty, but they were all in her way.

Moving as silently as she knew how, Genie walked down the center aisle, her ears and eyes wide open for any sign of Myers. In the dim lighting, shadows loomed larger than they should, and the noise of each breeze catching on litter scraped across already raw nerves. She'd circled through most of the upper floor with no success when Becca cried loudly in pain.

Spinning toward the sound, Genie didn't see Myers inch out from his hiding place and creep towards her from behind.

WHEN BECKY FINALLY came to her senses, literally, she was in a completely unfamiliar place. Somehow Genie had gotten her into another warehouse while she'd been struggling to keep her sanity against the evil pounding against her defenses. It had been only slightly better than that first "possession" in that she was expecting it and, therefore, had pulled her shields together as tight as possible.

Becky groaned as she got to her feet, unable to cut off the reaction. The room she found herself in was a huge, empty space with the skeletons of machinery strewn across the floor. Grimacing when glass crunched loudly underfoot, Becky froze and swept the area with her eyes as best she could, but didn't see much of anything in the artificial twilight.

"It's a terrible thing when the eyes start to go, isn't it?" a man called out conversationally.

Eyes locking automatically on the source of the voice, even though she couldn't see him in the dark, Becky called back, "I wouldn't know, my eyes are just fine."

"Not anymore."

Before she could move, something sprayed the air where she was standing; Becky cried out in pain when it hit her eyes. Even as she fell to her knees, Becky kept a tight grip on her gun. Tears flowed freely in response to the agonizing burn, but her sight didn't clear. She heard the click of lights coming on and footsteps moving across the concrete floor.

"Where's your partner, Detective Curtains?"

"Couldn't tell you, especially since I can't see worth shit anymore," Becky answered sarcastically.

"Ah, well that's too bad. If you would slide your weapon away?"

She shook her head. "I don't think so."

A gun cocked near her ear and he countered, "I really must insist."

Taking her thumb off the hammer, Becky slid the gun away from herself and waited. "So. After all this crap you've put me through, you're just going to kill me?"

"Oh no. Nothing like that," he assured her, almost pleasantly. "You're going to be found here by Vice, stoned out of your mind. And, once my associate has found your partner, we'll use your gun to kill her."

Fury ran through Becky and she strained to see him.

He chuckled mildly. "Don't feel too badly. You played a good game."

"You know that your own people are looking for you. You missed your chance to get away with this scot-free. Because even if you do to me what you're planning, they'll believe me once the drugs wear off."

"It doesn't matter."

"Doesn't it? Why go through all this if you're not going to get a clean win? Isn't that the point of beating someone? For everyone to know that you're the best? The only ones who think that are those two pathetic kids who worship you. You'll never have the respect of your peers," Becky taunted. "As far as everyone knows, I'm the strongest telepath alive. It's my voice that people listen to, not yours. Millions of people read the words that I give them, but no one even listens to you. They all think you're crazy!"

A fist slammed into her chin, knocking her forcefully backwards. It was followed up by a kick to the ribs that shoved her a couple of feet sideways. Becky couldn't even breathe to groan because of the fire searing through her gut. Fingers latched into her hair, dragging her up as he hissed furiously into her ear, "I am the best."

Becky grabbed his head, pushing her thumbs into his eyes as hard as she could. The soft flesh gave way and she doggedly hung on as he howled in pain, trying to get free. Using both of their pain, Becky flooded his mind with as much sensory input as she could, straining to reach the part within Helms that held his telepathic abilities. His mental landscape was as wild and bitterly cold as riding a white water river in the flimsiest of rafts, but she kept on.

Then Sharon, Daniel and Joel were there, as before, supporting her. They were joined by other telepaths until it felt like a warm blanket of love and determination surrounded her. Once everyone had linked together in a giant net, it was easy to use that strength and delve within Helms' mind to overpower him.

Helms' shriek of agony rebounded through the near empty warehouse as he collapsed insensate onto the ground, away from her, which was all Becky cared about. Before the scream died out, there was an exchange of gunfire, and then dead silence.

Becky came back to herself with shocking force when the connection to Genie severed without warning. Panic cut into her and she shouted, "Genie! Genie, are you all right?"

The ten seconds it took Genie to answer were about the longest of Becky's life.

"I'm fine! Just grazed," Genie shouted from above, pained. "What about you?"

Collapsing to the ground, Becky let the pain take her and succumbed to the welcome darkness now that she knew her partner was all right.

THE HOSPITAL ROOM was pretty much the same as the previous one her partner had occupied. Sitting on the edge of the bed, Genie asked anxiously, for the third time, "So they're sure it's only temporary?"

High on painkillers, Becky nodded and repeated, "Temporary blindness induced by um, something or other. And you're really okay, right? Not lying to me because I can't see for myself?"

"I'd never lie to you, Becca."

Becky felt fingers brush her cheek and sighed, the very thin edge of painkillers starting to wear off. She reached out and managed to snag the strong hand that so gently touched her. They were rather like a metaphor for Genie herself, Becky realized. Strong but gentle, heavy with rough calluses, but containing an overall elegance that couldn't be denied. *God, I've got it bad.*

"What is it?" Genie asked.

"We can't, we can't be more than friends, Genie. Or, at least I can't," Becky said slowly, trying to make sense of her fuzzy thoughts.

Genie sighed. "I figured that's what you'd say. It's just..."

When Genie's voice trailed off wistfully, Becky nodded and tightened her grip on Genie's hand. "I know."

"Am I interrupting?"

Becky's head turned towards Captain Carlson's voice and she released Genie's hand. "Nope. Just kinda making sure we're both okay."

"I understand," Carlson said, coming closer.

Becky grinned in his direction. "So what brings you to my humble hospital room?"

"I just wanted to congratulate you both on what a fine mess you've made."

Incredulous, Genie demanded, "Excuse me? We stopped a psychotic, cold-blooded murderer."

"You reduced a two-star, highly respected, even if lately nuts, Army General to a drooling non-entity that can't even be charged with his crimes," Carlson countered sharply. "You're damn lucky he likes to keep his trophies, or Detective Curtains here would probably be in a jail infirmary, instead of a hospital."

"What kind of trophies?" Becky questioned.

"He was following your career with obsessive paranoia.

complete with commentary," Carlson answered. "And the aluminum knife from the tourist murders helped, too. There are encrypted files on his PC, but we don't know what's in there yet. I'm thinking a lot of sick plans and details that I really don't want to read, but have to."

Genie remarked, "That's why *you* get paid the big bucks."

"Yeah well, forget about linking Doyle to any of this."

Becky felt Genie stand from her position against the bed, and heard the anger etched into her voice as she hissed,. "What? Why?"

Paper rustled, probably being passed back and forth, and Becky felt the fury in her partner increase just before the Captain said, "And that's just the summary of what his lawyers are going to have ready. I talked to the DA about it, but they aren't going to press any charges. Said that it's 'too circumstantial.'"

"Son of a bitch!" Genie exploded.

Irritated at being kept in the dark, Becky asked, "What's going on?"

"Doyle is claiming no knowledge of what Myers was up to," Genie explained furiously. "He says that if he'd known, of course he would have informed the police right away that the man was planning to commit murder."

Becky groaned, the drugs clearing up a little more as her mind comprehended what her partner had just said.

"What is it? Are you in pain?" Genie asked, anxious.

"Aside from a distinct and constant pain in the ass, no."

Carlson sighed, then changed the subject. "Detective Curtains, I have the misfortune to tell you that you're on unpaid suspension, pending investigation into this case."

Becky winced at Genie's mental and verbal snarl of, "They can't do that!" and made a note to train her partner on controlling her emotions in the very near future. It didn't help that her own defenses were down, with the drugs in effect, but they couldn't have Genie just tearing into everyone around her like that. Reaching out with her hand, Becky ordered, "Genie, calm down. They can do whatever they want."

Genie took her hand and gripped it tight. "What about her union rep? Can we get someone to intervene?"

Carlson sighed again. "Already went down that road, Marshall. They're going to wait and see what the Review Board comes out with. Believe me, I tried to *at least* get a paid suspension, but no dice."

"God damn it," Genie swore tiredly.

Becky tried to ignore the throbbing in her head. "Lovely."

"Anyhow. That's all I came to say. Oh, and get better soon."

"Thanks, Captain," Becky replied.

Genie nodded, adding disconsolately, "Yeah, thanks."

Becky heard the door close behind him and sighed again, heavily this time. It could take the Board weeks to come to a conclusion. Good thing she had saved for a rainy day, because it was pouring. "At least my health benefits can't be rescinded since I was injured in the line of duty."

"They'll probably find a way around it."

Her partner's anger and frustration washed over her. Becky tightened her grip on Genie's hand as she said, "Thank you, oh, ray of sunshine."

Genie pulled her hand free and walked away. When she spoke again, bitterness laced her words. "I'm sorry, Becca, but I just can't believe the crap they're saddling on you! It's not like I was sitting on my ass through all of this! Why aren't they suspending me, too?"

"Probably because with all the bad publicity, they're going to need one person they can point to and say, 'She's our bright, shining star and did everything right.' At least to the public," Becky guessed.

"What a crock! And how can you be so calm about all this?"

Grinning suddenly, Becky answered, "I'm on drugs, remember?"

After a few seconds of silence, Genie started laughing. When she could speak again, she said, "You know something, Curtains?"

"What, Marshall?"

"Life is never dull with you around."

Laughing, Becky mused, "Isn't that an old curse? May you live in interesting times?"

Still chuckling, Genie again sat on the edge of the hospital bed and answered, "Well, if it's a curse, then I'm completely screwed."

"You? I'm just an innocent bystander. You're the bad-ass."

"Bad-ass? Did you just call me a bad-ass?"

"I believe I did. What're you gonna do about it?"

They continued to banter back and forth, mainly because if they didn't laugh about the situation, both women knew that they'd have to cry with the disappointment.

Audio Excerpt from Rebecca Curtains' Journal—Year One

What the hell was I thinking? I wasn't, obviously. Well. Question number one answered: Genie wants me.

What a mess. What a friggin' mess. So the elephant's in the room. We both know how the other feels and still, we can't do a damned thing about it.

I know she wants to. I know her. Funny about that since we really haven't known each other all that long. Is it a cliché to say that I can see so clear now that I can't see at all? Insulting to blind men and women everywhere, maybe? I don't know, but then, I doubt it's actually the temporary blindness making me face up to things.

I get like this after a big case is solved. I have to drag every little piece out and examine my behavior, my choices, my decisions, everything. And though this doesn't have anything to do with the case, it has everything to do with my life and my choices.

We could get together and no one would be the wiser. We could. Everyone knows we already spend most of our free time together and not one word has been said about it to either of us. That tells me that people approve. Though I have to laugh, because it reminds me of what Thomas Mathisen has said, more than once, that I made Genie more human. Of course they'd want to keep us partners, even if romantically involved, because that means she won't revert to type.

But they aren't giving her enough credit. Genie has deep reasons for being how she is. I'm not yet privy to most of them, but I've got a pretty good idea. I think the fact that she's not completely antisocial or psychotic is a testament to her strength of will, her character.

So why am I still fighting against this if people don't care? Why am I so hesitant to become her lover in fact, not just theory? God, but I wish I knew. What I do know, is that if she mounts any serious opposition to not getting together, I'll probably crumble. I'm pathetic that way. I care about her so much, and want to be with her. Propriety and duty just aren't very warm comfort when you're blind and alone.

Or even sighted and alone.

Chapter
Twenty-Seven

"*TELL* ME THAT you weren't making out with Curtains in *broad daylight, on a public street.*"

Genie sighed at Carlson's question and pushed off from the office wall. She'd been running from the press for days now and it was seriously wearing thin. As was being without her partner. While her Violent Crimes coworkers were sticking by her and Becca, everyone else seemed to have developed an allergy to them both. Well, more than usual anyhow. "I'd like to, but I can't. Myers was coming right at us, so we had to do something to blend in."

Running a hand through his hair, Carlson said, "You couldn't have just ducked into a doorway or something?"

Genie shrugged. "There wasn't time."

Obviously stressed, Carlson pulled out a roll of antacids and popped one in his mouth like it was candy. Baleful eyes regarded Genie as he informed her, "Thanks to some helpful citizen, you can add 'conduct unbecoming' to the investigation already on Becca, and now you've got one of your very own."

"God damn it! Doesn't this shit ever end?"

Sighing, Carlson said, "You're on paid suspension until the investigation is cleared up."

"But Becca's still got the shaft on unpaid, right?"

"Pretty much," he agreed.

"Well, you know what? Fuck them and their investigation. We did everything right *and* Becca was temporarily blinded in the line of duty, and this is how they repay us? You can just take my badge and my gun, because unless Becca's reinstated, I quit."

The Captain accepted both items silently, then watched her leave. The phone stared at him for a long time before he made a decision. Digging out a battered address book from his top drawer, he looked up Sharon's phone number, then picked up the receiver.

It was time to bring in the big guns.

SITTING IN HER car, Genie stared out the window at the traffic whizzing by. Even though she'd spent the afternoon going over her options in her mind, the situation wasn't any better now, then when she'd walked out of Carlson's office. Genie had put her foot in it for real, this time. If Becca wasn't reinstated, they were both out of a job, but that wasn't nearly the worst part about the whole mess. The worst part was knowing that Becca felt something for her, something more than friendship, and refused to take that giant step off the cliff.

She snorted, not amused as she remembered the old-time Bugs Bunny cartoon. "Watch that first step, it's a lulu."

Shaking her head, Genie forced the depressing thoughts out of her mind and got out of the Jeep. Time to face the music, so to speak, and tell Becca what she'd done. Well, depending on how the other woman was feeling. If it had been a bad day, then the news could wait. She hit the buzzer. A woman asked, "Yes?"

"It's Detective Marshall."

The front door unlocked with an ear-grating noise and she pulled it open. She was upstairs in short order and knocking on the door. After a couple of minutes, the part-time nurse opened it. Genie flashed the older woman a grin. "Hey, Marta."

"Come on in, Detective," the other woman replied, smiling.

Genie saw Becca ensconced on the couch, eyes closed. Marta moved into the kitchen to give them the illusion of privacy, and Genie sat on the floor by her partner. "Hey, there. How're you feeling?"

Becca's eyes opened but they stared unseeing into space. "Amy called and said that you quit."

"Damn, that grapevine works fast."

"Were you planning on telling me?"

Grinning faintly, Genie answered, "Not if I could help it."

"Genie, what're you doing?" Becca wailed, hitting the couch with her fist. "We can't both lose out here!"

Capturing Becca's hand, Genie unclenched the fingers, brought the hand to her lips and kissed the palm before answering. "Unless you're on the job with me, I lose anyhow."

Becca reached out blindly until her free hand connected with Genie's shoulder and squeezed. "Genie, you know we can't..."

Losing patience, Genie exclaimed, "Yes, we can! I'm tired of pussyfootin' around this thing between us. Whether it came about because of us being partners, being linked in the noggin, or because we were meant to be, doesn't matter! I want you, Becca. I might even love you, I don't know. But I want to find out, one way or the other. I mean, think about it this way. Things can't get any more screwed up at work, so why *not* give this thing a shot?"

Becca was silent for a long time, clearly weighing everything over in her mind "This is insane, you know that? Everything's against this working out."

"That's your last grand defense?" Genie teased, relief flooding through her. "It's common knowledge that I'm certifiable. Did you forget?"

"Apparently."

Chuckling at the dry tone, Genie leaned forward and kissed Becca, enjoying their softness and her partner's happy, if belated, response. When she pulled back, Genie ran her fingers through Becca's short locks, massaging the scalp. Becca sighed deeply and leaned into the caress, obviously still worried about what would happen. Wanting to stop potentially damaging words from spilling out, Genie said firmly, "No matter what happens at work, I don't want to lose *you*, Becca."

Becca stared into space for a long moment before she finally replied with equal determination, "You won't. I don't know what the hell is going to come of this, if anything, but you'll never lose me."

Resting her head against Becca's midriff, Genie murmured, "Same here, partner, same here."

THOUGH THE ROOM was blurry and it was hard to make out minor details like, say, faces, Becky could see enough to know that she was facing the firing squad. They were both in dress uniform, facing the review board, and about to find out whether or not they were still cops and, on top of that, partners.

"Detectives Marshall and Curtains. This Review Board has spent a considerable amount of time and effort investigating your actions in what has been dubbed the 'Rogue Telepath' case," Commissioner LeBlanc began. "Many aspects of the case disturbed this entire Board, not the least of which was the fact that you hid the true focus of the killer. If we can't trust officers of the law to tell us the truth about what's going on, who can we trust?

"That being said, we have found that the only real wrongdoing in this matter, in your actions, that is, is just that. Failure to report pertinent information in an ongoing investigation. In response to that, Detective Curtains is put on suspension for a period of no less than thirty days and Detective Marshal the same, for two weeks. A note of reprimand will be placed in each of your records."

Becky thought that her knees were going to give out with relief, but she firmly told them to stay put and managed to keep her feet. That was it? It couldn't be that easy, not after everything that had happened.

"As for the other matter before the Review Board. Conduct unbecoming an officer. When the charges were added to the investigation, not all facts were in evidence," he continued, growing slightly flustered.

Becky's eyebrows rose with interest. The Commissioner blushing would be worth a lot in the gossip trade. She'd have to get the details from Genie, who could see it properly.

"It is apparently the, ah, intimate nature of a telepathic connection to strengthen the Psi-Agent's powers and, cementing this, this, bond, is the natural course of events. Therefore, the rules of fraternization in this particular case are waived. Especially considering that the productivity and solve rate of both detectives has increased since the start of the partnership. Should a...liaison...develop, or if one already has, no punitive action will be taken against either of you.

"And finally, as Detective Curtains has been off the job for twenty-six days, and Detective Marshal for fifteen, we will consider that time served and see the both of you back on the job on Monday," the Commissioner finished. "Dismissed."

Becky couldn't stop the grin from blossoming as she saluted, then turned to leave.

"Oh, Detectives?" the Commissioner called as they neared the door.

Both turned back to face the Board.

"We all wished to say, off the record, that you did as good a job as possible under the circumstances and to keep up the good work."

"Uh, thank you, sir," Becky replied, after a surprised moment.

"Yes, thank you, sir," Genie echoed. Out of the corner of her mouth she murmured, "Let's get out of here before something else comes up!"

Stifling a laugh, Becky turned and they left the room. She was surprised at the crowd waiting outside and, though she couldn't make out anyone unless they were directly in front of her, it sounded like the entire department, plus a few people, were present.

Mathisen called out, "So? What's the verdict, Marshall? They letting your sorry ass back on the force?"

"As a matter of fact, you will see both our lovely asses back in the office, come Monday. Time served and all that," Genie reported, lazily waving a hand in the air.

"They don't know time served until they've worked with you," Carlson complained. When the laughter died down, he continued, "For interested parties, Detectives Nickerson and Bailey are going to be enjoying sensitivity seminars for the next six months. Courtesy of me, and their own captain. Plus a year of community service out of the generosity of their hearts, for turning you guys in."

"Those sons of...!"

"Becky!"

"What?"

"That's my line."

Linking her arm with Genie's, Becky leaned against her partner. "I'm terribly sorry. Go ahead."

With a wink, Genie exclaimed, "Those sons of bitches!"

This time, everyone laughed as Becky and Genie walked towards the exit.

"Where do you think you're going?" Carlson called after them.

Genie called back, "We're off 'til Monday, boss! See you then!"

"You better be on time!"

"Yeah, yeah," Genie muttered.

They reached Genie's Jeep in short order, and Becky leaned against the door, looking up at Genie. "You know what?"

Genie leaned on the door beside her. "What?"

"We can pretty much make out wherever we want now," Becky commented, wriggling her eyebrows suggestively. This close, the damage to her eyes gave Genie a halo effect that had Becky itching to do devilish things to her partner.

Chuckling somewhat breathlessly, Genie asked, "Any suggestions?"

"How about right here?"

Before Genie could say anything, Becky grabbed the other woman's jacket and hauled her in for a long, deep kiss. Genie made a surprised noise in the back of her throat, but responded enthusiastically. It was fulfilling in ways that Becky had never expected, and made her want to stay right there, forever. Unfortunately, the need for oxygen forced them apart and she stared up at her partner with a smile, gasping, "How about we go to my place and get to know each other a little better?"

Genie grinned, but didn't move, keeping Becky pinned against the Jeep. "We could do that. Or we could go back to my place, instead."

With a shrug, Becky shoved her partner away and walked around the Jeep to the passenger's side door. She didn't care where they went, so long as they were in the same place. "Sounds like a plan to me."

Briefly closing her eyes against the light as they left the parking garage, Becky was surprised upon opening them to see where they were, and where they were headed. She grinned. Being with Genie was definitely a roller coaster ride, keeping her on her toes, but she wouldn't trade it for anything.

Genie glanced briefly at her, discovering the scrutiny. Arching an eyebrow, she prompted, "What?"

Becky laughed. "Nothing. Just enjoying the view."

Amused, Genie shook her head. "You're still blind."

"Not anymore, partner, not anymore." Becky reached out and took Genie's hand in hers, threading their fingers together, then faced forward again.

No matter what happened, Becky knew that the future would hold good things for them because now, they weren't afraid to go after what they really wanted: each other.

Never Wake
by Gabrielle Goldsby

Emma Webster hasn't left her house in over two years. After a brutal attack, she holed up inside, living a safe and quiet life, until the world goes quiet on June 5, 2008. At least, that's when Emma first notices the stillness. She can't be sure of the exact date because she's been cloistered for so long, but even a recluse such as Emma can sense when things aren't exactly right. It starts when her grocery delivery doesn't arrive. Then with some annoyance she notices that there have been no new posts to her formerly popular web blog. She searches other blogs in her web ring and notes that they, too, have been abandoned. Emma's unease grows as her food supply diminishes, expensive vehicles appear to be abandoned in front of her home, and the stray cat she usually feeds stops coming around. In desperation she posts a frightened, "Where is everyone?" to her blog.

Troy Nanson is a recovering alcoholic who awakens in a hospital with a headache and no memory of how she got there. When her calls to the nursing station go unanswered, Troy leaves her bed to search for hospital staff only to find them passed out in the hospital lounge. She tries to telephone her only living relative, but no one answers. Troy is forced to make her way home through the hushed streets of Portland, Oregon, where she passes a patrolman slumped forward in his car, several eerily still young men sleeping on a sidewalk, and a well-dressed man curled up on a bench at a train stop. At her brother's house, she finds him, as well as her dog, in a coma-like state. 911 won't answer, and a trip to a neighbor's confirm what Troy has begun to suspect - everyone else is inexplicably in a coma. Desperate and suddenly faced with her worst fear, Troy uses her brother's computer to search the Internet for an explanation of the phenomenon and instead comes upon Emma's post: "Where is everyone?"

What has happened and how long can their tranced-out neighbors last? Believing they are the only two people left awake, Troy and Emma meet. How can they solve this puzzle and make a difference when Troy has an overwhelming urge to drink, and Emma is terrified of physical and emotional contact with others? Two frightened women with the weight of the world on their shoulders must face their worst fears with only one another to help.

Will they manage to confront their fears? Or will their fright result in the destruction of all they know and love?

Other QUEST Publications

Printed in the United States
49796LVS00005B/235-291

9 781932 300536